a
sister's
place

Other Titles by Savannah Page

Bumped to Berlin

When Girlfriends Series

When Girlfriends Break Hearts

When Girlfriends Step Up

When Girlfriends Make Choices

When Girlfriends Chase Dreams

When Girlfriends Take Chances

When Girlfriends Let Go

When Girlfriends Find Love

a
sister's
place

a novel

Savannah Page

LAKE UNION
PUBLISHING

Published by Lake Union Publishing, Seattle

www.apub.com

Amazon, the Amazon logo, and Lake Union Publishing are trademarks of Amazon.com, Inc., or its affiliates.

ISBN-13: 9781503943179
ISBN-10: 1503943178

Printed in the United States of America

*For Heather, my sister, my friend, who's always
got my back (and my coffee).
This one was yours from the very start. XO*

Spring

1

Mimi

Dear Gracie and Juliette,

This is both a time of endings and a time of new beginnings. This is the first of five—five letters, five seasons. And this is also the last—the last of my letters, the last of my time here on earth.

How quickly the seasons change, the time passes. When you're just a child, the time between one Christmas morning and another feels like an eternity. When you have a child of your own, who eagerly awaits the jolly man in the red-and-white suit, you'll be reminded of your own youth and impatience and realize last Christmas feels as if it happened only a few months ago. When you have grandchildren, the time between one holiday and another, from one season to the next, seems to pass as quickly as a night's sleep.

Though my years have passed with great swiftness, they have been filled with much joy and love. I have lived a beautiful and full life, and I am grateful for each breath, each moment. Every fiber of my being clings to the hope that I will have more time, more moments to share with the ones I love, but in this circle of life there are beginnings and there are endings. We enter into the world on borrowed time—a lease—and there comes a time to depart. And my time is nearing.

I write this first of five letters to you, my dear Gracie and Juliette, because I wish to leave you with more than memories, photographs, and a final farewell. Through my letters I wish to bring you a smile, however small, during this sad time. To continuously remind you that even though I am now gone from this earth, I will always be with you, in your heart, your memories. I will be right by your side during the full circle of this new year's seasons.

With these letters I also propose to you a challenge, an opportunity. Unlike you, my dears, I was never gifted the fortune of a sister. I never had the chance to share life with a sibling. Never a moment to know what it feels like to slip into a big sister's shoes (figuratively and literally). To know what it feels like to help a little sister overcome a task too large for someone so small. But you, Gracie and Juliette, have had one of life's greatest experiences—sisterhood. I cherish the memories I have of watching you two little ones grow up as best friends.

I know life can be hectic, time never being in the abundance you need. Changes happen, physical proximities expand, and as life goes on, we find ourselves no longer living our lives parallel to each other but following our own paths—paths that can wind and strike out on their own. This is change, this is life, and this comes with age. No matter the distance or circumstance, I know you two love each other. I know you're grateful for each other. But I know time and physical distance have loosened the threads of your relationship. Not torn apart, no. Just loosened.

The bond of sisterhood, the friendship two women can have is something to hold on to—to cultivate and love. And so I challenge you.

Grandpa Harold, God rest his soul, and I have lived in our home since 1968. It has been in the Jones family since just after the war in 1947, when your great-grandfather Henry Jones Sr. bought his bride, Betty, a place to call home. 1402 Laguna Lane has seen three generations of Joneses under its roof; even your parents called it home for two years when they first married. It's a home rich with history, walls that have witnessed decades of conversations, experiences . . . lives.

It has gotten lonelier here on Laguna Lane these past eleven years since your grandfather passed, but these walls still remember the conversations and experiences that serve as this home's foundation. I am blessed to have your mother and father nearby and you, Gracie, just a short drive across town. I am fortunate to have had what I am certain was my last Christmas with the people I love most, right here in this living room. Once I pass, however, I will no longer be able to witness this home filled with the laughter of children, the songs of the holidays, the delightful cacophony of a family coming together for a Sunday brunch.

1402 Laguna Lane has been in this family for sixty-seven years. I wish for it to stay in the family for sixty-seven more. I wish for your children and your grandchildren to watch the spring's first tulip bulbs bloom just as your great-grandmother did. I wish for your children and grandchildren to dance under the garden sprinkler in the height of the sunny Santa Barbara summer just as I did. I wish for them to bake a pecan pie in the autumn and eat the delicious treat on the back patio steps and watch as the trees sway with the hearty push of the Santa Anas, just as your mother did with me. I wish for them to eagerly await Saint Nick (and cross their fingers for the impossible winter white to sprinkle down), just as you two did.

I have prepared my will, and, as you now know, I have left you girls both an inheritance and a task. As your great-grandmother Betty bequeathed it to Grandpa Harold and me, I wish to leave 1402 Laguna Lane to you, Gracie and Juliette. As for the task, your father agrees that this is the best choice. Your mother thinks this is a brilliant (and rather interesting) proposition. I do hope that you are not angry with me over my decision and method of going about passing down this home. You two were never sour with your Mimi, and now that I'm gone you can't very well go on holding a grudge against someone who just may pull a ghost prank or two in the house.

I know this will be a challenge. But what is life if not full of adventure and challenges that test our wills, our characters, our abilities, our preconceptions? What is life if not shared with those you love most dearly, in good times and bad, when convenient and when inconvenient?

This is the first of five letters and five seasons. Please know that I leave you this home and these letters, and that I give you this challenge, with only the purest of love and greatest intentions. I believe in you two. Gracie Dawn, with your loyalty and resolve, and Juliette Kay, with your zeal and tenderness, you will be able to grow from one season to the next, looking at each other next spring with new appreciation. You will even think that it seems like only yesterday you were reading this letter for the first time, yet feel as if saying good-bye to your Mimi happened a lifetime ago. Time eventually heals; life moves on.

I love you, my darlings. I know you can take on this task. You can call my home your home. You can create another generation of memories within its walls. You can share a sisterhood I wish I had, a friendship that's been there from the moment Juliette was born and Gracie became a big sister, a relationship that just needs some tender, loving care.

If you can't imagine doing this for each other or for yourselves, then I ask that you do it for me as one more favor to your dear old Mimi. (Well, and the P.S. if you don't mind, my darlings.)

Until summer,

All my love,

Mimi

P.S. The orange tree demands more love than the other beauties in the garden. It was a ten-year wedding anniversary present for your great-grandmother Betty. I find that in addition to regular watering, fertilizing, gentle pruning, and lots of harvesting, conversations under the orange tree have made it thrive. The orange tree's a friendly shadow, a fragrant friend, a delicious dessert, a keeper of secrets, a great listener, and a darn cheap therapist! Treat her kindly.

2

Gracie

Numb. All my senses are working overtime, but my fingertips and toes? I can't feel them. If out-of-body experiences exist, this must be what they're like. The sunshine-yellow-and-paper-white daisy pattern on the dress of the elderly woman across from me is so vivid (and offending) I squint. The consistent, crisp stream of the air-conditioning overhead chills my bare arms, which are now covered in thick sleeves of goose bumps. The murmurs in the cramped wood-paneled room are so loud I'm tempted to cover my ears like a small child pretending she can't hear what her parents are asking of her.

The taste of the pink lemonade, which was served with the chocolate chip cookies I neglected to try (because finding an appetite when mourning is like finding a needle in a haystack), still lingers on my tongue in a bitter-and-sweet combination. The scent of Mimi's pressed powder, remnants on my fingers from opening the compact I now nostalgically keep in my bathroom cupboard, is so strong I can't tamp down the well of tears that trickle slowly down my round cheeks.

A small yet firm hand cups my knee. I press my lips together and swallow back the freshly formed tears.

"This too shall pass," my mother says. She presses together her lips—lips just like my own, ones we both inherited from Mimi: plump, rosebud. Or, as Grandpa Harold called them, "pinup-girl mouths."

"This *too* shall pass." My mother swallows hard and gives my knee a squeeze.

This too *shall pass*, with the same heavy emphasis on the *too*, are the very words I heard my Mimi say to my mother when Grandpa Harold passed away more than ten years ago. I was fifteen, and while that was old enough to understand and commit to memory that mournful day, I cannot recall many details of the day we laid Grandpa to rest.

I do remember how forlorn my Mimi was, losing the only man she'd ever loved. I remember my mother saying it was too soon to have lost her father. To a fifteen-year-old, sixty-three seemed ancient. Now that I'm twenty-six, sixty-three doesn't seem that old. Certainly not old enough to die. I remember my Mimi comforting her only daughter, my mother, who was so weakened by sorrow she had dark rings under her eyes and talked not to or with but *at* my sister, my father, and me. *This* too *shall pass*. I can still hear Mimi bravely assuring my mother, as my mother assures me.

"I know," I whisper as my mother pulls me close.

She inhales sharply, biting back the tears. She gingerly rubs my arm, and in a convincing and consoling way says again to me, and as much to herself, "This *too* shall pass. It will pass. We will be fine."

"We will, Mom." I give her a kiss on the side of her head, her sun-streaked auburn hair dropping just past her shoulders in wide, heavy curls. "This *will* pass."

But it's too soon, I want to add. I restrain myself, knowing it won't make matters any better, only bring my mother to more tears. It will only make the reality of loss that much more palpable.

We all knew this day would come. Mimi had lived for seventy-four years, every moment but the last two weeks with her signature vivaciousness and passion. When the doctors discovered her advanced cancer last November, they informed us we should begin to make final preparations. Mimi had three months, four at most. Yet as she battled the cancer, kidney failure, and exhausting chemotherapy treatments, Mimi remained determined to give it the good fight.

None of us said it for fear of relying on false hope, but we all thought Mimi would have at least four months, maybe five, maybe six, despite what the doctors said. She was a strong woman with a lot of fight in her. She'd had no other choice, growing up in the throes of World War II, when sailors came and went (far more went than came) week by week on the Santa Barbara coast. At three she watched her father head off to the Pacific, with only her young mother to keep house until he returned. He never did return, but house was still kept. Her mother found work to support the family, and Mimi came into her own.

As her mother tended to her various jobs, Mimi learned to make her own lunch, get herself to and from school, and help with the wash. She fetched fresh eggs from the chickens out back for breakfast every morning, and after school she went from door to door selling the remaining eggs to help pay the bills. And every night before Sunday morning's Mass, she polished her single pair of shoes—a hand-me-down pair of saddle oxfords she wore every day until her mother discovered she'd worn them so thin her socks had become her soles. Mimi knew a new pair, even hand-me-downs, was a luxury her mother could not afford.

Mimi was resourceful, determined, hopeful. She was born to be a fighter, so when she didn't make it to five months or the hoped-for six, we were all surprised—and severely heartbroken. That she defied the doctor's expectations and made it a hair over four months? That was Mimi for you.

My stomach churns as I think about Mimi's last two weeks, which were spent in a coma. No matter what science or the professionals say, I believe that those final weeks were Mimi's private time. She could hear us, she listened, she even talked to us in her own special, spiritual way.

11

She wasn't in some kind of a limbo, nor was she already passing. No, Mimi had a plan. As a real spitfire with the warmest heart, brightest smile, and kindest soul, she fought for those four months and eventually let herself fall peacefully asleep. She knew her time was coming and made peace with the fact.

A few days before she set off for her final, private moments of peace in her coma, she reminded me that it's always important to give life a run for its money and take on its challenges with vigor. "But we have only a lease on life, Gracie," she said. I fingered the patchwork quilt that had decoratively dressed the foot of her bed for years. She had it pulled up to her chin, keeping her frail body warm.

"I know, Mimi," I said, trying to fight back the urge to cry, to wrap her in my arms, to beg for her not to leave me. Not yet. But, as Mimi encouraged, I stayed strong.

"Life's a temporary gift, and we have to make the most of it." Mimi's voice was authoritative despite heavy doses of painkillers.

I brought my fingers up to the side of her wrinkled face and brushed back a stray curly lock of grey hair. Looking into her grey-blue eyes—the same ocean color as mine, as my mother's, as my sister's, the Kay ladies' eyes—I nodded, letting her know I understood.

"And," Mimi said through a sigh, "when it's time to turn in the keys, you turn them in." She gave me that familiar, bright, rosebud-lipped smile. "The lights go off, the door closes—"

"Oh, Mimi," I cut in, not fond of the moribund turn.

She brought up her heavily wrinkled hand, the knuckles knobby as the roots of a centuries-old oak from years of arthritis. She snapped her fingers and said sprightly, "But you go out with a bang!"

My head snaps up, and I take a quick sniff in as I feel a hand grip my right shoulder. I come to from my daze and look to my right, thinking the hand belongs to my mother.

"Gracie." It is my father. His tan face comes into view. The first of the wrinkles that arrive with age, around his eyes and mouth, are drawn deeper than usual. He hands me a piece of paper, telling me they'll be starting soon. He asks if I'm all right.

"As well as anyone can be, given the situation," I say.

He hands me a pen from inside his suit jacket pocket. "The executor says it shouldn't take very long."

"It's fine." I wipe at my nose, the pen in hand. It feels like a brick between my trembling fingers.

Dad now gives Mom's shoulder a squeeze and whispers gentle comforts into her ear. I can't watch the emotional scene—my mother struggling to keep it together as she prepares to hear the last will and testament of her mother, her confidante, her best friend.

I glance down at the paper now in my hand. My eyes glaze over the phrases *Last Will, Miriam Kay-Jones, Deed of Entitlement,* and *Santa Barbara, California,* as well as some dates, bullet points, and legal jargon that should be crystal clear to a paralegal, but my mind goes blank. All I know is that the executor is already talking, reading Mimi's final wishes, bequeathing this and that and whatnot—

"Where's your sister?" Dad's voice rings through my daze once more.

"Hmm?"

"Juliette?" Dad glances about the stuffy room, where Mimi's family and closest friends have congregated. "Is she here already?" He cranes his neck, trying to peer through the open door.

"She'll be here," I say with assurance. "Late as usual, probably. But she'll be here."

Juliette has never been one to wear a watch, ask for the time, maintain a date book, or keep to schedules. I bought her a chic silver watch for her birthday one year, a leather-bound planner for Christmas another. As soon as I gifted them, I never saw them again. Juliette's more of a fly-by-the-seat-of-her-pants kind of woman.

To say she's inconsiderate would be rude and honestly incorrect, but *irresponsible* might cut it. If anyone believed in the motto "Fashionably late," it'd have to be my sister, Juliette Kay Bennett. She has a penchant for showing up to birthday parties and Thanksgiving dinners an hour late, falling back on the excuses of traffic, phone calls she couldn't abandon, and my favorite: an online bidding war. She was nearly always late for Sunday brunches at Mimi's, but usually excuses fell under the, as Mimi used to say, "naturally understandable and excusable" umbrella.

As Mimi would also say, "Juliette's heart is in the right place." I agree, but I'd like to add, "But her head's always somewhere else."

I know Juliette means no disrespect by her tardiness, and certainly never toward Mimi, whom she loved and respected just as fiercely as I. But while my mother and father just nodded and said they understood that she was five minutes late to Mimi's funeral last week because she was trying to make sure the florist added craspedia (Mimi's favorite) to the arrangements, I couldn't help but feel nettled. Juliette knew the importance of the craspedia, so why couldn't she have set her alarm clock five minutes earlier? Or planned her phone call and double-checked with the florist sooner? Why must Juliette march to the beat of some dingbat drummer?

If she's late to the reading of Mimi's will! I think sourly as Dad takes the seat to Mom's right. I glance about the stuffy room, hoping to see Juliette before the executor of the estate takes his seat at the center of the long oval table, large enough for a good two dozen people, if need be. For the reading of Mimi's will we are only half of that, and much to my disdain, Juliette is not yet among us.

I close my eyes, trying to drown out the mumbo jumbo of the low-volume conversations among the group as we await the beginning of the reading. I sink back into the plush chair and, for a brief moment, find myself back at Mimi's, in her warm and cozy living room. I'm sitting on her forest-green settee, the velvet one she said had been in the family since before my mother was in grade school. I can believe it; the fabric is worn and the style shouts early 1960s, but in a chic and sophisticated kind of way—a Mimi kind of way.

Settling farther down in my seat, I am whisked further back in time. I remember a moment from my past, sitting in the den. A bowl of lightly sweetened popcorn was in my lap; my feet barely reached past the end of the velvety cushion, and I was entranced by Tom and Jerry's shenanigans on the screen. I was crunching loudly, indulging in one of my favorite at-Mimi's-and-Grandpa's-house snacks, living the highest of life a five-year-old could imagine.

Suddenly there came a high-pitched shriek from the kitchen. Then I heard Mimi say, "You're a little mouse, just like that Jerry."

An unwieldy toddler flew from the kitchen, arms flailing dramatically overhead. "I'm not Jay-wy, I'm Ju-yet!" my two-year-old sister cried as she ran in my direction. "Gwacie, Gwacie!" she said shrilly as soon as she saw me. "Mimi's coming!"

Mimi appeared, pretending to be a tomcat, her fingers pointed at the sides of her head. She made a not-quite-intimidating meow. She crept on tiptoes closer to Juliette, who by then was scrambling to climb atop the settee.

"Help! Help! Gwacie!" my sister said through nervous giggles.

I grabbed her chubby little hands and hauled her up onto the settee. I was out of breath, popcorn flew this way and that, and Juliette squished her tiny body as close to mine as possible. She tried to stuff her face between my back and the cushion. "She's coming!" her muffled voice cried.

"You're Jerry and I'm Tom," Mimi said as she neared. "And I'm gonna get you."

"Mimi," I said. I gave her the serious eye. "*I'm* Tom, 'member?" I moved forward a skosh to help Juliette further wedge herself behind me, safe from the prowling, identity-stealing cat.

Mimi clasped a hand to her bouffant. "Oh! That's right!" She made dramatics with her eyes and breathing. "Juliette is Jerry and *Gracie* is Tom."

"We're Tom and Jerry and *you're* the Mimi," I said, giggling through popcorn munches.

"The Mimi!" Juliette screeched, jumping from her hidden space.

"*Your* Mimi," our grandmother said, taking a seat next to me. She pulled Juliette onto her lap, looped one arm around my shoulders, and said, "Park a piece of popcorn right here, Tom." She held out her hand and gave me a wink.

"Tom and Jerry," I said to myself, contemplating the nickname Grandpa Harold had given to us one afternoon. The cartoon had been playing in the background as Juliette and I busied ourselves with our dolls and collection of toy cars.

"I want some, too, Gwacie," Juliette begged in her high voice. She looked up at me with those identical grey-blues.

"We share." I placed two pieces of popcorn into her hand.

Juliette thanked me, then repeated to herself as she examined closely the popcorn, "We share, we share, we share." The words fill the heaviness in my mind, they become lyrical, and then—

"Hi, Daddy," I hear Juliette say. I look over at my sister as she scoots along the line of chairs. She gives Dad a hug, then Mom, whispering apologies in a harried tone.

Her long blonde hair is pulled up in her usual messy ponytail. Small tufts of hair are billowing out around the tie, adding to her already-frazzled look. Her leather messenger bag, strapped across her chest, is bursting at the seams, a colorful scarf trailing from it. The sleeve of her white linen blouse is pulled down, exposing her shoulder and thick black sports bra strap. It doesn't look as if she bothered (or had time) to put on more than a few quick swipes of mascara, the plum-colored rings around her eyes evidence of a lack of sleep. Yet, though disheveled and grieving, she still manages to be the same affectionate and warm-hearted Juliette she's always been. She's not quite as bubbly, but these past few weeks have been nothing short of heartbreak and tragedy.

"Gracie," Juliette says, out of breath. "Hi, honey." She squeezes my shoulder in a half hug, pressing my face against her waist as she takes the free seat next to me, the seat I've been saving for her and hoping wouldn't go unoccupied once the executor began his work.

"Hey," I mumble. I then add, "In the nick of time." I don't say it to be bitchy. In fact, I don't really know why I say it.

All right, maybe there's an undertone of intended bitchiness, but I don't want to be here. I don't want to hear the reading of my Mimi's will. I know it isn't realistic or even all that mature to think that your grandmother will live as long as you will—that you'll never have to go through life without her—but when the day actually comes, when reality hits, it's a son of a bitch, and the last thing you want to do is smile and convey niceties to a sister who's running late, causing a small commotion with her bedraggled persona.

Juliette takes a seat next to me. I brace myself for an excuse of "traffic" or "got lost." She clunks about as she removes her bag, runs her chair's wheels over the ends of her scarf, then backs up all the way against the wall, making a bit of a thump in an effort to right herself. Through an exhalation, she leans over to me and says exhaustedly, "I had to run to Mimi's on the way. I needed to grab something for her grave."

"You what?" I arch my eyebrows.

"I know." She rolls her eyes and smooths back some blonde flya-ways. "It sounds weird. Morbid." My eyebrows remain arched as she explains. "I forgot to put something in her casket, and then I thought I'd go put it on her grave when I remembered, but then it felt a little unceremonious."

"Huh?"

She shoves her bag under the table and scoots her chair forward. She smooths back her hair some more. "So I figured I'd do it after the reading of her will. That's kind of"—she shifts her jaw to the side and looks up for a second, searching for the words—"ceremonious, I guess."

"All right," a deep voice cuts into her explanation.

"I'll tell you later," she whispers.

I'm at a loss for words.

"Everyone looks to be here," says the executor in his deep voice, glancing at his watch. "It's time, so let's begin." He shuffles through some papers, and I look at Juliette. She's glancing at the paper Dad just gave her—the same one I have no interest in looking over right now.

How can she be so candid? I bite my tongue, contemplating the words *casket* and *grave*, which Juliette rapped off with ease. It's almost as if nothing's happened, as if the reading of Mimi's last will and testament is an everyday event like reading the morning paper.

I try my best to tamp down my frustration with my little sister. It's a familiar frustration that tends to broil when Juliette slips into that irresponsible "little sis" role of hers she knows so well. Or when she embraces her blithe spirit at the most inappropriate of times (today an epic example). Or when she blindly dives on into something because "Live in the moment!" is her credo, never mind the consequences.

"You look nice, Gracie," Juliette says sincerely. Her eyes dart from her paper to me, and she leans in close. She tells me with her eyes, a roundabout way of communicating we established in childhood, that she is sorry we're sitting here, having to endure this.

"Thanks," I say. My frustration fades. My heart softens at Juliette's words, her consolatory expression.

"I wanted to look nice today," I add as I glance down at my lap. "For Mimi."

I gently finger the cream satin fabric of the dress I wore for Mimi's birthday two summers ago. She said I looked like Joan Crawford in it, that it suited and accentuated my feminine curves, that the soft color contrasted wonderfully with my brunette hair, conservatively chin-length and layered as it's been since college. It's a dress I was on the fence about buying in the first place, *because* it accentuated my curves. Mimi said I should wear the dress more. This is the first time I'm wearing it since her birthday. This simple realization saddens me.

"Job accomplished," Juliette says. She reaches under the table and encloses my hand in hers. "She's probably laughing up there"—she nods upward—"at what I'm wearing."

A tingle of discomfort runs up my spine as I think of heaven, which automatically makes me think of death, which makes me think of Mimi. I recoil when Juliette says, leaning closer, "I went for a swim this morning, then couldn't find my bra." She motions to her still-exposed shoulder. "Had to wear this dirty thing." She sighs. "But Mimi would laugh. 'That's Juliette for ya!' is what she'd say, right?" She squeezes my hand before letting go and turning her attention to the executor, who's been reading for . . . how long now?

I sit up taller in my seat and force myself to be in the here and now, no matter the pain. It is the responsible thing to do. It is what Mimi wants. And whether my sister wants to crack jokes or approach the topic with insouciance should not be my concern at the moment. Now is about Mimi. Now is about doing what needs to be done, no matter how much it hurts or how much I wish it didn't have to be done.

Perhaps Juliette can't grasp—or appear to grasp—this concept and act accordingly because she is the little sister. She hasn't needed to step up to the plate on nearly the number of occasions I have. She's had her hand held more than I ever have. Even Mimi coddled her when I was told to, as the older sister, "Be sage, Gracie." On one hand I feel justified in feeling indignant, but on the other I feel as if I'm taking my anger over Mimi's passing out on a sister who's only marched to the beat of that different drummer because that's who she is. Her heart is where it belongs, after all.

I glance back at my sister and force a smile through the pain that tears at my heart, the sorrow that fills my being, the frustration that's building over Mimi's departure—frustration I've unfairly placed on Juliette's shoulders. Juliette's posture is a bit slack, her eyes intently focused on the paper as she jots down notes, then back up and focused on the executor, ready for the next round of note taking. I realize that perhaps I should be acting sage, being that older and responsible sister, and paying attention to what my Mimi's final wishes are.

"She *would* laugh, Juliette," I whisper, leaning near her as I take a pen in my hand. "You could always make Mimi laugh."

She flashes me a wink much like the ones Mimi always handed out, and I turn my attention to the executor as he reads, "'As for my estate, my home, 1402 Laguna Lane, I bequeath it to my two and only grand-daughters, Gracie Dawn Bennett and Juliette Kay Bennett.'"

Juliette and I look at each other at once. We knew Mimi's home would be ours at some point, but presumably passed down by our mother, who'd certainly inherit it from Mimi.

The executor of the estate reads on. "'The Deed of Entitlement will fall to Gracie and Juliette Bennett under the following circum-stances: Gracie and Juliette must both reside at 1402 Laguna Lane, Santa Barbara, California, for the entirety of one calendar year. If they succeed, they will be the sole inheritors and owners of the property, home, and all property assets, less those items already bequeathed, as stated in this Last Will and Testament. If they do not succeed—if they fail to agree to the terms or fail to reside together for one year—the property and home will be put up for auction, facilitated by my daugh-ter, Janey Kay Jones-Bennett, and son-in-law, George Aaron Bennett, the proceeds going to the YWCA. If one year is successfully achieved, Gracie and Juliette may decide the fate of the house. They may continue to reside in it, sell and split the proceeds, lease, whatever they wish.'"

I hear Juliette gasp just as I do, and we exchange looks again. I can't believe what I'm hearing. Mimi never breathed to me a mention of her rather game-like plans for the house; obviously this is news to Juliette's ears, too.

"The late Miriam Kay-Jones," the executor continues, "expresses her earnest wishes that her granddaughters accept the circumstances with which she bequeaths her home, noting in an additional codicil that it, and I quote, 'is a great desire for the home to remain in the family, but that it is a greater desire that I see my two granddaughters come to understand the meaning of sisterhood, hence the rather unconventional conditions. I hope that you will not view the conditions as a'"—he looks closer at the paper in his hand—"'gag, game, or last ride of fun on the merry-go-round for the old lady.'"

The room breaks out in soft, genial laughter. Juliette and I don't make a peep, don't crack a smile.

"'My wish is for you to take on this challenge as one of many in life,'" the executor reads. "'I send my love'"—he looks up from the paper—"'and wish you luck.'"

My mouth is agape. My tongue is dry. My senses are still heightened, but I'm afraid the out-of-body sensation is actually becoming an out-of-body experience.

"Uh, what the hell?" I hear Juliette breathe after what feels like a great length of time.

I look to her. Her mouth is open, her tongue probably just as dry. Her eyes are round with astonishment. "She's got to be kidding," she says.

The only words that form on my parched tongue are, "This is not happening."

3

Juliette

Mimi always had a strong will and a mind of her own, doing as she saw fit even if it went against the current. Most admirable, I found it. The conditions of her will, therefore, should come as no surprise. But despite the many weekends and sleepovers at Mimi's, holidays and after-school visits, late-night conversations and morning cups of coffee we shared over the past twenty-three years, a small part of me cannot believe what the executor of her estate just revealed.

In my hand I hold five sealed cream-colored envelopes—"a part of the Deed of Entitlement conditions," the executor said. Mimi's broad, looping, feminine handwriting is on the front of each; they're labeled with the names of seasons, SPRING on two of them. Evidently Gracie and I are to read these as each new season approaches. That is, if we agree to the conditions, agree to make Mimi's home ours for one year . . . *together.*

I look placidly at the sheaf of envelopes in my hand, a tiny breeze of comfort filling my sails as I consider that I hold Mimi's last letters. I hold some of her final words, her final wishes. I want to tear into them right away, with no regard for the seasons or her conditions, just so I can hear her voice, and I want to keep them sealed forever. As trite as it may sound, I take comfort in knowing that a piece of Mimi is still very much alive in her letters and fear that if I open them all, Mimi will no longer have anything to share, no more conversations that can be had. The end will *truly* have come.

I slip the letters into my overstuffed messenger bag, adjust its shoulder strap, and say to my sister, "Thanks for coming with me, Gracie."

"It's fine," she replies in a steely voice. She looks straight ahead, taking long and even strides across the lush, freshly cut lawn.

That's Gracie for you: focused on the task at hand, keeping a stiff upper lip. It's one of the characteristics I love and loathe about my big sister. That's just it—she's a big sister, and I think those determined and rule-abiding characteristics are some of the things that allow her to step into her role. Even make her a *good* big sister. Yet they're the same characteristics that can make her a bore. Rarely one to deviate from the rules or just live a little, Gracie stands strong as the responsible one, making little sis Juliette look all the more irresponsible, careless, and foolishly intrepid.

Sometimes I wish she'd just let go of expectations and give in to being real, raw, and open. Even now, as we make our way to Mimi's final resting place, she's got that lawyer aura about her. She's got her ramrod-straight posture, her head held respectably high. She looks as if she's on a mission. Granted, she teared up on the ride over here, but when I reached out to comfort her, she just shook her head, kept her bleary eyes on the road, and didn't say a word.

Our pace slows as we approach Mimi's final resting place, her grave adorned with bouquets. There are bright oranges and yellows (her favorite), with bursts of vintage-yellow craspedia, just as I know she'd want.

As we near, my gut tightens, my chest burns. Prepared as we may have been for Mimi's passing, with months' worth of preparations for her funeral, wake, and burial and all final arrangements made, I'm still taken aback at how unexpected her passing feels.

I roll back the forming tears and rifle through my heavy bag. My fingers have grazed the envelopes when Gracie finally speaks. "This is the first time I've been here since we buried her." Her voice is weak.

My fingers alighting on what I came here to give to Mimi, I step nearer to Gracie and tell her that it's my first time, as well.

"We knew this day would come," she continues. Her posture remains stiff, head slightly inclined in what I sense to be supplication. She takes in a breath, then exhales it slowly, controlled. "It *will* get easier." She looks to me, as if asking for reassurance, something Gracie never does as the sage and responsible older sister.

"Of course it will," I insist sincerely. "Here." I hold up a perfectly round, exquisitely bright Washington navel orange. I hand it to her and retrieve a second one.

"I'm not hungry." She limply motions to return the fruit.

"It's not to eat, goofy." I give her a loose smile. "It's for Mimi."

The orange tree in Mimi's backyard, the tree that's been in the family for generations, was Mimi's favorite item in her abundant garden. I have many memories of Mimi, Gracie, and me picnicking under its shade; Gracie and me plucking its fruit and playing grocer; caring for the blossoming tree with Mimi and gathering its fruit for midafternoon sweet snacks, homemade sorbet, and citrus pound cake. It might seem silly, but it felt like something I had to do—give one last orange to Mimi.

Overcome as I was with shock and emotion the day we buried her, it completely slipped my mind to tuck an orange into her casket. Now, though, with the final arrangements complete, her last will and testament read, and Gracie and me in possession of her final letters, it seems the time to make this small but meaningful tribute to our grandmother.

I explain this to Gracie. She thanks me for bringing her one, too, says the idea is creative. She rolls her orange in her hand, then brings it up to her button nose, which reminds me so much of Mimi's. "It smells like her," she says. A very small laugh escapes her lips, also the same as Mimi's.

I've dealt with twinges of jealousy through the years over how much Gracie takes after the Joneses. I'm a Bennett girl through and through. My nose is straight and thin, like my mouth, both of which are 100 percent my father's. I have long fingers like my father, which I'm often told must come in handy when I play the piano (because naturally I would with such fingers, and because my father's fingers fly across the ivories, filling our home with the likes of Mozart, Chopin, and Händel). I don't play the piano, but I have long Bennett fingers. They're nice fingers, nice hands . . . so long as you ignore the bitten nails and gnawed cuticles—from a nasty habit Mimi always scolded me for.

My complexion is creamy with a hint of sand-colored freckles, more Bennett than Jones. Gracie's skin, like our mother's and Mimi's, is flawless and a light-almond color. It tans gently under the Southern Californian sunshine every summer and glows all year round. Gracie has more feminine curves, a heftier chest—Jones traits of which I'm not necessarily too envious. I have some curve—just the right amount, I like to think—and am pleased the Bennett side kicked in there. I enjoy swimming and the occasional bike ride, and Gracie is a diligent jogger with a steady biking routine. If I had a nickel for every time she complained growing up (and still complains today) about how her more womanly features annoyed her during her sports routines, I'd be a wealthy woman.

Our grey-blue eyes, similar stature (I may be the little sister, but I'm proudly one inch taller at five six), ability to make taco tongues and say the alphabet backward without a single flub, love of Simon and Garfunkel, and near-identical paperclip's length of scar above the belly button (a blood sister mark that then seemed like a brilliant idea but now seems totally stupid, especially when it's bathing suit season) are a few of the clear indications that we are sisters.

If we were as close and by each other's side as often as we were as kids (and really up until it came time for Gracie to go to college), then perhaps it might be more obvious. *If* we, as twentysomething adults, had standing lunches at McQueen's Burgers on State Street or girls' nights out each Saturday, a history of trips to LA for shopping sprees or even routine text message exchanges and phone calls, then perhaps it'd be even more apparent.

But, as can happen in life, situations and people change, and the people who were once your best friends become friends, then distant relations—family members whom you love but see and talk to only when you find a free moment or when the holidays roll around. I guess you call it growing up and growing apart. I never thought the two synonymous, but such is the case with Gracie and me.

I love my sister and I love the memories of our close friendship growing up. I'd be remiss if I didn't say that I feel nostalgic for what we once shared, that I wouldn't mind having that today. But life gets busy. Things change. *People* change. And really, what's the point in trying to force something that maybe isn't there anymore? Just because you share a set of genes and used to be tight doesn't automatically mean you're cut out to be the best of friends.

And besides, with Gracie in California and me out in New York City, how exactly could we cultivate a close-knit friendship? To say nothing of our busy lives, she with her law-firm work, I with whatever multiple jobs I'm juggling to make rent. Things change, and you can fight it or flow with it, that's what I say.

"She's your sister, Juliette," I recall Mimi telling me as we strolled the grocery store aisles one afternoon when I was a junior in high school. "Don't hold grudges against her. She's your blood, your best friend."

"I wouldn't say that any*more*," I said with a dramatic eye roll.

"She may have gone off to college, but that doesn't mean she loves you any less or that you're suddenly less important to her."

"People change, Mimi." I tossed in a box of Froot Loops, a childhood favorite Mom forbade but Mimi allowed. "Gracie's making her life at college. And some day *I'm* going to go to college and I'll make *my* own life!"

"Oh, Juliette, you don't have to be so dramatic." She added a box of cornflakes to the cart, a favorite of late Grandpa Harold's and a preference of hers out of nostalgia. "You don't have to build a wall."

"Well, if I'm in New York then how exactly will we be able to stay best friends, huh?" I hopped onto the front of the cart's undercarriage and leaned forward, arms wrapping around the sides. "You know I'm going there?"

"And you should always chase your dreams, dear." Mimi searched the shelves of granola and snack bar varieties. "But don't forget that sisterhood is a beautiful, rare gift. Embrace it. Never take it for granted."

There is a heavy silence after Gracie and I set the ripe oranges among the colorful flowers atop Mimi's grave. We stand side by side, and I continue to reflect on that uneventful afternoon at the grocery store with Mimi—uneventful save for those simple words about sisterhood that have stuck with me all these years.

Mimi's conditions for inheriting her home are her final way of telling me, yet again, what she told me then. I try to find the sauciness in her last-ditch effort, the cleverness of her strong will's finding its way even after life. However, I can't help but think that this plan will inevitably fail. Gracie and I haven't lived together in eight years. A lot has happened since then. We are not the same little girls we used to be; we are two very different women. We have experiences not shared with each other and not mutually understood. We lead different lives. How is this going to work?

Gracie is the first to break the silence. "I guess we should read the first letter."

We look down at the letter labeled SPRING, a small number one scrawled in the corner.

"She really had this planned out, didn't she?" I say.

"She knew she had a set amount of time." Gracie's face is expressionless as she takes the envelope in hand. She runs a finger across Mimi's handwriting, tracing it slowly, methodically. "It is March. Spring is here."

The late-March date is not the only indication that spring has arrived. The louder chirping of the birds, the blossoming cherry trees and tulips, the warmer sun that hangs in the sky a bit longer each day, the flowering fruit and olive trees, and the growing number of farmers' market vendors, art dealers, and skateboarders that fill the streets, parks, and beaches are some of Santa Barbara's most cheerful indicators of this fresh new season.

And this letter, this first letter from Mimi.

Gracie flips over the envelope and is poised to open it. "May I?" she asks before proceeding.

I quickly consider the comfort in not knowing the contents of these letters, but with this one opened, that still leaves four. I can still hold on to Mimi for a while longer—one year, to be precise.

I nod, telling Gracie this is what Mimi wants.

"Juliette?" She pauses in her opening and looks me in the eyes. Her face is serious yet soft. She's been mourning and is trying her hardest to keep it together. "What do we do?" She swallows. "About the house? The letters?"

Exhaling loudly, I cast my eyes up at the cerulean sky. I search for a puffy white cloud, but there isn't a single one in sight. Spring has brought us one of her warmer and sunnier days.

"I mean, it's a bit peculiar, don't you think?"

I chuckle halfheartedly in response.

"We just move in . . . together, and . . ." She wags her head and brings the envelope to her side, looking spent. "This is absurd. The logistics alone." She pauses, waiting for me to respond, maybe waiting to think of an answer to her own question. Then she says again, "What do we do?"

I tighten my ponytail and cast a quick glance at the orange I gave Mimi. "It is peculiar," I say. I gesture to the envelope. As she finishes opening it, I turn to face my sister and say, "I don't think we really have a choice, Gracie."

4

Gracie

"Brunch was a good idea," I say to Juliette, who's seated across from me in the booth of a quaint diner a few blocks over from Mimi's home, where Juliette and I will be living for the next year.

God help me, I think. Barring visits and correspondence relating to Mimi in her final days, Juliette and I haven't seen each other or talked since Christmas. I know next to nothing of the life she leads in New York, and she's no more a part of mine. Now we're supposed to live together, around the clock, for one whole year? We'd be practical strangers living as roommates. *I don't know how this will work.*

"I haven't eaten breakfast yet. Figured you hadn't, either," Juliette says. "The grieving usually forget to eat." She pushes her scrambled eggs around her plate, maneuvering a few bits to her dry piece of wheat toast.

"Good idea," I repeat, distracted as the contents of Mimi's letter run chaotically through my head. *The logistics of a move. The implications if we don't agree . . .*

"Plus," Juliette says with a groan, her fork poised at her lips, "we need to chat about this house stuff." She takes a bite of egg-topped toast. "Mimi doesn't give us much of a choice, you know?"

"So you're feeling coerced, too?" I blurt out. It's a small relief, if *relief* is the appropriate word here, that I'm not alone in thinking this whole ordeal is insane. "You have reservations about it, too?"

"About living there?"

I nod as I pick up my fork, forcing myself to eat at least some of my pancakes. I was hungry when we ordered, and I know I should eat, but the stack of blueberry-and-cream pancakes no longer seems appetizing, to say nothing of healthy. *What was I thinking ordering these?*

"I love Mimi's house. We practically grew up there." She takes another bite of toast.

"What about living there with *me*? For a year? Isn't it . . . inconvenient?"

"Someone want the house all to herself?" Juliette says this with a teasing smirk.

"You know that's not what I mean."

She drops her half-eaten toast onto her plate, and a piece of egg bounces off it and onto the table. She licks her fingers and says, "Inconvenient? You mean because I live all the way across the country?"

"For one."

She just shrugs.

"Not to mention we haven't lived together in forever. We have totally different and separate lives. And the immediacy of this move," I point out. "It's all so sudden."

"So is death," she says, point-blank. "You can prepare for it as much as possible, like Mimi did, but it's not like she chose this." She piles more eggs onto her toast. "We didn't choose this house arrangement, but—"

"We do have a choice," I interrupt.

"Are you kidding me, Gracie?" Her brow furrows. "We don't have a *choice*. This is what Mimi wants, and we're going to do it."

She is right. Practically speaking, there is a choice to be made. But would either of us really consider selling? I can't fathom it; I would never do that to Mimi, to our family. "I know that," I say. "We *are* going to do it."

"So, see? We *don't* have a choice." She takes a quick bite. "Selling and donating to charity under different circumstances would be totally fine by me."

"Me, too."

"It's a noble idea."

"It is."

"But the home's been in the family for *generations*. You know as much as I do that you'd die to see the place sold, someone else moved in—"

"Our family history washed away."

"Exactly."

I heave a loud sigh and plunk my elbows onto the table. "I didn't see this coming. I just can't believe we're in this situation."

"You and me both." She takes another bite. "But look, I don't think it's that insane or as bad as you're making it out to be, Gracie." She chews some, then says halfway through her swallow, "Yes, it's bizarre. Yes, it's not really convenient. You've already got a nice place to live here. Neither of us really planned on making a big move right now." I nod repeatedly as she explains all the reasons I don't see how this arrangement is possible.

"And I live in New York," she continues. "It's inconvenient in a lot of ways, yes." She finishes her toast. "But what it comes down to is this: Mimi's death was inconvenient. Having to go through this and figure this shit out is inconvenient. I don't like it any more than you do, Gracie. It sucks." Her eyes become glossy and she swipes at her nose. "But this is what Mimi wants. I want to respect that. And I know you do, too."

"I do," I say, suddenly feeling childish for taking such a selfish perspective.

Of course it's a burden to have to figure out the logistics of the move and make choices I'd rather not have to make—to find someone to whom I can sublet my house, to pack up and move into Mimi's home and live surrounded by her memory, constantly reminded that she's no longer here. Not to mention I'll have to live with my sister. Sometimes I feel as if we're strangers, that we couldn't be more different from each other. Not exactly an ideal roommate match.

Juliette considers herself a liberal progressive, while I consider myself a moderate; she dates with abandon, I prefer long-term, intimate relationships; for Juliette, vanilla is the most boring ice cream flavor, whereas I believe it the ideal flavor because of its neutrality. Going braless, returning library books months overdue, and hitching a ride to LA instead of finding gas money are examples of the ways Juliette chooses to go about things differently from me. You will never catch me braless, my library books are always turned in early (and I never recheck them out; it seems unfair), and hitchhiking is not only essentially illegal but dangerous (as is driving until the gas meter reads *empty*).

Juliette and I live in different worlds. I have a serious career; she has her hands in all the cookie jars, not sure what she wants to do with her liberal arts degree from NYU. I have the goals of excelling at the corporate law firm where I work as a paralegal, someday getting married, buying a home, having children, maybe even getting a dog. Juliette's greatest ambition may be to become a full-time barista. She has a thick little black book, and I don't think children are anywhere near her radar. We want different things in life, we lead different lives, and now we're supposed to live under the same roof and somehow "figure this shit out," as Juliette says?

Despite my reservations, however, Juliette is right. Mimi is right. I know deep down that what my heart is telling me is right. Juliette and I have to move into Mimi's home, and we have to stay there for one year. We have to make it work somehow with the jobs, the sublets, the transfer of Juliette from New York City back home to Santa Barbara. We have to find a way to learn to live together again. We have to do it for Mimi, and we have to do it for each other. As Mimi wrote, we have to do it for sisterhood.

And if things don't work out well come the end of these four seasons, it is only one short year. In the grand scheme of things, in the brief window of time that life is, one year is only a tiny fraction of a life. And who knows? It could turn out to be a really great year. Juliette and I aren't enemies. We don't have any deep, dark resentment toward each other. We've just . . . grown apart. And now Mimi is trying to push us back together.

"Let's do it," I say at last, forcing myself to achieve a sense of resolve. "For Mimi." I consider taking a stab at the pancakes but still can't find the appetite. So instead I set down my fork and, the small mess niggling at me, pick up that stray egg of Juliette's with a napkin.

"All right, then," Juliette says. "I'll go back to New York, pack my bags, and then I guess we'll get this thing started."

"That easy? What about your job?"

Juliette just laughs, tossing her head back comically. "Please, I've got one tutoring gig and I help out a caterer when she's in a bind. Total under-the-table stuff. It's time for a change, for some adventure. This is a great excuse."

I cringe a little at her choice of words. Respecting Mimi's wishes is not an *excuse*, although what do I have to say for myself in regard to the words *obligation*, *coerced*, and *reservation* when I contemplate the impending move?

"And remember," Juliette says as she helps herself to my pancakes, "if we're doing this for any single reason, it's to keep the house in the family. Even if we come to hate the arrangement, we have to remember that. Nearly seventy years, Gracie. That's a long time, and I'm not going to be the reason that home with so much history and so many memories is sold off to some new family or some greedy developer." She takes another forkful of my pancakes.

She has a point, a very salient one that can't be overlooked. Normally I am the logical one, eagerly pointing out the practical over the emotional while Juliette gets caught up in passionate ruminations. Now the shoe is on the other foot, and it serves as the sliver of hope that Juliette and I will be able to do this.

"It'll be an adventure," she says with some enthusiasm.

"I'm not exactly adventurous, Jules." I push my plate closer to her. She can just have my pancakes at this point.

"All the more reason this is a great idea. You could use a little adventure. And I could probably use some of your order and routine." She winks. "A *little*." She holds up a bite of pancake for me to eat and doesn't relent until I take it. It's syrupy and fruity and sweet—delicious.

"Mimi knew what she was doing," Juliette says. "She was a smart cookie. And who knows, maybe once all is said and done, we'll be the best of friends, we'll love living together, and the house will be ours. Roomies for life!"

I raise a skeptical eyebrow, and a small smile crawls across my lips, the first in what feels like a lifetime. "You really think that?" I ask. I pick up my fork, ready to eat some of my breakfast after all.

"No." She licks syrup from her thumb. "But it's worth a shot."

———

I'm struck with incredulity that 1402 Laguna Lane, the home of my Mimi, my grandparents, and the grandparents before them, will be mine . . . mine and Juliette's. Presuming we can accomplish what seems like an impossible task. It is a gorgeous home, high on charm, charged with memories; it is a bittersweet honor that Juliette and I will live here.

I pick up the small collection of newspapers scattered about the dewy lawn—from a *New York Times* subscription that has seamlessly continued, from Grandpa Harold to Mimi and now to Juliette and me. I take a moment from the hustle and bustle of moving in to ponder the weight and import of this move, to take in the beauty this special home holds.

Though much has changed with Mimi's passing, and 1402 Laguna Lane will never be the same without her, and though my and Juliette's lives are about to change in many ways, Mimi's home is still very much the same.

It is painted the same light slate grey it has always been, with white wooden trim and accents to match the whitewashed picket fence that lines the front yard. It is a cooling color combo that complements the cheerful cherry red of the front door.

The home is one of the many Craftsmans in Santa Barbara's West Downtown area, among the city's charming Victorians, eclectic cottages, and classic red-roofed adobes. West Downtown is adjacent to Westside, the city's oldest neighborhood, rich with cultural history, stunning mountain views, quick access to the beach, and a level topography backing up to the rear side of the Mesa, which makes it positively idyllic for bike rides. From Mimi's home it's practically a straight shot to the harbor, and happening State Street is less than a five-minute bike ride away. The library, theater, cafés . . . they're all within easy reach by foot or bike. It is the perfect home located in the perfect wedge of Santa Barbara. Since I was born, it's been my home away from home.

I finish gathering the newspapers and walk up the front steps, sheltered by the wide and lengthy awning of the wraparound porch. I grip the front door's handle, give the old, heavy door a shove open, and find a calm in the warm, familiar fragrances of citrus and vanilla—signature scents of Mimi's home.

It took Juliette all of five days to fly back to New York City, pack up her life, and return to Santa Barbara. Standing among a small sea of boxes in the center of Mimi's living room—I suppose *our* living room—I'm both overwhelmed and underwhelmed by the fact that Juliette's life is all here, strewn about. She doesn't have all that much.

I, on the other hand, have managed, also in the brief span of five days, to tote most of my belongings the short drive over from my two-bed, one-bath bungalow. I've left behind almost all the furniture and large items, planning to sublet furnished, but I've still claimed Mimi's den, half the dining room, and one of the two guest bedrooms with my boxed-up life.

"It's going to take some elbow grease to get this place organized and livable," I say to Juliette, surveying the chaotic space. "It's a lot of extra stuff in a home that already had a place for everything, everything in its place."

Juliette shoves aside some boxes, blowing a loose strand of her long blonde hair out of her eyes. "It'll be fine. We just got here. It'll take time, but we'll make it work."

"True," I say with a nod. "At least you don't have a lot of stuff."

"It's called living paycheck to paycheck and sharing a *tiny* apartment in Brooklyn with three girls and a parakeet." She moves a box labeled Random Crap on top of a box labeled Books I Love. Juliette's labeling system makes me smile. Living with my sister is bound to bring about small moments like this from time to time, moments I know I'll need, with the hole Mimi left in my heart.

"A parakeet?" I say quizzically.

Juliette rolls her eyes. "Don't ask. It wasn't my idea." She sighs, looking at her display of boxes. "I love New York, but it felt good to leave behind that shoebox of an apartment."

She fetches a glass of ice water from the kitchen, hollering to ask if I'd like one, as well. I tell her sure and she returns with two familiar mason jars Mimi used as drinking glasses.

We stand next to each other, sipping our chilled water in silence. Looking on at the clutter about us, both of us probably having the very same thought: *What now?*

"I'll move in tomorrow," I say at last. I take another sip. "I still have a few small things back home I want to bring over. You going to crash here or at Mom and Dad's?"

"Mom and Dad's." Her face softens; she looks as if she's trying to fight back tears. "I need one more day. I'm not ready for this."

"I won't bite your head off, Jules," I kid.

"No, I know." She half laughs. "I'm just not ready for"—she waves a hand around the living room—"this. Living here, starting those letters . . ." She recalls Mimi's first letter: "This 'new beginning.'"

"I'm not ready, either, Jules," I say solemnly.

5

Juliette

I'm going to miss New York City. I've spent just one night in Santa Barbara, in my old childhood bedroom, since I turned in my Brooklyn apartment keys, and I'm already homesick.

No, I don't miss the cramped apartment or the grueling job market, nor do I miss the parakeet. I am looking forward to a new adventure. But for me New York City represented growth, a rebirth of sorts. It was nearly five years ago when I set foot on NYU's campus as a wide-eyed freshman, ready to make new friends, take fascinating English lit and art history courses, meet new and interesting East Coast boys, and learn the ins and outs of the city that'd first captured my attention when Dad came home with a rented copy of *Home Alone 2: Lost in New York*. Then came *Friends* and *Sex and the City*, and I was hooked. New York City had to be my home, much as I loved the flavor of SoCal life. New York called, and I answered.

Since graduation a year ago, finding work has been quite hit or miss, with mostly misses, but I keep a sunny outlook. There's been some barista work, the odd filing job here and the random tutoring gig there. None of it glamorous nor quite in line with what I studied, but it was still work that paid the bills (however minimally). It was still something that gave me a sense of purpose (however small). Eventually I'd find my footing.

Sure, I could've played it safe and studied something with job security, the way Gracie did. I could've stayed on the West Coast and lived with Mom and Dad or even Mimi and saved up for a place of my own, studying to become a teacher, an accountant, a lawyer.

But I've always sought adventure, something fresh, and longed to take risks. New York, NYU, and the liberal arts held that for me. And while I'm going to miss it, I'm pretty confident there's a heavy sampling of adventure in store for me here in Santa Barbara for the next year. Besides, not everything in New York was rosy. Life wasn't turning out quite as I'd pictured.

"We've got a dilemma," Gracie says as she pushes through the wide-framed cherry-red front door of the place we will now call home. She's carrying a double stack of filing boxes, one labeled Q1—2013, the other Q2—2013.

"Single-car garage, I know." I've been waiting for Gracie to bemoan the parking situation. It's a luxury to have a garage in Santa Barbara—most people resort to street parking. The garage is currently occupied by Mimi's old 1969 mint-green Citroën, which she bequeathed to me, no-need-for-a-car-in-New-York Juliette, so long as I agreed to the living arrangements. I've already prepared myself for Gracie's bitching about how she should have equal access to the garage for her car. She's that way: order, rules, fairness.

"No," she huffs. She sets the boxes down on top of two other similar boxes. "But now that you mention it, yes, that's going to be a pain." She fans at her lightly flushed face. "The bedrooms. Who sleeps where?"

"Flip a coin?" I say nonchalantly.

The choices include the largest bedroom with attached access to the only full bath, which is Mimi's room, the smaller guest bedroom with the walk-in closet, or the larger guest bedroom without a closet—walk-in or wardrobe.

I pluck a quarter from my wallet and am about to call it out when Gracie says, "I don't think either of us should take Mimi's room."

I pause to consider. It would be odd to take Mimi's room. Even if I won the coin toss fair and square, it wouldn't feel right to take it.

"Okay," I say. "It's easier, then. Guest room one and guest room two. We'll flip."

As expected, Gracie calls her side first (she always seems to get what she wants), and, also as expected, she wins and chooses the room with the walk-in closet. That's all right with me; she has more stuff anyhow.

"And the bathroom?" Gracie asks.

It's always been a frustrating matter, the single full bathroom. The home was renovated and the additional guest room added on years ago, but it is a 1920s Craftsman. For all its charm, with its original hardwood floors, Spanish tiles, wraparound porch, lush backyard garden, and single recessed garage, it lacks modern-day practicality and convenience, with the insufficient storage space, a fireplace that serves only an aesthetic purpose, and only one full and one half bath. It is a home with memories, a second home to us, and we love it for its quirks as much as for its charms. It will have to work.

"We'll have to figure out a bathroom schedule or something." Gracie answers her own question. "I don't know. We'll figure it out."

"No panic, Gracie."

"I have to be at the office every weekday at eight. Sometimes seven thirty, even seven." She looks panicked.

"Ha! No worries about me interfering with your beautifying schedule, then. I'll be sound asleep like a baby."

I gather Mimi's five letters, the opened one slipped neatly back into its envelope, and tuck them into the top center drawer of the dark wooden china cabinet in the dining room.

"Have you already found a new job?" Gracie asks.

I'm tempted to roll my eyes at the way my sister hops straight to career talk. It's her life. She eats, sleeps, and dreams her lawyer gig, and I'm sure I would too if I'd worked so hard in school to achieve that. If I had her brains and determination, her luck, then maybe that'd be my priority. But life's really too short to be stuck in an office all day, doing the same job day after day. Where's the adventure in that? To say nothing of the fact that I've only just arrived in town.

"Nope," I reply casually. "I will eventually. I mean, a girl's gotta eat."

"I can help you, if you like," she offers.

"I'm not a lawyer."

"Neither am I."

I purse my lips, confused.

"I'm a paralegal, Jules. There's a difference. I am employed *by* lawyers." She sighs, as if explaining the difference (is there one?) is going to take a toll on her.

"Fine, I'm not a *paralegal*," I correct. "What kind of work could I possibly do where you've got connections?"

"Don't get snippy." She stands from her seat atop a large box and heads to the front door, which is still propped open from her last trek in with what obviously is work she brought home. "I'm just offering to lend a hand," she says. "Maybe help you look through ads, let you know if I hear of something or see something at a coffee shop—"

"I'm a big girl," I say, defensive. "I've managed the last year on my own. I'm capable."

"I never said you weren't. I was just offering—"

"And I can do more than brew coffee." Her jumping to the assumption that I'll make espresso and warm up muffins makes my hair stand on end. While I'm perfectly fine doing that kind of work, and have in fact done it quite often, I resent the fact that that's the first thing that comes to my professional sister's mind. She might as well come out and say, "Little liberal arts Juliette, scraped by in the big city and now needs work. Should have gone to law school."

"Whatever." She holds up her hands, dismissing the conversation. "I didn't mean that." She makes her way to the door. "And I know you can do more than brew coffee. You're a bright woman, Jules."

Now I can't help but roll my eyes. "Forget it. Sorry. I barked for no reason. You don't have to patronize me."

Gracie just wags her head and disappears out the front door to retrieve what I hope, for both our sakes, is the last of the boxes to be moved in.

———

"Girls," Mom says, holding up her glass of Syrah, "I have to hand it to you. You've done a remarkable job."

"Especially considering the difficult time," Dad adds. He, too, holds up his glass of wine.

The four of us, the Bennett clan, are seated in my parents' family room. My feet are propped on the large wooden coffee table as I sit snugly on the accent chair. Dad is in his cushy recliner, Mom and Gracie on the love seat. If you swapped the topic of our current conversation from how the first week living at Mimi's together has been going for which summer camp we're most interested in, and if you pulled Gracie's layered, chin-length hair into two tight, curling pigtails and covered my left eye with that forsaken eye patch I wore to correct my lazy eye, you'd think it was another weeknight Bennett family dinner back when we were in elementary school. In some ways, not much has changed over the years.

"It's a work in progress, isn't it?" Gracie says to me with a small smile.

"One box at a time," I reply.

"It must be a bit weird being roommates again," Mom says.

Gracie and I shared a bedroom for only about two years, though we had the space; our parents thought it was smart for bonding purposes to let us share a room in the early years. Still, we were practically roommates up until we went to college. Sure, once Gracie started high school, and certainly once I did, we took to our respective rooms more often. However, for the most part Gracie always wound up playing in my room with me, and I always wound up reading in her room with her. Sometimes I'd slip into her bed at night to hide from the big bad closet monster, and sometimes she'd slip into my bed at night because she knew I was afraid of the big bad closet monster. Being roommates again after all these years of being away at school, after moving on with our lives, is not quite as second nature as tying your shoes. Though shouldn't it be? If we were so close before, shouldn't this roommate thing be like tying a knot? Or at least like riding a bike, even if the ride's a little shaky?

"It is odd," I chime in, "that we haven't bitten each other's heads off yet."

"Oh, Juliette," Gracie and Mom say simultaneously.

They do that often, Mom and Gracie. I see it as yet another thing they have in common. When they exchange glances after my comment, though, that's when I get steamed. It's as if Mom and Gracie look to each other to confirm that I am acting inappropriately. I know they've basically always been neighbors—Gracie was never one to wander far from home—and Gracie has a closer relationship with our mother than I, but they're not *that* close. And even if they were, they don't have to act like a double dose of Hayley Mills.

"Did everything arrive safely from New York?" Dad asks me, changing the topic to avoid even the slightest bit of the feminine confrontation he hates so much. Surrounded by estrogen, Dad's learned over the years how best to avoid bitchiness, quips, and hormone-induced mood swings and backlashes.

"Everything did. Thanks for helping me send it all," I say to my father as I bite my nails.

"Don't do that, dear," Mom says of my unrefined habit. She looks to Gracie and sighs.

I shamelessly bite some more with intention, just because of the mother-daughter shared sign and glances of exasperation.

"Juliette," Mom says in a signaling tone, followed by a stern, head-tilted look.

Dad tries the same tactic. "I've talked to the executor of the estate." He loudly clears his throat.

This isn't what I was hoping for—more talk of death, of deeds, of *the estate.*

"It's on the books, if you will, that you two girls are cooperating and set to see through Mimi's wishes," Dad says.

I look to Gracie, who's nodding.

"One year, and if you two carry through, the house is legally yours." He sips his wine. "If you renege, however, legally—"

"We know, Dad," Gracie says.

"And what happens after the year?" Mom inquires.

"The house is legally theirs."

"Will you two still live there?" Mom looks from Gracie to me with round, curious eyes.

I look up from chewed fingernails, look to Gracie, and shrug as she says, "I don't know. We haven't thought about it."

"Let's just get through the year first," I say with a small chortle.

"That's a sound idea," Dad says.

"We could maybe split it as a vacation home or something afterward?" Gracie proposes. "Take turns summering there or something."

"The year," I say with a rapid nod. "Let's get through the year and then decide."

———

Later that night, shortly after the grandfather clock in the living room chimes midnight, Gracie and I finish unpacking a few more boxes, then decide to call it a night. She has work early in the morning, a point she's made ad nauseam. Come six o'clock sharp, she'll need the bathroom.

We've been at a general routine for a week now. I don't see why she has to drive the point home time after time that she gets first dibs on the bathroom.

"I'll be out of here by seven fifteen," Gracie tells me, standing in my bedroom doorway. "The bathroom's yours then."

"I get it, Gracie. I get it." I don't mean to snap, but part of me knew that was what she was going to say when I heard her footsteps near, the old wooden floors creaking with each step, sounding her impending arrival. The predictability of her big-sister behavior to a little sister who's not quite so little anymore drives me batty.

You would think she would be sensitive to the fact that I've uprooted my life nearly three thousand miles away, that I've given up my job, my friends, my social life, my dream of making it in New York to slip back into a world where I, by default, fall into the role of the helpless little sister. You would think she would consider my fragile state since Mimi passed, and that nitpicking the minor, generally meaningless things in life like morning bathroom routines, how to load the dishwasher, and finding a fucking job could take a backseat for just a minute.

"What's with the attitude?" Gracie snaps back unexpectedly. She's raised her voice, something she rarely does. "You've been acting bitchy all day. For most of the week, in fact."

"You haven't exactly been a princess."

She takes two small steps inside my room, arms now akimbo. "Change doesn't come easily to me, Juliette. *What* about this has been easy? I had things figured out . . . for the most part." She flutters her lashes. "I had my house, my career, my routine."

"You and your routine," I say, exhausted.

"Yes! My routine. I had a *life*, Juliette, and now I've had to turn it all upside down, which, don't get me wrong, I'm doing because I love Mimi, but when you go and make this change purposefully more difficult—"

I'm flabbergasted. "How?" I shoot out. "How have *I* made it more difficult?"

"Your snide comments. Your nonchalance about this—this—this being an adventure, living here!" She waves a hand above her head.

"Snide comments?" I say under my breath.

"There." She points at me. "Like that."

"Wha—? Whatever."

"Your attitude is just . . . it's poor."

"Yeah, well, this ain't exactly a party, Gracie. In case you hadn't noticed."

"There! There it is again." Both hands fly to her head. "You're so blasé all the time."

I shoot up from my position on the floor, huddled over a splay of books. "Blasé?" I retort. "What do you want me to be? Happy? I'm dealing with all of this the only way I know how."

I feel myself deflate some. The book in my hand, *Paradise Lost*, drops slowly to my side. I grip the binding tightly, will myself to a state of calm, then close my eyes. "This isn't easy on you *or* me."

"God, I know. Sorry."

My eyes are still closed, but I know she's walking near. The floor stops creaking, and then I'm pulled into a warm and tight and forgiving embrace.

"I want this to work," Gracie says, eyes suddenly wet. I hear her sob into my ear, the side of her face pressed tightly to mine.

I can't hold back; I collapse into the day's first tears. I haven't had a day with a dry eye since Mimi passed. Usually I weep into my pillow at night or shed a tear when I walk down memory lane when I'm alone with my thoughts on the beach or in the backyard. When I last visited Mimi, my tears ran—an uncontrollable flood. I thought that maybe today would be the first tearless day, the beginning of the healing process, but now, as I cry like a helpless child in my big sister's arms, I tell myself that perhaps *tomorrow* will be the first tearless day, the first step toward healing.

"I want this to work, too, Gracie," I say. I bury my face in her chocolate-colored hair as I sniff back the tears. "I just want this pain to end. I want for us not just to live here for Mimi. We should make the best of a weird situation."

We pull back and appraise each other, both of us teary eyed and wet cheeked, our hair plastered to our faces. Gracie swallows hard and nods fervently.

"I want for us to get along," I say. "To do what Mimi intended by putting this . . . wild scheme together." We share a short, throaty laugh.

"Me, too." She keeps nodding. "It'll take some getting used to, living together. You know?"

"Do I."

"We'll do more than manage, though. I think we could be . . . I think we could learn to be close again, you know?" She gives me a questioning look, as if she needs to hear it from me, too, in order to believe it possible. "At least not rag on each other so much. We'll never last a year if we go on like this."

I blow out a puff of air. I am emotionally spent, struggling to keep it together, to refrain from falling prey to asperity. "Tell me about it," I say limply.

"Pinkie promise." Gracie holds up her pinkie. "As rough as it gets, in the most nagging and impossible of moments, we won't give up."

I look at her well-manicured pinkie, the nail painted a pearl color. "I can't promise we won't get on each other's nerves." I hold up my pinkie, the nail not quite manicured but at least painted, albeit a chipped mauve. "But I'll promise to try to be easier to get along with." I make an uncertain, questioning face.

"Me, too."

We lock pinkies and Gracie says, "To not giving up."

"To not giving up."

6

Gracie

"Gracie?"

I look up from the splayed manila envelopes and papers on my desk. "Good morning, Lee," I say to the associate who's responsible for the stacks of paperwork that have been consuming a good 95 percent of my time at the office lately. It's one of the more time-intensive cases so far this year at the corporate law offices of Donoghue, Sterling & White, the place I've called my second (sometimes first) home for almost four years now.

"Morning," Lee says with his usual expression—bushy brow furrowed, strong jaw squared, eyes deep in focus on the file in hand. He flips through some pages. "Have you finished annotating the memos?" His gaze stays trained on his papers.

I squeeze my eyes shut, trying to recall *which* of the many memos he's referring to. "Emmet . . . from February . . . ," I think aloud.

"Johnson and Emmet, that's right." He claps his file closed and looks at me, his expression unchanged.

"Yes," I say with certainty. How could I forget the memos that caused me to burn the midnight oil on a Friday and suffer the world's worst migraine the following day? "They're done. This afternoon I'm updating the files."

I love my work as a paralegal. Despite what many may assume, I have no aspirations to become an attorney. Being a paralegal is not a "step" but rather a well-balanced position. I'm a necessary piece in facilitating change and am able to be a part of something big and important. My work can be demanding and is challenging, and sometimes I take it home, but it comes without the extremely overbearing kind of attorney-related stress. There's no fretting over billable hours. No sapping courtroom dramatics and seemingly endless trials. No trying to make partner. Just the law and my place in it.

As I regard my desk, however, I am reminded that sometimes the job is more draining than rewarding, and not too far from that of an attorney. In the end, though, when my work on a case is done, and especially when a case is closed and the firm moves on, I'm reminded that what I do is important. I am a valued member of this small but successful firm, and my work means something. That's what I want: purpose.

"Update the files yesterday," Lee says. "We need the new contracts drafted, and for the McKenney–Lorde case we need those depositions scheduled ASAP."

"I'm on it." I quickly jot down a note for myself.

"Excellent." He sets his file on my desk. "This case will be behind us before you know it." He gives a half grin.

"And then the next one will be on our heels."

His half grin turns into a full, though brief, smile. He raps a few fingers on my desk before turning to someone two desks over, someone else, like me, who helps make his job easier. "You know it!"

My office phone rings as I bring my mug of black coffee to my lips. I've been chugging along full steam from the moment I stepped into the office a hair past seven, and I haven't had a second to enjoy my coffee, which is now tepid.

"Oh, good, I'm glad I caught you." Juliette's voice rings over the line.

I ask her what she needs. It's not the most convenient time for a non-work-related phone call. As always, her timing seems to be ironically impeccable.

"I'm trying to prune the orange tree and I can't get to the ladder." Her breath is short.

"It's probably in the garage," I say as I run a pink highlighter across a first-draft correspondence.

"I know it's in the garage, but it's in the way back, between the wall and Mimi's car."

"Your car," I point out. Though it makes perfect sense considering she doesn't have one, when I first discovered that Mimi had given her classic Citroën to Juliette, I was a tad jealous—its condition is just as mint as its vintage color, and riding around in that baby on the joyride-worthy streets and coastal roads of Santa Barbara, and Montecito and Ojai, too, would be idyllic. I suppose in my off time I could very well take those scenic cruises, but it's not quite the same in a Mitsubishi sedan.

"Have you taken that thing out for a ride yet?" I inquire. "Your license is still valid, right? You aren't scared you'll wreck it or something, are you?"

Juliette laughs. "Well, now I am. No, I just haven't gotten around to it. Everything I've needed lately is close enough to reach on foot or by bike."

Santa Barbara is one of the rare cities in California where having a car is not necessarily a requirement. Of course, being without one would be highly inconvenient in the long run. But seeing how Juliette has yet to find work and has managed to busy herself with things around the home, or at least no farther than a reasonable bike ride, it's understandable the Citroën has not yet left the garage.

"Gracie?" Suzanne, a fellow paralegal whose desk is just opposite mine, peeks her head over her monitor, brows raised.

I hold up a finger. "I'll help you when I get home, Jules," I breathe into the phone. "I've really got to go. I'm swamped."

"The tree really needs pruning, Gracie," Juliette presses. "At least, I think it does. You know what Mimi always said about not letting the branches touch the ground!"

"I know."

"They can be a bridge for snails and stuff."

"I know."

"I've been procrastinating, and now that I've put my mind to it I want to get it done. I'm worried I'll scratch the car with the ladder, though."

"So move the car," I say with a lighthearted laugh. This isn't rocket science.

"I would," she says in a tone that suggests this is obvious, not letting my sarcasm go unnoticed. "I can't find the keys. That's why I'm calling. Do you know where the keys are?"

Suzanne presses her lips together tightly, brows up as high as physically possible. "Jules, I've got to go. I'm sorry, I don't know where the keys are. Maybe call Mom or Dad. They might know. Maybe they have a spare?" Suzanne is now walking over to my desk.

Juliette starts talking again, mostly to herself, but I interrupt, saying, "Hon, I've got to go."

"Fine. I'll see you when you get home." She sighs a dejected-sounding sigh. "Hopefully not *too* late," she adds on a whining note.

"What's up?" I ask Suzanne before the phone hits the cradle.

"It's the Parker deposition," Suzanne replies with a sigh. "White wants me to team up with another paralegal and . . ." She twists her lips to the side.

"I'm the lucky sucker?" I take a quick drink of coffee, immediately regretting my ill-planned choice. I can't help but spit out the cold, muddy liquid.

"Come on, I'll brief you. It shouldn't be too tough." Suzanne motions for me to abandon whatever is at my desk—obviously far less important than this new task coming straight from the top.

As I stand, my cell phone vibrates and pings from atop a stack of papers. I glance at the freshly arrived text message as Suzanne says, "I'll buy you a drink tonight for helping me."

The name on my screen makes my stomach flip. *David.*

"Maybe we'll get a phone number, or one of us will get lucky," I faintly hear Suzanne say. Given that we are two of the few single ladies here at the firm, I know Suzanne is actually serious. I, however, couldn't be less interested.

"Yeah," I say out of politeness, a weak, nervous laugh following. I click my cell phone screen dark, not bothering to read the text message. As if I need any more distraction from work today.

"There's a new bistro/bar place that's opened up near the Arlington Theatre," Suzanne says as she leads the way, her patent black sling-backs click-clicking against the tile. "I don't know about you, but my romantic life needs a lift." She casts a glance over her shoulder and adds, "And judging by the hours you clock here, yours does, too."

I swallow, flash her a conciliatory grin, and say, "Something like that."

———

"Get out of here!" Juliette shouts into her cell phone. She's curled up on the wingback that Grandpa used to watch baseball in, a bag of Bugles in his lap, an iced tea on the end table adjacent, set on one of Mimi's many lace doily coasters. Those lace doilies are still all over the house, subtle reminders that this is still Mimi's home in many ways, that she is still here reminding us that the best way to deal with beverage rings is to prevent them. I notice Juliette's can of Coke neatly set on a doily, and I smile.

"He did *not* say that," Juliette barks at whoever is on the other end of the call. She's incredulous, staring ahead at nothing in particular, eyes round. She lazily winds and unwinds a strand of hair around a finger as she shrieks some more disbelieving remarks.

I'm teleported back to our teen years when Juliette and I, much to our parents' chagrin, discovered the beauty of the telephone (and what a grand distraction it was from homework). Juliette's always been the more social sister, the more popular among the crowds in junior high and high school. In grade school, even.

When it came time to plan our birthday parties each year, Juliette had a guest list the size of Texas. My mom sagaciously limited her to a tolerable number year after year, insisting that our home was only so big, a cake's slices could be only so narrow. As a young child, I took Mom's rebuttals at face value.

As I got older and Juliette's guest list still remained the size of a small country, even growing from one year to the next, and as Mom continued to throw out excuses (some rather far-fetched) for why she had to limit the list, I came to learn that Mom was playing that delicate and all-too-familiar game mothers come to master. My birthday party guest lists were never state-size. I couldn't even touch Rhode Island. Mom obviously didn't want my feelings hurt, didn't want there to be any excuse for her daughters to resent each other, to fill with jealousy. I appreciated the rules Mom set in order to keep the peace, to keep me from feeling that I had shortcomings in the social arena. Though I was far from unaware of the popularity of my little sister, ignorance (and avoidance) can be bliss.

While we both enjoyed phone privileges, Juliette enjoyed them far more often than I ever did, and I was all right with that. I still am. I know now that being the more introverted sister, the less dramatic sister, the sister who does not have a slew of acquaintances, is just as okay as being Juliette.

After a twelve-hour workday and a deposition that lasted for one-third of that day, however, the last thing I want to come home to is one side of a conversation that sounds as if it's being had by two fifteen-year-old girls. Juliette's shouts, gasps, and *omigod*s are borderline unbearable.

"He's such a douche, seriously," Juliette drawls into the phone as she gnaws on her thumbnail. "I told you Dirk was never serious material. His name alone! I mean, come on, Alexandra, you couldn't be serious. *Dirk?*"

I turned Suzanne down for that drink she wanted to have. The deposition had taken the little energy I had remaining. Right about now, though, I wish I were knocking one back with her.

I set my briefcase and purse on the dining table and, by rote, withdraw my cell phone. I'm suddenly reminded of the text message I blissfully ignored all day. I'm surprised I've managed to delay reading it; I haven't heard from David since . . . February.

"Finally!" Juliette says loudly, breaking my concentration. Feeling as if I'm caught with my hand in the cookie jar, I drop my phone atop the table and spin on my heels. "I thought you'd never come home." She tosses her own phone onto the wingback.

"Busy day," I say. I stuff my phone back into my bag. More blissful avoidance never did anyone any harm.

"Tell me about it!" Juliette does a ballerina twirl, her hands dancing wildly above her head. "You would be so proud of me." She's radiant.

"You found a job?" I've made a mental note to ask about her employment with less frequency, because she finds it pressuring, and I don't want to nag.

Juliette and I are finding a generally pleasant way to coexist under these less than traditional circumstances. When I go and, as she says, "rock the boat" by prying into her life, things get tense. We end up fighting, going to bed angry, and rethinking our decision to take on this yearlong project. I immediately regret my question.

"*Nooo,*" Juliette groans.

"Forget I asked." I hold up surrendering palms.

"It was so awesome!" She doesn't seem to be in the mood to go down that bickering road again. Her news must be too good to delay. "I drove! Dad had a spare set of keys, came over, the damn thing didn't start. Something about a dead battery?" She looks puzzled. "Anyway, eventually we took her for a spin, and Gracie, it purrs like a kitty cat."

I crack a smile and laugh. My sister's enthusiasm for the simplest things in life—deliverable sushi, the GEICO commercials, a car ride—can be endearing.

"And guess what else?" she asks, wide-eyed.

"You pruned the tree?" I dig through the kitchen cupboards, searching for something to whip up for dinner.

"I did. It's not exactly the job of Edward Scissorhands, but practice makes perfect, right?" Hands behind her, palms on the counter's ledge, she pushes herself up onto the counter. She bunches the overflow of her purple linen skirt between her legs.

I tell her I'm impressed she's caring for the garden. Mimi would be proud.

"The surface hasn't even been scratched, my dear," she says. "We've got to channel Martha frickin' Stewart soon. The garden's getting unwieldy."

"Oh yeah?"

"Dad said he hasn't seen so many weeds or out-of-control mint plants in the time he's known this home."

Grabbing a box of Rice-a-Roni, I look to Juliette with pursed lips. I shake the box. "Ate yet?"

She shakes her head.

"Well," I say, "then I guess we better figure out what we're doing and get to work out there."

Juliette and I used to tend to the garden with Mimi relatively routinely. As we got older, time spent in the garden was usually with tea and cookies rather than shears and topsoil. We still tended to the tomatoes (usually when we wanted to make a fresh batch of salsa or pico de gallo); we picked herbs every time we visited—mint for the iced tea, chives for the salad, basil for the pasta sauce; and we always gave the orange tree attention, whether by helping water it, picking its succulent fruit, or having conversations in its shade.

Managing the entire garden, though? The tomatoes, oranges, lemons, herbs, squash, and potatoes, not to mention the flowers and shrubs and trees? That was Mimi's territory; we were only ever assistants. Taking on her luscious garden will either break the two of us (to say nothing of the harvest), or it will bring us together (Mimi's plan, I am sure) and harvest will be plentiful (one can hope). Although there's still a good chance the harvest will be nonexistent even if the Bennett sisters get along merrily as they try to earn themselves a show on HGTV.

"I'm one step ahead of you." Juliette jumps from the counter, nabbing the Rice-a-Roni box from my hands. "I picked up some magazines and found some old gardening books around here." She returns the box to the cupboard. "We just need to do some homework first. Shouldn't be too tough."

"And that was dinner . . ."

"Come on." She plucks a set of keys from the windowsill above the kitchen sink. "We're going out for dinner. My treat. You're going to *love* the car."

"I've been in the car plenty of times before," I point out. I have many fond memories of hopping in that car with Mimi, Grandpa, and Juliette. Trips to Carpinteria and Summerland beaches, short rides to one of our many favorite diners, the ice cream shop, the grocery store, the pumpkin patch come Halloween.

"You haven't been in the car with *me* at the wheel, girlie." There's a sparkle in Juliette's eyes.

"Well . . . are you sure you want to treat? Can you afford it?" Again, I bite my tongue for jumping to job implications.

"And money-shmoney! It's not like I'm dead-ass broke. Besides, I'm making money. I've got a job."

I'd hardly call mowing our neighbor's lawn twice a week a job. For Juliette, I suppose it's a start.

She charges for the front door, picking up my purse on her way. As she does, my cell phone falls out and she nabs it before I can.

"Does McQueen's sound good?" She hands me my purse and phone, and I nearly miss her question because my heart is pounding at the sight of my phone. David's name and his unread text message refuse avoidance.

"Okay," I say, not really sure I've heard where it is we're going for dinner. It doesn't matter, though. I'll go anywhere if I can buy more time before I read and respond to David Nichol's text.

7

Juliette

You'd think I would have learned my lesson from partying hard in college, or the one too many weekends out since then. One drink is fine, two is all right, three is pushing it. Four makes me ask myself, "What were you thinking, Jules?" Four makes Gracie ask the same question of me.

I have a colossal headache, the ultimate price for staying out well past any reasonable bedtime, frequenting new bars, meeting new people, making new friends, collecting new potential romantic interests. In all the time of digging the Brooklyn night scene, standing in line for the hottest clubs in Chelsea, and toasting the night away on cheap champagne in whatever pub or lounge we could squeeze into (and afford) in the Village, I've forgotten how much fun a girl can have in her old stomping grounds.

Last night I took my sweet new ride to a relatively new bar across town. It was mostly a college-age scene, but twenty-three is still a very passable age for such a crowd. I begged Gracie to come out with me. "On a Wednesday night? Are you crazy?" she'd said. I know, unthinkable.

Since we've started living together I've realized just how much she lives under a rock, her social life not extending much further than her office and phone calls with Mom. Her love life is just as weak, if it exists at all. Unless she's secretly got something going on with one of those lawyers at her firm . . .

I doubt it. As discreet as Gracie is, she's also prim, proper, and proud of her high moral code. If she's in a relationship, it's one of the folders that go into her filing cabinet, so to speak. Though it would be private, details for her eyes only, her relationship status would be a known fact, labeled, part of her routine.

"How about Friday night, then?" I proposed, a heavy whine in my tone. She just stalled, then gave me the run-of-the-mill "We'll see" response. I told her that if she, like my car, doesn't get out there and use what she's got under the hood, it'll just stop working. She shooed me off, told me her hood was just fine (and none of my business), and wished me a good time, followed by a stern "Don't drink and drive."

I squint against the bright-white morning light streaming through my east-facing bedroom window. "Son of a bitch," I mutter, thinking early riser Gracie should have gotten this bedroom. Even though the window's covered with thick-paneled blinds, the near-summer sun is strong enough to seep powerfully through the cracks.

Rubbing my temple with one hand and shielding against the offensive sun with the other, I try to recall how I wound up home last night. I notice my car keys on the small nightstand, as well as a sticky note on a mason jar of water.

"Hope you had fun. (But not too much.) I'll pick up the car with you after work," reads the note from Gracie.

I sip some water and vaguely recall the cab ride home, shared with, as evidenced by the blotchy blue-inked name scrawled on my left hand, someone by the name of Rob. Making out the digits under his name would take a decoder. Looks like one potential romantic interest's been lost. Maybe next time. I grab my searing head—a next time that won't involve so much booze.

———

The orange feels ripe and solid in my hand. I rub my thumb across the lightly bubbled, waxy globe and think about Mimi, about the last orange I left for her. The habit came about artlessly. The first orange I brought for her, the one with a twin from Gracie the morning after her will was read, was ceremonial. The second orange, which I brought on a visit to Mimi's resting place alone a few days later, was an unintended gift. I'd originally brought it to snack on while I had my first private conversation with Mimi. Before I knew it, I was caught up in my emotions, my appetite lost, and, seeing how the first orange I'd placed had begun to shrivel, I gave Mimi another one.

When I came with the third orange, with intentions of giving it to Mimi, I also brought another for a snack. The delectable fruit, at its most ripe, was nearly as comforting to my soul as the conversation I had with my grandmother.

Now it's a habit. Every few days I find myself sitting atop the vibrant green lawn of the Meadows Memorial site where my grandmother has been laid to rest, sharing oranges with her. We talk about everything and anything, even secrets. Especially secrets.

We talk about the mundane, such as the weather, the tourists, if the menu at Meryl's Café over on Vittoria Street has anything unique on it, such as rose-flavored macaroons, lemon curd waffles, or eucalyptus and mango chutney on rye toast. We talk about life in general: how the garden's coming along (so far slow going, though nothing has wilted away yet); how Gracie seems to work too much (she really needs a social life); how I'm liking living at 1402 Laguna Lane (it's beginning to feel like home); how it's going living with Gracie (it has its ups and downs, but we're making the most of it); my job search. That's when we talk about secrets. It's the only time I talk about my secrets.

I have a lot of friends . . . they're all back in New York City. No one friend is really super close, no one nearly as close to me as Gracie used to be. I have friends, though, and some I consider relatively close confidantes. Well, *used* to consider close confidantes, I guess I should say. Maintaining friendships when thousands of miles separate you is proving to be difficult, especially since none of those friendships really had the sturdy, can-weather-any-storm legs required to sustain such distance to begin with.

I ran with a diverse crowd in college, most of them as far left socially and politically as you'd imagine those who flood the NYU campus to be. I felt at home. Like the crowd I ran with, I'm a pretty free-spirited kind of girl. I embrace the to-each-their-own philosophy when it comes to many controversial subjects. Although there comes a time—there *came* a time—when living free as a bird and raging against societal norms and expectations wasn't exactly all it was cracked up to be. Sometimes you can get in too deep, things go too far. I found it in my best interest to grow apart from the crowd over the years. For a number of reasons, come graduation, everyone bound to go their own way, most of my friends from that particular circle were no longer at the top of my recent-calls list.

The friendships I do still have are no longer the strongest and grow only weaker, more shallow and superficial, with each week that passes. My old roommates, for instance, no longer shoot the breeze with me about shitty days at work, fights (and sexy makings up) with boyfriends, and the gamut of things twentysomething girls trying to find their place in the city talk about. Gone are the days when we'd have late-night talks about everything from relationships to philosophy. I'm no longer in their inner circle, so to speak.

Time and space have planted themselves between us, and the great divide grows. As it grows, our correspondence turns from personal conversations to a barrage of questioning and facts. They'll keep asking when I'm coming back to town; they'll succinctly dish the gossip about who's dating whom and how vile or delightful the matches are; and then they'll make mention of who's trying to get shares with whom in the Hamptons this summer (and how impossible it is, as it is *every* year, to score a really cheap place), tossing out a "We wish you could join us!" but not necessarily as if they really *did* wish I could join them. It's not the same, and I know the divide will only grow with time.

My place is here for now; this is where I belong. Over time my life will take shape in Santa Barbara, just as it did back in New York City. Life's an adventure, after all. It's probably good I got away, turned in one adventure for another.

As it stands, though, what's a girl to do when her network of friends is no longer the reliable place for her to share her thoughts, concerns, and even secrets? Finding a friend I can turn to when I need a listening ear, or a nugget of advice, or a shoulder to cry on is considerably more difficult now.

My conversations with Mimi are more therapeutic than actual conversations. They make me feel that someone understands, someone listens, someone reserves judgment. I've thought about talking to Gracie, but she's so busy, and she wouldn't understand anyhow. Mimi's always listened. Even though I may not have divulged my grittier secrets and thoughts to her when she was alive, she was always a good listener.

When I called Mimi my junior year to tell her that I feared I'd failed my sociology exam and blown all chances of getting a passable grade come the end of term, Mimi calmed me down. She talked me out of dropping the course and told me to talk to my professor, see if I could retake the exam or nab some extra credit. If that failed—if "making an effort" failed, as she said—then I could drop the course, plan on taking it again next term, and cut back on the partying. I distinctly remember her lighthearted chuckle when she said that last part. She also said that a Jones girl had fun in her blood. She empathized with my trouble, having enjoyed one too many sock hops in her day.

When I rang the following week, telling Mimi that I had successfully passed a retaken exam, she told me she'd known I had it bagged. When I told her I had celebrated passing it with tequila shooters with some friends, she told me she would have done just the same. No judgment, no lecture. It was always the perfect give-and-take with Mimi.

Of course, I never shared with her that one night my senior year. I haven't shared that with anyone, save my circle back in New York. Judgments and lectures would certainly have flown; all hell would have broken loose had I shared the events of that night with my family. My parents, Gracie, even Mimi would have shrouded me in a suffocating cloud of disappointment and shame. Some secrets are meant to be taken to the grave . . . or shared at the grave.

Through my private conversations with Mimi now, I find release, escape, the comfort that a close friendship provides. I can talk to her about why I get so nettled when Gracie pries about my lack of a job, or that I don't want to have to explain why getting work isn't as easy for me as it is for her, or why I did what I did that foolish night in Brooklyn last spring . . . how I got to that point. I talk to Mimi and she listens. And sometimes you need a friend who will just listen.

There are two sides to every coin, though, and eventually you'll need that friend who will impart advice, assure you that everything will be all right, and say that there is no sin that can't be forgiven, even when you think shame has gotten the best of you. Eventually my conversations over oranges with Mimi will not be enough.

But for now, I think as I set Mimi's orange on her headstone, it is just what I need.

———

Mowing lawns isn't going to cut it in the long run. This much I know. But it's something. It's a start. It's been more than two months since the move, and I haven't found what Gracie calls "reputable employment." I do, however, have seven different lawns I mow throughout the week. Never fancied myself a gardener, but cash is cash and work is work, after all. I've had worse gigs.

I've been tending to Mimi's flower gardens pretty well. *Better Homes and Gardens* knows its stuff. Although I'd like to think that years of practice as a young child planting and watering the blooms with Mimi has more to do with it. The various roses lining the house are blossoming, and I've been snipping some and bringing them to Mimi. I have so many I've started to make hand-tied bouquets and bring them to the cemetery, where I sell a handful to the gift shop each week.

I'm hoping to find real work soon, something that pays an actual paycheck, requires set hours (and a sense of responsibility). I need something where I feel as if I'm *actually* using that degree I busted my ass for. If I could get a tutoring deal, that'd be nice, or even work at a bookstore or coffee shop . . . I don't know. It isn't easy finding work, and I'm not even asking for something glamorous, not expecting that dream job.

Until an opportunity pops up, I've got to make the most of what I have (and get Gracie off my back about finding a *real* job). I'm accustomed to getting by somehow. As of last night I have half a dozen brooches and hair ornaments for sale on Etsy. Not necessarily requiring that art history minor, but a creative outlet nonetheless.

The other day, while unpacking and organizing the contents of my very last box, I came across an old Bloomingdale's dress box of Mimi's under the bed. It was filled with craft materials—ribbons, lace, fabric scraps, vintage buttons, beads. I always favored craft hour in school and dreamed of making some kind of an artsy career for myself, so I decided to have some fun.

I shuffle through things in the den, searching for some envelopes or packing material. I've sold three of my brooches and want to run them by the post office before the mail is sent out.

Gracie's claimed the den as her space, for the most part, which is fine by me. Grandpa used to use the desk for reading the *New York Times* (a love affair he passed down to both Gracie and me), working his crosswords, and penning complaints or notes to companies about products enjoyed or loathed. Once he passed, and until now, the space was rarely used.

Gracie now has filing boxes, paperwork, and all sorts of office stuff in here. She brings her work home, and the den's the perfect place to do it. Save for the wingback in the corner, with a small 1960s vintage beverage cart and an overarching metal globular lamp completing the bookish area, the den is mostly an office. There's a long, shallow wooden desktop built into the wall, a large bay window above a good half of it looking out into the garden, two filing cabinets, and a swiveling office chair that looks as if it were picked up straight off the set of *Mad Men*.

I nudge some of Gracie's things around, not wanting to disturb her pristine order. She's a stickler about that kind of thing. I pull open one drawer, then another. I flip past the loose-leaf papers mixed in with coupons probably long expired. As luck would have it, I find the keys to the Citroën. There's a paper tag attached to them, the kind you see in garage sales or at antique stores, and on it is written JULIETTE'S RIDE.

A sting rushes to my heart. Mimi knew her time was nearing when she made this tag, when she began to assess who would become the new owners of the items she would leave behind.

As I slip the key in my back jeans pocket, a small smile tugs at the corner of my mouth. I think of how I miss Mimi, of how clever she was to devise this home-sharing plan. Summer's only a handful of weeks away. Though it hasn't been easy and I don't know if we'll really make it in the end, as that circled date on the calendar grows nearer I feel a sense of accomplishment and pride that we're almost one season down, one step closer to a goal achieved. To doing what Mimi wanted.

I survey the desktop, beginning to fear that the last of the envelopes went with the last of Grandpa's letters of complaint. I reach for a paper organizer. Nothing useful in it, and nothing useful in the thick binder next to it.

I'm nearly ready to capitulate when my eyes fall to a small floral-patterned box I haven't noticed until now. It's on the desk between a three-ring binder and a thick law book. I rifle through the box, finding receipts, scribbled-on Post-its, a hair band, a movie ticket stub, an old car wash ticket. No envelopes. Then I find a slightly worn photo of Gracie and—

"Where'd you put the biodegradable garden bags?" Gracie appears out of nowhere, startling me so I drop the box. Its contents spill out over the desk, making a ruckus. The photo remains in my grip as I look to Gracie.

"The bags. I thought you used them the other day when you were working on the hydrangeas?" She swipes an arm across her forehead. Her face is glistening with sweat from her work in the garden.

"This is David," I blurt out. I turn the photo to Gracie. "You and David." I flash her a schoolgirl smile.

Gracie darts over and yanks away the photo. Her already-flushed face instantly grows a darker shade of red. "What are you doing going through my stuff?"

Her response takes me by surprise. "I didn't mean to," I say with a baffled laugh. She can't seriously be upset with me. "Come on, Gracie. Chill." I peek at the photo clutched tightly in her hand. "It's just a photo." I plant a protesting hand on my hip. "Of an ex-boyfriend. Every girl's got 'em."

She regards the photo for a flash of a moment before stuffing it, and the rest of the scattered objects, back into the box. "Forget about it," she says hastily.

"We're sisters!" I exclaim incredulously. "Where's the fun in that relationship if we can't share woes about guys, huh?" I crack another smile, hoping to encourage some gaiety.

The discovery of this photo could be just the catalyst for a close sister-to-sister exchange, something we could sorely use at a time like this. At a time when we've lost one of the most important and influential women in our lives and need more support and concern and love than the occasional whisper through tears of mourning that "It'll get easier." When we need a hearty laugh, a practical joke, or just a lazy Sunday afternoon indulging in gossip or having a heart-to-heart to forget about our pain, to remember the simple joys of life. We could use a beat of normalcy now—sisters being sisters and doing . . . I don't know, what sisters do!

While we may share the roof over our heads, the memories trapped within the walls, and the pleasures buried in the garden, we do not share a sense of camaraderie. What lies beneath the surface is left untouched; it's simply about survival as roommates at this point, not rekindling a relationship. How will we get through three more seasons like this?

"There's no relationship to talk about," Gracie mutters. She pries the photo free from the box, eyeing it with what looks like a mixture of skepticism and longing.

"Exes . . . one-offs . . . serious relationships . . . *any* of it." I'm not about to give up on this chance to talk, to bond. "There's obviously *something* worth talking about. I mean, who prints out photos these days anyway, huh?"

As Gracie stares at the retrieved photo in her hands, I feel I still have a chance to get her to open up, to share a laugh with me, an anecdote. Something, anything! I gently give her shoulder a nudge. "I'll tell you about my last guy if you tell me about you and David."

Silence.

I point at the photo. "When was this taken? Were you on a date?"

She sets the photo in the box.

"Gracie—"

"I don't want to talk about it."

"Oh, come on."

"No!" she barks. "It's none of your business anyway."

"Sheesh, Gracie. I was just having a bit of fun. Try it sometime."

She angrily stuffs the box back into its place and half shouts, "Well, it's all fun and games until someone gets hurt, okay?" She fixes me with a pointed glare. "Please just stay out of my personal stuff."

I soften my tone, my face. "Gracie." I hold out a hand.

She spins on her heel, making her way out of the den in a huff.

"Gracie?" I call out, but to no avail.

I'm beside myself—did *not* see that one coming. I know Gracie and David had a serious thing going and it didn't end up the way Gracie had imagined. It's not a happy-ending topic, but it can't be something out of the *War of the Roses* playbook.

Crossing my arms over my chest, I look about the den in silence. I contemplate following her out to the garden and trying to smooth things over. I'm not sure how much good it'd do.

The man in the photo with Gracie is David Nichol. David was the love of Gracie's life, at least for her college years. I don't think she's ever been so over the moon for anyone else. She's not exactly an open book with her love life (or with much else, for that matter). David Nichol, though, was a tidbit of her life she couldn't hide. She met him when she was going to college at USC. They'd grown up only streets apart, unaware of each other, but it wasn't until college that they finally met and hooked up. They dated for a while until he went to law school or grad school or something. It was a mutual breakup, Gracie insisted, but she was torn up over it. She lost probably ten pounds, as well as her interest in going out on Saturday nights, mingling, dating, having fun, or a social life. I don't really know what went down between them because at that point I was off at NYU, living out my own relationship drama sophomore year.

Eventually Gracie came around, gaining back those ten pounds and not being *as* averse to having some semblance of a social or romantic life. She said she and David were on decent terms, just friends. When David returned home for the holidays or to visit his folks, they'd see each other, catch up. She said they had an on-again, off-again thing, whatever that means in Gracie's world. Whenever I asked, she'd clam up or dismiss it, saying it wasn't going anywhere anyway. What was the point? They were, after all, *just friends*.

The photo of the two of them, though, can't have been taken all that long ago, and that's what really sparked my curiosity. Sure, we've all got those stashed-away photos of long-lost loves. But this photo? Gracie's wearing the black-pearl-and-diamond earrings Mimi gave her last Christmas, a pair identical to my own. That means that *sometime* between Christmas and now, she and David have to have seen each other, have to have had some kind of a relationship. Judging by the way they look in the photo, I'd say something was going on between them. Something that was more than *just friends*.

Still alone in the silence, in the wake of Gracie's anger, I decide to do what I know Mimi, whose spirit is all around this house, would certainly frown upon.

I peer out the window, into the garden, watching Gracie blaze a choppy, angry path past the orange tree, past the lemon tree, and on to the tomato plants. I look at the small floral-patterned box and remove the lid. Returning my gaze to Gracie, who's now on her haunches, picking and pruning the unruly tomato plants, I blindly fish for the photo.

The Gracie in the photo is wearing a sparkling sapphire dress, the kind of dress a woman would wear only on a special occasion. She has both arms wrapped around David's waist, and she's kissing his cheek. David, who's wearing an open charcoal-grey suit jacket with a white button-up, top two buttons undone, and an expression that says, "She's with me," has his lips drawn up at one corner. He's looking into the camera with piercing blue eyes, made bluer by the stark contrast of his smooth jet-black hair. It looks as if they're in a restaurant booth or maybe a bar. As if they're on a date. As if they're an item. David's hand on her shoulder is gripping her tighter than it would if he were "just a friend."

February 2014 is written on the back of the photo.

Only three months ago. If Gracie and David were in some kind of a relationship three months ago, what happened between then and now, and how the hell have I been able to live under the same roof and not know a damn thing?

I slip the photo back into the box, clicking my tongue against the roof of my mouth. *Three months,* I think.

I situate the box back in its rightful place and silently pitch up an apology to Mimi, who I know is watching and clicking her own tongue, but in that *tsk-tsk* way she used to do when I'd sneak a second Popsicle I wasn't supposed to have before dinner.

Gracie's still tending to the tomato plants. She's working at a quick pace, most likely fueled by the unfortunate discovery. As she plucks and tosses and waters, caring for the tomato plants in very much the same determined way as Mimi (plus the air of hostility), I can't help but think that every woman has her secrets. Who am I, of all people, to get my feathers ruffled over my sister's neglecting to share the intimate parts of her life when I've got my own skeletons buried in the closet?

8

Gracie

That's just like Juliette, to go nosing through my stuff, asking me questions about something she *knows* is a sensitive topic. And what does she care about David and our history anyhow? We broke up four years ago and she's never so much as uttered his name since then.

In fact, as soon as she left for NYU, she couldn't have cared less what was going on in my life. She had her life, her friends, her relationships, and I had mine. Now she suddenly has an interest in David? In my life? Because we're forced to live together doesn't suddenly mean we're—*poof!*—best friends!

I've sometimes wondered what would have happened had Juliette and I gone to the same college or at least stayed within a few hours' drive of each other. Would we have remained the close sisters we were growing up? Or would time or distance have eventually found its way between us anyhow, resulting in the very divide that's planted itself between us today?

Regardless, Juliette's digging up my demons and wanting to chat nonchalantly about them as if we're the best of friends, closest of confidantes, is nothing short of pernicious.

I grit my teeth and prune the tomato plants too viciously—a vine that was once sturdy has now snapped in half. I curse under my breath as I finish off the damaged vine.

"Slow and thoughtful." I hear Mimi's voice as I place the broken vine into a bucket for compost. "A hasty gardener may get the job done quickly, but a patient gardener gets the job . . ."

"Done well," I finished for Mimi. I gently tamped down the soil with my small seven-year-old hand. I flashed a gap-toothed grin up at my grandmother, my face shadowed by her wide-brimmed sun hat.

"That's right." Mimi handed me my small plastic watering can, colored hot pink and yellow, a daisy sticker in the center. "Now, a small first drink," Mimi sweetly instructed in that smooth, kind voice of hers. She was the perfect teacher—patience in every instruction, kindness in every suggestion, authentic joy in every word of praise. "Make sure you try to avoid the leaves there. We don't want them to get burned."

"Like our skin!" I exclaimed loudly as I considered the oily screen that coated me. In my excitement, I accidentally sprinkled some water on the baby tomato plant's low leaves. "Oh no!" I cried.

"That's all right." Mimi showed me how to wipe away the spilled water.

"Did I ruin it?" I copied her slow and gentle movements, drying each leaf with a tattered rag.

"No, Gracie dear. Not at all. There's nothing that can be done that can't be made better. Did you know that?"

I scrunched up my face, not really sure what she meant.

I followed her to the next row in the garden, the row of slowly sprouting green beans. Only some months ago the beans had been nothing but carefully tilled soil in precise mounds Mimi, Juliette, and I had made together, again an exercise in patience over speed. I may have been born with a meticulous gene or two, but Mimi fine-tuned them with each afternoon we spent together in the garden.

"It means," Mimi began, "that mistakes can be made, but we can fix them."

"Like accidents?" I said. She told me I was on the right track. "Like when I accidentally broke Daddy's coffee mug? And when I helped him glue it back together?"

"You're a smart girl, Gracie."

"I didn't glue it so good." I laughed, my shoulders rising and falling with each tiny beat of laughter. "Daddy tried it after and water went all over the place. It was really funny . . . but it wasn't. His shirt was *all* wet."

"You made an effort," Mimi said. "An honest effort, and even if the glue didn't hold, you still tried. And that's what counts." She handed me a small plastic shovel, hot pink and yellow to match my watering can. "In the end," she said, grabbing her spade—larger than mine, wooden, professional, "all was made better. The effort and care made it better."

Ruminating, I set down my pruning shears and remove my gardening gloves. I take a seat on the soil, disregarding the moist ground and the mark that will inevitably be left on my jogging shorts. The sun is burning more brightly than it has all week. Summer is not far off.

Maybe I'm not being fair to Juliette. Maybe her showing an interest in David was an attempt—shoddy as it may have been—to connect with me on a more intimate level. Maybe she wanted to make simple conversation, make an effort. Maybe she actually cares about what happened between David and me. Maybe I was too harsh, too defensive, too guarded, too unwilling to make an effort.

David Nichol, the man who stole my heart and refused to return it, is so intimate and painful a subject I'm not sure I'd know how to share the details with Juliette. Aside from Mimi's passing, I haven't had a serious, emotional discussion with Juliette in years. I don't think I'd know where to start, what to expect.

I've never had the fortune of a very best friend, someone I could turn to in the darkest hours, in the most questionable of situations, with no second-guessing. I used to have Juliette, but then we grew up and she did her own thing. There was always Mimi, and Mom was good to talk to, too. And there was David, but none of them were the same as that very close and best friend.

I've always lacked that special relationship—that unique bond— a woman can share with another woman. Growing up, I had a few friends, but no one I'd share a split-heart best friends charm bracelet with, and in college my friendships weren't the type where you'd rouse someone from sleep at three in the morning just to gush about a date or plan a spring break trip south of the border. I don't know why, but I suppose some women are just handed that no-BFF-for-you card—the unluck of the draw?

Even if I could regard my sister as my best friend, how would I begin to build that bridge? How would I go from keeping things close to the chest all these years to suddenly confiding in someone I some-times feel I barely know? And if I did muster the courage, would Juliette reciprocate? Would she, too, open up? Would she understand me? Or would she judge?

Juliette's never been one to toss about judgments and make you feel like an outcast. Yet I still have to ask, *who* would she be within the circle of intimate sisterhood? Would she stick around when the going got tough? When we neared the close of a full year and had the option to go our own ways, would she still be here?

I have to be honest with myself. The unknown makes me nervous. I don't like to be vulnerable. I've been able to go all these years without having that close friend in whom I can confide. Why should I allow the passing of my Mimi, God rest her soul, to serve as the occasion for me to offer up my heart and feelings on a platter, in the name of a sister-hood that may or may not be there?

Sure, Juliette and I could try to form a bond over Mimi's passing, become more involved in each other's lives as we share a home together. What happens afterward, though? Does Juliette seek another adventure?

Do we go back to being sisters who talk on rare occasion, see each other for the usual family holidays, and that's it? Do I put my heart on the line and invest in a relationship that, like so many before, could dry up, maybe even leave me the worse for wear? Or, if I don't, could I be passing on a potentially beautiful experience? That dear friendship I've always wanted?

I dust the dark dirt from my kneecaps and stand, then dust my stained shorts and head up to the house.

I decide that if Juliette wants to make an effort, it's not only the job of the older sister to oblige, it's the right thing to do. I should at least meet her halfway.

Besides, I think I'm feeling more unsettled at the way I treated Juliette over the discovery of the photo than I'm feeling angry at the fact that she found the photo and that it exists in the first place. If I'm so upset that it exists, though, one might ask why I've bothered keeping it all these months.

Flinging open the back door, I smile to myself, somehow feeling comforted in the fact that I, and I alone, know very well why I have that photo and why I intend to keep it. And why the secrets behind it shall remain secrets . . . at least for now.

———

"So the girl *does* drink!" Juliette says, a flabbergasted look about her. She takes a hearty pull on her wine. Her hair's done up in a high, mussed bun. She's wearing bright-blue, sparkly eye shadow that reminds me of the covers of some of the old albums of Mom's stashed in a trunk in Mimi's bedroom. I half expect Juliette to belt out a few verses from Bonnie Tyler's "Total Eclipse of the Heart."

"I'm not a prude, Jules, contrary to what you may think of parale-gals who take their work home," I say after a sip of Chardonnay.

"Well, it is only wine." She winks. "And thank *God* you're out of that office and letting loose. It can't be healthy to be so committed to work like that."

"As opposed to . . . slacking off? Not caring about my job?" I snicker and take another sip.

Though I was initially opposed to going out for drinks on a Thursday, the light buzz, upbeat music, and contagious friendly atmosphere of the wine bar remind me that getting out of my shell was a good idea. Juliette said she wasn't about to move from letter one to letter two of Mimi's without having shared a drink on the town with her big sis. "It's unconscionable," she said.

"You look fabulous tonight, Gracie," Juliette compliments me. "You can do some damage in that number if you want to."

"Ha-ha." I roll my eyes at her comment and the ridiculous wardrobe episode we had before we got to the bar.

"You'll be smokin'!" Juliette had exclaimed, holding out a glittering champagne-colored tank top as she searched for appropriate "going out" attire for the evening.

"Not that," I protested.

"Oh, zip it. Put it on," she demanded anyhow, and I did, but only for her amusement. She seemed to get a kick out of playing dress-up. Maybe she was conjuring up childhood memories of when we'd try on Mom's heels and Mimi's clip-on earrings, the way I was. "It's fab!" she gushed. "You have to wear it. You'll turn so many heads."

I laughed, insisting that (a) the tank, which is too slutty when worn solo, would have to be paired with my blazer, in particular the charcoal-grey one with the three-quarter sleeves, which was an outfit for the office rather than the club; and (b) I had no intention of turning guys' heads. Especially at a bar. When has that ever turned out well for women who are interested in finding *real* love?

Juliette told me I could "totally pull it off!" before eventually relenting. She dug out a slim black shirt with a black lace overlay and said it wouldn't turn as many heads, but that with the right necklace I could draw attention to my cleavage. Suffice it to say, I abandoned any addition of jewelry to the outfit, especially a necklace. And, though I was skeptical at first, I'm enjoying myself out on a school night with my little sister, dressed in the least slutty yet most bar-appropriate outfit possible, talking about our week, the evening's bar scene, and if Juliette should return the call from a guy she met on East Beach.

Though I'm not as well versed in flirting with the opposite sex, I do my best to give advice. I lob her a few softball questions: "Are you attracted to him?" "Did he seem nice?" "Are you interested in dating right now?" "Does he seem like relationship material?"

She answers a gusty "Yes!" to the first few questions, but at the last one she cackles and replies, "Relationship? I don't do those too well, Gracie."

I don't know if it's the wine or the merry atmosphere, but I raise my glass and say, "Hear, hear. To women who don't know how to do relationships." I take a heavy slug. "To hell with men."

Juliette leans forward, both elbows on the table, her glass poised at her lips. "Relationships may not be my thing, but that doesn't mean I've sworn off men."

"It's all the same." I hiccup and laugh, again not sure if the wine or the atmosphere is to blame. "Relationships, dating . . ." I wave a dismissive hand. "You're either with someone and have a successful relationship, or you're alone."

"Don't be so narrow-minded, Gracie." Her tone is still light enough that I know she's not pulling out the insult card. She is galled, though.

"If it's not a relationship, then what is it?" I ask.

She wags her head, bottom lip slightly jutting out as she considers my question with the same regard Oppenheimer would have given to quantum mechanics.

"Fine, *dating*," I say at last. "That's testing the waters, seeing different guys. I suppose you're not *completely* alone. But you're not *with* someone, you're not *committed* to one person." I don't know if I'm making any sense. I shut myself up with a drink of wine.

"There's dating, and then there's being in a relationship," Juliette explains. "And then there's playing the field, maybe?" She laughs. "I don't know. Why do we need to label everything?"

"I'm a labeler; it's what I do." That gets a smile out of her.

"Testing the goods, having fun, not strapping yourself down . . . call it what you like, you don't have to be in a *relationship* with every man you find intriguing." She laughs to herself. "If that were the case I'd have a heck of a time monogramming bath towels." She shrugs. "I don't know. I never really find myself in relationships. The few times I have, they didn't turn out so great."

"And I'm in the same boat," I point out. "I'm twenty-six. By now I thought I'd be picking out china patterns, maybe even already happily married and searching for the best day cares. I'm nowhere even close. Same boat as you with relationships. Men!"

"No." She hunkers low to the table, eyes locked with mine. "I avoid relationships because dating around works better for me. You avoid relationships *just* as you avoid men, Gracie. You're closed for business. In every way."

"I am not." My tone is stern.

"You lament you don't have a boyfriend, but dating seems to be out of the question. Gathering a number or just hooking up for pleasure's sake is neither here nor there—"

"Excuse me if I'm closed for that kind of business." I look down at my lap with raised eyebrows, and this gets a laugh from Juliette that's so loud we actually do turn some heads.

A table of four guys looks over at the commotion, the freckled, ginger one gesturing a toast with his foaming beer as he sets his eyes on Juliette. Juliette returns the flirty gesture, then looks back to me. She's bubbling with laughter and tells me she loves my dry humor.

"You don't have to hit the sack with the guys in order to put yourself out there and have some fun." Before taking another drink she adds, "Although I highly recommend it."

I suppress a groan. "Is that the plan with this Graham guy? Hit the sack and see what happens?"

"Come on, Gracie. Let me help you out. I *never* get to help you out like this."

I furrow my brow. "What are you talking about?"

"Let's get you some action. Let me set you up." She casts about the bar, and I tug at her wrist.

"No, no. Not here," I plead. "Not at a bar."

"Fine, but be open to letting me set you up?" She looks at me with eager eyes.

"I don't think so."

"You're no fun."

"Not yet," I quickly say, because she's so keen on hooking me up with someone that I'd hate to make her feel as if I don't appreciate her and her best intentions. She thinks a good lay will help right things, and there's no need to point out how flawed her methods are. So I indulge her. "Later. But not now," I say. A half-truth.

She gives a vague shrug before taking another sip.

"So are you going to call this Graham guy or what, Jules?" I change the topic. "You obviously like him. I'd vote for a date. Maybe slowly get to know him, leave yourself open for a relationship . . ."

She makes a sour face—nose crinkled, lips puckered, eyes crossed.

"Okay, okay. Forget my advice. You going to call him or what?"

Juliette whips out her cell phone and pulls up Graham's number. "Since it's a night of going out on a limb, you with your Thursday-night bar scene, I think it's only fair I give the guy a chance. Right?" She taps the "Call" button.

"Because calling a guy back is going out on a limb for you?" I tease.

"No." She brings the phone up to her ear. "But going out with a twenty-year-old lifeguard with a Bart Simpson tattoo would be."

"Oh, Juliette." I toss my head back. "No good can come of this."

"That remains to be seen," she says with a sultry look in her eyes. "Want me to see if he has a brother for you?"

"Juliette."

"A cousin? A friend?" She points to her phone. "It's ringing. Hurry. Decide."

"Oh, Juliette."

"You haven't been out with someone in forever, right?"

I bite my lip and dart my gaze to my drink. "Juliette, stop."

"Maybe he's got a brother." She says this with a jesting smile. "It's worth asking."

"Only if he has a companion Homer Simpson tattoo," I tease.

Juliette clinks her glass to mine. "Touché, sis." Then she answers the phone with an expert trill—syrupy, sexy, signature Juliette. I really should take notes.

————

"We're making progress. Slow, but something," I say to Mimi as I situate the ladder underneath the orange tree. It is a gorgeous, sunny June afternoon. The signs of the light morning rain and dew are scant, save for the edge of a rainbow still peeking over the Santa Ynez mountain range. When I breathe in the citrus scent of the orange tree—a big, deep, long breath, eyes closed—I know without a doubt that summer is upon us. Nothing beats a Santa Barbara summer. Nothing.

I pull from a hard-to-reach branch deep inside the tree some dried leaves. I watch them flutter to the moist ground below, where they meet the small collection of postharvest fruit that never dropped.

"Juliette and I are having some fun together." I continue my rambling. "I think, when the moment's right, we bring out the best in each other."

I tell Mimi about the routine Friday-night drinks Juliette and I have come to share at the wine bar on lower State Street, which is quickly becoming our favorite watering hole. Even when work's bogging me down, I find a way—going in early or staying late on Thursday, if need be—to keep up what has become a genial way to bond with my sister.

"We've even started to go for bike rides together on Saturday and Sunday mornings," I say as I ascend the ladder to its midway point. "That is, when she's not in the arms of some guy who's caught her eye." I can almost hear Mimi laugh at this tidbit.

I'm no saint, but it takes more than a lobster dinner or a ride on the back of a motorcycle along PCH for me to drop my panties. Juliette's motto is "Life is for the living," and she applies this not just to her career and politics but also to men. It's fine, if that's how she wants to live. But when her life choices bang against the thin 1920s wall that separates her room from mine, reminding me of what is, much to my dismay, missing from my life, I begin to resent our living arrangement, my sister's attitude toward life, and this whole trying-to-bond sister thing that one minute seems to be working and another seems to be a hopeless, frustrating cause.

"I don't know, Mimi," I say. "We're just two very different people. We don't have nearly as much in common as we used to. *Can* such people become close friends?"

I snip with care some unwieldy twigs and branches. I'm mindful not to prune too heavily and risk the limb sunburn that can happen in the summer, something I remembered Mimi's warning of long ago only *after* Juliette and I went to town trying to keep the low-hanging branches from reaching the ground. Eventually we'll get the hang of this.

"I love my sister, Mimi," I continue. "Of course I love her. Very much." My tone becomes defensive. "I guess it's normal to have disagreements and different preferences even when you're friends, when you're close sisters, but you probably don't go and live together, be with each other twenty-four-seven. Hearing their business . . . it could drive *anyone* batty." I snip a weak branch deep in the shade of the tree, and before I can catch it, it falls to the ground, knocking free two more late oranges.

"It's not easy," I breathe. "Not black and white." I pluck the fruit from the ground and blow off the dirt. Maybe it will be salvageable.

"But I think your plan's working, Mimi." I place the oranges in a bag, hopeful they'll taste just as ripe and juicy as the oranges did back during the peak harvest season. "It's not easy, but I think it's working. We just can't give up. That's the key."

Juliette and I have still got a ways to go, but we're talking. We're having some fun together. We're trying, and I'm sure that's precisely what Mimi predicted we'd do at this stage.

What is to come, I don't know. I'm scared, a bit apprehensive. But Juliette's adventurous take on it, though mind-boggling and impish at times, is somehow strangely comforting. She's a reminder that I'm not going through this loss and this yearlong challenge alone. She's a reminder that I have not only a sister through all of this but potentially a friend.

Summer

9

Mimi

Dear Gracie and Juliette,

Summer! Oh, how I love the way the sun kisses my skin golden. How I love the scent of the salt in the heavy summer-morning air. It complements the bitter taste of a cup of coffee in such a peculiar way. I'll never get tired of the gentle roll of the waves upon the sandy beaches and the way they lap along the docks in the copper night. The days are longer; the nights glow more intensely and coat the great Pacific in glitter. School is out; the children and grandchildren are home. The garden is plentiful, as are the morning bike rides and the evening strolls. Oh, how I will miss the magical summers of Santa Barbara, the summers at 1402 Laguna Lane.

As summer now visits you, dear girls, I hope you revel in its beauty, enjoy my favorite season together, in good company. By now you must be all unpacked, settling in well, and hopefully getting along well enough. I am sure this adjustment hasn't been easy, but if anyone can do it, it is you two.

You were such close sisters when you were younger. You loved each other fiercely. Though you've spent some time apart in recent years, I am confident you'll pick up as if no time has been lost. There will be tiffs, and maybe you'll even resent my concocting such a plan. I am certain, though, that there is nothing you two can't overcome together.

Don't give up. Life is full of ups and downs, and it's better to experience them together, with someone who loves you in the way only a sister can.

If you find yourselves in a bind, tempted to give up and carry on with your lives as they were before I knocked you for a loop, perhaps a small history lesson will encourage you?

I know you understand how special this home is, as it holds so many dear memories for you two, and because it has been in the family for years. It is also a special place to each generation. I believe it important to keep it within the family. It has kept the Jones, Kay-Jones, and Jones-Bennett families very well, and I hope it will keep future generations well, too.

Your great-grandparents Henry Jones Sr. and Betty Mills bought this home in the summer of '47. Back in '38, Henry and his brother, Saul, opened up their own deli, right here in Santa Barbara. They were nothing but children: Henry seventeen, Saul eighteen. Their grandparents had come into a nice sum of money what with all the gold in the city long ago, making their parents quite wealthy at the turn of the century, when the city was booming. Thank heavens the Great Crash didn't hit them too badly.

Henry and Saul, with a gift of their family's fortune, opened Jones Bros. Deli. Then Uncle Saul felt the call to duty and went off to Europe to join the war effort. Henry, medically unfit to enlist and bearing the responsibility of a new wife and a young business, stayed home, and things were a little rough.

Then Pearl Harbor happened—the country was a real mess, girls—and come '43, once Saul returned home in one piece, your great-grandfather Henry went off to fight in the Pacific. It was any wonder the deli survived, to say nothing of the turmoil I am sure the family underwent with one son after another off to war, but you come from determined and strong stock, Gracie and Juliette. Never forget that.

After the war, the deli picked up, Santa Barbara grew, and that's when your great-grandfather Henry spotted the charming 1920s Craftsman on 1402 Laguna Lane. He and your great-grandmother Betty made the house a home; they planted the orange tree in 1948! (How is my favorite tree faring? I imagine wonderfully—you two were always my happy little helpers in the garden.)

As I've already shared in my first letter, Henry and Betty left the home to your grandfather and me. We lived here with them the first year we were married (1958), then made it our own ten years later when Henry Sr. passed and Betty eventually remarried and moved away. She left the house to us, the deli to Grandpa Harold's older brother, Henry Jr.

Unfortunately, Henry Jr. shut down the deli in 1973 and left town.

But your grandfather was eager to try something different. Wise man that he was, he invested in some orange groves, began work in hotel management, and never made me want for anything. But I digress, as an old lady will when she reminisces!

I have known no other home since, and I wouldn't have it any other way. Like your grandfather and me, your parents lived here when they were first married. And now you two, a new generation, call 1402 Laguna Lane your home.

It warms my heart to think of the new memories you two will make here, fills me with an indescribable joy to think of the bond you will rediscover. If you're ever doubtful of the arrangement, and if this history doesn't inspire, then look around the home, the garden. Sit under the orange tree and talk to me, lie down on the living room settee where you used to watch cartoons together, turn on Simon and Garfunkel and dance in the kitchen (I'll be right there with you). Take comfort in knowing that everything you see in the home has a story, is a part of history. And you are a part of that story. It is something you two, Gracie and Juliette, can share and make your own.

I imagine it's been rather trying this first season. Juliette, I hope uprooting yourself from New York City wasn't too much of a strain and hassle. I am certain, however, that no matter the trying circumstances, you two will have a splendid summer together.

Revel in this opportunity. Life is short. Don't take it for granted. Grow close, turn to each other when times are tough, savor the moments together when all is well. And enjoy this most beautiful season together. I wish I could be there with you right now, snacking on saltwater taffy on the wharf or sitting under the orange tree and talking about how fragrant the honeysuckles are this time of year. I am with you in spirit, though. Always and forever.

I love you, my darlings. Stay strong and stay together.

Until autumn,

All my love,

Mimi

10

Juliette

Mimi was right: it's magical. How could I have forgotten how magical Southern Californian summers are? The winds dance in my hair, loose curls tumbling like golden waves, flapping harder as I increase my speed. I cut my rapid pedaling for a beat, leaning forward and coming to a half-standing position as I round the wide-arcing curve. I hang a right, rolling through the "Stop" sign with nothing more than a brief yield at the one-way street. A quick nod to Mrs. Parsons watering the lawn of her gorgeous corner lot as I finish out my turn. More hearty pedaling, the wind still carrying on its dance in my hair.

My morning ride to Bluejay's is briefly slowed as I await my turn at a busy intersection where picturesque Victorian and adobe homes back up against a scenic park. Dogs are walked on leashes by women wearing baseball caps, ponytails pulled neatly through and swaying in perfect step, just like their sculpted hips. Guys are getting in their morning jogs, bypassing the small line of cyclists waiting to proceed through the traffic.

I love that Dad dug out my old ten-speed from high school. When I arrived home from New York City, he had it all polished up. New tires, a shiny new coat of mint-colored paint (to match the Citroën), and even a new bell. Even though sometimes I like to give the wheels of the Citroën a spin, just for the fun of it, getting around home on a bike is easiest and quickest, and I love the feeling of freedom and fresh air as I zip along the streets.

As soon as I enter the coffee shop, the friendly jingle of the brass bells announcing my arrival, I say a cheerful good morning to Pete, the familiar scruffy face I see on the mornings I come to Bluejay's.

"Morning, Juliette!" Pete hollers. He gives a slow, lengthy wave over his head, a towel in hand.

"I've forgotten how brilliant this town is," I say. My morning bike rides, which often lead me to my new favorite coffee shop, are invigorating. They really make me appreciate the choice to uproot for a year.

I ferret in my bag for my wallet. "New York in the summer?" I say to Pete. "It's hot and muggy and loud. That is, when everyone hasn't vacated for the shores." I find my wallet and pull it out triumphantly. "Then the place is just a freakin' ghost town." I blow some of my windswept hair out of my face. "Don't know which one is worse."

"Nothing beats the California sun, man," Pete says before emptying wet coffee grounds into the knock box.

Pete's a burly kind of guy, the type you'd think would run with some salty sailors—thick arms and chest; dark-olive skin kissed by the sun for decades; a thick, long brown beard. He's fortysomething but doesn't seem a day older than twenty with his jovial surfer-boy lingo accompanied by a contagious laugh, his Hollister and Quiksilver T-shirts and colorful collection of cheap flip-flops, and his preference for drum-heavy and musky acoustic guitar tunes—coffeehouse tunes—which he hiply streams into the shop via Spotify on his equally hip MacBook Air, shakily perched on an old wooden shelf behind the counter. He's the quintessential laid-back Californian that I've, I realize, really come to miss.

"How long have you been away?" Pete asks after he checks if I want my favorite Italian-import bean or the Santa Cruz–roasted specialty I recently discovered.

I tell him, "Let's go local," before adding that I've been gone from California for too long.

I pull out a ten-dollar bill, the tip Mr. Silver gave me for lawn duty yesterday. I'm holding on to the twenty-dollar tip from Mrs. Parsons, wedged at the bottom of my wallet. I've had my eye on a fabulous swim-suit at Anthropologie, but I can't bring myself to part with the $119, plus tax. I'm not exactly broke. Not exactly head above water, either. I've got my share of the groceries to cover this week, and the Citroën could sure use a fill, not to mention a wash.

On the bright side, I sold three brooches yesterday and eight last week, and my bouquets clear out at Meadows Memorial each week. I haven't picked up any more lawns; almost everyone in the neighbor-hood who doesn't hire a professional lawn-care company is already a customer of mine. To be honest, I'm all right with that. It's exhausting work under the summer sun, and it's not as if it's a dream job. It's paying all the bills . . . *Well, almost all,* I think as the darling one-piece vintage-style navy suit flashes to mind.

"Will it be the usual this morning?" Pete asks. "Or can I interest you in the fresh lemon poppy-seed muffins we just pulled from the oven? Meyer lemons. From my backyard."

"Good-bye, croissant, hello, muffin!"

I'm sure I shouldn't be splurging on frilly coffee and baked goods, but I pick my battles. Maybe I'll snag the suit on an end-of-summer clearance and be able to sport it at East Beach next year . . . or the Hamptons, depending on where things go.

With a smile, Pete rings up my muffin and Americano. I hand him my ten, drop the coins in the tip jar, and, though I'd rather tip more generously, reluctantly return to my wallet the remaining change.

"*New York Times?*" Pete knows one of his more frequent customers all too well. He flips through the stack of newspapers on the counter.

"Actually, today I think I'm going to do a bit of writing." I wave about the leather-bound notebook I found in the Village last summer.

"You doing journalism? Writing a novel or something?"

"Ha." I take a seat at a long bar in front of a window with a view of a line of quaint boutiques. At half past nine, shops are slowly beginning to open; no signs of shoppers yet. Give them an hour and they'll be bustling, the usual mix of affluent housewives, sleepy trust-fund babies, and college kids home for the summer.

"I wish that were the case—then I'd be making a buck, right?" I say with a jesting smile. "Just some poetry, for fun." I fish a pencil out of my bag.

"Hey, you still looking for a job, Jules?" Pete's voice rises in interest. He finishes brewing my coffee before disappearing into the back.

"Yeah," I say when he returns. "You hiring now?" I asked Pete back in April if he could use some experienced help around the shop.

"With the college kids back for the summer, I think we *are* going to need an extra set of hands around here." He sets my muffin and coffee in front of me and holds out an application. "I've already got a couple of applicants, so I'll probably make a decision soon." I take the double-sided application from him. "If you can get that in within the next few days, that'd be great," he says as I scan it. I flip it over, quickly glance at it, flip it back over.

"I can't make any promises, but I think your application will be at the top." He gives me a pat on my upper arm.

Still scanning wildly, I nod and thank him.

"Well, I'll let you get to your poetry." He claps his thick hands and saunters back behind the counter. "Let me know how that muffin tastes. Lemons were *riiiipe!*"

I'm beginning to feel hopeful at the prospect of working here as I run my eyes up and down and across the application. I would love some real employment, and I know how to do barista work. It'd sure beat what I'm doing now, and it'd be the most real job I've had in a long while. And this actually looks like an application I can fill out. Good-bye, lawn duty. Good-bye, crossing my fingers that more brooches and bouquets will sell. Hello—

"Damn," I whisper under my breath.

The feeling of hope visited for only a brief, although joyous, moment. I take a big bite of muffin, roll my eyes, and turn my attention to my poetry.

My kryptonite's hit again, the ever-present question on applications: *Have you ever been convicted of a felony?*

———

As with poetry, or really any craft or creative outlet, baking can soothe the soul. I tend to write poems or craft more often than I bake, but when I do pull out the mixing bowl, I can slip into a private peace. With poetry, it's just me and my words; baking, me and the recipe. I turn random words into a flowing poem, a mess of ingredients into a delight for the taste buds. In a way, I take nothing and create something.

It's in the moments when I feel that I don't have control over my life, when I feel that I'm going nowhere, that I find myself flipping open my leather-bound notebook (or turning on the oven) more frequently. I don't need *much* control—a bit of disarray or chaos in life is healthy, keeps you guessing. I love the unexpected. Well, most of it.

Sometimes the lack of control, the lack of a destination, can clutch me with a grip so tight I feel as if I can't breathe, as if I'm being cornered. It's been this way for a year now with work. My love life, okay, isn't really stable, but it's mine, it's what I choose. My new living situation isn't traditional, but it works and it's actually, all in all, going pretty well. My professional life? What's that? I feel as if I've pissed away my professional career, four trying years at university and my bachelor's in

English literature and art history all for naught. All because of one stupid decision. All right, perhaps a string of ill-thought-out choices that led to one ultimately stupid decision. My past haunts me and traps me.

I think I've escaped the cornering for a fleeting moment, finding ways to make it with my unconventional methods of employment. All's right with the world, then reality hits. I go and pick up an application and I realize I'm in that same stupid corner I've been in for a year now. Hopeless Juliette Bennett.

I wrote some poetry about seagulls and clouds and general nonsense in search of clarity at Bluejay's. Now I'm churning brownie batter, trying to get myself in the right frame of mind. Mimi always said I could do whatever I put my mind and heart to. She failed to mention that included making screwy choices.

I take a lick of the brownie batter, savoring its rich chocolate sweetness as it melts on my tongue. Of all the desserts to bake, it's odd that I've chosen to make the dessert that started it all.

The lingering taste of the brownie batter on my tongue and lips whisks me back to high school and that first pot brownie. Then on to high school graduation and the biggest high I'd ever experienced up until that point. It all seemed harmless then, and if they're taken as isolated incidents, I suppose no harm was ever really done. The worst effects were conspicuous red eyes that made my parents threaten to take away NYU; the permeating fragrance of patchouli incense that nearly ruined my favorite coat; the bed of prizewinning lilies of Dawn's mom's that we thought, in our hazy state, would look divine plucked and tossed about her living room.

Then I flash to the end of my sophomore year at NYU, when my partying and not-so-refined habits started to become more serious.

It was a mixer at some fellow English lit major's apartment. It wasn't my first party; I'd been to plenty of rowdy parties back in high school at homes of kids whose wealthy parents were conveniently out of town. Those weren't that different from the parties my freshman year at college, filled with the requisite booze, beer pong, promiscuity, and dope. The liquor was just in greater abundance, the drinking games varied, the promiscuity was seedier, and the dope was not just dope.

"It'll change the way you write," said Matthew, a smooth-talking philosophy and English lit double major with retro Coke-bottle glasses that somehow lent a very sexy vibe.

"I don't know," I said, nibbling my pot brownie. I never considered myself among the hardest of partiers. A nice hit now and again, maybe a brownie, a few drinks, fun on the dance floor lip-locked with some hot guy, maybe take it to a room for something more, that was to be expected. I turned to Matthew and said, "I don't do drugs."

Matthew reached into his pocket and withdrew a tiny bag, like one that spare buttons come in attached to the tag of a new blouse. Inside were small rainbow-colored pills. "You're doing 'em now, babe," Matthew said with a nod to my brownie.

"Weed should be legalized." I took a sizable bite. My head felt both heavy and light, a sensation that never got old.

"I thought you were for all drugs being legalized?"

He had a point. We'd been a part of the rally together with NYU Progressives last term, and if I wasn't mistaken, he had actually made posters with me that touted the very line he'd just served.

"Yeah, but that doesn't mean I want to use them myself," I stated with pride. "Some"—I raised the brownie—"okay. Not all."

I wanted it to go on the record that while I might support the legalization of drugs, I also responsibly supported widely available and cost-free rehabilitation centers and services. I'd done a study in high school sociology class about the drug culture and policies in the Netherlands. It was highly enlightening and reshaped my whole outlook on the topic. However, I was beginning to feel too baked to run down my laundry list to Matthew. Instead I pushed away the bag of pills and told him I wasn't interested.

"I'm not charging you. Have one with me, for free." He opened the bag, dropped two into his open palm.

"What is it?" I dared to ask.

"Just some E. Harmless. It's nothing."

I set down my brownie. "If it's nothing, what's the point in taking it?"

Matthew seemed stumped by the question. He brushed it off with a roll of his head. "Come on. It'll energize you. You'll feel *raw* emotion and you'll write some *amazing* shit." He inched closer, hooking an arm around my shoulders. "Something that'll blow the minds of the profs."

"I already write amazing shit." I shoved him playfully in the shoulder. "I don't need that stuff. And neither do you."

"You've never tried it, I take it?" He raised one dually inquisitive and accusatory eyebrow.

"No." I slunk out of his grip and stood from the lumpy-cushioned plaid couch. "And I'm not going to start now."

The ringing of my cell phone brings me to, startling me. I drop the spatula in the brownie batter.

"I was beginning to think you weren't going to call me back," a deep, raspy voice growls through the phone. "Was our first date *that* bad?"

"Hey, Cary." I pour the batter into a baking dish, cradling the phone in the crook of my shoulder. "It was not bad at all."

Cary's a guy I met at Bluejay's. He's in town, back home from Cornell for summer break. We got to talking about the East Coast, a mutual fondness for New England clam chowder, and how not enough people appreciate the sorbet-pink-and-tangerine sunsets on Hendry's Beach.

Conversation flowed easily, we made each other laugh, and Cary, standing at six feet, eyes like turquoise, shoulders broad, and smile warm and inviting, was poster-boy handsome. Needless to say, I didn't hesitate when he asked for my number.

Our date at Hendry's Beach (of course) to watch the sunset was more romantic and intimate than most of my first dates. In any ordinary circumstances I'd have thought it a bit cheesy. But it's summer in Santa Barbara, with college kids on vacation, and my date book is wide open. Why the hell not? Contrary to the seductive gaze Cary fixed me with when we kissed on the wet and sandy beach, the gentle lulling of the ocean's rippling waves setting the perfect mood, he later pulled the gentleman card. It took a lot of self-control not to try to convince him otherwise.

His call for a second date isn't exactly surprising, seeing how he acted a gentleman. He did say he'd call. My coquettish smile as he tells me he's glad I picked up the phone, that he's glad we met, are evidence I'm just as happy that he called, that we met.

"How about I take you somewhere Friday night?" he suggests with an insisting tone.

I'm about to tell him that sounds great when I remember my standing girls' night out with Gracie. I ask if tomorrow would be better, even tonight.

"Someone can't wait to see me again," he teases.

"Someone's already got plans on Friday," I quip back with ease. I plunk the empty bowl into the sink, then slide the dish of brownie batter into the oven.

"Another date. I see. All right, all right. You're a beautiful woman. Shouldn't be surprised."

"I've got a date with my sister," I say with a light laugh.

"Fair enough. Tonight, then? How's seven sound?"

———

"Hey!" I say in a flurry to Gracie as soon as she walks through the door, home from work.

"Hey, Jules," she says in a tired tone. She sets her things on the settee. "Where are you running off to?"

I dart in front of the small gilded mirror in the living room to make sure I don't have any lip gloss on my teeth. Giving a quick fluff to my hair, which I've decided to wear down, loosely curled, I spin around and face Gracie. "I've got a date."

"When do you *not* have a date?" she says with a laugh. She begins to flip through the mail. "Who's it with?"

"Cary, the guy I met at Bluejay's."

"I thought his name was Eli?"

"That was the guy I had a date with *at* Bluejay's." I slip my tube of nude-colored lipstick into my purse.

"What happened to him?" She asks this with a stuttering kind of laugh.

"He was a Wiccan. Turned out he was trying to recruit me." I toss up my hands at the thought of the interesting (to say the least) round of dating I've had in the few short months since I've been in town.

New York, especially the NYU campus, provided a range of characters in the dating pool. I enjoyed the variety, the no-strings-attached view many of them ascribed to, and was pleased to find my pickings here weren't all that slim in comparison. As with anything, though, there are hits and misses, and sometimes a girl really misses.

"And Cary?" Gracie abandons the mail and walks over to me. "A Scientologist trying to recruit you?"

"Ha-ha." I stick my tongue out at her reflection in the mirror. "Just a nice guy."

"Serious material?"

"You and your serious material. I suppose in your book he'd probably be 'serious material.'" I make air quotes. "Goes to an Ivy League."

"And?"

"And he has really smooth lips, a nice ass, is pretty laid-back—"

"Enough." She gives my shoulder a shove. "Why do I bother asking?"

"It's just *fun*." I turn and look her in the eyes. "You know? That thing you should do more often?"

"Yeah, yeah." She pulls a loose thread from the side of my black-and-hot-pink, floral, high-waisted skirt.

"How do I look?" I hold my arms out, awaiting an honest but kind assessment. The kind of assessment a sister—a friend—gives.

She tells me to do a spin, then asks what shoes I plan on wearing.

"Sandals would be the most practical," I say. "Easier to kick off."

She groans. "You plan on hooking up with this one, *too*?"

I put a hand on my waist. "Gracie."

"I'm teasing you. I just don't want you hurt."

"Ah, Gracie, that's sweet you're worried about me," I say, tone sappy. "I won't get hurt. I've done this many times before." I rest an assuring hand on her shoulder. She glances at it, then at me, eyes trying to understand.

"I'm a big girl," I say.

"I know."

"And this big girl's got to get herself out on a sexy date!" I turn back toward the mirror.

"Where you going?"

I tell her the sandals are probably the better choice because Cary and I will most likely go to the beach again.

"That's romantic." She gets a far-off look in her eyes.

"It was romantic the first time around."

She touches my matching brooch, made of black organza and tiny pink-and-black beads. "Nice," she says. "You made it?"

"Yup! Sold one just like it, too." I glance back at the mirror, this time checking to see if dried mascara has flecked under my eyes.

"That's turning out to be real work for you, huh, Jules?"

"Eh," I say breezily. "Wouldn't call it that. Still need a real job, but hey. No one's hiring." I shrug evasively. "Got to go."

"Have fun. Be safe." She returns to the pile of mail.

"Oh, and I baked some brownies." I point to the kitchen with one hand and slip on a pair of black flip-flops with the other. "And I stopped by the farmers' market the other day. Bought a ton of blueberries."

"More?"

"Fresh and for super cheap. Of course!" I've gotten into the habit of picking up some every Tuesday morning. "Made muffins with them."

"So you've decided to open up a bake shop?" Gracie kids.

"See ya later."

"See ya," Gracie calls out as I dash out the door.

———

"I haven't done this since I was a kid," I shriek as I hold in one hand the yellow plastic handle, made for a child's small fingers, and gingerly guide the string with the other.

"Kite flying is just as fun for adults," Cary says. He focuses on the slowly waving and rather steady motions of the kite.

The evening wind is just right—a strong-enough breeze to keep the kite afloat, and coming in gentle sweeps to make it dance. "And I think someone *has* done this recently. Look at you." Cary places a hand on the small of my back. "You're a pro."

The rainbow kite continues its steady dance above Shoreline Park as the wispy evening clouds roll in and hover, Santa Barbara's evening weather routine. Wake up with the clouds and the mist, go to sleep with a cloudy blanket.

Suddenly a gale-like wind pulls the kite with such force I nearly lose my grip on the tiny handle. "Oh no!" I tug at the string as I achieve my grip again. My hasty motions make the kite twist and twirl rapidly.

"Maybe not such a pro after all," Cary razzes.

"Wait . . . a . . . minute." I keep a hawk-like focus on the kite, biting the tip of my tongue as my hands carefully maneuver the toy.

Another heavy wind picks up, and rather than sending the kite to the doomed end of its dance, carries it higher into the sky.

"Spoke too soon." Cary removes his hand from my back. From the corner of my eye I see him lie down on the beach towels we laid out on the grass. He brings his bottle of Newcastle, beach contraband wrapped in a not-exactly-discreet paper bag, to his lips.

Like our first date, our second is just what I like: relaxed, entertaining, no frills. It's perfect for me. Cary represents the lightheartedness I crave. No stress, no obligations. Just fun. A perfect release in a world that's been challenging the past few months.

I loosen my grip on the kite some and glance over at Cary. He's smiling, sipping his beer, seeming to delight in the kite-flying activities as much as I do, even in his passive state.

Suddenly the string pulls taut and slips from my hand, and before I can regain control, the kite nose-dives to the ground.

"Oh no," Cary and I say in unison. He laughs. "What goes up must come down."

I drop the kite at his feet and spiritedly take a seat next to him. I lean over him, reaching for my own paper bag–covered bottle of beer. My elbow grazes his waist, the bare skin exposed between the hem of his plain white tee and his board shorts. I give him a small smile, then grip the neck of the bottle as I lean farther over. My chest now grazes his waist. A hand grips my calf, and, leaning back on my elbow, beer in hand, I say in a kittenish way, "Someone's not quite as gentlemanly this time around."

Cary smiles. He has a hint of a gap between his two front teeth, the kind you might get after neglecting to wear your retainer once the braces come off. It's irresistible.

"A gentleman?" he says with a laugh, head tossed back. He takes a drink.

"Yeah." I purposely settle in closer, the side of my torso resting on his lap. I take a drink.

"And how exactly was I a gentleman?" He's still smiling, but his lips are now drawn together.

"Oh, you know . . ." I run some fingers through my hair. My curls have become loose, the normally thick strands having taken on a kind of disheveled, cotton-candy texture—what Gracie calls my signature messy style.

"I do?" Cary says.

"Yeah. Romantic beach, sweet kiss good night."

"You expecting something more this time around?" That gap-toothed smile returns, and I can't help myself. I turn on the seductive charm: bottom lip bitten, brows raised, beer bottle swirling in one hand, fingers dancing along the exposed piece of very tan skin above his shorts.

"If you're thinking sex in a public park, I'm not that kind of girl." I take a quick pull of beer.

"No?" Cary's smirk grows. "Sex on the beach?"

I shake my head.

"Damn." He's clearly disappointed.

"No," I say with a laugh, "I totally am." My fingers dance to his belly button. "Third date, maybe. *Never* the second."

"Then I should ask you out on a third."

I give another laugh, this one louder. I grip my beer tightly and pull myself up. I straddle him and he abandons his beer, sinking back on two prone elbows.

"Maybe . . ." I hem and haw some. "We should enjoy the here and now."

"That's how you are, huh? Live in the moment?"

My beer poised at my lips, I look off across the crisp green lawn, then say, "Try to. Yeah."

He slowly raises himself upward, one hand on my thigh. He draws small circles with one finger.

"I just like to have fun." I shrug cavalierly. "It's been a tough year. Trying to find myself and follow my credo—life is for the living, have fun, it's short. You know?"

"Totally." His hand makes smaller, slower, looser motions on my leg. "I don't know if you're *that* kind of girl," he starts in an unsure way.

"Third date. That's the rule."

He laughs and I say, "Okay, rules are broken from time to time, but I'm standing by it."

"That's not what I'm talking about." He moves his hand from my thigh to my waist and eases back on one elbow comfortably. "But good to know. No, if you're cool with it, I've got some weed. Only if you're cool with it. You know? Live in the moment, life is for the living, have some fun . . ."

I polish off my beer and cast about. Shoreline is usually a pretty popular place for kids and families to hang out, but it's rather empty tonight. In fact, aside from a guy and his black Labrador several yards off, and a fellow kite flyer who looks as if he's packing up and going home, the place is dead. If we did spark up, no one would know.

Once upon a time I wouldn't have hesitated a single second, but that was then. Things have changed. I've changed. You'd still probably find me in a nationally-legalize-marijuana rally—my progressive politics have become only more progressive over time. But as with many things, just because I think they should be legal and accepted doesn't mean I necessarily want to make use of them. I promised myself last year that I wouldn't go near another illegal substance, and what happened to cause me to make such a promise is all the reason I will need to stand strong in my resolve.

Cary reaches into his pocket, lifting me up off his waist some. He holds up a rather thick joint. "A few hits? If you're cool."

"You do this often?" I don't know why I ask. Not like it matters. Curious, I guess.

"Only when school's out of session." He fishes some more in his pocket. "Was baked all freshman year and failed a psych elective." He flips open a Zippo. "Not going to do that again. How about you?"

"If by 'that kind of girl' you mean someone who *is* baked all the time, then no." I take the Zippo from him in a flirtatious way, tucking it behind my back. "'That kind of girl' who has before and one too many times back in school? Not just during the summer like she probably should have?" Cary and I share a short laugh. "Then yeah. I'm 'that kind of girl.'"

He holds up the joint. "I'm cool if you're not up for it. Just thought I'd ask."

I regard the white-rolled contraband for a lengthy moment, my turn down memory lane recurring so rapidly I forget where I am for a second, forget that Cary's awaiting an answer. A chill runs up my spine.

"Juliette, you've got to pay up sooner or later," Matthew's voice peals in my ears as I eye the joint Cary offers. "I'm not a bank. Can't just give you loans like this."

"Oh, chill," I said lazily. I hiked my book bag onto my shoulder. "You'll get paid as soon as I have it."

"You said that the last time." Matthew trailed me closely as I made my way across campus. I was late to class, as usual. Professor Thompson was going to have my head if I was late again. Three for three would be the week's record, and I couldn't afford to be docked as much as 10 percent of my final grade because of it.

"Look, I've got to get to class. I'll pay you when I have it. Right now I'm broke," I said to Matthew.

Matthew tightly gripped my arm. He gave me a shake and stepped so near I could smell the cigarettes on his breath. "Listen, Jules. I can't cover for you anymore. *I've* got loans to make good on, too. You pay me, I pay my guy. That's how this works."

"I don't have it," I said harshly, clearly.

"My guy doesn't care. I don't care. You've got to be fair, pay up."

"How much?" I closed my eyes, mentally scolding myself for being so stupid as to rack up a debt I knew was more than I could pay off before the end of the term. The monthly allowance my parents sent was enough to cover my metro ticket, the occasional movie or dinner out, some groceries, and, when I had change to spare, my marijuana habit.

"Two fifty." He kept his voice down as a group of students meandered by, one of them making a questioning face as he glanced at Matthew's grip on me.

I shrugged free, rubbed at the red mark he'd left behind on my arm, and said, "Yeah, if I had two fifty you think I'd be calling McDonald's a quality dinner? I don't have that. I'll get you what I can when I can. I'm going to be late to class. I've got to go."

"Juliette." Matthew's voice was still low, his face mere inches from mine. He raised his hand to grip my arm again but thought better of it.

Instead, to further drive his point home, he tightened his words, deepened his voice. "I don't think you understand how serious I am, how serious my guy is. It may be a light drug to you, but my guy needs payment for"—he cast about suspiciously—"harder stuff. Expensive stuff."

"Look." I was on the fringe of becoming furious. I turned to face him straight on. "Your pathetic E and coke habit isn't my problem. You get your own shit sorted out."

"My *point* is that the guy I—*we* owe money to deals a lot, *a lot* of shit. Not just easy fare like weed and E. He doesn't play around with small feed like us. We pay up or—"

"Or what? Get bumped? Hit? Whatever you want to call it? It's two hundred and fifty bucks, Matthew. I'll get it when I can. You take care of your tab. That's none of my business. You know what I think of your stupid, nasty habit anyway. You can't control it; it controls you, and don't you dare threaten me because of it."

"Don't act all high and mighty, like you haven't been seen doing a line off a dirty frat bathroom sink."

"Shut up!"

"You're no different from me, Jules."

"Like hell I'm not! I don't do that crap anymore."

He looked at me, smug. "But . . . ya . . . did," he said, singsong.

"Yeah, and I was stupid. And I'm stupid now for still finding myself having to deal with you."

"Yeah, yeah."

"Just shut up and leave me the hell alone."

He heaved a long, heavy, angry breath. "You still owe me, Jules."

"What do you want?" I was at my wits' end. "I'll quit buying. There." My habit had gotten out of control, especially last term. "I'll get"—I grabbed my head, trying to calculate how much I could siphon off my next direct deposit from my parents—"one hundred to you in a week. That work? The rest the next month?"

Matthew, eyes closed, shook his head, slow and dramatic.

"It's the best I can do," I said. "What more do you want? A blow job?"

For a second, he seemed to consider the proposition.

"You're sick." I began my trek to class.

"Wait, wait, wait." He rushed in front of me, impeding my progress once more. Surely I was going to be late. Again. "If you're serious, I could throw the idea out there. There are plenty"—he laughed in a scheming way—"of girls around here who do favors to fund their habits."

"No way."

"Jules." He gave me a sideways look, a chunk of greasy hair dropping over one eye. "You make your rounds around here. Don't pretend to be a prude."

"Fuck you, Matthew." How dare he put my sexual lifestyle up for examination, up for sale. "Cash. When I have it, you'll get it. Until then, back off."

"One week, Jules."

"One week?"

"I wouldn't be harassing you like this if I didn't think it was serious." He pushed his hair back, and I could finally read the nervousness that glazed his face, that shone in his glassy eyes. "I'm in deep myself. And then with your two fifty and half the guys from the Sig Ep house with some fat-ass coke tabs . . . I owe. *Big*-time."

I couldn't come up with that kind of money in one week. No way. It wasn't going to happen.

"There might be a way you could pay it back quickly." Matthew's voice became low once again. He drew close, pulled out his cell phone, and told me he'd text me a number. "This is a guy who needs a second hand."

"A second hand?"

"Deal."

"I'm *not* dealing."

"It's not really dealing, per *se*." He drew out the last word. "You just make the hand-off. No money crosses your hands, so you can't get in trouble. Just . . . hand it out. Some sorority girls, a couple of fellow English lit girls." He bumped his arm to mine, chummy-like. "Super simple. Let me work out some things and I can get you the gig. It won't clear your tab, but it'll help." He leaned closer, looking off to the side. "It'll definitely buy you more than a week's time."

I stared down at the ground, at the tips of my scuffed Converse. If it was harmless and it'd help get me out of the mess I'd gotten myself into, and it sure as hell was better than handing out sexual favors that, despite my penchant for keeping things easy and fun with the guys of NYU, I was not prepared to hand out, then why not?

"Fine," I said at last. "Let me know what you hear. Until then, leave me the hell alone." I roughly rearranged my book bag on my shoulder and stalked off to class, late again.

"Juliette?" Cary asks. "Juliette?"

"Hmm?" I say, the joint he's holding up coming into focus.

"Everything okay?"

"Yeah." I give a nervous laugh. "Sorry."

"Lost you there for a bit. You already took a hit or something?" he kids.

I draw the Zippo forward, hold it in my palm for Cary to take. "I used to do this, but not anymore. I'm not comfortable with it."

Without much of a thought, Cary shrugs and tucks the Zippo and joint away in his pocket. "That's cool. Bad experience with it or—"

"You could say something like that." I shrug it off, not wanting to talk anymore about it.

11

Gracie

"Case. Closed." Suzanne gives me a triumphant look. She raises a mani-cured hand, awaiting a high five, and I oblige.

"Think that one was a record," I say, feeling extremely satisfied that the lengthy Newman–Jetty case is now concluded. "Fourteen months?"

"Fifteen, technically, but who cares at this point?" Suzanne gathers up the first-draft contracts I've filled out and laid on my desk. I now need her to take a stab at them. "Back to the grind." She gestures to the new load of work.

"Never ending." I take a seat behind my desk and turn on the computer monitor.

"You should celebrate. Pop some champagne or get yourself a massage." Suzanne's always up for celebrating just about any com-pletion at the firm, be it an actual closed case or the close of the workweek.

I pull out my cell phone and scan through the reminders:

Deposition prep at 1:30

Lowry mtg. at 3:30

E-mail Lee SWL case files

There are six or seven unopened e-mails, all work related, a text from Juliette that reads Just saying hi! with a smiley emoji following, and then there's another text—from David.

Suzanne's prattling on about something—a new client, a coworker, I'm not really sure. It's been two days since I heard from David last, since I responded to his surprising text message alerting me that he was in Santa Barbara visiting family for the Fourth of July. I said only, Hi. Been a long time. It was a bold move, I thought at the time.

Now I feel it was a stupid one. A stupid, thoughtless, pathetic move. But had I not replied, left him hanging just as I'd done when he texted out of nowhere back in April, I don't think I'd feel any less stupid, thoughtless, or pathetic.

Only in town until Sunday. Would love to see you. Please call, David's text reads.

"I'm going to step out for a smoke," Suzanne says, catching my attention as she knocks on my desktop. "Celebrate the close of one case," she says, fluttering her lashes, "and prepare for that annotation."

"Have fun with that," I say vacantly, still very much preoccupied with the text.

"Don't forget to treat yourself. Celebrate. Live, girl," Suzanne says with a peppy trill as she spins on her high heels.

"I think I will," I say under my breath once Suzanne leaves. I click in the response field of the text and type out a truly bold reply: How's today sound?

———

It's been months since I've seen David Nichol. Since February twenty-third, to be exact. We left things in the wrong place then, but I didn't know what else to do. I was so hurt I felt I had no choice but to tell him I never wanted to see or speak to him again. It was what transpired that weekend in February that made it easy to ignore his message back in April. The same event makes responding to him now extremely difficult.

Yet in spite of the contradiction, for some reason I am sitting here on a bench of the pristine, red-tile-roofed office park, with a granola bar lunch for one, contemplating agreeing to meet David later this afternoon.

He eagerly asked to meet for lunch almost the instant I sent my text message, but that wouldn't give me enough time to consider whether I actually *should* meet with him. I needed time to process this decision. It wasn't one to be made lightly. I suggested we meet for a drink, happy hour or something. That gave me until the end of the workday to make up my mind.

I nibble at my bar, consumed with all the what-ifs. What would happen if I *do* meet David today? What would happen if I *don't*? I'm high on success at the office with my finished case, and I've been watching Juliette carry on with a romantic life (as much as I may disapprove of the way she does it), so I'm inclined to just go through with it. Meet David! See what happens!

What harm can come from a drink together? The damage was done long ago. Could meeting today be a step toward recovery? Toward mending broken bridges and reclaiming something we once had, be it friendship or something more intimate?

What does David so desperately have to say that he's tried yet again to contact me despite my hesitation to answer? Can this meeting be nothing more than a chance to ask a few questions, to have some questions answered?

Why shouldn't I see the man I once loved with every fiber of my being? The man whose face I still see when I contemplate marriage, a future partner, the happy wedded life? As far-fetched a possibility as it may seem, I can't help but fantasize about a life shared and lived with David, a life as Mrs. Gracie Nichol.

Be that as it may, I can't dispute that while David is the other half of my (broken) heart, he is also my cross to bear. He is that lost love I hope will either return or eventually dissolve. Today's meeting, I decide, could be that one step closer to trying to solve this six-year puzzle.

I thought I'd gotten my answer in February when all hope was lost, but a woman desperately in love can find herself doing some of the silliest things. And seriously contemplating meeting David this afternoon seems like one of them right now.

I hug an arm across my stomach and watch a couple, about my age, cross the street hand in hand. They're smiling. He says something to her that makes her laugh. She quickly grabs the top of her floppy straw hat as the wind is about to kick it up, and he helps her keep it tight on her head.

I fall into a daze watching the couple examine the menu of a French bistro. I imagine telling them that it is the most romantic place, that they look as if they're in love, they're happy, the restaurant is just the spot for them on this summery day. Oh, and don't forget to order the crème brûlée for two! I start to consider the halcyon days of love.

David and I used to look like that couple. He was my first real love. He was my only love. We were a great match, both USC juniors pursuing a career in law. We both believed the Beach Boys would never go out of style, viewed living outside California as the eighth deadly sin, and wanted to take our law careers as far as we could. That last part would eventually become the Achilles' heel of our relationship.

Come my junior year, I knew the attorney path wasn't for me. I'd set my sights on a paralegal program, which I began as soon as I graduated, living with my parents until I completed the certificate and landed an internship at one of the finest corporate law firms in Santa Barbara, Donoghue, Sterling & White.

David's path, however, led him to law school up north, in Sacramento. That summer before he left and I moved back home, we agreed it was in both our interests to technically separate.

It wasn't a "*breakup* breakup," as I remember David so clearly saying, both hands comfortingly gripping my arms. It was a mutual understanding that while we cared deeply for each other—still loved each other—it hardly made much sense to carry on a long-distance relationship for three years. Not when we both had "the opportunity to possibly meet other people, other people who could make us happy here and now," he said.

I put on my brave face, told him that the amicable breakup (a breakup, that's what it was, I won't rose-color it) was a good idea. I agreed it'd be nice to still catch up when he visited family during the holidays. Then I cried into my pillow, my heart broken into a thousand tiny pieces.

But what was I to do? We'd agreed our careers were important. He wasn't about to turn down his full ride up north and his chance to study law; I wasn't going to quit my paralegal studies and leave the city I loved, where I wanted to make a home for myself, for my future family.

That's how we ended up in a ratty situation, what I like to call "the off-and-on bullshit years." While David was in law school, I lived my love life on his terms. Well, I suppose if I had *actually* lived my love life on his terms I would have dated other guys, even gotten myself into a real relationship as he suggested we do—as he even did! When he found himself out of one relationship, that's when I'd come back into the picture. I could always be counted on for convenient dates during Thanksgiving holidays, his mother's birthday weekend, and any other random trips home that occurred when he was unattached. When it worked for David, I was the apple of his eye.

It wasn't the way I'd ever planned for my love life to go. But it was all I had, and instead of wising up and moving on, my broken heart and unrelenting love for David made me hold on to any string of hope.

When he landed a dream position at one of Sacramento's biggest firms straight out of law school, plucked ripe and with enthusiasm like something out of John Grisham's *The Firm*, I found myself clinging even more steadfastly to pitiful hope. I was determined to take what I could get, because I couldn't imagine letting go of David. If all I could have from him was bits and pieces, I would take them. And I did.

I glance for a moment at the bare ring finger of my left hand. I see David's familiar face—thin lips, coal-black hair, cobalt-blue eyes. Butterflies invade my stomach. The words *false hope* flood forward. I crumple the remains of my granola bar inside its wrapping after taking one last small bite.

Over the past year, before February happened, David and I were more off than on, his career as an up-and-coming lawyer taking off, his trips back home to visit family becoming fewer and further between. Sometimes, as when he came in for a whole week for Christmas or when he celebrated his parents' thirtieth wedding anniversary last summer, we met every day. Sometimes we made love, sometimes we dined at ritzy restaurants in Montecito or took romantic trips to Ojai. Sometimes we just shared a plate of fish tacos on Stearns Wharf and held hands as we walked along the clunky wooden slats of the pier.

However fleeting, I savored my moments with David; each meeting instilled in me the hope that we were one step closer to making things work out, somehow. Each day spent together somehow meant the next day spent together would mean we were falling more in love, more in line with paths that would eventually become one and the same.

But as his visits grew more infrequent, our contact dwindling, I found myself clinging to memories and hope. I neglected the harsh reality that at best I would only ever be "that girl David sees when he's not seeing someone else." I foolishly and desperately accepted this turn of fate—something was better than nothing. But then even that abysmal situation went up in smoke. Serious smoke.

In February, David betrayed my trust, lost my respect, broke my fragile, incompletely healed heart.

That evening we had a romantic dinner, he stayed at my place (as he often did), we made love, we talked (although only in vague and fantastical terms) about how we could possibly make something work together in Sacramento, Santa Barbara, maybe someplace new like San Francisco or a sleepy town like Carmel. I knew these were only bloated ideas, nothing that would ever come to fruition. His ambivalent air suggested he thought the same. Still, I clung to those impossibilities and absurdities with fervor. Love can do that to you. It can hold you so tight, with such a suffocating grip, you bend to its every whim no matter how painful it is, how foolish you come out looking. *Love is blind* is a gross understatement.

When David broke my heart on the twenty-third of February, I swore I would never see him or speak to him again. He was never to contact me again. We had, honestly, broken up nearly four years before, and it was finally time to seal Pandora's box and chuck the thing off the deck. David and Gracie could be no more.

I still loved him, though. Fool that I am, I still do today. I worry I will always love him, because I haven't been able to fall out of love with him and in love with someone else. I am afraid of being hurt again, of finding someone I think I can love but may be only settling for. David's reaching out to me is either another run-in with false hope . . . or is it proof that having waited for the man I love is about to pay off?

My love for David keeps me second-guessing my intuition to turn away, to just say no. I think of what he will say to me if we meet today. What does he want? Will I end up being that in-between-relationships girl yet again? Will anything have changed since February? The thought is gut wrenching, causing a pungent taste at the back of my throat.

"No," I say aloud, half surprising myself. I wag my head. I ball the wrapped granola bar in a tight fist. "No, Gracie."

I decide that I have learned my lesson. I am no longer to be dependent on David. I deserve to be happy, to find true love that is *not* unrequited.

With what I think feels like resolve, I throw away my poor excuse of a lunch and wipe the crumbs from my pants. I readjust my sunglasses and find the strength to tell myself that I am *not* chickening out. I am *not* missing out on a chance to determine what could *be* with David. It could be false hope at the end of the line or a chance for true happiness.

I feel sick to my stomach at the uncertainty in my decision, but I have been at these crossroads before. I know how it ends. I don't know if I will ever get over David, but seeing his face, feeling the warmth of his embrace, hearing his deep voice, will only set me back further.

Not allowing myself one more moment's hesitation, I quickly type out a text message to David.

Can't meet. Sorry.

My heart aches and my stomach continues to churn when I'm back in the office, trying to get into the frame of mind needed to sort through the SWL case files before my next appointment. They ache and churn even more when I notice the incoming call on my cell phone.

David flashes on the screen. The vibration scratches my every nerve. Without a second thought, I hit the "Ignore" button.

He's hurt me enough, I tell myself. *Not again.* Not *again.*

I don't know, however, if I am truly choosing to ignore David because I know it is what's best in the name of moving on, or if I'm afraid of loving him even more, afraid of his breaking my heart again. I think it's a bit of both.

———

"She left yesterday," I answer my mother, lackluster. "To Ventura . . . or was it Montecito?" I page through the *New York Times* on this lazy Friday-morning holiday. "One of the two. She's staying with friends for the Fourth."

I set the alarm for eight, fully intending to take a morning ride or jog around the neighborhood. But I hit the "Snooze" button so many times that the paper and a cup of black French press had become much more appealing. It will be three whole days of peace and quiet on Laguna Lane, just what I need after the whole David ordeal. Aside from catching up on the news, getting my caffeine fix, and visiting Mimi, my schedule is wide open. I haven't had a day off since Mimi passed. Suffice it to say I haven't had a moment to zone out and relax in a long while, to step away from everything for some me time.

"She didn't invite you?" Mom asks.

I tell my mom that it's all right, that it didn't sound like my crowd anyhow. "Plus she went with a guy she's dating," I add. "Don't ask me which one. He invited her. At least"—I pause and take a small pull of coffee—"I think they're dating. Maybe they're just friends. Who knows? She's always with *some* new guy, Mom."

"I don't want to hear this." I am sure Mom's blushing rosy at the mere insinuation that her younger daughter is caught up in some tawdry romance. "She's always finding the wrong guys."

"I know."

"I guess they're not *always* wrong," Mom says in that sweet tone she uses when trying to soften a blow she's inadvertently struck. "They're just never . . ."

"Right?"

"Yeah. Never the right kind of man."

David's charming face and warm smile suddenly come into view, just the way they did last night when I tried to push away all thoughts of him, of us, as I crawled toward sleep. Then I knew my choice to default on meeting had been a wise one. It came down to self-preservation.

But now . . . now the moment to meet has passed. Now some time has elapsed, and I've been able to ruminate on what could have been *had* we met. Did I really make the right choice?

I can't ignore the pang of longing, the cutting curiosity, and all the questions that will go unanswered by my not meeting David. Why did I back out? I'm hopelessly and foolishly in love with him. Don't I deserve some answers? Would meeting him *truly* be such a disaster? The uncertainty is killing me, and Juliette's insistence on "living free and having fun!" running about in the back of my mind is not making me feel any better about my choice.

Mom sighs breathily into the phone and I temporarily scrub the image of David from my mind—a practice I've come to master over the years. "I just worry about Juliette, Gracie," Mom says. "You know I always have."

"You're not alone, Mom."

"You're worried about her?"

"Yes, of course." I switch the phone to my other ear. "Always."

"Do you think she's safe?"

"I'm sure she's being smart." I assume she's tamer these days, but one never knows with Juliette.

"I do worry . . ."

"I do, too. She's an adult, though."

"I know that," Mom says in an admonishing tone.

"It's her life. She's always reminding us of that, you know?"

"Does she seem happy?"

"Sure. I guess. Doesn't really say otherwise. And Cary—or Eli—seems like a nice guy . . ."

I consider that I haven't met either one; I'm not even sure either of them is the one she's spending the holiday with. "From what she tells me," I quickly add, "I'm sure she's safe and having fun. Truth is, I find it best not to think too much of what might be wrong or could go wrong. You'll get a splitting headache."

"That's sweet that you worry about your sister, Gracie."

I've always worried about Juliette, but Juliette's always made it a point to declare herself competent, an adult, never a charity case, and fully capable of dealing with the valleys of life just as she can the peaks. I once made the mistake of telling her that I thought one of her high school boyfriends a most unsavory choice—I'd caught him making out with another girl in a car in the Rite Aid parking lot. It was all, "Gracie, you're just jealous that you don't have a hot football-player boyfriend, or any boyfriend for that matter!"

Part of that was true, and maybe a tiny part of me relished telling her that her wildly romantic ride wasn't all that wildly romantic. Always-Popular Juliette. Always-Dating Juliette. It became antagonizing.

Yet I hurt for my sister more than anything. I wanted to tell her that it'd be all right, that she could do better than some two-timing footballer who'd no doubt peak in high school, that I was there for her.

She found herself a hottie on the baseball team a couple of weeks later. Seemed to forget all about the cheater in the Rite Aid parking lot and the shoulder I'd offered if she needed it.

"Well, what are you going to do for the holiday?" Mom asks, because for the first time in a long while (most likely because Mimi is no longer with us to celebrate, hosting the usual backyard barbecue) she and Dad have planned a Catalina getaway for the Fourth. I'm left to my own devices this year.

"No clue."

"Whatever you do, dear, have some fun." Mom signs off with her usual hugs-and-kisses sentiments, telling me Dad also sends his love. Then I return to my coffee and morning paper, preparing myself for a wide-open day of . . .

I pan over the kitchen, shifting in my seat at the small table in the corner by the back door. I can't even count the number of lunches and conversations Mimi and I had here at this cozy table over the years. Though the home is empty, this thought makes me feel warm and in the company of others.

Still unsure what I'll fill my day with, I spot the white milk-glass vase on the windowsill. Empty.

A sad smile tugs at the corner of my lips as I think of how Mimi always had freshly clipped flowers in vases all around the house, especially on the kitchen windowsill. I decide to snip two roses from the backyard and place them in the vase. The fire-engine-red blossoms brighten up the room *and* my spirits.

I finger the envelope propped by the vase, SUMMER written on it in Mimi's beautiful cursive. It's hard to believe this is the first summer I've spent without her. Harder to believe that Juliette and I have been living in her home for going on four months now, living here without her, moving together from summer to autumn just as she wished.

I touch the roses, their petals soft, and breathe in their scent. Their fragrance is faint, aromatic in a noninvasive way. They almost smell like the fresh-washed laundry scent David's pressed shirts give off.

Then, with the resolve of a woman on a mission, the scent of the roses enveloping me, I unexpectedly do what I've endeavored not to do this quiet holiday weekend. Mimi always said that life was for the living, and Juliette's never one to let me forget that. So, despite my better judgment, the endless considerations, and the heaviness in my heart, I cast caution to the wind and pick up my cell phone.

I know myself well. I will sit here all day, most likely taking that delayed jog or bike ride, maybe rooting about the garden some, then find myself alone in the silence and darkness of the night with a glass of wine, listening to the sounds of fireworks blasting and neighbors celebrating, and eventually giving in to my heart's desires and calling David. Or I could just call him now.

I decide against the delay—the gnawing, wearing waiting—and I call the man who still holds my heart, even if he's promised it to another.

———

"Gracie Dawn," David's strong, steady voice says as I open the front door. He's standing on our porch, where he's stood some times before, holding a beautiful bouquet of flowers. Last time it was crimson roses—a February guarantee. Tonight it's a garden blend—daisies, mums, some local greenery. I can't tell if his bouquet choice is indicative of the way he feels about me or about the meaning of our meeting. Regardless, I take the bouquet with my widest of smiles.

"David." When I say his name, my heart lifts, my smile is solid. I want to remember this moment forever. The moment when I lay eyes on David after all this time, when I neglect to remember the parts of our past I've prayed to forget. "I'm happy you could make it."

I hold open the door, gesturing for him to enter. It feels like a peace offering, or at least a truce. It feels like the start of something, but what I don't know. And, as I catch a whiff of the scent that's signature David, I don't really care.

"I've been *hoping* you'd agree to see me," David says with earnestness.

His voice hasn't changed, and neither has his walk, his smile, his subtle humor and lightheartedness. He walks both boldly and tentatively through the door. It's as if he's saying he's happy to see me but concerned about what the evening will reveal. He's sure and unsure, happy and sad, relaxed and scared stiff. I feel the exact same way, and I find a bizarre sense of comfort in this duality.

I tell him the flowers are lovely and that he didn't have to.

He steps near, our toes almost touching, the door still wide open. I think I can hear his heartbeat, just as well as I heard it when my ear was pressed against his chest that last night together in February. He's so close I swear I can hear his soft, perhaps nervous, breathing.

Feeling myself blush, I hold my arms open and glance to the side, preparing for a hug—a hug between friends, nothing more. I never know what to expect from David.

"It's so good to see you again, Gracie." My name comes out in a drawling, seductive way, the same way he'd say it after we'd make love and he'd look into my eyes, kiss my cheekbones, then my nose, and finally my lips. A tingle runs up my spine, and my mouth feels dry.

Slowly he wraps me in an embrace, and I can't decide if it's a just-friends hug or one that's shared by former lovers who have many questions to ask, lost time to make up for. Both options are likely, and while I try to reason why it's more likely the former of the two, David squeezes me tighter and whispers into my ear, "I've missed you, Gracie." He draws back, eyes locked with mine. "I've missed you so much."

Mentally cursing myself for not preparing to be swept off my feet so quickly, I find myself spluttering, "I-I've missed you, too." I can sense my blushing increasing. "Let me put these in water," I blurt as I rush to the kitchen to fetch a vase. "They're so lovely, I'd hate for them to dry up."

I'm babbling in an effort to calm my frazzled nerves. David has such a pull, such a magnetic charm with me. It's taking the tenacity of a bull not to fall into a puddle of tears and tell him I've missed him more than he can understand, that I've never stopped loving him, that I'm a pitiful single girl who's never been able to move on.

The few seconds of solitude in the kitchen as I arrange the bouquet in one of Mimi's most beautiful blue-glass vases buys me time to calm down, to get my emotions in check.

"I thought we could make dinner together," David says, entering the kitchen. "Or we could go out. Whichever you like."

I don't know from where it comes—perhaps the very back of my mind, the persistent aching question that begs to be answered, damn the place and time—but I spit out, "Better to make dinner here than to run the risk of being seen in public."

I bite my bottom lip. The words sound uglier once they've been said, uglier than I intended. At least the ball is now rolling. It's time to answer some questions.

"Gracie, let's not do that." David approaches with an extended hand. His brow is knit, lips drawn down, eyes entreating. "I know we have some talking to do, but not like that."

"You owe me an explanation." I'm not usually one to make unavoidable demands, and certainly not one to lead a conversation, so I surprise myself with my gumption. David does, after all, owe me an explanation for why he's decided to visit me after all this time.

"I do." His voice is calm, and his face relaxes. His eyes open wider yet are still entreating.

Not saying a word, I wait for him to carry on.

"Wha— Now?" He looks confused.

"Yes. Now. I think you owe me at least that." With a bravado that comes from some unknown place, I take a seat at the kitchen table. He takes the seat I push out for him with a nudge of my foot.

"How about you start with why you called me after all this time?" I swallow the lump that is beginning to form in my throat. "I told you to leave me alone."

"Things are different now. I had to see you, Gracie. I had to talk to you." He places his hand—a hand that is strong yet smooth, with long fingers and well-kempt nails—on top of mine.

With his thumb, he gently rubs at my hand. It feels so small and vulnerable under his. Part of me wants to pull my hand free, tell him that he has to explain himself before he can work his charms on me, seduce me, possibly pull me into his lies and deception once more.

Another part of me wants to grip his hand tightly, pull it to my lips, kiss his fingertips, feel his hands touch my neck, my collarbone, cup my breast, pull me tight as he lays kisses along my nape, my shoulders.

"Gracie." His voice is low and does nothing to quell the desire that's building for me to be with him once more, in the closest of capacities, in the most secure of embraces. "Gracie, I want to tell you everything. I want to be honest with you." I nod, urging him to go on. "I want to tell you the truth."

As I look into his eyes, I see them clouded with pain, not with the passion or the love I want to be there. David is keeping something from me—that much hasn't changed since we last saw each other.

"Okay," I say, voice small.

"It's just . . . it's difficult." He looks past me.

He's afraid to tell me. Afraid to tell me the truth? How he feels about me? Where he sees us going? That he loves me? That he doesn't love me? The multitude of possibilities is almost heartbreaking. I want so desperately to know this truth . . . but I'm terrified.

I suddenly can't think straight, I don't have control over my senses, and I don't want him to do anything but hold me. Hold me, in the silence.

Tears well in my eyes, and before I can blink them away, David has me in his arms. He's rocking me so softly, so soothingly that I fear I'll nod off right here, right now. I want to escape in his arms, in his comforting touch, in the protection that I feel he can provide for me now but will no doubt refuse me come tomorrow. Come tomorrow when he will inevitably tell me that he cannot see me again, that I must move on, that he is still with her.

We won't make it to tomorrow morning, though, partly because he says he promised an early-morning beach volleyball game with his father and brothers, but mostly because my demand for answers keeps me from waiting until a new day.

"You can tell me." I meet his eyes. "Please. Whatever it is."

He pulls me tighter, closer. I melt. "How about dinner first?"

"David."

"Come on." He gives me a light shake, as if to convince me whatever he has to share can be shared only on a full stomach. "It's been some time since we've seen each other, talked. We've got some catching up to do, wouldn't you say?" He raises both brows.

And there's that charm. I'm helpless, putty in his arms. I find myself shrugging, smiling, and saying, "How's spaghetti sound?"

Though I'm a mess of emotions, we eventually slip into easy conversation, almost seamlessly. It's welcome. It's nearly as comforting as being held in his arms. It's what I've craved for months. Our conversation about the local farmers' market and the weather, and the deeper subjects—Mimi's passing, the story of us that we slowly and cautiously approach—is comforting and familiar. Like talking with an old friend.

It's a saving grace to talk to someone other than Mom, Dad, or Juliette about Mimi's passing, the yearlong challenge Mimi's left us, the emotional ups and downs. David already knew of Mimi's cancer back in February. I told him about her deteriorating health and how the doctors hadn't given her much time. He was a rock for me then and before, since the moment the doctors diagnosed her last autumn and I was a terrible mess over it.

He didn't know of her passing until now, and he says he was devastated when I didn't answer his call in April. I tell him about what I was going through, and he says he wanted to be there for me. That's when, over some of the leftover blueberry buckle Juliette made before she left town, after a homemade dinner of simple spaghetti and meatballs, David and I begin to talk about us.

They're the words I've been itching to ask all this time, since the moment he contacted me back in April. I search for some of the earlier swagger that got me through our initial reunion.

"So, the truth," I say. "You want to tell me everything?"

"Gracie."

"I've waited." My eyes lock with his. "Long enough."

David says nothing.

"Are you still engaged?" I finally ask.

He inhales long and slowly, eyes cast downward.

"Answer me." My words come out with a vigor and confidence that I put on only for show. Inside I'm quaking like a kitten in a downpour. "Answer me."

"It's complicated," is his shifty answer.

I let go of his hand, stand from my seat next to him. Feeling incensed, arms crossed over my chest, I try to formulate my next question.

Nothing comes.

"You have to understand that I still want to be with you, Gracie." He stands and attempts to walk near me, but I sharply raise a halting hand.

"No," I say, biting back the sting of tears. "'It's complicated' isn't an answer. You're either with her or you aren't." I grip my head with both hands.

Oh, how I wish his reply had been different! Why must the pain grow stronger? The truth be the very thing you hope never to hear? Why must love be such a heart-wrenching experience?

"Listen." David's hands wrap around my arms before I can notice his approach. He pulls me tightly into his chest, pressing a hand to my lower back. "It's complicated, and I don't want to drag you through all this. You've been through so much with Mimi and—"

"No. Don't."

He exhales in response.

"I don't understand. Then . . . why did you call me? Why did you want to see me?" I look up into his cobalt eyes. "Why? Why, if you didn't want to hurt me, do you *continue* to hurt me like you do?" I can't hold back the tears now. They sting as they fall, but the sting is nothing compared to what his words do to my heart, my soul. "Why, David?"

"Because, Gracie." He holds my head in his hands. "Because I love you." He presses his lips tightly to my forehead, pulling me closer into his warm chest.

I fall limp, helpless against the love that's held me captive for years. A love that at times felt unrequited, at times innocuous, other times forbidden. A love that I thought I'd lost but, as I can see and hear and feel now, was only repressed.

"I love you, David." My words sound whimpering, but I mean them with every ounce of passion I have inside me, and then some. "I've always loved you. But I don't understand." My lips are quivering, my stomach is wavy, and I lean into him. I'm poised for a kiss, but a kiss that can't be had until I know, until I know for sure.

He doesn't come in for a kiss but holds me in his arms, eyes locked with mine. He looks to be lost in the moment, taking a mental photograph of it, perhaps because it may very well be lost forever, never to be replicated.

I summon the courage. "And you love her?" I can't hide from the truth any longer. I thought I wanted to hide in the dark, to believe, because he showed up at my door and now because he'll say that he loves me, that he does not love her. That there is no *her*.

Hiding from the truth, though, is how we wound up in this mess in the first place. There is a *her*, and he loves her. He is with her. I can feel it. I can read his sad eyes, his rigid body language, the words unspoken.

"It's complicated," he repeats, those words that hit like a poison-tipped dagger.

"Thank God we didn't do something stupid." I wriggle free from his embrace, rub my hands through my hair. "Like last time! God, I'm an idiot. To think you really came back for *me*. For *us*."

"Gracie, don't do this."

"And you say you *love* me!"

"Please. You have to understand that this isn't easy for me."

"And I suppose you think this is easy for me?" I push back my mussed hair.

"No." He wags his head, eyes downcast, shoulders sagging. "No, I don't. And I'm sorry."

"I am, too." I gather his things—his keys, his sunglasses, and the flowers I tear free from the vase. "You should go." Water droplets spray between us as I wrench out the bouquet.

"Gracie," he pleads.

"No." I hold his things out for him to take. "You can't play both sides, David. You used to, but not now. Not anymore."

"It isn't like that." He takes his sunglasses and keys and tells me to keep the flowers.

"Well, when it isn't like that," I say, throwing the flowers on the kitchen table, "then you know where to find me. Until then"—I charge into the living room and open the front door—"don't contact me. *Please!*"

Dejected, face gone pale, David steps onto the porch in the blackened night that's filled with the cloudy smoke that always lingers after the celebrations of the Fourth.

"In fact, maybe even when you do pick sides, don't come to me. It's too painful."

"Gracie, you don't mean that."

"You can't keep stringing me along."

"I don't want to."

"Yet you continue to. Answer me! Are you still with her? That's all that matters right now."

He can only sigh, then whisper out a pathetic, "Yes and no."

"Good-bye, David." I am determined to get through this departure without another shed tear, without heaving across the room everything and anything I can get my hands on.

"But I love you."

I press the side of my face to the open door, one hand gripping ever so tightly the interior handle. Trying to maintain my balance, my knees wanting to buckle and give way this very instant as I say the hardest good-bye—even harder than the last one. I say, "And that's what hurts the most. That you can love someone and still hurt them so badly."

With nothing more to say, I close the door on David. For now, for tomorrow, and forever. Though I close the door on the man I love, I can't yet close it on the love I have for him. The love that, though not unrequited, is unquestionably painful and forbidden.

12

Juliette

I've been so diligent about getting my shipments out on time. I know I'm not the most responsible person—I always forgot to take out the trash on my trash nights when I was a kid, even after Mom made me that helpful star-sticker chore chart; I neglected to study for almost every Spanish vocabulary quiz in college because I thought winging it with a shot of tequila and a can-do attitude would be enough to get at least a B. My Etsy orders, though, I am very dogged about. It's what many of my customers compliment me on when leaving their reviews. "Ships fast!" "Order completed quickly and satisfactorily!" "Beautiful brooch; fast shipper!" I'm certain my timeliness and these positive reviews are the main reasons I'm selling a good dozen pieces each week.

But now? Now I can't find the brooch I planned on shipping today. With the lag provided by the holiday, I can definitely kiss that glowing review good-bye. I might even get my first negative review. Then I'll be doomed to pulling lawn duty for eternity, at least as long as I live in Santa Barbara.

"It can't have gotten legs and walked away!" I say to myself.

I've dug through all my bedroom drawers, searched under furniture, in the bookshelf, in my messenger bag, the dining table, even the stack of mail. The brooch, no bigger than a coat button, is so finely detailed with vintage glass beads that even if I did make another one, I'd need a day or two just to find replacement materials and another day to tediously stitch.

"This is great! Just great!" I've resorted to turning the den upside down, including the no-touch items on the desk that belong to Gracie.

Even though she claims this space as hers, I've found it convenient to do some of my more intricate work here, as I did with the small brooch. The lighting provided by the desk lamp and the long surface at which to work made this particular project much easier.

Gracie complained once about the material scraps, thread pieces, and even loose beads that wind up in desk drawers, the computer keyboard, and sometimes the area rug. While I work I like everything splayed about—easy access, easy to grab things when needed. I try to keep the place as tidy as possible when I'm finished.

"What's going on?" Gracie says as she enters the den.

"My brooch! It's just . . . gone!" I'm flabbergasted. The den now is in such a state of disarray that even I find it to be well past acceptable standards.

"Calm down." Gracie lifts some pieces of fabric and stacks of paper from the desk. She casts about. "When did you last see it, and where?"

"I don't remember exactly where. When? Before I left for the Fourth." I'm trying not to panic any more than I already am. In the end, it *is* just a brooch. The customer may get their order late and I may get a snarky review, but the world won't fall apart. Still, I can't help but feel incandescent.

"Dammit!" I cry. I finally find something I can do well and consistently and I have to go and flub it up. *Typical Juliette!* I think as I shuffle through a desk drawer I've already checked.

Gracie offers to help, but not in her usual careful and meticulous way. She, too, raises her voice. "This place was a pigsty before you left, you know. No wonder you lost it."

I can't argue with that. As I recall, I left the den in slipshod shape. I was so keen on not being late to the carpool to Ventura that I neglected many of my to-dos.

"Well, it's not a pigsty now." I put a hand on my hip. I quickly look back at the desk, give a halfhearted laugh, then say, "Okay. It *wasn't* a pigsty before I turned it upside down in my search." I rub at my temple. "You cleaned up in here, then?"

She nods in an annoyed way. "Yes. Someone had to."

"Oh, don't high-horse this, Gracie. Shit happens."

"All too often." She rolls her eyes, and I twist my face in surprise. The heavy and obvious eye roll; the lazy and carefree eye roll; the sardonic, wisecracking, and even flirtatious eye rolls—those are my moves. Gracie rarely, if ever, succumbs to such an easy and childish display of emotion.

For the time being, I dismiss her atypical behavior and ask her if during her cleaning she happened to see the brooch or anything that might have *looked* like a brooch (it was so tiny, after all). She says no, but that maybe it wasn't left in the den in the first place.

"It can't be anywhere else," I say fervently. "It's here. It has to be." I lift the trash can from under the desk and notice that inside are handfuls of my fabric scraps, papers with design sketches I made, even one that has an address on it. I may have doodled all over it, but it was still a valuable piece of paper that I needed for my work.

"Gracie!" I hold up the trash can. "Did you throw this stuff away?" I pull out a handful of felt and organza, the edges all cut jagged, the material tattered and basically unusable, save for a few larger chunks.

"I threw some things away." Her voice rises an octave, in innocent defense. "Just *trash*, though."

"Oh crap." I begin to rummage through the trash can. "That thing was so small it probably hid in what you *thought*"—I roll my eyes, absolute resentment behind this roll—"was *trash*. Thanks, Gracie. Thanks a lot."

I mutter unpleasantry after unpleasantry, throwing organza, lace, ribbon, felt, and fabric behind me. I unroll a ball of paper, then reroll it and chuck it behind me in one direction, another ball in the opposite. "I can't believe this!" I cry. "Why would you do this?" I near the bottom of the trash can, no sign of my brooch. "Huh? Why? Can't you just let things be for one damn weekend?"

"I'm *always* letting things be!" Gracie's outburst takes me by surprise. I slowly return the trash can. "I'm always sitting back and letting things happen, passive. If you picked up after yourself more regularly, then maybe things like this wouldn't happen!" With that, she angrily spins around.

"So that's it?" I call after her. "Just storm off?" My sister doesn't lose her cool like this. And she doesn't just abruptly turn away from a heated discussion. "Okay, Gracie, I don't know what's going on."

"I'm going to help you." She fixes me with an inscrutable expression. "It's what I do. Bend over, take it, and don't dare ask for a fucking thing in return."

She waves her gardening gloves at me, then hands me my mine. "We're going to dig through the garbage. If that damn brooch is so important to you, let's find it." She pulls on her galoshes, slips on her gloves. "It's important, right?" She looks at me, deadpan.

"Well, yes . . ."

"Then suit up." She touches my galoshes with the tip of her booted foot. "It'll be dirty work, but it's important to you and it's my damn fault we're in this mess. Come on."

We pull three different trash bags from the garbage can out back. The summer heat has done a number on the waste, the stench not ideal so soon after breakfast.

"Why didn't you just leave the mess alone and let me clean it up?" I ask as we sort through a bag of trash. "Think I wouldn't get to it or something?"

"I was angry. Cleaning helps."

"Did you clean just the den or everything?" I crinkle my nose at the stench. "Then maybe we can just find the one bag you threw out."

Gracie yanks open a well-tied bag. She raises one brow and says, "I cleaned *a lot*. Bathrooms, kitchen, den . . . literally went around with trash bags, the vacuum—"

"Okay." I hold up a gloved hand as she carelessly upends her bag onto the ground. "I get it. Our job will not be easy."

I sort through what looks like kitchen trash, past spaghetti, banana peels, a bouquet of flowers that don't look as if they belonged in the trash quite yet. "What pissed you off so much you went on a mad cleaning frenzy?" I hold up half the bouquet of flowers. "You even threw out the good stuff."

Gracie snatches the bouquet and tosses it into the garbage can. "I don't want to talk about it!"

"So secretive," I mutter. "What with the flowers and all, you'd think someone had a date, maybe . . ." I flirtatiously pucker my lips, bat my lashes, trying to lighten the mood some.

"Secrets, huh?" She roots about another bag, dumping its contents haphazardly. There's so much emptied trash I can't see her feet anymore. "Want to talk about secrets?"

I laugh listlessly. "Okay. Whatever." Not sure where she wants to go with this rant, I begin to sift through a large black trash bag, one that looks promising yet daunting because it's so heavy.

"When were you going to tell me you got an application to Bluejay's?" Gracie's question comes out of left field.

"Uh . . . huh?"

"When were you going to tell me that you have a job application and *haven't* filled it out? When were you going to stop lying about not being able to find work. Huh?"

"Ah, cleaning? Right," I scoff. "Call it what it is—*snooping*. So you're snooping on me? That's great!"

"You can't keep going on like this, Jules." She shakes her head, like a mother scolding her child.

"Like what?" I hold my arms out and turn to the left, the right. "In a pile of shit? That's right. I can't! I'm done arguing with you."

She grabs my arm as I turn to leave. "You can't keep going on not working," she spits out, "refusing to fill out job applications. You know, just because you don't have to pay rent doesn't mean you should be lazy."

"I *am* working!" I point angrily at the trash. "You're sabotaging that!"

"Yeah, because I *purposely* threw away your brooch." She yanks open another bag of trash.

"What job applications I choose to fill out or throw away are none of your business. And since when did it become okay to go through my stuff?"

"Since it was okay for you to go through someone's personal belongings. Photo of David ring a bell?"

"Eye for an eye, eh? That's how we're playing this now?" I groan. "Real adult, Gracie. Real adult for someone who's always harping on me to *be* an adult. Such a hypocrite."

"Fuck you, Jules. You don't know the half of it."

"Because you don't tell me!" I throw a trash bag down, arms rigid at my sides. "Because you're a damn shell, closed up and silent. Don't blame me for your faults!" I take a step toward her, shuffling through the heaps of waste. I can feel my nostrils flare as my temper rises. I should be gagging from the odor, but I'm so angry I'm intent only on finding out what Gracie's MO is.

"What are we talking about?" I finally say. "I accidentally found a photo of you and David. BFD. You use that as a reason to go through my stuff? Find a stupid application for a stupid job I'll *never* get?"

"You don't know that."

"Yes!" I scream, angrily retrieving my discarded bag. "I do!"

"Whatever, keep lying to yourself," she mutters, picking through the trash.

"You're one to talk."

"I'm not lying, I'm searching for the truth." Gracie's voice, her pitch, the tears that follow, throw me completely off guard.

"Gracie?" I instantly drop the bag and rush to her side. She's nearly dry-heaving, her sobs so intense her entire body is shaking, her shoulders bobbing up and down. "Gracie, honey." I rip off my gardening gloves and wrap her in my arms.

"It's hopeless. Utterly hopeless." She drops her face onto my shoulder, still sobbing earnestly. "I'll always love him, but he doesn't respect me. One lie after another." She pauses to wail and let out more sobs that rattle her whole body. "He says he loves me, but if he doesn't respect me, if he can't even be *honest* with me, how can he really love me?" She looks up at me, tears wetting her face, hair in her eyes. "How?"

"Oh, Gracie." I rub her back, trying to soothe her rattled body, her saddened heart. "It'll be okay. I'm here to listen, to help."

Then, from nowhere, Gracie breaks into a bout of laughter, interrupted by some sobs and sniffles. "It's apropos, wouldn't you say?" She gestures to the mess we're surrounded by. "My love life is nothing short of a pile of shit."

"Oh, Gracie," I say through a quick beat of sympathetic laughter. "If you can still find your dry humor, you're holding your head above water higher than you think."

"Treading," she says loosely as we crunch our way, still locked in an embrace, across the mess of refuse we've made.

I no longer care so much about the brooch or the poor review that will be sure to follow, and I don't mind that there's a giant mess we'll have to clean up eventually. My big sister has never needed me before, and now that she does I'm not quite sure what to do.

As Mimi always said, though, "Sometimes all someone needs is for someone else to listen." And so, for Gracie, I will do exactly that.

———

I pour Gracie her favorite warm-weather drink: Diet Coke with a wedge of lemon and a handful of ice, the same beverage she's favored since she was a teenager. The way she puckers her plump lips to take a sip, eyebrows both raised a hair as the fizzy liquid is drawn up the straw, makes her look just as she did back when we were teenagers. She's even got her legs pulled up and crisscrossed, hunching forward in her seat next to me on the settee.

"Thanks," she says midsip. "I needed this."

I tuck a knee into my chest and turn toward her. "Never underestimate the power of an ice-cold soda on a hot summer day."

Gracie's calmed down, no more tears or heartbreaking tremors. I try to keep the mood somewhat light nonetheless.

As soon as we returned to the house, Gracie began spilling about David Nichol and the insanity of the past few months. She was letting out information so fast I barely had a second to grab her the Kleenex box and fetch her her therapeutic beverage.

"I don't know what's come over me." She sighs, long and heavily. "Guess I've finally cracked."

"Anyone would," I say. "I can't believe you've kept this bottled up for so long." Had I gone through even a fraction of what she has, I would have cried like a baby long ago. But that's Gracie for you, the reserved one in the background. Even when we were children, when we had to perform in the annual school play, it was Gracie who worked behind the scenes—back in wardrobe, the curtain puller.

"Trouble is, even though things are technically finished—" She looks to me, as if for confirmation. I just nod for her to continue. "I don't know what to do. I feel like I need to *do* something. But what?" She gives me a puzzled expression. "Isn't that stupid?"

"No." I firmly wag my head. "Not at all. Your feelings are never stupid. You can't fight how you feel."

"But I can fight—I can control—how I react."

"Gracie, you reacted as anyone in your situation would have reacted. Stop worrying yourself to pieces. David's a jerk and what—"

"No. No, Juliette. David's not a jerk."

"He has a fiancée!" I'm thunderstruck. How can she defend the asshole?

"He says it's complicated, and I *know* that's a bull excuse. It doesn't erase what he's done, but it also doesn't erase the feelings I have for him." She takes a quick sip of her Diet Coke. "And it doesn't mean he's a jerk."

I dramatically crash my head against the back of the settee. "Gracie!"

But I hold my tongue. This is one of the few times my big sister has wanted to open up to me. One of the rare moments she's talked about her romantic life and about David in such a volatile context. I want to be an open ear and a shoulder for her. Throwing out disparaging remarks or accusatory comments isn't going to invite her to continue to open up, or to open up ever again.

"I'm sorry," I say. "You love him. Those feelings are real—"

"Legitimate," she cuts in, and I smile.

"Yeah. Legitimate."

I pause for a moment as she takes one contemplative sip after another. I let things settle for a second before I pry.

"So how long *has* he been engaged?" I ask as she continues to nurse her beverage. "How long have you known?" She's now biting the tip of her straw. "If you don't mind my asking."

With an exhausted sigh, Gracie sets her glass on one of Mimi's many lace doilies. She sinks down in her seat, turns her head to me, and says, "David and I've been on and off for years, you know?" I nod.

"Usually whenever he was in town we'd catch up . . . hook up." She begins to blush ever so slightly. "All while he was in law school, if he had a girlfriend and if he was in town, we'd see each other, but *just* as friends." She really hammers this point home, making sure I know she's never been one to tread even remotely near home-wrecker territory.

I tell her that I believe her—of course she wouldn't do such a thing. In all honesty, I would *never* have pegged Gracie as the kind of woman who would wind up with a man who treaded these waters. Gracie was always so virtuous, always opting for the moral high ground, a lover of law and order and following social conventions. This afternoon conversation is taking me for a spin.

"When he didn't have a girlfriend, obviously he'd tell me." Her blushing returns. "We'd kind of hook up, and, well, that's kind of how it had always been. Ever since we left USC. That was our"—she uses air quotes—"'relationship.' Pathetic, I know." She blows a puff of air up.

"Last Christmas he was here," she continues. "We saw each other, we did our usual David-and-Gracie on-and-off thing." She gives an embarrassed sniff. "But when he came over in February, February *twenty-third*, because he happened to have some business in town . . ." She furrows her brow. "Come to think of it, I don't even know if that's true or not, but who's keeping track of the lies at this point?" Another sniff.

"When he was here, we got together, but it was different. I really felt like we could make something work with the distance. I was hopeful at Christmas—we had such a great time together, so natural, friends all these years, and . . . it was just so happy, so nice. So comfortable. You know?" A faint smile crosses her lips.

"Come that next visit, I was more than hopeful. I was kind of, like, *sure* things would work. We had such a pull, such a connection." She looks me square in the eyes. "We *belonged* together, Jules," she says with emphasis.

I place a hand on her knee and give a small nod. I believe her. Most women our age have been there at least once before.

I gave my first-love card to Miles Colwell, the captain of the high school football team. I also gave him my V card, so a week after we'd done the naughty-naughty and I heard he was lip-locked with some girl in a drugstore parking lot *not* picking up a prescription for his grandmother, I was a wreck. The rumors had been floating around school that my card wasn't the only one Miles had acquired. But rumors aren't necessarily true, so ignore the rumors I had, and hook up with Miles I had even more. What else is a girl in love to do?

However, discovering there was no medication for Grandma was too much to bear. I can distinctly remember the feeling of blood boiling when Gracie confirmed the rumors. I lashed out. For a moment I hated her. I hated Miles; I hated everyone and everything.

It was nothing a few drinks in the garage and hooking up with some twice-as-hot baseball player couldn't fix. But still, it hurt like hell. I can, at least in some small way, understand where Gracie is coming from.

Gracie carries on. "We had a really romantic time in February, and then—" She quickly clamps her mouth shut, swallows, then says, "He told me he was seeing someone. That he didn't really know why he was playing both sides of the fence."

"He used that phrase?" I interrupt.

She sniffs a laugh of disbelief. "Yeah. A winner, right? He said he'd had a girlfriend. A girlfriend since last autumn." She claps a hand to her head. "I can't believe he would keep something like that from me. That he would, well, play both sides of the fence!"

"Had he ever done it before?"

"I asked. Of course, who knows if he told the truth? No point in hoping for that anymore. But he said never. Every time we ever got together, he was in between girlfriends, single. For some ridiculously sick and twisted reason, he decided that Caroline—"

She darts her head to the right, fixing me with a hard gaze. "That's her name. David's fiancée. Caroline." She makes a gagging sound. "He decided that Caroline wasn't enough. I had *no* clue at Christmas. *No* clue, Jules! A tiny part of me feels like this is my fault because I could have asked him if he was seeing anyone."

"It's not your fault. No. No way."

"But after three years of the same routine I figured . . . you know? He *wouldn't* visit me and romance me and *sleep* with me if he had a girlfriend! A *fiancée!*"

"Absolutely."

"I knew something was a little off, though." She sets down her Diet Coke and wraps her arms across her waist. "After dinner and a walk on the beach and our night together at my place. Like"—she squints in recollection—"I felt like we could really build something together, but I also felt like he was keeping something from me. That something was unsettling for him. Something was on his mind." She glances at me. "And then, like out of nowhere, over breakfast at that darling French bistro—"

"La Chez?"

She nods. "The one and only. With the killer eggs Benedict."

I smile, grip my stomach, and pretend to drool over the one-of-a-kind breakfast.

Gracie appreciates my attempt at levity and says, "Anyway, Benedict Arnold himself . . ."

I can't help but poke my finger in her arm and tell her that she really does have a fabulous and acute sense of humor.

". . . tells me there," she continues, "in public, probably to keep my crazy female emotions at bay, that he can't lie anymore. He's engaged to be married! He's been seeing her for, like, six months or something."

She loosely waves one hand about, and with the other reaches for her Diet Coke. "Said he wasn't sure what he was doing, that he was confused, that he loved his fiancée but that he didn't want to lose me.

Anyway, it was over then. I told him I never wanted to see him again. He'd hurt me more than I ever imagined someone could hurt me. Someone who *cared* about me! How could he do that? And to poor Caroline."

"I'm sorry, Gracie." I rub her back some. "I'm sorry you've had to go through this."

"Still going through it. Out of nowhere he contacts me in April." She makes a serious expression and tells me that she refused to have contact with him then. "Then for the Fourth," she says. "Only this time I answer."

"Because you still love him."

"I'm stupid."

"No."

She shrugs. "Whatever. I know I probably should have just let things be. Let him go and get married, never met with him this weekend. But part of me really wanted more answers. I wanted to know *why* he was contacting me again, after all that had happened in February. He was engaged to be married! Why's he trying to contact me still?"

"Is he still engaged?" The question is absolutely worth asking.

"I don't know."

"You didn't ask?" I can't believe it.

"Oh, I asked! He said—here's another winner—'It's complicated.'"

"Lame-ass Facebook relationship status, lame-ass answer." I steal a sip of Gracie's drink but crinkle my nose as soon as the aspartame settles onto my tongue. I slurp out an ice cube to wash away the taste and quench my thirst.

"He said he was and wasn't with her still," she says limply. "I don't know what it means, and I probably shouldn't care. If he can't say no, then I have no business seeing an engaged man." Gracie, for the first time this whole conversation, looks satisfied, assured.

"I wonder why he decided to tell you he was seeing someone else," I say, puzzled.

"Wedding date nearing." Gracie cackles in a deprecating way. "I asked him, in February, if he had been engaged in December. The last time we had sex. Not that hooking up once with an engaged man was any less painful, but, I don't know. It feels better, at least infinitesimally, to have done it only once, not twice."

"You didn't sleep with him this past weekend?"

"Good God, Jules!" She looks absolutely appalled.

"I'm sorry." I immediately regret asking. "I didn't mean anything by it."

"I am *not* that woman, Jules. I am not."

"Sorry."

"They got engaged on New Year's. A few days after we'd been together. Can you believe that?"

"Damn."

"Then in February he told me all about how, even though they were engaged, he wasn't so sure about it, about her. He felt like things were happening too fast. They'd been seeing each other for only a few months. I don't know. He said he was just in a really weird place and wanted me to be patient with him while he figured things out."

"And you said hell no."

"Exactly. Told him I never wanted to see him again."

Suddenly her face gets a cloudy look to it, her gaze shifts from me to a point far off on the opposite side of the room, her creased brow and tight lips kind of melt down, her shoulders become loose. "But I still did it once." Her voice is weak but lingers in the air heavily for what feels like an eternity before her next words. "I can't hide the fact that I did it once. The shame, the guilt, the pain. I slept with another woman's man. And I still love him. I'm the fool, Juliette. I'm a damn fool!"

"You're not a fool. You can't help who you fall in love with. And David deceived you. You can't blame yourself for something you had no idea about."

"I know, on a very logical level, that that's true. It doesn't make the pain and the guilt any less, though."

"I know." I give her a sympathetic hug. "But as you're always saying, like Mimi always said, 'This too shall pass.'"

She sniffs through a fleeting smile and tilts her head so that it rests against mine. She sinks into my hold, and I tighten it. "I told him to leave. To figure out his life and leave me out of it."

"And if this 'It's complicated' excuse with Caroline can be resolved," I say, "if he doesn't end up marrying her, do you still want him to stay away?"

"I told him to."

"Do you *want* him to?"

She gently rolls her head against mine. Her silence and her weak lopsided smile tell me that her head led her to say one thing, but her heart is saying something else.

———

"Thanks for listening, Jules," Gracie calls out as I slip out of the bathroom and through Mimi's bedroom and pass by Gracie's wide-open door.

She's in her bed, the rim of the rose-patterned top sheet drawn expertly across the lightweight cream blanket, tucked under her armpits. She takes off her reading glasses and places them on top of the hardback she has open, page saved, on her chest.

"It was nice talking," she says. "Like . . . it's good to have a sister I can talk to. It's nice you're just in the other room."

"My pleasure, Gracie." I pull from my hair the ruffly tie I used when rinsing my face for the evening. "Anytime."

"You're a good listener, you know?"

"I'm here anytime you want to talk."

"I am, too. If there's *anything* you want to talk about, Jules, I'm here."

146

This has always been the case, and on many occasions I've taken her up on her offer to lend an ear and give me sage advice. As the big sister, Gracie was the requisite first step to solving most of my troubles when I was younger.

I've always prided myself on being independent for the most part, but if I needed help with algebra homework, a ride, someone to listen to me blow off steam about how unfair Mom and Dad were being, Gracie was there.

For a lot of the difficult stuff, too. The difficult stuff, that is, that I knew she could help me with and wouldn't think less of me for. Like what to do when the college freshman blues hit so hard I was tempted to drop out and move back home, enroll in the community college.

I've always known that Gracie's been there for me, and that's comforting. But there are *some* things that a sister can't understand. Some things you keep bottled up inside for fear of a judgment so harsh there would be no redemption in any corner.

"I know you are," I tell her nevertheless. "Thank you."

"Anything." Gracie's voice is filled with urgency.

I tuck my bathroom bag under my arm and chuckle. "All right. You've got it."

"Jules." She props herself up on one arm and faces me. "I'm sorry about what I said earlier, about you living here rent-free and not getting a job and all. I was out of line. You are working. You're not lazy."

"Only after five and on the weekends," I kid.

"I'm serious. I'm sorry."

"Thanks."

"And you're looking for work." She raises an inquisitive brow.

"Mmm-hmm." I take a step deeper into the hallway, ready to call it a night.

"If you need help filling out the Bluejay's application, I can help."

"I'm capable of filling out a job application intended for a tween."

"Are you going to fill it out?"

"You're prying, Gracie. Nagging."

"Sorry." She shifts, about to lie back down, but returns to her propped elbow. "I want to help you, if you need help. Or if you want to talk about it or want help finding a different job—"

"Not now." I bite my tongue, calling forth every ounce of patience I can find not to erupt. I want to tell Gracie to let me be and live my life the way I see fit. So long as I'm not messing up her plans or encroaching on her life, why should she care what I do for work, if I fill out some stupid application or not?

"When you're ready?" Her face pleads with me.

"Fine." I grip her doorknob. "When I'm ready."

"Good night." She blows me a kiss. "Sleep tight."

"Don't let the bedbugs bite," I finish, sealing it with a blown kiss.

13

Gracie

"Think we should have more tomatoes than this," the note on the refrigerator reads. "Also, unripened lemons dropping off tree. More fertilizer? Water? Will pick up fertilizer from store on way home. Can you please water? XO Juliette"

I let out a disgruntled groan. Throughout the spring, Juliette and I seemed to have a decent handle on the garden. We pretty much left things as they were and watered, weeded, pruned some, plucked ripe fruit. Once summer came along, our tasks were still routine, although perhaps things slowly began to fall by the wayside. If we don't do something fast, the whole garden runs the risk of drying up before autumn. There will be no small squash and cute gourds to grace the kitchen and dining tables this year, as Mimi had each harvest.

Truth be told, Juliette and I have been spending more of our summer riding bikes and going to the beach together than tilling the earth and reaping a bountiful harvest. Gardening was what we both did together with Mimi as children. We share many fond memories of time spent in that backyard, and Mimi left it in our care, to pick, prune, sow, and reap to our hearts' content. But a shared appreciation for zipping by on two wheels, the sea air whipping freely through our hair, was doing the trick of sisterly bonding just fine.

Well, that and the whole meltdown I had about David last month. Juliette really helped me through that rough patch. She said all the things a broken heart needed to hear, even tossing out jokes and coming up with welcome distractions. She got in the habit of inviting me out to join her and her new group of friends for dinner or drinks now and then. I agree to it some of the time, as they are nice and have welcomed me into their relaxed circle.

But Juliette's crowd isn't exactly my type—the very laid-back, carefree, dream-it-and-it-will-come sort. They're a group that considers capitalism the most deceiving of religions in the world and views participation in the Occupy movement as being as much of a full-time job as the ones held by those "bloated men in suits."

And, as I learned at our most recent night out at a bar together, they think my little sister should definitely hitchhike with them to South America. When Juliette mentioned she'd love to go somewhere unlike anyplace she'd been before and find raw inspiration for her poetry, her new pals insisted their thumbing-a-ride approach would provide just what she was looking for. Suffice it to say I understand better now why Juliette has such disregard for convention. She's always been an energetic spirit, and her natural desires are only encouraged by her circle of friends.

Regardless, I appreciate the invitations, and I appreciate the company. Though they're not my usual circle, everyone is affable, and the time spent with Juliette, and the time spent as a friend, has been very welcome. And I have to admit, slipping out of routine and relaxing, learning to "embrace life!" as Juliette says, has been nice.

Sometimes I lose myself in work and forget to have fun. I focus on the pain of having lost Mimi, of having lost David, of the responsibilities that are required of me, and I forget that there's still time to smile, to have fun, to embrace life. As time goes on, as the days turn to weeks, broadening the span of time between loss and the present, remembering to embrace life and the good becomes more natural. Learning to let go becomes easier.

Every week or so since the weekend of the Fourth, Juliette has asked if David's tried to contact me again. She's ready to rally to my cause like bees to honey. I appreciate it, and surprisingly I don't feel claws come out when his name is spoken, or when the incident over the holiday is mentioned, or when the possibility of his contacting me is brought to mind. Juliette, with her carefree attitude, warm spirit, and zest for life, puts me at ease whenever I hear the name David. She could ask all she wanted about him (luckily, though, she doesn't too often), and I'd understand she was doing so only with the best of intentions, only to let me know that she cares for me and is looking out for me, that she doesn't want me hurt. She's as much a part of the process of learning to let David go as is time. I need her. I'm grateful to have her not just in my life but one bedroom over.

Now, when I open up the freezer and discover that there are even *more* blueberries packed in there, fresh from the farmers' market, I no longer mumble to myself, "Why does she make living with her so difficult?" When the mountains of blueberries come pouring forth like lava from a mountaintop, the frozen marbles dancing all over the kitchen floor, leaving flecks of water and occasional purple dye in their wake, I don't shout, "Juliette, I'm going to kill you!" I'm tempted to, especially when an unexpected avalanche came pouring forth on my once-white, now-purple-polka-dotted blouse one morning.

My encounters with the blueberries, with Juliette's chronic lateness to dinner at Mom and Dad's and to meetings at Mimi's grave and in getting up for a morning bike ride, are all just not-so-subtle reminders that I live with my little sister whom I love, my little sister who would probably clock David good if he ever set foot on our front porch, my little sister who's got my back, who loves me. Though she's sometimes difficult to live with, she is the only roommate I would ever want.

———

When Juliette arrives home at twenty past seven, after I've spent my evening home from work watering the entire garden and gathering the unripe, wasted lemons from the ground, I ask if she found some good fertilizer. "The organic kind that Mimi liked?" I say.

"Forgot," she answers casually. She flops down onto the long sofa made for three. She drapes an arm over her face. "Slipped my mind. I lost track of time getting my fliers out."

This is Juliette's latest attempt at finding work. She's advertising private tutoring for elementary school kids needing help with reading, English, spelling, even entry-level Spanish. It's something she used to do back in New York City, evidently.

"How'd that go?" I ask.

"One hundred made and printed, spread across every Santa Barbara café, bookstore, grocery store, library, you name it!" She rolls her head on the sofa arm and looks at me, her own arm still draped over her forehead. "I hope at least *someone* will bite, what with school starting up again soon and all. We'll see. It can pay really well."

"I'm sure," I say positively as she bounds from her seat with unexpected urgency.

"I'll get the fertilizer tomorrow." She gives me a face that says she swears she won't forget, because she knows it's safe to assume I dutifully did the watering. "Promise."

I follow her into the kitchen. "You know, maybe this weekend we can do some real work out there? Really get our hands dirty. You're right, I do think Mimi had more tomatoes at this point in the year."

"Sure." She plucks an orange from the fruit bowl and tosses it in the air a few times. "Just not when I've got plans. Maybe Sunday?"

"You got another hot date?" It never ends with Juliette.

"You love living vicariously, don't you?" She blows me a teasing kiss. "I can get you set up, Gracie." She licks away the orange juice dripping down her hand. "I've got a lot of single guy friends and friends who know single guys. Say the magic word."

"When I'm interested, I'll let you know. So, who's the hottie?" I, too, pick up an orange. Juliette's making it look irresistible. "Cary?"

"Oh, nah. This is some guy I met on the beach." She licks her lips and shakes her head. "Cary and I stopped seeing each other weeks ago. He went back to school. Just some summer fun, you know? And he was kind of a stoner. Not really my type."

This is news to me. I was under the impression they were still together. Guess it's time again for the whole out-with-the-old, in-with-the-new song and dance. And that my hippie sister finds a stoner not her type? I don't know if I'm more surprised or impressed. Maybe she is more grown up than I take her for.

"I didn't know that," I say, feeling a tiny bit hurt that I wasn't included in what I figured would be a juicy bit of sisterly or girlie gossip that might be shared on, say, one of our bike rides. After having spilled about David, I'd think Juliette could feel free to talk to me about stuff like this.

"Yeah, no big deal," she says breezily. "Just a summer fling." Unable to sit still, she leaps from her seat at the kitchen table, throws the remainder of her orange in the trash, and rinses her hands. "You know, I'm feeling like a swim."

"A swim?" Though a Southern Californian born and bred, I've never been one to fancy a swim in the great Pacific. Sure, I go in, but just to wade a bit, maybe tread in barely deep water. For me it's never recreational, as it is for Juliette. It's not that I saw *Jaws* one too many times, or can't swim, or have a fear of drowning or of depths to which I cannot see. I've just never much liked the idea of floating or swimming or playing about in a giant, unpredictable force of nature. Not my thing. Not to mention the Pacific isn't exactly warm.

It's always been Juliette's thing, though. She dove in fully clothed, even skinny-dipped. If she felt like a swim, off she'd go. I was mildly surprised she'd chosen New York as her college destination. She used to sneak out for a late-night swim with friends in high school all the time, sometimes even with boyfriends. I always promised I'd cover for her if Mom or Dad found her missing, but I feared I would flub and spill the beans under parental pressure. Thank goodness I never needed to cover up.

"A swim?" I repeat. "At this hour?"

"Of course! It's only swimming," Juliette replies eagerly. "Can do it at *any* hour. Want to join?"

"You're not going alone, are you? It's not safe at night."

"It's not night. It's still light out! Come on, Miss Priss. It's perfectly safe." She wipes her freshly washed hands on the back of her torn-cuffed blue-jean shorts. She grabs my hand, leading the way. "Summer's almost over. We have to enjoy the last days of the midnight sun!"

"Midnight sun," I say with a laugh. "We're not exactly in Norway."

"You know what I mean. Come on. It'll do you some good after what I bet was a long day at the office again." She raises her brows, awaiting the answer she knows I'll give.

"Ten hours at the office is, sadly, not the longest of workdays," I say. I reach for my car keys, reluctantly agreeing to Juliette's evening-swim plans.

She snatches the keys from me and says we'll ride our bikes. "Make it a real summer-night thing. *Mimi* would insist we enjoy the summer, you know?

Summer is leaving as fast as it arrived, and Juliette and I have certainly made the most of it. We picked barrels of lemons and limes together, went on countless routine bike rides in the neighborhood, had barbecues on the patio with Mom and Dad a number of times, took regular trips to the beach and Stearns Wharf. We even turned on the sprinklers in the front yard on a particularly sweltering day and danced in them to the tunes of Simon and Garfunkel like carefree teenagers.

And yes, when Mr. Silver walked by with his two Rhodesian ridgebacks, I sheepishly waved and told Juliette we were too old for this, abandoning the frivolity. But we cranked up the music again one Sunday afternoon, in the backyard, when we decided to give the garden a much-needed session of weeding and watering, and we danced some.

This year's summer, though not quite what it could be were Mimi alive, and even despite David's disastrous return, has turned out to be one of my favorite summers of my adult life, one I know I will always remember as the summer I got to spend with my sister.

Juliette and I hop on our bikes, just as when we were kids, and pedal down Laguna Lane toward a favorite slice of beach, where the waves are weak, the current gentle.

———

I regret not having grabbed the *Times* from the pile of mail I haven't read yet, having rushed to the office quite early this morning. Had we driven my car, I would have at least had the romance novel I was halfway through.

No reading material to enjoy as the sun sets over the water, I close my eyes and listen to the sound of the waves rushing up on shore, then trickling back into the wide sea. Back up the shore, down again. Whoosh . . . whoosh . . .

Occasionally I pick up Juliette's shriek or laugh as she runs up onto the beach, then splashes and bodysurfs back into the water. She calls out my name twice, then a third time before I finally open my eyes. She's popping up from a quick dive, hands waving wildly overhead. "Take a dip!" she yells.

I shake my head, and she pleads on. So much about this night is like a flashback to childhood. Juliette's insisting on taking the most scenic (though longer) bike route from Mimi's to the beach. My scolding her for flying through a "Stop" sign much too fast. Juliette's telling me she'll race me to the shore. My locking up not just my bike but hers, which she abandoned in her giddy rush to dive into the ocean.

"It's beautiful!" she cries. Arms akimbo, she's standing rather far out, though the water comes to only just above her knees. She's wearing nothing but her white cotton bra and panties, soaked through and sheer. I'm grateful it's dusk and we're not occupying the slice of beach with anyone else.

I reject her invitation once more and instead close my eyes, return to the solitude to which the sound of the rushing waves sends me. I pretend it's another day at the beach with Juliette, Mom, Dad, Mimi. It's a day filled not with work or deadlines, not with reminders to take care of the electric bill or that one of us needs to remember to pick up a carton of milk tomorrow. Not with the daunting image of a garden that's in need of serious care or the phone number of an ex-boyfriend that I'm both tempted to call and tempted to delete from my contacts list. Not with any worry, any care, any *thing*.

I hug my arms to my body, burying my hands inside the baby-blue cable-knit sweater of Grandpa's—my "beach sweater" that I've had for more than a decade, its stitches loose and wearing thin.

I crack open my eyes, expecting to see Juliette even farther out, a distance she prefers, especially given the low tide. I squint against the evening light in search of her. The sun is only a half globe now over the water. It's large and a severe orange, like the geraniums that line the brick walkway to the front door. I spot Juliette as she pops up for air. She's still in the shallows, though the tide is starting to come in. She's bodysurfing, catching one low wave, diving in, riding it out for as long as she can. The ride is brief, and she darts back to the water and plunges into the next wave, dancing in the ocean without a care in the world.

I can't help but smile as I look up into the sky, painted with the gorgeous colors of sunset. A few seagulls fly overhead, either squawking their alertness for their evening meal or announcing the call to nest. Thin sheets of clouds advance. Restaurants, streets, and the occasional beach house lamp are lit up. It is a classically beautiful Santa Barbara summer night. A beautiful reminder of why I love the place I have always called home.

I bring the limp and baggy sweater cuffs to my face. Grandpa's scent of pipe tobacco mixed with chocolate and oranges has long since disappeared, but the familiarity the sweater holds is still a comfort. I close my eyes again as a chill comes in, the expected evening marine chill.

Juliette calls out once more that I should join her. "Come on, Gracie!" I am imagining her not twenty-three but ten, not here on the beach with just me but with Mom and Dad, and Mimi and Grandpa, as well. It is another memorable summer, another family outing that, when experienced, may not seem all that eventful, but in retrospect is one of the many simple joys that you recall when you're having a rough few weeks, a difficult year, and need to be reminded that life is short— an adventure, as Juliette is prone to saying.

"The water's not that cold," Juliette says. "Come on. It's fun!" I watch as she dives yet again, full of a child-like vigor. Life is an adventure.

All right, I think as I whip off my sweater, revealing a ratty USC T-shirt I slipped into before making my watering rounds in the garden. I roll my cuffs halfway up my calves and take off for the water.

Juliette makes an excited shriek as I advance into the ocean, only deep enough for the water to come to midcalf. "It's cold." I state the obvious. I rub hands over my arms.

"It gets warmer." She waves me in.

I firmly plant my toes in the sand. Again, something that takes me back to childhood. As the gentle waves roll in, the icy water dances across my feet, up my ankles, and nearer my pants. I dig my toes in deeper. The water runs off, and I feel the curious sensation of losing my footing. Considering I call Santa Barbara home, the sad fact of the matter is I do not come out here, to the beach, nearly as much as I should. As they say, if you live in Paris, you tend to dismiss the Eiffel Tower.

The sensation occurs again and again, Juliette's cheerful shrieks carrying on as background noise against the rushing waters. I tell myself I need to work on being more in the moment, being more spontaneous, engaging in more of the simple pleasures that make life the beautiful and short-term gift that it is. *A lease*: Mimi's words come to mind. I've started by abandoning my wish for reading material and giving in to the call of the ocean, following Juliette into the water, though only a fraction of the way.

After more coaxing from my sister, I think, *What's a little more of a push?* I take a few steps farther into the water. I'm nearing Juliette; she's still flapping around like a kid.

The water is no longer ice-cold as it greets my feet, my ankles. There's the crash of a larger wave, and the water that rushes up and soaks the bottoms of my pants and the dry parts of my skin is indeed cold. I shriek through a guttural laugh.

"Get in, Gracie!" She looks on at me with persuading eyes, head cocked to the side. It's as if she's saying, just as she did when we were children, *Don't be such a scaredy-cat, Gracie. Get in already!*

"Here goes!" I shout back. My pants are already wet, but the water quickly becomes far less cold as I spend more time in it. I take off my T-shirt and toss it onto the sand, the chilling breeze immediately making me wish I hadn't worn such a sheer bra. I cup my breasts and wade deeper into the water until I meet Juliette, now chest deep.

"Holy cow," I say, dramatically chattering. "It's cold."

"You crazy girl. You've got your pants on."

"You're in your panties. *Who's* the crazy one?"

Juliette holds her nose with two fingers and does a swirling motion with her upper body and head, arm waving above before she disappears under the water.

I attempt a shallow tread as the waves rock me to and fro, the sand below coming and going as the tide rolls in. A hand slithers across my leg, then my stomach.

Juliette's head pops up, her hands gripping my waist, and she tells me she'll race me to the buoy several yards off. She then breaks into a smile and tells me she's kidding as my face goes long.

She used to love that game when we were younger, loved seeing how far she could go, how thin a line the shore and how tiny the robin's-egg-blue lifeguard stations could become. Only once did I agree to join her in her race to the buoy, deciding that fear shouldn't hold me back. I panicked halfway out, though. We were many yards offshore, and the distance from both the land and the ocean floor threw me into an anxious state. Since then I've kept to the shore, the shallows, and sometimes, as now, a little farther out, where one can still bodysurf and usually stand on two feet.

"I bet you can't hold your breath as long as I can," Juliette says, treading.

"Bet you I can." I brace myself for the icy cold shock and quickly dunk my head, smoothing all my hair back as I come up.

We swim out some, the tide having brought us closer to shore. As we put some distance between ourselves and the beach, Juliette flips to her back and begins to lazily backstroke. She says we should do this more often. I tell her she's right. Maybe not the whole running out half-naked in the freezing ocean at night, but some version of it. At least the beach part—the time spent together that doesn't have anything to do with gardening tasks, tidying up a house, or arguing about who will cook dinner (or pick it up). Time doing nothing but a lazy, feel-good pastime.

"I come out here a lot, you know?" Juliette says. It seems she's forgotten the breath-holding contest she was so enthusiastic about. I don't remind her. "Was actually here this afternoon. After I did my fliers." She returns to treading. "That's how I met the guy I'm going out on a date with this weekend. His name's Geoff, with a *G*." She cackles. "So pretentious, but he's a volunteer for the Red Cross, so how bad can he be? Told him I'd donate blood. That's our date. So *not* pretentious, right?"

While I should be struck with the giggles at what Juliette's calling a date, with how absurd but really rom-com-like it is, I'm struck instead by the fact that she went to the beach after passing out her fliers. Not that I'm keeping tabs on her, but why did she say she lost track of time with her fliers and therefore couldn't get the fertilizer? Why go to the beach and, evidently, pick up guys when she had something to do? Despite my ability to cast caution to the wind for a moment and dive into the water, I pull a classic Gracie and pry like the nosy big sister. "You were already here?" I ask.

"Yup!" she answers. "I come here a lot, to swim. To just hang on the beach." Her tone and attitude are so casual. "I know." She rolls her eyes, the kind of eye roll that says she can read my mind. "I should be doing something more productive with my time than lazing by the beach."

"Summer isn't here forever," I say, trying to make her feel as if I'm not putting her under the microscope. But, yes, part of me can't help but feel the unjustness in her "lazing by the beach," picking up guys who will only become castoffs after a few dates once she's grown bored of them, while I'm slogging away at the firm, being a responsible adult, doing something meaningful with the degree I earned.

It bothers me not just because, let's face it, a day at the beach is *much* more appealing than time spent looking over contracts and annotating memos under fluorescents. What bothers me most is that I want the best for Juliette. I want her to live up to her potential and do great things with her life, and I find it hard to believe that her world of opportunity can be found on the shores of a California beach. She's twenty-three years old, college educated, fortunate to not have massive amounts of school debt or even traditional bills, and she's squandering her opportunities, her chance to find what she wants to do here and make something of herself. She's just so uncommitted. I don't understand it.

"It's inspiring out here. I come here to think, to write poetry," Juliette carries on. She's lying on her back, making slow treading motions. "To draw and stuff."

"Oh." I feel guilty for jumping to conclusions, passing judgment. She has mentioned how she'd love to get a career in the arts going, doing something that she's passionate about. Maybe this is her own way of trying to do that. I don't have to understand it, I just have to acknowledge it, respect it. That's what Mom has always told me when I complained of Juliette's disregard for convention, her need to do things her own way. Like when we agreed to go half-and-half on a spa package for a Mother's Day gift one year, and a week before, Juliette decided a mother-daughter collage of the three of us was more personal, "more Mother's Day–ish."

"It helps clear my head," Juliette says.

"With Mimi." I jump to this conclusion because I think that if I were to escape to the beach to draw or write poetry, needing to clear my head, it would be because of the loss of Mimi, the deep thinking her challenge has been forcing me to do as I consider my life, my relationship with my sister. Then again, I'd probably want to clear my head with David, too.

"Yeah, and other stuff. Life," she replies. "It just helps center me, calm me. Figure shit out."

I sniff in response, understanding this completely.

"Forty-two," she says.

"Huh?"

She dunks her head below the surface, then swiftly pops up and smooths back her long blonde hair, made caramel by the water. "Forty-two," she sprays out, treading. "Seconds I can hold my breath. Not a record, but best this season." She holds her nose. "Ready? One—"

I wipe my eyes as she calls out "Two," I hold my nose, and on "Three!" we simultaneously submerge ourselves in the dark-green water, and the countdown is on.

14

Juliette

"No, it says half a cap, once a week." Gracie reads out the instructions on the back of the bottle of fertilizer.

"What does that even mean?" I swipe a muddy hand across my forehead. "They don't mean pour half a cap onto each plant. We'd be here all day!"

Gracie tries to wipe away some of the mud she says I've smeared on my face, but it's such dark soil it doesn't come off. "Half a cap per gallon," she clarifies.

"We're going to need a hell of a lot more than a gallon of water to take care of all these vegetables!" I take another muddy swipe across my face.

"Easy calculation." She grabs the watering can and fills it from the hose. She explains how we'll go about this.

"We'll still be here all day." I huff and puff some, then read the back of the fertilizer bottle for myself.

"Patience, Jules," she says with a smile. "Gardening and impatience do not go hand in hand."

The fertilizing does take some time, but we manage to move things along more efficiently when Gracie hauls out two buckets and an extra watering can from the garage. Before we know it, the entire garden is properly fed, the roses and cacti even getting the special blends of fertilizer they need.

"Job well done!" I say with pride as we survey the garden. "Ready to call it a day?'

"Mimi's notes"—Gracie consults the legal pad—"say we have to be sure to heavily fertilize the orange tree in the summer. Good thing we've checked this." She waves the pad about.

"Yup."

"And the Santa Anas hopefully won't come in too hard this year."

The gusty, hot winds can be particularly hazardous to citrus, but Mimi's citrus trees have done well over the years. They're positioned so they can get reflected heat from the house's walls, and because of the way the walls are situated, the trees are relatively well protected from hearty winds that might sweep through the garden.

"And she says we won't have to do the cacti again until the spring!" Gracie looks at me in a surprised and pleased way.

I feel a small flash of pain at the thought of next spring. Next spring our challenge will be over. What then?

I glance at Gracie. She looks as if she's having the same sudden thought as I.

"Spring," she breathes out.

"Time flies." I once read that the days are long but the years are short. As we make progress with the challenge Mimi proposed, I am reminded of this message with every letter and season. We have all this time to rediscover a sisterhood, to even discover a piece of ourselves, perhaps, yet it feels as if we have only scratched the surface.

Gracie loops an arm around my shoulders and rests her head against mine. "Time does fly," she says with a sigh. "But I think we're making the most of it."

"Yeah . . ."

She points to the orange tree, the one thing in the garden that hasn't wavered under the desultory caretaking of the Bennett sisters, and says, "Mimi would be impressed."

"The one thing we haven't killed," I say with a dry laugh.

"Hey! We got some tomatoes this year."

"Enough for a batch of pico and salsa."

"Which was to die for, Jules. Seriously awesome." She gives me a nod of approval. As she removes her arm from around my shoulder, she suddenly leaps back and erupts into shrieks and screams.

"What?" I cry in alarm.

"Omigod! Omigod!" She's launched into a crazy, arms-flailing, legs-skipping kind of dance. She nearly falls into one of the healthier tomato plants. I scramble to reach her, pulling her forward and trying to figure out the source of her fear.

"What is it?" I pan wildly, investigating her arms and back as she squirms about. She's spinning like a dog chasing its tail.

"A bug, a bug. A huge bug!"

Then I spot it: a large praying mantis is clinging for dear life to the back of her shoulder. "Calm down," I soothe, trying to still my sister. It's hard to keep from laughing. "She won't harm a hair on you. Just chill."

"What *is* it?"

Gently I urge the praying mantis onto a spade. "Hardly a black widow." I show her the source of her anxiety.

"Oh jeez." Gracie wipes at her forehead, painting it with mud, surely now a job to match my warrior paint.

I can't contain myself. Gracie's eyes are so round, her nostrils flaring, certainly her heart beating from her rambunctious break dancing routine. I move the spade closer, making a *wooo-wooo* sound. I make a slight yet sudden jumping motion toward her and she relents. She throws up her hands and runs deeper into the garden, screaming. She leaves me in uproarious laughter as I safely guide the startled insect back into the garden.

"You're so mean, Juliette. That's not funny!" Despite her wails and protests, she's laughing, telling me I'm going to wake up with a mustache painted on.

———

I trace a finger across the soft leather binding of my journal, made supple from the countless times I've stuffed it into a tightly filled bag and lugged it from one contemplative place to the next. I'm rarely without it. Yet despite how often I carry it, open it, and rifle through its inked pages, many fresh cream pieces of parchment remain.

Sometimes I'll start a line or two of poetry or begin a sketch, then drift into memory or contemplation, abandoning my work. My journal sort of provides the impetus, and from there I can search for clarity, come closer to answers, to peace.

Often I complete a poem or a sketch. Today, however, I do not. It is one of those days when everything around me seems dull, my mood glum, and nothing can pique my interest. Maybe it's the ending of the summer season, maybe it's the nearing of opening another letter of Mimi's, maybe it's just the uncertainty of life right now. Maybe, even, it's the feeling of being held back, of being trapped, of not knowing where to turn or what to do. The lack of response to my fliers is partly to blame, and I am also certain that the realization that Gracie is wrong is what is taking a toll on me.

Gracie said the other day that we are making the most of our time. We still have plenty of arguments and disagreements, sometimes even tossing out a flippant, "I wish we'd never become roommates!" in the heat of the moment. But we are making progress. There are plenty more enjoyable days than difficult ones.

The question of whether *I* am making the most of my time is what gnaws at me. Moving to Santa Barbara was to be a new adventure, and while I'm feeling more at home here, rekindling my relationship with Gracie and learning to live in a world without Mimi, my past still holds me down. I feel as if I've lapsed into inertia.

I glance down at the page, at the poem I've begun in my search for peace as I struggle with the hauntings of my past. *Equilibrium* is written at the top, two sharp lines scratched beneath. Below it I've written:

> Moving forward, falling back.
> Waves. Like waves.
> Pull of one force, push of another.
> Sand. Like sands of time.
> Falling

The words come to an abrupt halt. It is the second incomplete project I've given up on today; the first is a neglected brooch I chose to abandon for some time at the beach.

As soon as I finish reading the scant words I have managed to write, I return to where my train of thought was just a minute ago. I slip the pencil between the pages, close my journal and my eyes, and fall back onto the sand and into memories of life back in New York City.

My roommates, Cassie, Sam, and Alexandra, and I had made a cramped apartment intended for one, maybe two, into a home for four. Even in Brooklyn, though, and even with four NYU bachelor's degrees among us, it was the best we could do. With rents notoriously high and the job market not exactly booming, life wasn't quite what I'd thought it would be nearly one year out of college.

It was, however, more than I would have gotten had I run back home. I loved home, loved my family. It wasn't as if I had been running away from anything awful by going to school so far away. I'd just wanted something different, to get away, to flex my independence.

Generations of my family had lived in Santa Barbara, and I'd thought it would be best if I went as far away as possible for school. Started a new chapter in life, something different, discovered myself.

Returning home once college ended would have seemed, even though I'd given New York four years, like giving up. I wanted to try to make it for myself straight out of school, not turning to the safety of my parents' home until I could get on my feet or enroll in a graduate program, seeking shelter from the real world for two, three more years. (Plus I couldn't afford grad school. My grades weren't good enough for a grant, and I saw no reason to go into debt with loans for an advanced degree I didn't even want.)

Had I been able to secure myself a job *before* commencement, things might have looked different at that point. Maybe I wouldn't have wound up, fresh out of school, a bridge-and-tunnel girl in a roach-infested apartment I could hardly pay for. I did have a couple of tutoring gigs for junior high and high school students that I carried with me from my time at school, however; though they weren't ideal jobs, they covered the bills.

Truth be told, I had no idea what the hell I wanted to do out of college. Because I had never really thought past senior year. And "something creative" wasn't exactly direction enough. I think I figured something would kind of fall from the sky, right into my lap. That I'd have a bachelor's, and from NYU, and that would be my Charlie's-got-a-golden-ticket deal. So it wasn't a degree from one of the "Big Three," and so my GPA might not have been high enough to get me a fancy Latin title at commencement, but I finished school, at a reputable one at that, and I finished well in my area of study, with nothing less than a B in all English and art history courses. Surely I could have found some kind of decent job out of college, right?

I suppose, however, that even if I'd had a shinier GPA from an elite institution, I would have still found myself crammed in a shabby Brooklyn apartment with three roomies, barely scraping by doing a job appropriate for a high schooler looking for part-time work rather than an NYU grad—all because of that last term at school. All because I chose to say yes to a hit I shouldn't have, because I agreed to pass along a bag of drugs I had no business carrying. Because I had done it many times before, without consequence, and because I foolishly figured I could do it again, one more time.

The back of my throat burns when my thoughts move to the last-minute trip I took out here to Santa Barbara to visit Mimi when I first learned of her cancer. It wasn't the last visit we would have together; I would, thankfully, see her again one more time before she slipped into her coma and passed.

But when I think of that last-minute trip, what stands out in my mind is that I was faced, for the first time, with the potential last chance to see her alive. And I held a secret that would crush her. She often told me then that even though she wished I were as brief a drive away from her as Gracie, she was happy I was chasing my dreams in New York. Said she knew I'd do something big and special and important. That I'd find just what I was looking for.

The obstacles I'd put in front of myself, though, said otherwise. "Am I making the most of my time?" I now repeat the question aloud. Then I think, *Would Mimi be proud?* Both questions have the same obvious answer. How I can overcome the difficulties I've gotten myself into, I am not sure. In fact, I am no surer of what I'm looking for now than before. I know, as Gracie reminded me, that I can make more of my time. I just need some help. I need some courage, some direction. I need my Mimi.

I feel an overwhelming sense of loneliness and guilt wash over me, so I decide to pack up my things and take a drive. No amount of poetry or isolated contemplation is going to help. At times like this, a girl needs her Mimi.

———

"I know I can't feel sorry for myself," I say to Mimi as I sit next to her headstone. "I did this to myself; plus I've never been one to fall into the self-pity trap."

I hug one leg to my chest, my chin resting atop my knee. Though still touched by guilt and frustration, I can feel their grittiness slowly slink off as I visit with Mimi. "I know I'm making excuses sometimes. It's easier." I crinkle my nose at the admission I'm embarrassed to have made.

"I saw an ad in the window of an art supply store. Still haven't had any bites for tutoring yet, but school's just started up and I'm sure kids will be coming home with those first grades soon." I chuckle softly as a childhood memory visits me. "I remember coming home with that first C in math," I say to Mimi. "It was the first-quarter report card in third or fourth grade. Remember the deal Mom and Dad made with me?" I run my fingers along the young grass that covers Mimi's resting place. "If I brought my grade up a whole letter I could go to Disneyland with you, Gracie, and Grandpa? That was a good time. Remember the teacups? Grandpa *hated* those things, but we loved them."

A faint smile—a smile you can't fight when recalling happy childhood memories—glosses my lips. I close my eyes. I can feel myself on the dizzying ride, and I can feel my hands brushing against Gracie's and Mimi's as we give it our all turning the center disk, sending ourselves into a tighter, quicker spin.

"I remember your necklace flying, Mimi. Isn't that funny? The things we remember?" All loneliness just melts away now; it spins off into the wind, dances about like Mimi's pearls.

I take one of the oranges out of my bag—a store-bought one, as the season for Mimi's orange tree has passed, but still tasty, still symbolic. I begin to peel it. I peel it just the way Mimi taught me.

"Start near the navel," she said. Then a small and careful thumb mark. Follow a ring, round and round you go. Lifting and moving gently. "And someday," she said, "when you practice enough, you'll be able to peel it in one clean peel." She'd demonstrated with patient and impressive precision. Over time I came to master the art of peeling an orange.

"Maybe I should apply," I say before putting the first ripe piece of citrus into my mouth, "at the art supply store. It probably doesn't pay much, but it'd be more normal than what I'm doing now. It's somewhere creative. Following a path I'm interested in . . ." I raise my voice at the tail, as if I'm seeking Mimi's approval.

I eat another piece of fruit and say between munches, "I just don't want to fill out another dumb application just to be reminded of my past. I don't want to face the facts. That's chicken, I know. But at Bluejay's, some little no-name coffee shop, they had the question on there. 'Ever been convicted of a felony?'"

I roll my eyes and pop another piece of fruit into my mouth. "I didn't go by for my usual coffee and croissant for a week; I was too embarrassed to lie about why I didn't end up applying, isn't that ridiculous?" I'd told Pete that the lawn work was keeping me busy, a partial truth.

"I'm just *so* tired of running, Mimi, of being faced with mistakes from the past. I always believed that wrongs could be righted, that second chances are real, that life's too short to spend it on regrets." I twist my lips to the side and watch as two birds fly freely overhead, chirping as they sail. "Trouble is, I don't know what to do. Where to begin." I look back to the headstone. "What should I do, Mimi?"

A lengthy silence falls and another gusty breeze kicks up, a cluster of fallen amber leaves chasing one another across the finely cut lawn.

Finally I say, "Gracie's a lawyer—" I stop and correct myself. "Correction, a *paralegal*. She's snippety about that. Anyway." I take another bite of orange. "I'm sure I could talk to her about my options. What she thinks, legally. I mean, there's probably no real way out or anything—a crime's a crime, a record's a record. And even if I told her, she'd probably just jump to conclusions and judge and then we'd ruin the good thing we've got going on together. Which, by the way, isn't that bad." I finish the orange, licking my lips and fingers in satisfaction.

"Maybe I should talk to Gracie?" The idea not only flits about my brain, but it's screaming loudly. It is as if Mimi has whispered the words straight to me. Perhaps she has. "Not just for legal advice," I say, "but for support. Someone to talk to. Of course I enjoy these conversations with you."

I finger Mimi's name—MIRIAM—on the headstone, brush my fingertips across the dates at the bottom.

"Gracie would probably judge, though. You know she tends to do that? And she doesn't even have to come out and say anything. Her face will say it all."

I immediately think of the look Gracie gave me when I told her I was going out of town with some friends for the Fourth of July. After she'd disdainfully spit out, "Let me guess, probably a party held by *some guy* you randomly met on the beach!" she gave me that look.

For the record, it was not a party held by *some guy* I randomly met on the beach. It was a party hosted by a girl named Brea, whom I happened to meet while waiting in the line of a club's bathroom during a rather lousy date. But Gracie was so quick to judge she never bothered to ask.

The look Gracie gave me then was the same look she gave me when I told her in junior high that I padded my bra to get boys' attention, or when I told her that I was faking a stomachache to stay home sick because I failed a math test I didn't want to have to show Mom and have her sign. It's the same look she gave me when she, on Mom's heels, came into my room and watched on as Mom told me the jig was up and I had some explaining to do, some extra credit in math to request. Gracie said afterward that she told Mom only because she knew there was no other way out for me—it was in my best interest to get it over with and quickly. She may have been right, but the betrayal annoyed me. The judgment and the superiority she certainly felt, looking so smug when she came in to do the right thing, felt more like an act of betrayal than the actual betrayal of running to Mom.

I have an incredible knack for getting myself into trouble, and while Gracie will have my back sometimes (she always came up with some excuse for why I was home late from a date or school; I am still grateful), she is always the first to rush to judgment, to tell me she told me so, or to say that if I would have just come to her I wouldn't have wound up in such a pickle.

Most of the time she is right, and much of the time I have run to her side for help, but sometimes a girl's got to try to grow up a little on her own. There is no doubt in my mind that if I come to Gracie with what happened last year, the judgment of all judgments will rain down hard.

"I don't know," I mutter to Mimi. "I could talk to her and just suffer through whatever judgments she'll make." I roll my eyes. "I don't know how I can open up about this one."

In an effort to distract myself from falling into more self-pity, I remove the other orange from my bag. "I brought you a super-ripe one today, Mimi." I set the orange on top of her headstone. "Trader Joe's finest."

Sometimes the previous orange I've left for Mimi will still be here, often still ripe and ready to eat. Sometimes it'll be shriveling under the sun. Sometimes it's just gone. Maybe the groundskeeper removes them, thinking it unlikely that a griever would be leaving fruit to rot as a memorial, or perhaps a bird or some other animal steals off with them. I know it's silly, but I like to think that when an orange has disappeared, it's because Mimi has taken it.

I stand, slip my bag across my chest, and decide that the best solution to inertia is doing something—taking that first step, making that first push, making a decision—whether or not you are prepared for what will happen when you do.

"Gracie opened up about David, you know?" I say, both hands gripping my bag's strap. "She spilled all the details about him and . . . Mimi, I'd never seen Gracie open up like that. She was so vulnerable. So honest. Maybe it's time I do the same?"

I pause, as if to let Mimi answer. In a way, she does. I can picture her standing right here with me, and she's telling me that the choice is mine. No one else can make it for me. I can choose to confide in my sister now or later . . . or never. But if I choose to keep to myself what is bottled up inside, I cannot continue down this disparaging and embittered path. I cannot expect to move forward without assuming the risk of falling back.

"I've decided. I *am* going to talk to Gracie," I say at last. "I don't know when," I quickly add, "but maybe she can help? Maybe it'll just feel good to talk to my sister."

I readjust my heavy bag and tell Mimi that I'll keep her posted on what happens.

Before I descend from atop the slightly sloping hill, at a position where I am still able to see the tip of Mimi's headstone, I turn around. If my eyes aren't playing tricks on me, I'd say the orange has disappeared.

I squint, cup a hand over my eyes. I am still unable to clearly see an orange. I smile and turn back to my car.

15

Gracie

From the china cabinet, I pull out the envelope with AUTUMN written across it and set it in the middle of the dining table—a reminder of next week's visit. I know we will not need reminding, but just the same I set it out. It sits there like a good friend who has something new to share.

"Sure," I say to my mother over the phone. She's been running on and on about a new salad recipe she found online. "I'm sure it'll taste delicious."

"It has crab."

"Crab's tasty. What's wrong, you don't like crab?"

"I don't think your sister likes crab."

I pause for a second, not sure if Juliette likes crab or not. "Well, she loves sushi," I say.

"Will you ask her for me? I don't want to make a big old salad filled with crab if no one but you and your father will eat it."

I pick up the black high heels I kicked off the moment I got home from work and return them to their space in my closet. "What about you?" I ask.

"Oh, I won't eat this salad. It calls for mayonnaise and cilantro, and I hate mayonnaise and cilantro."

I laugh and assure her that at least I'll eat it.

"So then you're coming for dinner?"

"Yup." I take a seat behind the desk in the den and look at the calendar on the wall, unable to miss *BBQ* scrawled in red marker.

"And your sister? She's coming?"

"I think so." I lean back in my chair and swivel around.

"It's on a Sunday." She sighs. "I should hope she can make it. What could she be doing on a Sunday? Is she doing all right?"

"She's coming, Mom," I rush out. Juliette said she'd come. Though just because she agreed to the plans doesn't necessarily mean she'll remember them. But I try to dismiss the chance Juliette may not make it, because Mom does tend to fret over my little sister. Often for good reason. A family barbecue, however, is not one of them.

"She's all right, isn't she?" Mom pries.

"Mom." I half laugh, half groan. "We've already talked about this. Everything's fine. And we'll be at the dinner."

There's a loud pounding on the window from behind, and I yelp, nearly falling backward in my seat.

"Gracie!" Juliette yells from outside. She pounds some more.

"Hey, Mom, I've got to run." I hang up the phone and turn toward Juliette, clutching my heart and giving her an expression that says, "What is the matter?"

"You want to go to a festival?" she shouts, her face practically pressed against the glass.

"What?"

"A! Festival!" she screams louder.

"I hear you," I shout back.

She tosses a hand at me and disappears, materializing in the den a few seconds later.

"There's some solstice festival in town," she says excitedly. "I got off the phone with Brea and she and some of the girls are going to go tonight." Her cell phone is in one hand, a wooden bucket filled with lemons, limes, and the last of the year's tomatoes in the other. "It's like a fair. Want to come?"

I shrug. I'm not one for fairs; the last time I went to one was with David. It was during one of our "just friends" periods, and I was head over heels in love with him. I spent the night pining like a lovesick schoolgirl as we rode ride after ride, while he talked about how law school was turning out to be all he'd dreamed and how the connections he could make with professors and well-connected students were beyond anything he'd imagined. Suffice it to say it was not the finest fair excursion.

"Come on!" Juliette urges. "It'll be good for you to get out. The weather's gorgeous." She holds up her bucket. "I've spent practically all day outside. And I'm sure you haven't so much as stepped a foot outside your office all day?" She gives me a sideways glance. "You could use it. We both could."

"I could," I say, noting that it had been another busy day at the firm, with a pitiful twenty-minute lunch break. "All right," I succumb. "I'm not a third wheel on one of your dates, am I?"

Juliette laughs away my comment and tells me to change out of my pantsuit and into something more comfortable. "Just Brea and some of the other girls," she says. "It'll be fun. We're meeting them in a half hour. Hurry, hurry."

———

Much to my delight, the festival is a lot of fun. There are the usual fair-like elements: large rides like the Ferris wheel, a carousel, bumper cars, and a plethora of kiddie rides, and the requisite fair booths with silly target games, their tented ceilings lined with cheap neon-colored stuffed animal prizes. There are some arts-and-crafts booths, with things for sale as attractive as amateur oil paintings and as kitsch as ceramic animal figurines.

Some musicians, their instrument cases opened and littered with shiny tips, are among the expected magic and balloon-animal acts. There are some people handing out pamphlets about preserving sea life, and there's a booth with people in yellow smiley shirts who are part of the free-hugs craze. As Brea just said, "This fair's a nice blend of carny-meets-craftie-culture eclecticism." Among the usual fried fair foods to buy there's a booth handing out complimentary vegan snacks and an organic wine-tasting bar, where the girls and I have decided to linger.

Though I have met with these girls only a few times for dinner or drinks with Juliette, and I don't know anyone that well, I like Brea most. She's not the typical friend I've known Juliette to make. She's obviously a free spirit and jovially opinionated—she didn't hesitate to engage in the free hugs that were offered, she enthusiastically took one of the sea life pamphlets and inquired about donations, and at least three times tonight she's told Hazel, the one with the long dreadlocks and heavy, glamorous cat-eye makeup, that her dreads are looking ratty. She also seems grounded and goal oriented. Not to say the others aren't, but she is the only one seeking a college education and knows what she wants to do with her future: she's a premed junior at UCSB with a steady boyfriend of three years, also premed. (The other girls, as I've gathered, either don't believe in the "stifling monster of education intended for the elite" or have dropped out.)

Brea's nice, and she and all the girls, particularly Juliette, make me feel welcome in the group, as if I've been hanging out with them all summer. I'm glad Juliette encouraged me to get out tonight, even though this is not my crowd or my scene, never mind its being a school night.

Hazel and Corinne, both waitresses at a restaurant where Brea hosted over the summer, pass around tiny sample cups of a Sonoma Pinot Grigio.

"What's this one?" Juliette asks, examining the cup.

"A white," Corinne says, deadpan. She motions to Vanessa, who is either Hazel's or Corinne's ex-roommate from a cut-short freshman year at college. Vanessa, like Corinne, prefers to inject sarcasm into every other sentence. She takes a sample cup and adds, "An *organic* white."

Juliette rolls her eyes and takes a sip.

"So you think Bailey will hook up with that coworker?" Corinne asks Hazel.

Juliette leans next to me and informs me that Bailey is another "one of the girls" who couldn't make it tonight because she had to pull the evening shift at the country club where she works. Bailey has a knack for hooking up with coworkers, evidently, and the bets are on about the new club lifeguard.

"She always does," Vanessa says.

Brea nods her head. "Jake," she says, referencing her boyfriend, "says he's a nice guy, the new lifeguard. Knows him from high school." She reaches out for another sample cup, asking if I'd like another one.

"Sure," I say. "Maybe a merlot or a Syrah?"

"That'd be red," Corinne says to Brea with a snicker. Brea tells Corinne she's going to end up with a red stain all over her white skirt if she doesn't quit teasing.

The girls continue with their gossip and teasing, and I interject a good-natured laugh here and there, ask for clarification at times when I'm not sure whom they're talking about or what event they're referencing. As the conversation moves past the latest Thursday-night television lineup and toward the next national election, Juliette pokes me in the ribs and asks if I want to go on a few rides.

I look off into the distance at some kind of roller coaster. The *rickety-rickety-whoosh* sounds the tracks make as the carts ride along it give me pause.

"Nothing too scary," Juliette says, reading my mind or expression, as I'm not being so subtle about the tension I feel as I watch cartloads of people rushing by on the coaster, screaming. "No roller coasters," she adds.

"Sure." I finish my wine sample, and Juliette asks who's up for rides.

Juliette, Brea, and I team up for the Ferris wheel while Vanessa, Hazel, and Corinne opt for one of those pendulum rides, the kind of ride that would surely induce vomiting, especially after the chili cheese hot dog and cotton candy I ate earlier.

It's a fun night, even though the second time around, the Ferris wheel makes me wish I hadn't eaten the entire bag of kettle popcorn I grabbed between the jaunt on the bumper cars and the go at the dartboard. Juliette does a brilliant job of keeping me up to date on what's going on in conversations that lose me. It's a side of her I've never seen. I always had my friends, and she had hers. The circles never overlapped. But tonight it feels good to be included. I can't help but swell with a bit of pride as I see that among a group of women Juliette calls her friends I am one, and the one she seems to most enjoy spending her time with.

Eventually everyone but Brea makes her way home. The three of us give it a go at a smack-the-mole game, and Brea wins a teddy bear. I end up three moles away from winning a prize.

Juliette wins, too, in her own way. I don't think she smacked a single mole, but the sandy-blond guy with a UCSB hoodie playing next to her is amused nevertheless. He tells her in the most flirtatious way that her game isn't the mole one so it *must* be one of those shoot-the-water-pistol games. She takes him up on his flirtatious gesture, they play a few rounds (she does horribly), he wins a betta fish, and then he gives it to her—gives her the fish!—along with his number.

I stand by, gobsmacked, and Brea just laughs and says, "Only Juliette could get a number *and* a pet from a guy she's just met."

Juliette makes her way back to us, all smiles. "So, who wants some more cotton candy?"

"I'm calling it a night," Brea says with a yawn, her prize teddy bear tucked under her arm. "My first class isn't until two tomorrow, but I've got a research paper that needs serious attention."

I tell her good luck, and Juliette thanks her for coming up with the idea tonight.

"Totally," Brea says. She gives Juliette a hug. Then she looks to me and gives me a friendly hug. "I'm glad you could come out with us, Gracie. I hope we weren't too much of a bore."

"Oh, no. Thanks for the invite," I say. "My opinion of fairs—or festivals—has totally changed now. It was fun."

Juliette laughs and says, "The last time I was at a place like this was at a carnival in Jersey I hitchhiked to one weekend. Worst but *funnest* decision ever."

"You're a crazy girl," Brea says to Juliette. "Hey, I'll talk to you later!"

"Definitely. Hey, wait!" Juliette holds up her plastic bag containing the purple betta. "You want a fish?"

Brea laughs. "That one's all yours."

"So now you've got a *pet*?" I say to Juliette once Brea leaves. The two of us lazily walk among the thinning crowds.

"And a number." She holds up and twists her arm so I can see the inside of her wrist.

"You going to call him?"

She shrugs. "Probably not. I mean, I got a pet fish out of him, so I'd say I've already scored."

I laugh. "We're really keeping that thing?"

"Why not?"

We turn toward a less populated area of the festival, nearing the carousel.

"This was nice," I say after a long beat of silence.

"It was." Juliette looks over at me, then back at the fish. "I miss this, Gracie."

"This?"

"Hanging out like this, like when we were kids. It's fun." She swings her arm some, the poor fish on his own festival ride.

"It is," I wholeheartedly agree.

As Juliette strides toward the carousel, smiling and swinging her arm with greater weight, I can't help but reach for the fish.

"Hey, you want to ride the carousel?" She doesn't seem fazed by my taking control of the new pet.

"Another ride?"

She looks back at the slowly spinning horses. There can't be more than three children on the ride. "Yeah! Why the hell not?"

I splutter a laugh in reply, then tell her that I'll ride so long as I get the black stallion, the horse I always clamored for at Disneyland due to my love of *Black Beauty*.

"Totally! So long as I get the white horse with the pink saddle," she says before bounding to find her own childhood favorite.

———

"Can you believe it's that time again?" I ask Juliette one evening as she follows me into the bathroom to get ready for bed. We fell asleep on the sofa together watching television, and now it's well past one o'clock. I am grateful I arranged to take the morning off work tomorrow. "We should try to get to Meadows Memorial before ten," I add.

"Why? Don't you have work?" She rubs at her eyes.

"I told you I'm taking the morning off." I dress my toothbrush with paste.

"Oh. Right," she says through a yawn.

"Plus, there's going to be a funeral held at ten and we don't want to be there."

It happened last time, when Juliette and I went to Mimi's grave to read aloud her summer letter. We arrived at the tail end of a funeral not five yards away. Most of the bereaved had filtered out, but there were still some who stayed behind, which made the whole reading-our-letter-aloud thing awkward.

"Got it," she says, her toothbrush already in her mouth. "You're right. I can't believe it's time again." She tilts her head back to keep from losing her paste, mouth foaming.

"I know." I pause for a second before putting my brush in my mouth. I stare at the melty white paste, raising one corner of my mouth in a disbelieving smirk. "It's hard to believe."

As I bring my brush to my lips, Juliette says, "It's hard to believe we've been sharing this bathroom!" The foam now drips down both sides of her lips. I laugh so powerfully at the sight of her that I spew toothpaste all over the mirror.

"Great," I say. I pull the brush from my mouth and point at the mess I've made. I spit the remainder of my paste into the sink. "I'm the one with bathroom-cleaning duty this week, too." I wink in jest, and Juliette nudges me with her hip, clad in nothing but a pair of men's tighty-whities, her usual nighttime attire.

"You'll learn to brush your teeth just like a big girl someday, Gracie." Juliette puckers up her white-foamed lips and smacks out a kiss.

And that is the way Juliette and I close out the season of summer at 1402 Laguna Lane.

The following morning, we each pick a ripe lemon from the tree, a suitable in-season replacement for the sleeping orange tree, and grab Mimi's letter entitled AUTUMN. We ride our bikes through the unexpected drizzle all the way to visit our grandmother.

And that is the way we welcome the season of autumn.

Autumn

16

Mimi

Dear Gracie and Juliette,

Autumn! My favorite season may have just passed, but there is no question that the winds of autumn bring with them a beautiful and refreshing newness—a chance for nature, the garden, even ourselves to experience the change necessary for growth.

Albert Camus put it brilliantly: "Autumn is a second spring when every leaf is a flower." Autumn, with the falling of the leaves and the approaching hibernation of the garden, is a visible mark that time passes, and that as it does, there is a chance to grow, to become more vibrant, a chance for revitalization as we begin to move from one year to the next.

This season I challenge you dear girls to continue to lean on each other for support, to grow close, to stand strong despite any hurdles that may seem impossible to overcome. Continue to move from one season, one year, to the next, growing together and learning something from each other every step of the way. You have crossed the halfway mark, and I am so very proud of you. Don't give up.

Gracie, your loyalty will be your greatest attribute as you push ahead. You are a dedicated woman. You are eager to teach, to help, to please. You love with all your heart. All wonderful qualities. You've always made sure everything's just the way it ought to be, and you're not afraid to work hard to achieve that. As a little girl you were eager to get things just right. Careful attention in the garden and top grades in school. Never had to be told twice to do your home-work. As a young woman you had your sights on a clear career path. You've pleased your parents and your Mimi by staying close to home, and you've made a fine home and life for yourself through your hard work and ambition. I couldn't be more proud of you.

No doubt the past few months have been trying for you. Change isn't among your favorite things, espe-cially change beyond your influence or control. Learning the balance of being a good older sister and a sister—a friend—is bound to be difficult. I know my Gracie Dawn. You will try to fix things. You will try to keep order. You will try to instruct and shape things the way you see fit. Your determination to do this is a great quality of yours, but it is your loyalty that you will have to fall back on when your determination makes you too thickheaded.

Juliette, you have a tender soul and a zest for life that I simply adore. You are not your sister's stark oppo-site, but you two are different. You're eager to learn, and in your own way, at your own pace. The emotional response is more natural to you than the logical. It's one of the things I enjoy most when we spend time together. When you were young, couldn't have been more than four, you drew a family portrait. You made all our heads—yours, Gracie's, your parents, your grandpa's, and mine—in the shape of hearts. "Because I love you," is why, you said. "Because families love."

Your passion is the source of so much of your joy, Juliette. It is also the source of so much of the trouble you find yourself in. You haven't been an easy child for your parents to raise. I am sure your living with Gracie is a challenge to the both of you. You are a sensitive soul, and instead of being guided by logic, you will listen to your sensibilities. When something needs to be fixed, you will have to hold tight to your tenderness, a quality that will never go out of style and one that will carry you when your passion leads you astray. Remember this.

Gracie, stand strong and stay loyal to your sister. She is the only sister you will ever have. When she turns up the music too loudly, or forgets to close the refrigerator door, or decides to disappear for a weekend getaway without so much as saying good-bye, remember that there is no one who could take her place. There is no one in the world who loves you as Juliette does. Remember that everything wild and impulsive she does, she does because she is passionate. It is with this very same passion that she loves her big sister, looks up to her, needs her.

Juliette, remember that Gracie loves you and wants the best for you. Let your delicate sensitivities shine through when she's trying to help, to instruct. There is no ulterior motive behind her actions. She may need to relax some, learn to turn up the music, maybe even take an evening swim now and then. (She is still deserving, however, of an explanation when you suddenly leave town, young lady.) But you have to respect her impulse to help you stand when you fall. You must remember that when you think you two can't be any more different and might not be able to make it through this challenge, your unconditional love for each other is the glue that holds you together. Two people can love each other and show their love in different ways. Embrace that. Celebrate that!

Above all, don't sweat the small stuff. Life is simply too short. And when it comes to bigger elephants in the room, for your dear Mimi, please do not tear each other down. Work together. Because you are both Bennett women—strong women—you can accomplish anything. Strong on your own yet stronger together. Learn from each other when you're lost. Help each other stand when you're down. Be what each is missing in her life.

I imagine, despite the hiccups now and then, things are going well. You're finding your rhythm, have grown rather accustomed to things on Laguna Lane. With half a year behind you as roommates, I am sure you have learned so many new things about each other, started including each other in weekend plans, and I bet you're even enjoying it so much you can't really imagine why you ever stopped being so close. You are very different women, but you are as compatible as cinnamon and sugar.

Whenever in doubt, look to the fallen leaves of this season as flowers and remember that we are here on borrowed time, that it is never too late to grow.

Until winter,

All my love,

Mimi

17

Juliette

The temperature is a comfortable midsixties, pushing seventy. It seems to be rising as the day progresses. As if summer has returned. The steady breeze in the afternoon is now kicking up to gustier levels, the palms lining the street swaying to and fro high above. It's still temperate enough, though, to enjoy a walk around the neighborhood, a book under the shade of a tree.

I went for a morning bike ride, enjoyed a late-afternoon coffee at Bluejay's, and Pete from Bluejay's was kind enough to help unjam the ancient car tape deck, so now I've got some sweet Simon and Garfunkel—Mimi's favorite—streaming through the tinny speakers. There's a bounce to my step today—an unexpected bounce that is quite welcome after a rough couple of weeks.

I still haven't heard back from anyone regarding tutoring, and it's frustrating. I've stopped bringing bouquets to Meadows Memorial because the flowers at this time of year aren't all that varied or abundant, so that's a few fewer bucks a week. The lawn duties are still going well, but that's not exactly exciting. My Etsy shop is so-so. I've kind of lost steam, though. There have been days when I've been uncharacteristically low, no doubt due to the realization that half a year has already passed by, in a flash. Where has the time gone?

I've been meaning to talk to Gracie and have been meaning to apply for the job at the art supply store, Keating's. Yet when I think I've gathered my nerve, as after a good journaling session at Bluejay's or after taking a long bike ride along the coast, I'll find some excuse to put off both those tasks. Gracie's busy with work . . . she's on the phone . . . there's something on TV I want to watch.

Sometimes my journaling or exercise will have elevated my mood so much that, once I've gathered the nerve, I realize I'm in a good mood. I no longer feel as if I need to sort out troubles. I'll rationalize with myself and Mimi (who seems to keep whispering, "You have to make a choice," as she waits for my next move), thinking that if I'm happy the last thing in the world I want to do is to bring myself back into an unnecessary low. I've gone this long without confiding in anyone, so what's a little longer?

"Hey, Mom." I answer my ringing cell phone as soon as I exit Trader Joe's, arms cradling a paper bag full of groceries. "What's up?"

"Oh, good, I was afraid I'd miss you," her high voice peals through.

"I'm about to get in the car and go home. Perfect timing. What's up?"

"Oh, just trying to figure out what desserts to make for the barbecue," she says in a distant and distracted way, as if she's consulting a list of dishes to serve. "You're coming, right?"

I've already told her twice I would come, although the reminder this close to the date is helpful. Gracie, though, wouldn't let me forget.

"Family dinner this Sunday?" I say.

"Yes. You know it'll probably be the last barbecue of the season? It's starting to get cold."

I laugh, thinking of the not-so-subtle difference between a Southern California and a mid-Atlantic autumn. "I'd hardly call upper fifties cold, Mom."

"Too cold for barbecue," she states. "So you're coming? You won't forget?"

"I would never miss out on Dad's famous burgers."

As I approach my car, I heave the bag of groceries higher on my hip and say, "Hey, Mom, I'm going to hop in the car and hit the road, so is there anything else you need to know before I go? Want us to bring something? Some wine?"

"We've got it handled," she says, still sounding distracted.

I'm about to tell her I'll talk to her later when she says, "Juliette, are you all right?" Her tone is laden with concern.

I laugh into the receiver. "Yeah. Why wouldn't I be? Are *you* all right?"

"Well, I'm just calling to make sure you're okay, that everything's good."

I stop a few feet short of the car and ask what's really going on. Is there something she doesn't want to tell me? Some bad news to deliver?

"I only love you, Juliette. I'm your mother, so I worry about you." Her tone is no longer filled with concern, rather smothered by that familiar maternal mushiness that I appreciate on holidays, in particular Christmas and birthdays, but loathe when it comes during out-of-the-blue phone calls like this.

Usually what follows is a string of highly charged worries: "Are you getting enough sleep?" "Are you doing drugs?" "Did you drink too much?" "Are you dating the *right* guys?" And, though we've graduated from this one, I had to suffer countless times through "Are you having trouble in school?" There's always the "You do know we love you very much?" (Yes, I do.)

And then the classic one she now delivers: "I'm your mother, so of course I worry about you." To this I'd like to ask, "Do you *really* give this kind of drilling to your other daughter?" I can't imagine she does, seeing as how Gracie's always seemed to be the ideal child, more in line with the expectations that our parents set for their children, never raising hell, never cause for concern.

"Mom, I'm fine." I sigh. "There's nothing to worry about."

I unlock the car door. I heave the bag of groceries into the passenger's seat, on top of two recent parking tickets. One ticket just because I double-parked once for literally *three* minutes to pick up something from the drugstore. The other one because I parked in a loading zone, again for only three or so minutes.

It was ridiculous. The first parking ticket that I received, when I first started driving the Citroën, cost only forty bucks. I paid it, and then when I acquired these, I figured it was really no harm to the city if I waited awhile to pay them. Forty bucks here and there can surely wait when it comes to a city as wealthy as Santa Barbara. My wallet, however, could benefit from the postponement.

I'm slightly tempted to mention to Mom, as I toss the two tickets to the backseat, "If you want to worry, I *have* racked up some parking tickets." Instead I let her explain why she's really calling.

"Gracie mentioned you were clearing your head a lot lately," Mom says. "So naturally I'm concerned about you. What's going on?"

"What?" I slide behind the wheel.

"Don't get upset. She loves you. She only mentioned you were clearing your head or something, on the beach. Frequently, I guess."

"Why are you and Gracie talking about me?"

"We aren't *talking* about you, Juliette."

"Uh, yes. That's what you call this."

"If it's nothing, then why are you getting so upset?"

"Because!" I'm practically shouting now.

Mom continues to blather on about her and Gracie's concerns, and I'm trying to keep my cool. I know there's a better way to handle this than by blowing my top, but I've grown tired over the years of having to hear secondhand from my mother something that I told my sister.

When I was a freshman in college, I called Gracie complaining of the famous "freshman fifteen." I was terrified I was going to bloat into a balloon, having already gained a hearty eight pounds in the first three months. Next call from Mom she asks, and I remember it brilliantly, "Halfway to the freshman fifteen isn't that bad."

I asked her how she'd known, and she bashfully said she figured it was the case. "I was a college student, too, once, you know," was her explanation. I neglected to poke and prod about the real source of Mom's information, knowing Gracie had been the little bird. But when Mom "casually" asked if I was on the birth control pill after I'd told Gracie not even two days earlier that I had met this guy I really liked in my Psych 101 class, I called her out on it. I called them both out.

I grew to accept (though I disliked) Mom's incessant maternal fretting. It comes with the territory of motherhood, evidently. But Gracie? Why? I never understood why Gracie felt the need to share some things with our mother. Just because I didn't ask her to pinkie promise or swear her to secrecy didn't mean I wanted all my laundry—dirty, clean, or wrinkled—aired to our mother.

I'd like to believe that things have been changing since Gracie and I've started living together, that perhaps we are forging a unique friendship where trust plays a crucial role. Then I go and hear that she's still running to Mom with stupid frets, niggles, and concerns, even when they're so irrelevant, like my writing poetry on the beach, for Chrissake! I just want to toss up my hands and say, "Forget about it! A real friendship, *out* of the question!"

"Gracie doesn't tell me these things to make you angry or go behind your back," Mom says tenderly. "She loves you and is concerned about you. She says you're having a rough time?"

"Mom." I bite my tongue, lower my voice.

"It's not just Mimi, is it? What's going on? Is it boys? Is it the job hunt?"

"Mom."

"Gracie can help you with the job thing. She has a talent with résumés. You know she helped with Mrs. Parsons's daughter's résu—"

"Mom!" I steel my nerves. "Everything's fine."

"We're only concerned because we love you."

"I know. There's nothing to worry about." I take a deep, shaky breath. "If I want to share something with you, I will. If I want to share something with Gracie"—I want to say, "I'll think twice," but I don't—"then I will."

———

"Gracie?" I muster all the strength I can not to explode as soon as I enter the house. I plunk the bag of groceries on the kitchen table when I notice she's not in the living room or the den. "Gracie?" I shout louder. No reply.

"Look at these geraniums, Jules. I'm amazed that they're still so vibrant," Gracie says when I find her in the garden. She points to the line of colorful flowers along the back side of the house, matching the ever-vibrant ones along the front walkway. The winds are evident from the swaying palms and blowing leaves of the tall trees in the garden. The geraniums, however, are almost smiling in the sun, barely moving.

"They're so beautiful," Gracie admires. She's got a mason jar of iced Diet Coke in one hand, her other hand on her hip. She surveys the garden barefoot, dressed in a pair of yoga capris and a worn T-shirt, and she has a peaceful, pleased look on her face.

"I mean, the tomatoes have gone to crap." She glances at me through the small slit above her sunglasses. "Yield this year would totally shame Mimi. Lemons are looking strong and healthy, though. And the—"

"What's your game, Gracie?" I shoot out. My cool was gone as soon as I hung up with Mom. It's time I put to rest what's been bugging me for years.

"My game?" She peers over her sunglasses again, this time a longer, sharper gaze. The wind suddenly catches Gracie's hair; a thick auburn sheet covers her face for a quick beat before the winds whip her hair the other way. "My game?" she repeats, nonplussed.

"Yes! I'm *depressed*, according to Mom!" I jump to the most goading of things Mom shared before I signed off the pointless phone call. "She's"—I angrily place a hand on my hip—"concerned about me because I'm writing *poetry* at the *beach* by *myself* and going for evening *swims*? What's that about?" I toss up a hand. I look at her, incredulous.

Gracie pushes her sunglasses farther up her nose, eyes now fully covered. She takes a drink of her Coke.

"Well?" I bark.

"Jules, it's not like that."

"Bullshit it's not like that. I can't trust you!"

"Oh, please. Trust? It's hardly a matter of trust. All I did was mention in *passing* to Mom that we had a fun evening swim together."

"Sounded like that's *exactly* what you said."

The winds now catch my hair, a wild mess blowing across my face and leaving it just so, as if to encourage my state of annoyance.

"I mentioned, all right, that you went to the beach by yourself a lot."

"Mentioned?" I push back my hair, but the wind has other plans, another wild dance across my face.

"Innocently mentioned!" Gracie snaps.

"Yeah, whatever." I roll my eyes, angrily tucking as much hair behind my ears as possible.

"Look, I told Mom you were really seeming to get used to living here, back in California. You're making this your home. You've got some nice friends. You're comfort—"

"Cut the crap, Gracie."

From nowhere, she raises her voice. "I *did* say that!"

"Whatever else you told her sure didn't sound as rosy." Without giving it much thought but needing to calm my nerves with a mindless task, I charge to the garage and grab the hose.

"I said you were writing poetry," she says, her tone defensive. "You were being creative. Isn't that what you want to do? Write or paint or—"

"Let's not change the subject." I shoot a strong spray of water at the base of the lemon tree.

"Don't hit the leaves." Gracie lunges forward, trying to take the hose from me.

"I've got it!" I lower the hose so as not to hit the leaves and burn them, as Mimi always seemed to have to remind me. I shout, "Subject! Don't change it, Gracie!"

"Whatever, Jules." She tosses back a careless sip of soda, pushing her dancing hair out of her face. "You're making this out to be more than it is."

"No, no I'm not. You've always done this. Always going to Mom with random information about me. It can hurt."

"What are you talking about?"

"Don't act like you don't know." I reposition my angle when I notice, in my haste, that I'm spraying the bottom layer of lemon leaves again.

"I told Mom you go to the beach, you write poetry," she says. "Big whoop!" I wag my head. "She asks why. I say, I don't know, because, as you told me, you like to figure shit out that way." Her tone is condescending.

"Oh, that won't ring alarm bells for Mom. Dammit, Gracie."

"She asked if you were depressed, I said I didn't think so, but of course I'm no doctor. You know Mom. She gets an idea and she follows it and—"

"An idea *you* put there. Thanks a lot, Gracie. More crap to deal with."

"Get off your high horse. It's not a big deal in the grand scheme of things."

She's right, but then—I release the handle on the hose, the water stops, and I toss the hose to the ground. "No." I charge to her. "No, no, no, it *is* a big deal. It's a big deal to me."

Her sunglasses are now atop her head. "How do you mean?" She squints in confusion.

"It may not seem like a big deal to you. But when you tell Mom something I've told you, even if it's not a secret or a big deal—" I pause, feeling as if I'm going to break down into tears. I don't know why. It's not as if I'm particularly sad or emotionally vulnerable over Gracie's revelation to Mom of my beachside poetry habits.

In my pause, glancing at the orange tree that stands tall behind Gracie, then looking into Gracie's eyes—she looks concerned and curious, eager to know what it is I have to say, why I am so enraged—I realize why it is difficult for me to stand here, failing to control my emotional faculties.

I motion to the patio chairs, we take a seat, and I explain to Gracie—nothing held back—exactly how I feel. It is both painful and relieving.

This lack of trust with Gracie has played a role, all these years, in why I've been able to easily fall out of close friendship with my sister. If I can't turn to her in complete trust with something as trite as my love of solitary time on the beach, with my journal, how can I tell her intimate secrets? Thoughts? Fears? The kinds of things a woman should be able to share with a best friend, a sister?

It isn't so much the fact that my mother is made privy to such information against my wishes (although letting her in on it usually does more harm than good), but rather that this sharing is proof of a lack of trust, a form of betrayal, regardless of the intentions behind the sharing. And it hurts.

A lack of trust is not the crux of why we've grown apart over the years, I reassure Gracie. There is no *one* reason, rather a number of things: time, physical and emotional distance, lack of things in common. And *yes*, a lack of trust plays a role.

It is not as if I distrust my sister. There have been plenty of times, in fact, that Gracie has kept her word. There were the late-night trips to the refrigerator sometimes as kids, when we pinkie swore it was a Bennett-sister secret. When Gracie found out my sore throat was caused by a kiss with Timmy Fowler on the playground and not the water bottle I shared with my friend Carly Prescott, she swore she'd never tell anyone. And she kept her word. It is the consistent assurance of a confidence between *just two* that is missing—total trust.

If Gracie and I are to draw closer, if we're to create a meaningful friendship, we have to be honest with each other, we have to trust each other. If we don't have that, then all our attempts at rekindling a relationship, all the positive steps forward that we are making together will have been for nothing—a surface friendship, nothing with roots.

"It—it hurts," I say to Gracie.

"Jules," she breathes. Her face falls, her brow furrows.

"It's like . . ."

"Yeah?"

"It sounds silly, but . . . with stuff like this, I feel like we don't have a friendship between two, but a kind of . . . familial relationship among three." I swallow the knot in my throat. "*Only* a familial relationship. There's no room for an honest and close and personal friendship between us."

"I'm so sorry, Juliette. I didn't know." Gracie gives a long and breathy sigh, a sigh of disappointment. "I'm not even aware," she whispers. "I never intend to hurt you, you know that?"

"I know." Relief slowly creeps forward. It feels good to confide, to confront, to share.

Gracie sighs and says, "Now that I think about it and look at it this way—" She holds up a hand. "As a three-way friendship . . . I guess I'm not doing anyone any favors."

"*Some* things, not everything, but *some* things are all right to be *just* between sisters. You know?"

"Yeah."

"Between friends," I say with a one-shouldered shrug.

"I do it to talk, Jules." She crosses her arms over her chest. "Mom and I talk a lot. She's my mother *and* a friend."

"I know."

"I'm not blaming you or pointing the finger, but when you went off to NYU it was like you just . . . ran away. You were so determined to get out, to do your own thing, to get as far away as possible. You can't begrudge me for choosing to be close to our mother. *She's* always been down the road."

"I don't begrudge you that. And I wasn't running away, Gracie. You know that." She does. I've made the point time and again that I was not running away by going to NYU but running *to* something. What exactly was I running to? I've never quite pinpointed that, but I was running toward a creative dream, toward something new and adventurous.

"Mom and I have a good relationship," Gracie says. "And I guess I don't think about some of the things I say to her. We have a friendship and, like you said, things between friends and . . ." She shakes her head quickly. "I'm sorry."

"I am, too." I rest a hand on her knee. "I know you voice your concern to her because you love me, because you're worried."

"You do seem depressed now and then, Jules." She looks at me imploringly.

I blow a puff of air upward, slap my hands to my thighs, and say, "I've been better, that's for sure." I stand. "But I've been worse."

"Do you . . . do you want to talk about it?" she asks cautiously.

A large gust of wind sweeps through the garden, knocking over a watering can and sending it rolling across the lawn. It hits the base of the orange tree, coming to a halt. The wind, however, only increases. The air feels heavy and as if the temperature has risen five degrees in five seconds.

"The Santa Anas," Gracie says, taking her glass in hand and standing.

"I don't miss everything about home." I grab a handful of my now-ratty hair and twirl it into a temporary rope.

Gracie fetches the watering can. Under the shade of the orange tree, she pulls free some loose leaves and drops them inside the can. She looks dreamily up at the tree, then back at me. "Do you?" she asks in even, confident tones.

"Do I want to talk about . . . stuff?" I look at the ends of my hair, buying myself a small amount of time to consider.

Gracie plucks a lemon from the lemon tree and polishes it on the back of her pants before making her way to the back door. She looks back at me with a small, encouraging smile. She says nothing. She doesn't have to.

I give the garden a quick survey, a rush of confidence filling me as my eyes fall to the orange tree. I let loose my rope of hair, and the wind immediately catches it. I turn to Gracie and say, "You know? I think I do."

18

Gracie

"You've gotten into trouble—gotten caught—for smoking," I say to my little sister as she sits here before me, very much assuming the role of the little sister who's impuissant, apprehensive, turning to her older sister for support and advice.

I have taken a few hits off one joint in my entire twenty-six years. I didn't find the experience all that thrilling. It was actually quite boring, and I wasn't fond of losing awareness of my surroundings and control of my actions, reasons why I never found the appeal in getting drunk, either.

Juliette's preferences, however, differ greatly. I will never forget the look on her face when she rushed to tell me that she'd just tried her first joint. She was only a freshman in high school, ever the party girl, three years ahead of my own encounter with marijuana. She was excited, fearful, and eager all at the same time. Her high had worn off only a few hours earlier, and she was already enthusiastically talking about her "next time."

She said she'd felt invigorated and fearful by doing something she knew she shouldn't be doing. She loved the risk. What if someone were to catch her? What if she were to do something to jeopardize her future college plans? All the what-ifs fueled her mad curiosity for the next time and the next after that. I never considered her a pothead, but I'd have been a fool to think she hadn't formed some kind of habit, one that at least played a significant role at parties.

I warned her time and again that she should be careful, that she shouldn't risk her future, shouldn't burn off her brain cells, act irresponsibly, participate in something illegal—my list went on. She'd brush me off, or tell me she lit up only once in a while or that marijuana wasn't even a *real* drug and so I shouldn't worry about it. Or she'd erupt and tell me I was being a prude, judgmental, a fun-sucker. Eventually I stopped asking about her party habits, and she stopped telling me.

Juliette rubs at her face with both hands and groans. "Yeah, I've gotten into trouble before, but never this serious." She takes a moment to answer my interrupting question before revealing her secret of secrets. A secret that, and I quote, "Is *not* to be shared with Mom or Dad, ever. Promise, Gracie!"

I promise. As far as I know, Juliette has been able to keep her illicit behavior largely under the radar, rather impressive considering how often it seems she gets high, but she isn't invulnerable to being outed and punished. And before, when she was, my worry for her rose considerably. I feared it'd be only a matter of time before there were serious ramifications.

I say, "Mom and Dad grounded you for like"—I try to remember—"a month?"

"Two weeks," she corrects. "Came home way too soon after smoking, red eyed and still out of it. I couldn't go to the spring dance because of it."

"'Springing into Sophomore Year,'" I say, remembering not so fondly my own dance.

I remember with even less fondness how angry and shocked my parents were with Juliette. My father was disappointed but had little time to voice his concern, since he had to calm down my panic-stricken mother, explaining that adolescence is a difficult time and different for every teenager. I remember her exclaiming, "But Gracie never did this!" (She never did learn of that one time.) All that did was cause Juliette to launch into a diatribe about how perfect I was, how hopeless she was.

"It was probably a lousy dance, by the way," I say to Juliette. "Mine was."

"Yeah, well, that wasn't the only time I got caught." She rolls her eyes. "Mom and Dad caught me doing it once in the back of Mary Kerry's car. Remember that one? My junior year?"

I was already deep in my college studies then and not always on top of Juliette's high school life, although I would hear on occasion from my mother some details of the goings-on at home. But I also went home just about every other weekend, and almost the moment I pulled up in the drive the weekend after the Mary Kerry incident, Mom rushed out to tell me the big no-no little Jules had done.

I sniff a genial, easygoing laugh. "Mary Kerry. That was really cruel of her parents."

"God, I know. Horrible name."

"But this last time?" I urge Juliette to finish her story. "This last time that you got into trouble?" I'm not sure how bad it is. With the buildup and the nagging suspense, she's making it out to be a hair more serious than I originally imagined when she said "secret" and "pinkie swear."

"Contrary to what it sounds like," she says, "I wasn't *always* high."

"Just at parties."

"Not always. And I don't do it anymore. I swear." She states this with conviction. "Not since what happened last spring."

"Okay."

"I'd be an idiot to do it after what happened. Then again, I was an idiot to *let* it happen."

"Jules." I place a hand on top of hers. "It's okay. I won't judge you."

I mean what I say. I want her to open up, to confide in me. If she will feel a fraction of the release and comfort that I felt when I told her about David, I will implore her to share.

At last she tells me, her eyes cast downward the entire time, bringing her fingers to her mouth to bite her nails. She tells me how she got in too deep with her habit. Contrary to her assertion that she wasn't *"always* high," she spent a considerable amount of time her junior year at NYU stoned. Her first two years, it was more a rare "here-and-there habit," but she eventually racked up a bill she couldn't pay.

When she says she was offered the possibility of cutting a deal with her supplier, making the handoff to a number of fellow students, my jaw locks. I try with all my might to keep from making a judgmental face, gasping, spitting out a "You *didn't?*" with incredulous eyes. Maybe things are just as bad, just as serious, as I feared.

Juliette presses on, eyes still focused downward. "I eventually came clean with what I owed," she says. "And I said I was out. I didn't want to make handoffs anymore. I cut back *significantly* on how much I smoked, didn't want to wind up running up another bill."

Her eyes dart to mine, as if asking if I believe her. I nod fervently, encouraging her to go on, reassuring her that she's my sister, why would I not believe her?

"Then it was one stupid, *stupid* night." She squeezes the bridge of her nose, eyes shut tightly. "So stupid. I was high. I needed a buzz to make my last handoff, because I was so nervous. It wasn't my usual kind of work. I owed a girl a favor for helping me with some homework. She agreed to help me with some lame, really tough math course that was a prereq. I neglected to take it until the last minute, and—" She wags her head, dismissing the information as extraneous. "Anyway, she knew I was a go-to girl for weed and said if I could get her some, she'd call it even with the study help."

"Okay."

"But she didn't just want weed. She wanted some . . . some E." She looks at me, fear evident in her eyes. "Ecstasy."

"I know." My stomach is churning as my fears snowball.

"I didn't want to do it, but then she threatened to tell the dean what I'd been doing if I didn't get her what she wanted, and . . . it was a total mess. So I got her some stuff. Only a few pills. It was practically nothing. But then . . ." She sighs. "Then I got caught. *Big*-time."

"You never exchanged any moneys, did you? I mean, I guess you exchanged services with tutoring . . ." My legal brain begins to kick into overdrive as I realize Juliette may have been in further over her head than she knew, and certainly more than I could have ever imagined.

"No. No way." Her tone is firm. "I knew *that* would be stupid. I knew that much was illegal."

"Juliette." I close my eyes for a second. "*All* this is illegal."

She gives me a pointed look. "Gracie—"

"I'm sorry," I blurt. "Sorry. Go ahead."

She clears her throat. "I had a debt to pay, and I didn't know how else to fix it. And the threats to the dean—"

"It's okay."

"I didn't exchange money. Ever."

"Good." I pause, then ask, "And New York isn't one of those states where making a"—I use her terminology—"*handoff* is viewed as the same as a deal where moneys are exchanged, is it?" I'm not an expert in drug crimes, but this grey area is vaguely familiar from my legal studies.

"Bingo!" Juliette taps her finger to her nose. "Such bullshit."

I can't help it, this time I do gasp, and rather loudly.

A cloudy unease covers Juliette's face, and she looks at me entreatingly. "I didn't get busted for dealing, let me make that clear. Calm down, sis."

"That's good." My fears are allayed slightly.

"But I had weed *and* E on me. And some coke—"

"Coke, too?" I spit out this question so sharply Juliette's eyes grow round.

"Yes." Her voice is small.

"Jeez, Jules . . ." I grip my head. The room begins to feel as if it's spinning.

"I told you it was a shitty situation."

I brace myself for whatever surprise is around the corner.

"And I was pretty high. I was with a group of friends who were also high, some high on E, some on coke, I mean . . . a real fucked-up bunch, let me put it bluntly."

I nod repeatedly, trying to process all that is being revealed.

"I'm making the handoff, and then two of the guys started to get into a fight and there we were, on the corner of a street, total club scene, I mean, how stupid was I to do this on a *Saturday night*, near a *club*?"

I want to tell her all this story is stupid, but I refrain. I'm so angry with my sister for having gotten herself into this level of trouble. I always warned her!

I tighten my hands into fists, try to remain calm and listen on, judgments and criticisms and cries of worry screaming in the back of my mind. It is taking every ounce of strength I can muster not to erupt.

"Cops bust the fight," she raps off, "drugs are everywhere, we're fuckin' high, I'm caught with my hand all the way in the cookie jar, the weed and the E still in my pocket. Thank *God* the coke I had on me I'd already handed off."

"*Two* deals?"

"Not really. The coke was for a friend. It was a favor." She shakes her head. "Another stupid move. God, I deserve the punishment."

"Did you . . . spend time in jail?" I can't believe I'm asking this of my sister. She's been a bit of a wild child, but this? Jail?

"One night." She doesn't look at me.

"Jules," I say in a lengthy whisper.

"I was lucky it was only one night. Some of them were seriously busted. We're talking court! And *serious* jail time!"

She looks at me now, eyes wide. "Apparently if you have so little weed on you in New York it's not required that you spend the night in jail or something. I don't know exactly. There were like six or seven of us, all high and carrying, and then the fight was crazy. One guy in the fight brought out a knife and . . . well, you can't really blame the cops for just locking us all up for the night, you know? It was chaos." She begins to chew at her nails.

"I didn't have much weed on me," she says. "Which helped my case. But the E didn't win me any favors. And the crowd I was with? Busted. I didn't know what to do, so I cooperated with the cops."

"That was probably the best thing you could have done," I jump in.

"I broke down, cried, told them that even though I was high, the drugs weren't mine. I was high on only weed. I mean"—she chuckles—"come on."

I'm not amused. I'm staring at her with a stupefied expression.

"I told them I never used E or coke or anything hard."

"That's good."

She presses her lips together and looks off to the side.

"You haven't, have you?" I ask, afraid to.

She just looks at me.

"Jules?" I cannot hide my shock.

"A *few* times! Calm down, Gracie." She touches my shoulder. "Honestly, I'm clean. I don't do that anymore. I took E honestly not more than a few times."

"Oh, Jules."

"And I've done only like *two* lines of coke in my entire life. Okay?"

"Oh, Jules."

"What? It was peer pressure. I was stupid. Everyone was doing it . . . and it was so easy. I wanted to try it."

"Jules . . ."

207

"Don't judge me! Please, Gracie." She's pleading, her hand tightening on my shoulder. "Please."

I swallow the knot in my throat as Juliette fixes me with a hard gaze, forcing me to meet her eyes. It can't be easy, coming clean like this, having had to go through what she did. I nod and tell her it's okay, that she can go on. "I won't judge you," I say.

"It was a stupid thing to do, I know," she says. "I'm done. Honest, never again. I don't even smoke weed anymore, all right? Clearly"—she rolls her eyes—"it can get you into some serious trouble."

"So you cooperated with the cops?" I force myself to get back on track, not to linger on the words running wildly in my mind and not to scream out loud: *What were you* thinking, *Juliette? How could you put yourself at risk like this?*

"Yes," she says. "I told them I'd made a few handoffs but *never* accepted money in exchange. I totally cooperated, even outed my supplier, swore I was done with the habit—as if that helped, I don't know." She rapidly wags her head. "I didn't have a previous record, unlike some of the others. I got a misdemeanor, first-time offense. All in all, I was lucky. Extremely lucky. Problem was, though, it was considered public use. Under the influence in *public*, with a bag on me in *public*, because the cops searched me in *public*. Voilà! Out in public. God, I don't want to relive it. It was awful."

"Oh, Jules. I can't believe this."

She casually shrugs, one eyebrow raised. "My driver's license was suspended, too. Six months. Stupid, because what good did a license do me in New York City anyway? And as a college student?" She snickers. Leave it to my zany little sister to find levity in such a moment.

"Ended up with unlawful possession—thankfully with no intent to distribute—and I paid my fine, got a misdemeanor stamped in my record, license suspended. The cops told me second time around I could face real jail time, more serious implications." She covers her face with both hands and moans. "It's so horrible. So embarrassing."

"Jules." I reach over and stroke her arm. I'm at a loss for words, bowled over by an admission I *never* saw coming. Then the words just flow: "It's in the past." My voice is soft, low, comforting.

"I wish!" She peers at me through the gaps between her spread fingers, like a child playing peek-a-boo. "It's on my record, Gracie, so I relive this shit every time I want to apply for a job. Every time there's that stupid little box about being convicted of a crime."

"A *misdemeanor*, Jules. Petty-theft shoplifters can get them. Doesn't mean they're doomed to unemployment for the rest of their lives. That can*not* keep you down."

"It does."

"I have to do my homework." Immediately I'm in legal mode, ready to crack open books, research the law, Juliette's options. "This shouldn't be a problem for you with filling out job applications."

"I've heard that if you don't tick that box about crime on an application, you can get into trouble. Like, you won't even be considered for the job if they find out you have a record and hide it. And I'm not a liar. I'm not going to lie."

"Of course not." I'm not condoning a lie, I'm simply wondering if there are other options, if Juliette's really facing the trouble she thinks she is. "Have you ever talked to a lawyer about this?" I ask.

"And how would I pay one?" She looks at me with a blank expression. "With weed?"

"Not funny." I tuck some hair behind my ears. "*Me*, Jules," I say earnestly. "You should have come to me with this. I can help you."

"Just call you out of the blue—my sister I rarely ever talk to—and tell you I'm in jail and fucked up?" She rolls her eyes.

I don't know what to say. I cross my arms over my chest and search my mind for solutions.

"Companies say they don't discriminate," she says, "but they do. They see that box ticked and my application goes in the trash, Gracie." She makes a shooing motion with one hand.

It's sad but true. It has become an epidemic. With stringent marijuana laws on the books in many states, those who have committed crimes and served time are coming back into the workforce, but they are saddled with this tick-the-box question. There can be no getting ahead, overcoming mistakes of the past.

"I'm sure you can get it expunged, if it's really on your record and something you have to let employers know about," I say. "You are not the only college student who's gone through this. You're not doomed. There's a way out."

"Mowing lawns," she says limply, "filling out applications that don't ask about a criminal background."

"You're not a criminal." I reach out for her arm, stroking it again. "It's going to be all right, Juliette. I promise."

"Can you really promise that everything will be all right?" She looks at me with a weak, dubious expression.

I consider the question for a second. I think of the corner I felt backed into with David, even the improbability of Mimi's yearlong arrangement. Then I give a small smile, a few consolatory pats to her arm, and say, "I can. We'll figure it out together."

"You don't think I'm a loser?" Her voice is weak.

"Omigod, no." I pull her into a hug. "No, I don't think that. I'm your sister." I pull back, place both hands firmly on her shoulders. "I love you."

"Thanks for not freaking out . . . too much. I wasn't sure how you'd react."

"Granted . . ." I shrug one shoulder. "It's not my area of expertise, and I think you live on the edge too much. Too dangerous. And *coke*?"

"I know." She groans.

"But I love you." I grip her tightly. "You got into a mess and now you need to find a way out. You're not alone. You're not the only one with burdens to carry or shit to deal with. Don't forget that."

She cracks a smile, a short beat of laughter slipping out. "Guess so."

"You should have told me a long time ago." I quickly calculate the months we've been living together, the time she's spent not filling out applications, the time she's had to carry this burden by herself.

"Yeah. It feels good to finally share."

"And as for that little box and the job?" I shake my head, as if to say that this can't be as big a deal as she's making it out to be. It isn't a small ordeal, but this is far from life-altering.

"Not that easy, right?" she says.

"There's no reason you should be afraid or unable to get a job. And not just a job. A career!"

"Hold it, career girl. I'm not ready to put on the pantsuit here."

"I'm not saying you have to," I add. "I'm saying that this stupid mistake is not going to keep you from doing what you want. You just have to find out what it is you want, and go for it."

———

The following day, I come in to work an hour early. I ask an ambitious (or perhaps just overloaded) first-year if he can pull some narcotics-related legal material from the shelves, and anything on New York penal codes.

I'm not exactly working within my jurisdiction or expertise, but basic research to get a better grasp of Juliette's situation shouldn't be too difficult. I'm sure even Juliette herself could do the homework, but I didn't pry, didn't urge. I want to do this for my sister, a proverbial olive branch extended to show I do care about her, love her, that I'm still sorry for making her feel all these years that I've dragged Mom into what should have been a two-way dialogue between sisters.

I find small pockets of time throughout the busy day to educate myself on the subject. Lee has come by for a fourth time now, asking if I've made any more progress on the Lowry deposition. The firm is engaged in the usual deposition-scheduling battle. One side wants it quick and painless (as in, we don't want to give the opposing side too much time to dig up dirt), refusing to allow the deposed to meet for more than two days. Our side, sure there is dirt to find and that two days is hardly enough time to uncover it, is pushing for four. I am the lucky paralegal who has to schedule it, sitting in the middle of the back-and-forth battle.

"They won't agree to the three days, six hours. They want two days, five hours," I tell Lee.

"Dammit!" he growls. He dramatically pounds a fist against the doorframe of the conference room.

"You have a counter?" I've grown tired of calling to propose new times. I really shouldn't have to be stuck in this position. Traditionally I contact the client and check with the representation here to make sure everyone has the same date and time on their calendars. Lee, as has become habit since he's begun spearheading the hottest, biggest, latest case, is trying to pawn off the paltry tasks on any paralegal, first-year, or intern with whom he crosses paths. For deposition scheduling, I'm the unlucky sap.

Lee paces the room in the same dramatic fashion with which he pounded his fist. "I'll deal with it," he says under his breath. He glares at Suzanne, who enters the room carrying a stack of books. "If you want to get anything done, get it done yourself."

"Hey!" Suzanne protests as she passes by Lee, who nabs the top book from her stack.

"What is this?" Lee holds up the book and looks at me. "Bennett? You working on some new case I don't know about? Did White end up getting that Burbank case?" His jaw locks, face beginning to redden as he leaps to the conclusion that someone else has stolen the Big Case Spotlight.

Suzanne sets the stack next to me and holds out her hands to take the book back from Lee.

"I told Lowry's office I'd call them back in five," I tell Lee, abrupt. I look at my watch. "That was four minutes ago. I suspect if you want

anything more than two days, six hours, you'd best give them a call."
I don't have time for rankling comments and nose poking from Lee.
There's work to be done, and I've always been diligent about my work,
making deadlines, staying late to complete unfinished tasks. He has no
business questioning me.

"All right, all right." With a furrowed brow, he returns the book
to Suzanne.

"God, sometimes," Suzanne says once Lee leaves the room. She rolls
on her wheeled chair, leaning back and stretching an arm to shut the
glass-paned conference double doors. "Pester much?"

"He's right," I say. I look through the books Suzanne's brought in.
"I'm working on a case, so to speak. Thanks for bringing these." I hold
up the book I've started pawing through, the book Suzanne says one of
the first-years added to her stack, per my request.

"No problem. I assume they're for the Lowry case?" She cracks open
a thick folder, preparing herself for a long day of annotating, research,
and whatever random task Lee will hurl our way.

"Yes. Except for one book." I page through the book I hope will be
helpful in my quest to right Juliette's wrong. "Someone I know needs
a little legal help."

"Representation?"

"No, nothing like that. Just some 1L work, you could say."

I decide the book will most likely prove helpful, but now's not the
time for it. Right now I have a mountain of annotations to do with
Suzanne. I slip the book into my briefcase and turn my attention to
the Lowry case.

"Who's it for?" Suzanne pries as she wields a chunky hot-pink
highlighter.

I grab the yellow highlighter and turn to page one of the documents
before me. "For a friend," I say.

"It's been a while since we've been able to do this," Dad says. He adjusts some dials on the outdoor grill, a long stainless-steel spatula in one hand.

"Dinner or barbecue?" Mom asks. She sails out from the house and onto the back porch, her waist-high navy-blue apron floating along as she sets a plate of sesame seed–covered hamburger buns on the patio table.

"Both," Dad replies. Smoke billows in a heavy cloud when he opens the grill. "Well done, right, Gracie?"

"Yup!" I answer.

"Blackened for Juliette?"

"Like a meteor," Juliette says from her seat next to me. Both legs are tucked underneath her. She's wearing blue-jean shorts, one of her beloved pairs with torn cuffs, despite the fact that it is hardly shorts weather. I can't help but smile at her quirkiness. "With lots of cheese, Dad," Juliette adds with enthusiasm.

"One cheddar slice for me," I tell him.

"I'm glad we could do this, too," Mom says cheerily. She fastidiously arranges the condiments, the plates of lettuce, tomato, and onion, and a variety of beverages in the middle of the table.

"You know, it's so nice to be able to have you girls down the street like this," Mom says as Dad hums some Mozart or Beethoven piece while flipping burgers. "We can have such nice family dinners together, like the old days."

"Mom's getting sentimental," Juliette kids, nudging me with her elbow.

Family meals and barbecues like tonight were usually on the calendar once a week, at least a few times a month, before Juliette and I moved in together. They were one of the perks of living close to family. And even though the dinners and brunches haven't been as frequent since the move, due to the unusual circumstances of the year and Juliette's and my finding other ways to keep our weekends and evenings full, we still get to enjoy a home-cooked meal as a family now and then.

We all dig into our delectable burgers, cooked expertly, per order, when Dad asks how work at the firm is going. I tell them the workload is heavy. "But that's nothing new," I say with a smile.

"You still love what you do?" Dad asks between hearty bites of his cheeseburger.

My father, and my mother, too, for that matter, has always encouraged me to seek a career that I'm passionate about. Dad's a successful and accomplished architect, having worked with a prestigious Santa Barbara firm for decades, Mom a freelance stationer who has her designs in a number of small coastal city paper and party supply boutiques.

They raised Juliette and me to believe that if you do what you love as a career, you'll never work a day in your life. And that when you work with passion, you do your job to the absolute best of your ability.

There is most certainly truth to this line of thought, even during the days when I want to tell Lee that I am overwhelmed, overtasked. Researching Juliette's brush with the law has reawakened the knowledge that I don't want to be anywhere else, doing anything else.

"Absolutely," I say.

"And speaking of work . . . ," Dad says with pep. He looks to Juliette. "I hear you may have landed yourself some work at an art shop?"

"Arts and crafts supply store," Juliette answers.

"Keating's?" Mom inquires.

"Keating's, yeah," Juliette says between bites. "I applied." She glances at me for a fleeting moment, and I'm filled with pride for my sister. "They don't need help anymore, at least it isn't advertised in the window like it used to be. I still had an application lying around and figured, what the hell, you know?" She looks to me again.

"Lawn work might slow down, since it's not summer anymore," Mom says. "Probably a smart idea."

"Juliette's been killing with that," I jump in.

"Oh yeah?" Dad looks at Juliette with that usual warm and encouraging smile of his. For a second you'd think, with his glowing eyes and infectious smile, that he was Mimi's son. He chuckles, looking even more like a Jones.

"If my gardening skills wow you, I just might blow you away with my saleswoman skills if I get the job at Keating's."

Juliette and I share a smile. It's the first step, Juliette's putting in an application. She said she hadn't come across "the little box," and I assured her that a misdemeanor and a felony are two very different things. She had no reason to fear that stupid (and controversial, irrelevant, and discriminating, I might add) box. What's to come of her record I don't know, but she should not let one mistake in her past keep her from searching for a career she's passionate about. Repercussions are one thing, giving up another.

Things at work have been moving pretty fast lately. Suzanne and I are overloaded with Lee's random assignments, plus our regular tasks, not to mention the extras that come with signing on a new and large case. I haven't had much time to dedicate to figuring out the details of Juliette's predicament, but I encouraged her to apply anywhere she was interested in, period. I'm proud that she's making this step. She deserves to be happy. If mowing lawns is it, all right. If working at an arts and crafts supply store is it, go for it. Whatever it is, I want her to find what makes her happy, work toward it, and just do it.

————

Little did I know those words of encouragement I'd given to my sister would be the very words I'd fall back on when a familiar little

216

name and number appeared on my missed-calls list one early Friday evening.

I didn't know if I should return the call, respond with a text, or wait for him to call back. The instant I saw *David* on the screen, my stomach flipped, and all I could do was shove my phone inside my bag to delay a decision.

Besides, he could have pocket-dialed my number by mistake. Never finding the courage or confidence to pursue the matter, I'd kept my phone in my bag, out of sight.

Hours later, however, I am still in a state of disbelief. I can't wrap my head around the missed call. With my phone still neglected, I decided that the usual Friday girls' night out with Juliette would be best spent in a long evening ride along the waterfront, stopping to watch the paddleboarders and kayakers float atop the calm harbor waters. Distract myself. Remind myself that there is more to my life than trying to win David's attention and heart. The call, at least for a while, can wait.

Unable to resist the call to the ocean, Juliette, ignoring the overcast sky and cooler autumn temperatures, decided she needed a quick dip and has left me to my spot on the sand, where I sit now, ruminating on my decision to neglect my phone, to delay the inevitable.

How can David be calling? Why? I begin to contemplate the situation in the peaceful silence. I retrieve my cell phone for the first time since I tucked it away, and I gaze at it in hesitation.

What part of letting me learn to fall out of love with him does he not understand? And what part of putting us in the past and his relationship with his fiancée first does he not grasp?

I resist the urge to throw my phone—an urge that is, surprisingly, greater than the one to hit the "Return Call" button. I must steel myself for another painful episode of learning to let time and silence between former lovers work its magic. With every attempt David has made to reach out, regardless of the outcome, I have found myself right back at the doorstep of unrequited love. And now, against my will, I've found my way back here yet again, thanks to a simple missed call.

I turn on the screen, and I notice I have a voice mail. I swallow the lump in my throat. *Could it be from him?* I think, knowing with both absolute certainty and dismay that it is. David's call is my only missed call.

I look up from my phone, set my sights on the lapping waters of the ocean. Juliette's dived under the water. There isn't much wave action; Leadbetter Beach is a calmer section. I train my eyes on the horizon. The sun has already set, but it still provides just enough light for me to make out Juliette's head as it pops up, her hands flying above.

My thumb is trembling over the button that will call my voice mail in an instant, reveal the message that David has decided I must hear.

What harm can there be in listening to the message? I consider. *No more harm than the harm that's already been done by the phone call.* The damage was done the moment David decided to call. The curiosity, the weak flame of hope that still shines, urges me to listen to the message. To maybe even return the call.

I am relieved when Juliette, shivering and saying she is "crazy-balls crazy" for going in the water, returns. She bundles herself in a beach towel, kicking up sand that blows in my hair, brushes against the side of my face. I disregard the nonsensical habit of sand flinging that she's never outgrown, I'm so numbed by the unexpected.

"I built up a sweat on the ride," Juliette says. She drops down next to me, loops a damp arm through mine. "Phew! Thought the dip would do me good, but *brrrr* it's cold." She leans in close and peers over my shoulder. "Whatcha got there? That Les guy from work hounding you?"

"Lee," I say.

"Lee-Shmee. He probably just needs a good lay."

I hold the phone up to Juliette without saying a word, without letting another second pass by that I don't let her in on the biggest bomb that's been dropped since the Fourth of July.

"Shit," she mutters.

"I have a message." I look at the phone. The "Return Call" button is burning on the screen.

"Did you listen to it?"

"No."

"Are you going to?"

"I don't know." I do know. I know that I will never be able to let this message go unheard. "What would you do?"

Juliette looks stunned when I ask her this question. It takes a second for her to respond. Her soaking hair is hanging in thick cords around her face; her lips are a deep cabernet red, chattering lightly. She deadpans for a while.

"What do you expect to hear?" she asks. It's not what I expected her to say. I figured she'd say something along the lines of "Ignore the bastard!" or "A listen won't hurt anyone." Her response is a question I haven't even considered. What *do* I expect to hear? What do I expect of David? Of myself?

"I don't know, really," I say. "I want to listen."

Juliette gingerly takes the phone from my hands. "I can understand that. Hear me out, though. Do *not* do things on *his* terms, Gracie."

I nod. We've had this talk before. I know how it goes.

She hands me the phone and I listen to the message, biting down so hard on my tongue I taste a faint trace of blood as David's voice—that sexy, cooing, deep voice of his—rings in my ear.

"Gracie, I know I'm probably the last person you expected to hear from. I'm sorry, but I just—I just had to call you." David clears his throat nervously. "I'm going . . ."

I focus on Juliette's wide blue eyes as I listen to the remainder of the message. When David says the unexpected, my mouth drops open. Juliette mirrors me, and as soon as the message concludes, I slowly bring the phone down to my lap.

"Well? What? What?" Juliette's on pins and needles. "What'd he say? Something big? Crazy?"

I hold the phone out to her, gesturing for her to listen for herself. Before she can snag it out of my hands, I tell her in a trancelike state, "He wants to see me. At Thanksgiving. He'll be in town."

"Oh bullshit!" Juliette takes the phone. "He's not playing games with you like this anymore."

"He says he has something he wants to tell me." I swallow hard.

"What?"

"I don't know. He didn't say."

19

Juliette

I feel so terrible for Gracie. I've never loved anyone the way Gracie loves David. Sometimes I find it hard to understand how someone so wonderful could love someone so awful.

I suppose it isn't entirely fair—I don't know David that well. What I do know of him personally dates back to when he and Gracie were actually going out, and he wasn't a bad guy. This whole on-and-off phase of theirs (to say nothing of the secret fiancée), however, casts a very gloomy pall on anything positive David ever had going for him. The way he's toyed with Gracie's heart like this, back and forth . . . it burns me up. I don't understand how Gracie could still want him, could still love him.

I'd like to believe that if I were to find myself in such a position, I would not let myself be pulled one way and then another. I would not allow myself to live on his terms the way Gracie has, no matter how much I thought I loved him. I wouldn't let love blind me so that I'd put myself second.

I don't let myself get anywhere near that kind of situation anyhow. I live on my terms. If the right man comes along, all right, I'll be amenable to seeing where it can go. But it hasn't come to that yet. Maybe someday it will. If and when it does, I'll do my damnedest to remember the hurt and suffering I see in Gracie's eyes each time David reaches out, each time he loves her in return, then breaks her heart all over again.

The thing with love, though, is that it can be all-consuming. It can drive people to do some of the craziest things. In the name of love, people can lose sight of themselves, who they are, what they want, even whom they think they see in the person they love. And because of the insane force that love is, I cannot judge Gracie and her feelings for David. I cannot fight the helplessness I feel to do something to ease my sister's pain, to slap David silly and make him see what he's missing, what he's doing. I can't, because love is an unpredictable and unexplainable force.

Wishing I could offer her the help and support she offered to me with my legal issue, I found myself doing the only thing I could think of. I invited Gracie to join me and some of the girls for drinks. It'd be fun and a chance to get out, to get some distraction going. She's had my shoulder to lean or cry on—she'll always have that. I've told her she deserves a man who can love her unconditionally and to believe that she deserves that. I've given her the best advice I could give: "If you feel you *have* to call David, you have to do what you feel is right, for *you*. Otherwise leave it be. Let him go."

As much as I resent David's coming back into Gracie's life, Mimi always said that the heart wants what the heart wants. I can't begrudge anyone that, but of course I'll be damned if I encourage my sister to go about trying to get it in a way that will only leave her bruised, bloody, and battered.

"Are you sure you don't want to come?" I beg of Gracie one last time before I head out to meet the girls. "Brea asked if you were coming."

"Some other time," Gracie says with a grateful smile. "You have your fun. I think I'd just like to stay in tonight."

I'm about to ask if she's going to mope, feel sorry for herself, or get angry and go on a mad cleaning spree again, but I think better of it, reminding myself that it has barely been twenty-four hours since David called. Gracie has all the right in the world to sit and stew some.

"Tomorrow," I say instead. "Tomorrow you and I are going to go do something."

"What?" She looks hopeful, eager to hear what interesting and distracting thing I may have planned.

I twist my lips to the side. "Um, I don't know yet. Whatever it is will be totally cool and distracting." I flash her a reassuring smile.

"There is a movie I've been wanting to see . . ."

"Movie it'll be!"

"Cool."

"Of course you can *still* join tonight."

"No." She motions for me to go on without her. "You have fun. Say hi for me."

———

Before I walk through the front door shortly before midnight, I notice a lamp is still on in the living room. "Gracie?" I say as I enter the house.

I'm about to call out her name again when I spot her asleep on the sofa, one arm covering her face, the other resting on top of a book that's spread open on her stomach.

"Oops," I whisper, careful not to make any further unnecessary noise. I peek at the book she's reading—*Penal Law* something or other I can't make out.

I glance at the coffee table, where she has a neat pile of paperwork; a cluster of pens, pencils, and highlighters; an opened bottle and half-drunk glass of white wine; and her cell phone. She must have been doing more work for that Lee character. *Poor Gracie,* I think. *She could have used a night out more than any of us.*

I give her a light kiss on the forehead and whisper, "Good night, sis."

———

The scent of baked waffles in the morning sets my olfactory senses into high gear. It's as if Mimi is right here with me, telling me to stir in the blueberries carefully, to add in only the paste-like interior of the vanilla bean, not the twiggy casing. I can see her wrinkled and arthritic hands carefully stirring the batter about in the large teal ceramic bowl that she always used when baking anything—cakes, pies, pancakes, waffles.

I've even turned on some Simon and Garfunkel, just as Mimi and Grandpa used to do when dinner was being prepared, when Gracie and I would help Mimi with the breakfast waffles. The song "Scarborough Fair/Canticle" fills the kitchen with its melodic notes, dancing with the aroma of butter and vanilla.

As the chorus begins, Gracie enters the kitchen. "Good morning," she says groggily.

"Morning, Gracie." I flash her my most chipper smile—quite chipper for eight o'clock on a Sunday morning, I should note.

"You're up *early.*" She yawns, stretches both arms over her head. The hem of her oversize college tee, one of her usual nightshirts, rides up just past a pair of jogging shorts. "Are you Juliette? Where'd my sister go?" she teases. She treads lazily across the kitchen floor. "Oh, I drank too much wine last night." She grips her head.

"Been there, done that. Hungover?"

She rubs at her temples. "I don't think so. Only had a couple of glasses."

"Couple of glasses for you could be a couple of glasses too many."

"So true." She rubs harder. "Ugh. Anyway. How was last night?"

"Super fun. You should have come out. The girls asked about you."

She takes a seat at the kitchen table, says, "Maybe next time," then leans forward in her chair to look at our pet betta fish swimming lazily in its bowl in the center of the table.

"We really should name him." I close the lid on the waffle iron and turn the handle 180 degrees.

Gracie laughs. "How about Fish?"

"I don't think so." I lean against the counter.

"You name it, then." She sits back in her chair, knees pulled into her chest.

"Fish is your serious suggestion?"

She rubs away the sleep in her eyes.

"I won him," I say, "you name him."

She looks to be considering a name for the pet that, nothing short of a miracle, is actually fed and cared for, never mind the negligence in name giving or that we'd probably forget he was here if it weren't for the spotlight location of his bowl, a location Gracie cleverly insisted upon. "So last night . . . ," Gracie says instead.

"Yeah?" I'm afraid to hear something about David. Surely her pregnant pause and shift in conversation topic has to do with him. I hesitantly ask, "David?"

She nods.

"Something bad?"

"No," she asserts rapidly. "Nothing bad. Something good, actually." She rubs at one temple. "Well, I *think* good." She shakes her head. "Don't really know."

"Spill the beans, sis," I say, relieved. I take a peek at the waffle. Not finished yet. I know Gracie likes them a tiny bit gooey. I prefer them an even golden on both sides.

"You'd be so proud," she says. "I didn't call him at all."

"Good for you!" I am proud. "And the part that you *think* is good?"

"He didn't call again."

"Good. Definitely good."

"But I want to know what he has to say, Jules," she whines.

"Well, if you want to know that, then you'll either have to call him or wait for him to call you again."

"So logical," she mutters. "Since when were you the logical one?"

I laugh and say, "Guess you're wearing off on me and I'm wearing off on you."

"Yeah, well . . ."

"I'm proud of you, Gracie. Not letting him call the shots, you know? That's the way to do it." I check the waffle once more. It's reached golden perfection. "Is that why you hit the wine a little?" I venture.

"Yes." Her reply is dry. "It was all I could do *not* to call him. Had two and a half glasses."

"Holy hell, call AA!" I bang the spatula against the edge of the sink. "Gracie Dawn Bennett's gone on a bender!"

Gracie laughs, then holds her head and says I'm being far too loud, far too early, especially for someone who's had far too much to drink.

"There's more good news," she says. "I finished my homework last night on your misdemeanor."

Gracie says this so breezily it kind of makes me recoil. Then, I remember that my run-in with the law isn't as life altering as I've made it out to be all this time. A misdemeanor is *not* a felony. I don't have to report my stupid mistake on a job application. Background checks, though . . . that's a different story. The point is, I've learned my lesson, and I don't have to live my life on the terms of my mistake.

"Turns out," Gracie says, "there are two types of background checks done for jobs. In California there are private checks and then government ones."

"Oh?" I say interestedly.

"Not all companies do background checks, either. Remember that. And not all checks show everything, like an expungement or eradication."

She's losing me. I tell her I'm not sure where she's going.

"If you're in a government or law or health field, for instance, then you're subject to the government check without doubt, and everything is on your record. All convictions. Even ones that you had expunged. Like if you petition a court to have something 'removed from your record,' so to speak?"

"Yeah?"

"They'd more than likely be cleared from a private check. But government? No. But you don't want to be a lawyer or nurse or go into a government line of work, so . . ."

"Okay, so that's good news, right?"

"Definitely."

"And this expungement thing?"

"I've looked into it. If you want, two years post-action, we can try to have your misdemeanor erased."

"Really?" I can feel my entire face glow.

"Yes, but like I said, we have to wait awhile. I'll look more into it when the time comes."

"But this won't be a black stamp for the rest of my life, you're saying?" I pour batter onto the hot iron.

"No, Jules." She gives me a comforting smile. "Even if you couldn't get an expungement, it's not a black stamp for the rest of your life. You went to jail for *one* night, not prison!"

"Yeah, well," I say, not wanting to get into the "Slip into my shoes and then tell me what you think" speech. Gracie's been a doll helping me; this is excellent news.

"You have a misdemeanor. You are not a felon. You are not a criminal. You made a very *stupid* mistake and, quite frankly, were lucky. Things could have been worse."

"I know."

"You've paid; you've learned your lesson. It's time to move on." She sprinkles feed into the fishbowl. "Point is, stop letting it rule your life."

"And this background check thing?"

"When a company does a *private* background check, which is *not* always the case, don't worry. Just be honest with them. That's the best you can do. And if they don't check, then you're fine. You're a hard worker, have a degree, good grades, you're smart . . . Don't let anything stand in your way, 'kay?"

I nod excitedly. This is great news. Excellent news! Sure, it's not an expungement and clean record, and it doesn't erase what happened, but it's a reminder that I don't have to let some stupid mistake in the past ruin my future—or my present. As Gracie sagely said, I don't have to hide in fear and embarrassment. I just have to put my mind to something and believe in it, in myself. All I had to do was reach out to a sister who's always been there.

"And when you decide to puff up again, just make sure you're in a state where it's legal," she says with a sly expression. "Second offense isn't pretty."

"I know." I roll my eyes. "I'm done with that. As tempting as it may be with a hottie on the beach." I think back on Cary and his offer.

My thoughts quickly turn to how my marijuana habit brought me into the circle of friends who also chose harder drugs, how that led me to the path of makeshift dealing, to a night spent in jail, to a fight that could have ended so much worse.

"No," I say with steadfast resolve. "Lesson learned. Unfortunately, the hard way. I appreciate the help, Gracie. Thanks."

"My pleasure."

"Harold," Gracie then says from nowhere.

"Huh?"

"Harold," she repeats with a smile. "I think we should name the fish Harold."

"As in Grandpa's name?"

"Actually. Didn't think of that. But I guess. I was thinking of *Harold and the Purple Crayon*. He's purple." She points to the fish.

"Harold it is," I say.

"Harold and his magic purple crayon drawing his world *just* the way it should be." Gracie smiles assuredly, but more to herself than to me.

I smile, too, enjoying how good it feels to be that much closer to not just coming to terms with my past but also embracing the here, the now, and welcoming whatever future will be had at 1402 Laguna Lane with my sister, purple crayon in hand.

20

Gracie

It was no bigger than a thimble, but it was far shinier—a very shiny silver with the most delicately etched *G* in the center. It was simple, yet lovely. It was the kind of necklace a mother might buy a daughter, maybe even one a father might buy his little girl, the kind of necklace a girl might give to her best friend. It was also the kind of necklace a man might buy for the woman he loves, the heart-shaped pendant a small symbol of his feelings, the monogram a personal touch, one that might even be a stamp of possession.

For me, the necklace has come to be nothing more than a keepsake of a better time, a memento tucked away in my jewelry box. It was, however, once the necklace that a man did buy for the woman he loved, or thought he loved. It then became the necklace that had been given by one friend to another, a reminder of the something special that had once been shared between two lovers. That perhaps, like thinning threads of an old tapestry that refuse to let go, was a lingering piece of what had become a very peculiar relationship.

I remember the day I received that necklace, the silver heart and chain both a shiny-sterling new, the *G* cut so clearly. I was twenty years old, in love, and on Thanksgiving break from college, spending it with my new boyfriend. The weekend was monumental. It was the first time David would meet my parents, the first time I would meet Mr. and Mrs. Nichol.

Nerves were dancing; the cheer of the holiday and all its festivities was palpable. Preparations for the traditional Bennett family smorgasbord Thursday afternoon were underway. It was, by tradition, a lazy and jovial affair of daylong gorging with intermittent periods in front of the television to watch the football teams gain and lose yardage.

Preparations for the traditional Nichol family feast for Thursday evening were also under way, with the added accoutrements of fine china, crystal goblets, and cloth napkins. David had astutely warned me of his great-aunt and her penchant for giving newcomers the third degree. He'd also given me a heads-up to avoid his sister's pumpkin pie, but that her green bean casserole could not be missed.

I, in turn, told him that after five minutes of talking with my Mimi, he'd agree I had the best grandmother ever. And that if my father asked if his loyalty lay with the Anaheim Angels or the Los Angeles Dodgers to say something about the San Francisco 49ers. Drive my father as far away as possible from the politics of California baseball. Jokes would be exchanged around the Bennett table, while talk of the stock market and new business opportunities would make their rounds around the Nichol table.

That Thanksgiving was the first holiday of what I hoped would be many that David and I would share, looking back and laughing about how different our two families could seem, yet how well we fit into each other's worlds.

It was a young relationship—only two months at that point—but a part of me was sure that David and I would come to look back fondly on our love story, telling our children that while we hadn't met until college, we had been right under each other's noses all that time, growing up in the same small town and only miles apart. And though we hadn't gone to the same high school, we surely had passed each other at a local coffee shop, brushed shoulders at a party or concert or on the beach. So close, but not yet ready to meet. We would tell them that love's a funny thing, that it's beautiful and peculiar and, as I'd touch my heart-shaped necklace that I'd still be wearing after all those years, it was unexpected.

The autumn air was crisp and salty, the breeze from the Channel whipping around the tight corners along the vintage shops and high-end boutiques that lined manicured State Street. Most of the small shops were already closed for the extended holiday weekend, some beginning to shut down for an early close.

David and I'd been walking along the pristine sidewalk, hand in hand, having enjoyed a light lunch—a spontaneous outing made necessary after Juliette and Mom launched into an argument over the ethics of consuming meat. Juliette had recently decided she would become a vegetarian, and that meant eating a good half of the Thanksgiving meal would be sacrilege.

To steer clear of whatever drama was surely continuing at home, David and I decided to take a long stroll. We were headed toward the beach when he stopped me in front of a jewelry shop in Paseo Nuevo. I remember the elegant pearl earrings on display in the window, as well as the matching pearl necklace, and a variety of thin gold rings. I remember most, however, my necklace. The one in the display had the letter *A* etched on the heart. It was very delicate, understated. Simple and sweet. I commented on it casually, saying that I liked that it wasn't a locket.

"Heart necklaces always seem to be lockets," I said.

"You don't like lockets?" David asked.

"I haven't really considered whether I like lockets or not." I'd never had the occasion to contemplate romantic pieces of jewelry. No man had ever bought me one, unless you count the pink plastic ring Erik Newman bought me from the twenty-five-cent toy machine outside Buster's Burgers when I was seven.

"I like the heart shape," I said. "And the monogram is nice."

I was ready to move along with our walk, tugging his hand as I stepped forward, when David said, "I wonder if they have a *G*." He raised a curious brow, then led the way into the shop.

My fingers grazed the necklace's shiny heart-shaped pendant as David asked, "What do you think?" He appraised the necklace with the letter *G* that hung gracefully around my neck.

I gently ran my fingers along the thin chain. It was the perfect length, coming to the ideal point below my collarbone and a good three fingers above my breasts. No matter what shirt or dress or blouse I wore, the lovely little heart would always be seen.

"It's beautiful," I said. I looked at my reflection in the handheld mirror the young saleslady had offered after she fastened the necklace around my neck.

"It is," the saleslady remarked.

"Then it's yours." David surprised me.

"No. No, David." I had no idea what the necklace cost, but even if it wasn't all that much, I didn't expect David to buy it for me. It was too soon for jewelry. We'd only recently become exclusive. The meeting of the parents and the sharing of a sacred holiday were big-enough firsts for the weekend. I couldn't accept the necklace.

"Do you like it?" David inquired eagerly. His cobalt eyes were sparkling as he smiled. I could see he wanted to buy me the necklace as much as I wanted it—though I would never admit as much.

"It's beautiful. I love it." I held the mirror back farther, falling more in love with how the simple yet elegant necklace matched and dressed up my whole outfit—black three-quarter-length cardigan over a black T-shirt, fitted cargo pants with the ankles cuffed twice above a conservative pair of silver ballet flats.

"We'll take it," David said to the saleslady.

I continued to protest that he didn't have to, that he shouldn't. He said, having already paid and leading the way out of the shop, that it was done. "Enjoy it. It was made for you."

The breeze had picked up considerably in the brief time we'd spent in the shop. An afternoon rain was on the radar, and David and I still hadn't made it to Stearns Wharf for the saltwater taffy he insisted on having while in town.

I stopped for a minute nevertheless, boldly tucking a thumb in the rear of his navy dress slacks, pressing a hand to his chest, and I kissed him. He brought both hands to the back of my head, the intensity of our kiss increasing, never mind the public display of affection we usually shied away from. We were more the conservative and private type, keeping the more intimate moments, like a deep and passionate kiss, for times when we were not on the side of the street for any and all to see.

But I didn't care where we were, I didn't care who watched us embrace and kiss as if we were love-struck teenagers. I felt so happy, so content, so at peace with everything in my life right then and there. I had found a man who wanted what I wanted out of life and who wanted to share it with me. So it was a new relationship—that was so much the beauty and appeal of it. It was magical.

Call it a goofy reaction or first-real-love giddiness, but I had gotten my first piece of jewelry from a man—a heart-shaped piece of jewelry! I wasn't sure then if that was David's way of telling me he was falling in love with me, but one month later, when we'd walk the very same streets during Christmas break, I would know for sure that he had. He would stop me, take both my hands in his, and tell me he loved me. I'd be wearing the same necklace, I would tell him I loved him, too, and I would feel that overwhelming sense of joy and pure happiness that fill a woman when she's in love.

Our love was so real, so all consuming, I would never in a million rational-thinking, practical-cautioning, pragmatic-reasoning years imagine that David and I would not be together forever, that there would come a day when I would take off that necklace for one final time, that we would not have that serendipitous love story to share with our children.

"You still want to watch the latest *Modern Family*?" Juliette says, peeking around the corner into my bedroom. "I've got it queued up."

Startled, I drop the necklace back into the place where I've kept it for so long.

"Are you okay?" Juliette asks. She gestures with a nod to the necklace. She knows precisely what I'm tucking away.

I close the small wooden jewelry box, slip it into the top dresser drawer underneath my panties and bras. "Yeah. Just reminiscing."

"He hasn't called? Texted?"

I shake my head and slowly close the dresser drawer, as if the slow, drawn-out movements will buy me time to snap out of my daze, my longing. As if they will give me just the amount of time I need to close the door on the foolish hope that David will call, that that necklace could ever mean again what it once did.

"Maybe he will tomorrow," Juliette says, tone hopeful. She leans against the doorframe, arms hugging her chest.

"I thought it was best he didn't call again," I say. "That we move on?"

Juliette doesn't say anything.

I sniff a small laugh. "I want him to call," I admit to her, to myself. "I want him to call because I want to hear what he has to say."

"Of course. I can imagine."

"And because it'd be a sign—dumb as that sounds—that he does care. That he wants to . . . fight for me." I shake my head at the absurdity of what I've just admitted.

"I know." Juliette pushes off from the doorframe. "Love's a bitch, Gracie." She gestures with a nod for me to join her in the living room. "We need some *Modern Family*."

———

We've both faded off to sleep, right here on the settee in the middle of watching TV, and are startled awake by the ringing of my cell phone.

235

"What time is it?" Juliette grumbles. She takes hold of my wrist and tries to read the face of my watch. She doesn't get a chance to make out the time, because I'm searching for the loudly ringing phone. "Is it already tomorrow?"

My search is halted for a second. I panic, worried I've slept in, will be late for work. I glance out the front window. It's pitch-black, save for the golden glow of the porch light.

I breathe out a sigh of relief, then pull my phone free from my purse. I'm about to blindly answer it, a small part of me concerned that a call coming in at such an hour—twenty past ten, I hastily notice on the grandfather clock—can mean only bad news. But I stop. I stare at the screen.

"Shit," I breathe. I look to Juliette with pleading eyes. "What do I do? What do I do?"

"What?" She's rubbing her eyes with her palms. "Who is it?"

"Who do you think?"

"No."

"The one and only."

"Shit."

The ringing continues. I feel my toes tingle in anticipation, the recognition that my window of opportunity to answer the call will be over in one, two, *maybe* three rings.

"What do I do?" I shriek, jumping from my seat.

"Do what you feel!" Juliette blurts out right as I bring up the phone, finger ready to either answer or ignore the call.

"I'm answering," I say with a sudden sense of vindication.

"Be strong." Juliette makes a pumping action with her hand, and I steel myself.

I intake a deep breath and press the "Answer" button. I exhale heavily but quietly, then say, as calmly, as coolly, as rationally, in as controlled a way as possible, "Hello."

"Gracie?" The sound of David's voice is like butter melting on a hot day. It makes my knees weak. I save myself from collapsing from the mixture of overwhelming nerves, the surprise of his call, and the appeal of his voice. I grip the back of a dining chair, but I can't will myself to take a seat. I think that by remaining standing I'm somehow standing my ground.

"Hi, David." I'm surprised by how controlled my tone is.

"I hope it isn't too late," he says.

"No, it's fine," I lie. I'm just so happy he called. I'm glad I won't have to wonder what it is he's wanted to tell me. I'm relieved that he's called *me*, that I'm not the one running to him for once. I glance at Juliette for support and she gives me a thumbs-up.

"How are you doing?" His voice is still, collected.

As unpredictable as David can be, I am certain he is not calling to shoot the breeze. But, not wanting to turn the light mood sour in record time, I carry on with the banalities. "Fine," I half lie. "How are you?"

"Could be better, has been worse," he says with a sigh.

I know that sigh. It's the kind of sigh David makes when he's relaxed, when he's talking for talking's sake, as when I'd ask how class went, what he thought of the new deli we'd tried the day before, how he wanted to spend the weekend. He would raise his arms in a wide-arching stretch, maybe throw out a light yawn, then put his hands behind his head and *sigh*.

In a flurry, I try to sort through my whirl of thoughts. I want to ask a million and one questions, as always seems to be the case after a lengthy time away from David. I glance over at Juliette again. She's on the edge of her seat, chin in her palms. She's staring at me wide-eyed, eager, perhaps a twinge terrified.

Empathizing, I give her a crooked smile, grip the back of the chair harder. "Worse?" I say to David, unsure where to start. What does David want out of this conversation?

"Yeah. God, Gracie, it's so good to hear your voice." He sighs again. The same sigh. This time it's as if I can see him, as if he's sitting right here next to me. "I've missed you a lot. It's so good to talk to you again."

"Are you all right?"

"I've been better, but it's not as bad anymore."

I can't handle the weakness in my knees anymore, the beating around the bush with pleasantries, the banter. "It's good to hear from you, too," I say, taking a seat next to Juliette. Immediately she drapes an encouraging arm around me. "Is that why you're calling? Because something's happened? What's 'not as bad anymore'?"

"I just—I just need someone I can trust and who understands, who really knows me. You've always been that girl, Gracie."

It wouldn't surprise me if my cheeks are blushing red at David's charms. He could always make me feel like a girl in love. Ironic, because he also had a knack for making me feel like a girl whose heart had been shattered.

"I've been trying to call you for weeks now."

"Weeks?" I am certain I haven't missed more than that one call from him Friday night.

"Been trying to gather the nerve for weeks," he clarifies. "I've needed some time to think. I actually took a small vacation from work." He scoffs. "That's how bad it was, how much I needed to get away. I went to Big Sur, where we stayed on that weekend getaway we took years ago. Remember that?"

How could I forget? It was only the most romantic trip I'd taken, to a bed-and-breakfast surrounded by redwoods and wisteria, with a balcony with a view of the river, no decent phone or Internet connection, no televisions or computers to detract from the romantic setting.

"I had to clear my head," he continues. "I never miss work, you know that. That should tell you how messed up I was."

"Are you okay now?" I can't hide my concern for David. His voice has taken on a weak tone, something it rarely, if ever, does. He sounds vulnerable.

He doesn't answer my question. "It did me some good, though," he says instead. "And I've thought more about it over the weeks. And now I just really want to talk to you."

"Okay . . ."

"Did you get my message?"

"Erm, yes." I consider lying about why I didn't return his call, then figure what's the point? "I told you I needed space. That if we couldn't be together, then I—" I swallow away the suddenly formed knot in my throat.

"I know," he interrupts. "I *had* to talk to you again. So much is going on, and I've given it a lot of thought, calling you."

"What's going on?" I make sure my voice is steady and determined. It's time to do away with banal conversation. "Tell me, David. For once can you be honest with me?"

He sighs that familiar sigh, then says, "For the past few months, the wedding's been on and off. We've had a date set, we change it, back and forth, back and forth."

I want to laugh out loud—"back and forth" is what David does. It's all he knows. Instead, I sound an *mmm-hmm*, encouraging him to go on.

"With all that on-and-off, I had a lot of time to consider getting married. Caroline and I'd started fighting more," he admits. I cringe at the sound of her name, and Juliette's embrace tightens in solidarity. "I told her about us. About how we had gotten together over Christmas. And in February—"

"How you'd deceived me. Us!" I cringe some more when I put Caroline in the same boat as myself.

David remains calm. "I told her, and that was kind of the straw that broke the camel's back, guess you could say."

Was he seriously trying to be funny? There was no humor in any of this. "Infidelity will kind of do that," I spit back. I look to Juliette, clench my jaw, and shake my head violently.

"I wanted to come clean, Gracie. I can't get married with lies hanging over me."

I shake my head some more. I want to blurt into the phone, "What is the point of this call?" Tears are beginning to form, stinging my eyes, stinging the back of my throat.

"It wouldn't be fair to Caroline, to me . . ." The tears really begin to swell. "Or you."

"What do *I* have to do with this, David?"

"The wedding's off, Gracie."

"Off?" I furrow my brow, taken aback. "Off-off? Or another on-again, off-again off?" I can see Juliette roll her eyes.

"Off." His voice is unbending. "Caroline and I broke up. The engagement, the wedding, it's all off."

I can't think of anything to say at this point. I am absolutely, positively flabbergasted.

"Gracie? Gracie?"

"Uh-huh," I stutter.

"I have to see you." His words are imploring. "I've taken time to think this through, to think about the engagement, about you, about how I feel. I only want to see you. Just see you in person, to talk."

"I don't know." I nervously look to Juliette. I hadn't considered this a feasible option, and never under such circumstances! I know self-preservation should be a priority, but what about fate? Serendipity? What about my chance for happiness and a future with the man I love? Would I be fair to myself—would I be really honest with myself—if I refused this opportunity? Things are different now. David is single. I am single. We're friends, former lovers, who want to talk.

"Please," he says. "I understand if you hate me."

"I don't hate you," I cut in earnestly. "I don't hate you, David."

"I understand if you don't want to see me. It's selfish of me to even call you like this, when you told me to let things go. It hurts me to hurt you."

"Yes."

"But that was before—"

"Before you found yourself single, needing fill-in-the-blank Gracie again?"

Juliette gives me a squeeze and a shake. She's smiling and mouthing, "Good girl!"

"It's not like that, Gracie."

"It's sure as hell how it feels."

There's a lengthy silence that falls between us, giving me time to consider my next move. I may no longer be standing, my knees may still be weak, but I'm resolute.

"I haven't stopped loving you, David," I say, and Juliette pulls back. Her face goes long in surprise. "And when you hurt me, the pain I feel is a thousandfold to what you think you feel, because I love you. Because I'm afraid I will always love you. And . . ." I exhale, a small sense of relief washing over me as I say precisely what is on my mind. "And because I love you, I'm going to be a complete idiot, a total fool, and agree to see you. I'll talk to you."

"Thank you, Gracie."

"But David, listen to me." My posture is rigid, words sharp. "If your fucking wedding is back on, if you're back with Caroline, if you've so much as gone out for friendly *coffee* with Caroline between now and whenever we're to see each other, don't bother. You move on, you let me fall out of love with you, and don't you *ever* call me again. Got that?"

"Got it."

"We'll be through forever."

241

"How's Thanksgiving sound?" he asks, and I look to Juliette and shrug. It's all I can do in response to her expression of sheer bafflement.

———

"I'm in shock!" Juliette says, stalking across the bathroom, waving her toothbrush in the air. "I'm in shock over so many things!"

"I know, Jules." I dry my freshly washed face. "I said I'd stand my ground, but then I buckle, fall for his charms."

"Not just that, but you spoke your mind. *How* you spoke your mind!" She plunks down on the closed toilet seat. She's wearing her men's tighty-whities and a shrunk-in-the-dryer Lakers tank, and her hair's done up in a high-set bun. She looks as if she could be the female partner if *Risky Business* had a duet scene. "You said the F word. Go Gracie!"

"I let it slip now and then, Jules." I laugh at her petty observation.

"I think you handled the whole thing with great aplomb." She rapidly cleans her teeth.

I run a brush through my hair a few times before pushing it back with an elastic headband. "I doubt using the F word is acting with aplomb."

"Well, whatever you want to call it." She spits into the sink. "You did your best. Don't you think?"

"I guess." I've been so high on emotions since the call, I haven't had time to really process it all in the last hour that Juliette and I have been rehashing the whole conversation. I sit on the edge of the tub. "You think I'm stupid for agreeing to see him? Again?"

"Who cares what I think? You have to do what's best for you, Gracie."

"Still, what do you think? *Surely* you have an opinion. Your eyes nearly bugged out when I said I'd see him again."

"I think"—she finishes rinsing her mouth—"that you did a damn fine job of dealing with an unexpected phone call." I do think I've scored points for acting so composed under pressure. She drapes the hand towel around her neck and says, "I think you followed your heart."

"I did. I want to see him. I want to talk. Either to put things to rest for good, without him having this big secret, this wedding, this other woman, or to see if there's something there for us."

"You think there is?" she asks in a soft and genuine tone. "Think there could be something?"

"I think there's always *been* something, Jules." I look across the room, a contemplative peace making my nerves finally calm, my lids growing heavy with sleep. "And I don't think that's just me fantasizing. David and I share something special. He was my first love. My *only* love. I'm glad I took the call. I'm glad we're seeing each other."

"And you're glad he and his fiancée broke up?"

"Yes," I say. "I am."

"I'm happy for you, Gracie." Juliette follows me to my bedroom. "I'm proud of you. I'm glad you're a step closer to getting what you want, whatever that may be." She gives my cheek a big kiss. "But if he breaks your heart again . . ." She clenches her jaw.

"I know."

Juliette turns out the lights and tells me that she wishes me a great day at work tomorrow if we don't happen to see each other in the morning. She's going to sleep in and wait until it gets warmer before she does her Monday lawn mowing, a job that she's been very appreciative of recently.

Her tutoring search has been fruitless, and the position at Keating's didn't pan out, which Juliette had predicted, since the store was no longer looking for help. She seemed all right with it, pleased she had at least applied.

Just before she shuts my door, she blows me a kiss good night and tells me to get my beauty sleep—to give my thoughts about tonight a rest.

"I love you, Jules," I call out just before she closes my door. "Thanks for being supportive."

"Right back at ya."

Left in the darkness, with mental and emotional exhaustion quickly beckoning me to sleep, I think on Juliette's words.

Am I a step closer to getting what I want? I am both thrilled and angry over David's contacting me again. I'm thrilled that that door between us has only been closed, not locked for good. We may or may not have a chance at love together, but at least we're talking. There's still hope; David's still someone relevant in my life.

I'm angry because this was never how it was supposed to be. We weren't supposed to break up in the first place. We weren't supposed to see each other in an on-again, off-again fashion, and never when he was engaged to be married! He wasn't supposed to call me back. This wasn't how things were supposed to wind up. And now he's got a broken engagement on his hands, now he wants to see me, now he wants to talk.

I am left with mixed feelings, frustration, and I fall asleep thinking, *Is this even what I want after all? Do I want David? At all costs?* I don't know, but I'm determined to find an answer.

21

Juliette

My sailboat sketch was all wrong yesterday, the sails not very sail-like, the scale and depth not all that realistic. Today, though, the creative muse seems to be doing exactly what she's supposed to. My sketch looks just like its real-life model in the harbor, although the pluming sails are imagined. Its deck is long and wooden. The scale is accurately drawn in relation to the sea of neighboring boats, as are its sails and the detailed lines and curves of the bow.

I've been coming out here daily for the past week, sketching mostly, not too much poetry lately. It's that time of year again, the holidays.

That time when stores haul out their Christmas trees or decorate their palm trees (although before Thanksgiving seems sacrilegious). The time when streetlamps and theaters don tinsel, coffee shops are filled with the aroma of pumpkin spice, and stores fill with customers who leave in droves carrying seasonally appropriate bags in red and green, gold and silver. That time when families come together, when you take the time to remember what you're grateful for, whom you're grateful for. That time when you remember the ones who are no longer with you to celebrate in person, yet who are always there with you in spirit.

Melancholy has struck me this season, mostly because this will be the first Thanksgiving that Mimi will not be with us celebrating. She won't be able to make her famous stuffing, nor will she be able to find some quirky excuse to give Gracie and me a Thanksgiving present. Christmas and birthday gifts we understood. Easter Mimi defended, in the name of the candy-delivering bunny. Halloween baskets were what Mimi called an open invitation to an extra little something-something for the holiday. (Homemade doughnuts or a My Little Pony tucked into the basket when we were kids, gift cards when we got older.)

Thanksgiving gifts, on the other hand, we never understood. But she enjoyed the gift giving, and we had come to look forward to it. It was one of the many things that were uniquely Mimi. It is one of the many things that I will miss this time of year and the years to come.

Soon enough it will also be the first Christmas that we will spend without Mimi. It's just around the corner, and before Gracie or I know it, the second-to-last letter will be opened. Another season will have come and gone.

They say the first year is the hardest when grieving the loss of a loved one. It's not just the raw recency of the loss that makes even the simplest or most trite of things seem intense, palpable. It's experiencing those firsts. It's that first spring without her, that first Fourth of July fireworks show, that massive shopping trip to Trader Joe's for the Thanksgiving meal, that first leap from one year to the next, the first of everything in one lonely year.

Drawing and escaping to the shore help me cope with the loss and the pain that come this year with the holidays. They help me put things in perspective, too. I've made Santa Barbara home again, I've made some friends, found some work, grown closer to Gracie. Watching Gracie go through whatever is developing with David gets me to thinking about life and what I want out of it. Gracie's always known what she's wanted: a career in law, a home in Santa Barbara, to marry David. Though it's an obscure and messy path she's blazing, at least she's got a path. At least she's working on it.

I, however, don't really know where it is I am going or what it is I should do. I got so accustomed to leaning on the crutch of my misdemeanor that I didn't really give myself a chance to consider the options. New York City was great, and being broke and struggling to overcome employment challenges kept me preoccupied, albeit disenchanted. I still only just graduated from college last year. I wasn't supposed to really have things figured out, anyhow.

As I consider the possibility of Gracie's getting back together with David (anything seems possible), and as we near the end of the year, I wonder if where I am actually meant to be is here in Santa Barbara.

Unsettling questions rain down hard. What will happen when Gracie settles down, with David or whomever? What will happen to Mimi's home when the challenge is over? Will Gracie stay here? Will I? Will we, together? And if so, for how long? Is that even what I want, to stay here? I want to be here for Gracie, and I enjoy our arrangement. Who would have thought it'd work out so well, even with the occasional disagreements? But eventually we will both move on—Gracie will do her thing, and I will do mine, whatever it may be.

I encourage Gracie to put herself above David's needs, to look out for herself, to do what is best for her. Yet I neglect to take my own advice. I'm twenty-three years old, and I don't know what I want. Part of me acknowledges that that's okay. I'm young, and the world is wide, made even wider by the revelation that my brush with the law isn't as bad as I thought. I don't *have* to know what I want or know who I am just yet. I have room to grow.

Another part of me, however, knows that if I continue to sit and wait for something to happen, eventually reality will hit, just as it did when I tried to get a job I really wanted senior year but ended up blowing it thanks to my dirty drug habit. The same reality that hit when I graduated and realized the real world was a bit harsher than expected. I will find myself wondering where the time went, wondering if I'm being the best I can be. Mimi always told me to grab my star and shine. I know there is room to grow, opportunities to seize, but I've been treading, head barely above water. I'm not shining.

Suddenly incensed at my feeling of inadequacy, yet not feeling sorry for myself or rooting about in the sand here for excuses, I consider my sketch complete and tuck my journal into my bag.

Gracie's right. Mimi's right. Hell, even Brea's right. Yesterday Brea asked if I'd gone into Anthropologie and talked to the manager as I'd been thinking of doing. I told her, bashfully, that I was still planning on it but hadn't gotten around to it yet. It was a half-truth. I could have gotten around to it, but I was nervous. I remember all too clearly what happened the first and last time I applied for a job there. I don't want to hit another wall of rejection.

Brea said, "You don't get it if you don't ask." Plain and simple. It was just like the star and the chance to shine that Mimi, and Gracie, talked about.

I text Gracie that I'm on my way home and that I can pick up something for dinner if she likes. Then I pack my things, and, noticing that it's not quite six yet, I make one more stop along the way.

———

"This was a sweet idea," Gracie says, leading the way two steps ahead of me over the kempt lawn of Meadows Memorial on a cool, crisp late-Thanksgiving morning. "You're so creative. The oranges and now this."

"This is one straight out of Mimi's book," I say. "Gifts for Thanksgiving." This gets a small laugh out of Gracie.

We stop at Mimi's headstone and admire the cornucopia of autumn flowers laid down by our parents. Our oranges still tucked in my bag for later, I bring out my Thanksgiving gift for Mimi. It's the sketch of the sailboat I finished the other day, framed and signed, "With love for Mimi, XO Juliette." I place it next to Mom and Dad's gift.

"Happy Thanksgiving, Mimi," Gracie says. She sets down a half-finished bottle of My Sin perfume, a gift from Mom from a vacation to Paris. Mimi cherished that perfume, used it sparingly for years. Mom always told her there was no point in keeping something quite literally bottled up "for a special occasion," as Mimi would insist. Mom would say that the material possessions we covet would become of no use to us when we passed from this world to the next. "Enjoy them now, because tomorrow it might not matter," I can hear Mom say in that salient way of hers, so much like Gracie.

"That's a sweet and creative idea," I tell my sister, pointing at the bottle.

"She loved it," Gracie says, nostalgic. "I'm sure she'd be wearing it today if she were here." She dabs at the corner of her eye with her pinkie. "Now she can." She takes one more item from her purse.

"What's that?" I ask.

"One of the last roses from the garden. From her favorite bush."

"The Juliet garden rose." It was only the most beautiful of roses in the entire garden—lush, eternally folding petals in the creamiest of peach blush.

Gracie sets the rose on top of the headstone, her fingers gliding gingerly over the frilly folds of the unique petals. "We wanted to bring Thanksgiving to you, Mimi." She takes her orange from me and places it alongside the rose.

"Happy Thanksgiving," I say, following suit with my orange.

"Should we?" Gracie's brows are raised.

"You start."

She clears her throat, then proceeds with the Bennett family Thanksgiving tradition. "What am I thankful for this year?" She pulls her waist-length black wool coat tighter to fight the cold. "I'm thankful for second chances. Juliette's idea to give *you* gifts for Thanksgiving this year, to carry on your funny tradition. You can't be with us at the table this year, but thanks to Juliette's ingenuity, this is kind of a second chance for us to carry on the tradition. Also!" She pulls her coat tighter as the winds kick up. "Second chances with David. I know, Mimi. I know."

Gracie is talking as if Mimi is right here in front of us, as much a part of the conversation as she once was. Gracie is talking with such ease, such candor. It's comforting.

"You had your doubts about David," she says. "Well, who doesn't?" She casts a glance my way. "I don't know what will come of tomorrow, but it's a second chance of sorts. I'm nervous, but I'm excited."

I rub Gracie's back. I'm glad she's happy, that she's staying positive. She's been sitting on this second chance with David for a month. Hell, far longer than that, if we really get down to it. Tomorrow they'll finally see each other for the first time post-engagement. I have no idea what will come of it, and neither does Gracie. Thank goodness there will be pie and wine and all the trappings of the holiday this afternoon to distract and keep us from bursting from suspense.

"And I'm—" I begin, but Gracie cuts me off, saying she's not yet finished. She says this in a whining tone just as she used to when, as a kid, I'd try to cut in the middle of her story or jump to the punch line of her joke.

"All right." I laugh. "Floor's still yours."

"And I'm grateful for *another* second chance." Gracie grabs my hand. "For a second chance with Juliette." She looks to me. "This year has been really rough, but it's also been really great. I love you, Jules."

Now the tears are going to spill. I thought I could make it through our visit to Mimi today without a single tear. I was going to be brave. After all, I have some great news to share.

"I love you, too," I say to Gracie with a stiff upper lip. We embrace, and I know that if Mimi were here right now, she wouldn't only be on the verge of tears, too. She'd also be beaming, ear to ear. Then again, I'm pretty sure she is right now anyway.

"Okay, okay." I wave at my flushed face. "My turn. You may be the older sister, but I've always been the attention whore." I nudge Gracie in her side. "This year I'm grateful for challenge and encouragement," I say. "Without them I don't know where I'd be right now. I'm grateful that you proposed your crazy scheme, Mimi, and I'm grateful for your encouragement through your letters, your spirit." Gracie nods in agreement. "I'm grateful for the challenge that life's given me. Last year I got into some pretty big trouble. The challenges to overcome it gave Gracie and me a chance to bond. Not exactly the *best* way to bond. But she was there for me and has helped me, and she challenges me to be the best I can be. She encourages me."

"Ah, Jules."

"And I've got some good news to go with that!" I root in my bag some. "You can't keep this gift, Mimi, but I can show you."

Gracie looks on in curiosity as I pull out a piece of cream paper. "Ta-da!" I cry joyfully. "It's an application. For Anthropologie. I'm going to fill it out. You always said to find your star and shine, and . . ." I look fondly at the application I'm so proud to have solicited, not without a fight. "I'm trying to figure out what I want and go after it. May sound stupid, this job, but—"

"That's awesome, Jules." Gracie looks at the application. "It's not stupid. If this is really something you want to do, then go for it."

"I think so. I mean, you never know until you're actually doing it, but yeah."

"That's great. So they're hiring?"

"No," I say with a chuckle. "But I didn't let that stop me. I asked for their manager and kind of begged for an application."

"Well, even if they're not hiring, companies usually always accept applications. I'm sure as soon as something opens up, you'll get the job.

You're just the girl. That store is totally your fashion, and you'd be so good with helping people pair things, put together outfits . . ."

"Maybe," I say in an uncertain way.

"Absolutely! No maybe about it. You have this, Jules. That's the perfect place for you."

"I'm not applying for a sales position." I can't hide my growing smile. This news will surely take her by surprise. "I'm applying for a design spot. Like the window displays, the floor displays."

Gracie's got a flabbergasted look about her—eyes wide, mouth open, lips drawn up at one side in a proud, intrigued smile.

"That's why it was kind of tough to get an application out of them. They have a special program for those spots, and they usually don't hire from outside for it, and . . ." I wave my hands excitedly. "Anyway, I'm not going to let that stop me. I've been stopped before." Gracie raises a brow. "I got an application, period," I carry on, "and I'm filling it out! I'm going to try my hardest for the job."

Gracie smiles. "That's awesome. How did you find out about this?"

"Uhhh, a girl I knew in New York did it." I turn toward Mimi.

"Have you tried for it before? In New York? You said you were stopped before—"

I tuck the application away and interrupt Gracie. "You know, I've always admired Anthropologie's displays and just thought, *That's the coolest job ever!*"

Gracie just looks at me.

"Creative . . . fun . . ." I flash Gracie a bright smile, not really wanting to talk any more about it, not wanting to jinx my chances.

"Yeah . . . ," she says in a drawn-out, not-so-sure kind of way.

"And I mean, the store discount I'm sure they give to employees can't hurt!"

"Yeah." She gives me a small squeeze. "Well, I'm proud of you. And it's something you want to do? Something you're really interested in?"

"I think so. Give it a try, at least." I shrug. "You never really know until you try, right?"

"Well, happy Thanksgiving, Mimi, for sure!" Gracie says. She wraps her arms around her waist, pulling her coat tight. She bounces up and down on the tips of her toes. "So much to be grateful for. The year may have started off crappy, but it's getting better!"

"Yeah." I wrap an arm around Gracie and make fast rubbing motions to try to warm her. "Let's head to Mom and Dad's. It's getting cold out here, and I'm sure the turkey is, too."

I turn to Mimi's headstone, eye the oranges, the cornucopia, the bottle of perfume, the sailboat sketch. "Happy Thanksgiving, Mimi."

———

"Oh. My. God. Jules!" Gracie gasps as she sets into the back of the Citroën a case of cabernet sauvignon Mom had on reserve at Bell Court Wine Company, a Bennett holiday routine. "What are all these?"

"What are all what?" I bounce gaily to her side of the car. It's funny how only earlier this week I was melancholy about the holidays, and now I'm feeling electrified. I'm finding my star, one small step at a time. I got to spend some of the holiday with Mimi after all, I'm picking up cases of holiday wine with my big sister, loading them into my car—the coolest vintage ride in town—and we're on our way to celebrate a day of feasting and gratitude with our parents, toasting and eating until our pants pop. Oh, and I gathered the nerve to pick up a job application. Does it get better than that?

"These—these—*tickets*? Parking tickets!" Gracie is hollering.

"Oh, those." I dismiss them with a lazy wave of my hand. Nothing's going to get me down today. "I've been meaning to pay those. Had to wait for that extra cash. They're so stupid. I mean, like thirty or forty bucks or something. What's the point? And parking around here is a *menace*. I'm sure *everyone* gets tickets!"

"Jules." Gracie shoves aside the wine and plucks up the handful of tickets. She counts them out loud. "*Three!* Please tell me you've paid *some* of these."

"No," I say in an offhanded kind of way. I don't see the big deal. Seriously. If we're going to talk rap sheets, I've done *far* worse than this. Gracie knows that. "I've paid, like, two of them, but that was a long time ago. These are new."

"You've gotten *more* than these?"

"Yeah."

"Jules, you can't collect these like you do stamps or notches on a dashboard!"

"Ha!" I point at her as I walk around to the other side of the car carrying the half case of Riesling. "You're funny, Gracie. Witty. I'll let the last one slide." I wink. "Haven't gotten lucky in weeks, so it's not *completely* applicable."

"Jules, this isn't funny."

"Lighten up, hon. I'll take care of them. I honestly just forgot about them. I have the cash. I'll pay."

She sighs dramatically, hands tossed up in the air. "You can get into trouble if you collect these. If you leave them unpaid."

"Wait. Not like permanent record or something? You've got to be kidding me." When will I catch a break?

"I don't know exactly. But you don't ignore these types of things. You'll get fined fees!"

"Tickets for tickets?" I laugh at the absurdity.

"Jules. I'm serious. Pay them. Don't make a habit of this."

"I know," I say honestly. "I know I need to pay them. I don't want to get into any more trouble with the law. I really just forgot they were there. Got used to tossing them back there." I chuckle. "Honest."

Gracie looks utterly unamused. "The backseat of your car is hardly the best place to put things that need immediate attention. You don't have bills back here, do you?"

I secure the wine, then take my seat behind the wheel. "Come on, Gracie. We're going to be late."

"Wouldn't want to be late, now would we?" Her sarcasm is not lost on me.

"Stop the teasing." I start the car, and Gracie finally gets in, though she won't relent. She taps the tickets into a neat little pile on the dashboard.

"We're writing checks for these right away," she instructs. "Putting them in the mail today."

"Post doesn't work today."

"Doesn't matter. This should have been done a long time ago."

"I love ya, Gracie." I flash her a smile as I crane my neck to look backward as I reverse the car. "You need to take a chill pill."

"And you need to take a responsibility pill. Pay your parking tickets."

"Maybe someone'll get laid tomorrow." I wiggle my brows.

"Not funny. Don't tease about that."

"Okay. Okay." I hang a quick left. "Sorry."

"How does anyone get this many parking tickets anyway?" Her voice is raised an extra two octaves, she's still so stunned.

I laugh in response.

"You're a handful, Juliette. A handful." She puts the tickets in her purse. "Only you."

"You know you love me."

———

The following morning, the refrigerator packed with Thanksgiving leftovers we happily took from Mom, my belly still full from one too many helpings of mashed potatoes and gravy, I brew a pot of coffee and consider it breakfast. I fill the Minnie Mouse mug Mimi and Grandpa bought for me at Disneyland when I was young—"Juliette's special hot cocoa mug," Mimi called it—and retire to the front porch.

Though the porch wraps around the front of the house and on to about a third of one side, making a very expansive and welcoming spot to relax, it has never gotten near the visits the backyard and garden have.

As I blow on my coffee, seated on the porch steps, I survey the front yard. The lawn is green, the fruitless plum tree off to the right still clinging to its aubergine-colored leaves. The variety of flowering bushes that line the entire porch are more green than colorful, and the geraniums are still managing to hang on. The wooden bird feeder situated near the shrubbery, ivy vines covering the three legs of its stand, has two happy, chirping diners. The palm trees—two quite large, one rather stunted—stand at the far left of the property. They provide the requisite coastal touch to any Santa Barbara home.

I bring my mug to my lips and take a sip. It's thick, black, rich. Just the way I grew to like it, since that's how Dad brewed it, how I came to know my first drink of coffee. I pull my bare legs up under my baggy sweatshirt. I wrap my fingers around the hot mug and close my eyes. It's the perfect start to a day off. The only sound I can hear is the birds chirping. Not a single hum of a lawn mower, *tick-tick-tiiiick* of a sprinkler, mail lady making her rounds, clicking the mailboxes open and closed, not even the sound of a single passing or distant car.

The garden is tranquil, magical. Below the aromatic orange tree is always a favorite place to sit. Rarely do you catch much noise in the garden, whereas in the front yard you usually can't avoid the occasional car driving by, the passing neighbors walking dogs, pushing strollers. But today it's as if the world has stopped, as if time has stood still. It's lovely.

"Morning." Gracie breaks the silence and joins me on the porch, a mug of coffee in her hand. Her hair is mussed, flyaways all over the place, some of the shorter layered pieces that were pushed behind her ears falling free as she bends down to take a seat next to me. She's dressed in a pair of plaid pajama bottoms and a long-sleeve tee. Her feet, like mine, are bare and sporting red toenail polish.

"Two sisters, straight out of bed, loungin' on the porch," Gracie says with a laugh, reading my mind. She stretches her long legs forward. "Thanks for brewing." She holds up her mug—her childhood hot cocoa mug with Daisy Duck on it.

"Think it's going to be a pretty day," I say as I look up into the blue-grey sky—overcast, as almost all mornings are here. "Weathermen say so, at least."

I shake open a piece of the day's *New York Times*, conveniently tossed on the front porch, a daily treat. I take another sip of coffee.

"Business? Arts?" Gracie says. "What are you going to read?"

"I'm taking the front page. You want Business or Arts?"

"I'll take Arts to start."

I hand her a portion of the newspaper and take another drink when she says, "Can you believe Dad's talking early retirement?"

"It's crazy, right?" I say in a high voice, recalling how surprised I was by Dad's news yesterday.

"Did not expect that to come up at the Thanksgiving table." Gracie meticulously folds the paper to the particular article she wants to read.

We used to share the newspaper just like this, swapping sections over breakfast. Gracie always strove to keep the paper in some sort of order, making clean folds as she progressed with her reading. Part of the appeal of reading the *Times* was that I could, unlike with a book, just flip it open, lazily page about, crinkle and wrinkle as I got my fill of the goings-on of the world. Sometimes Gracie would smooth out the wrinkled pages when it was time to swap, muttering that I wasn't the only one reading the paper. Over time she'd ignore the wrinkles or smooth them out a few times and leave it at that, not saying anything. I got better with my lazy form of reading. Gracie was right, after all: we were sharing the paper. This small memory, these habits that were formed ages ago, put on pause for years, have returned, and in full force, as if we never stopped. It makes me feel good, fills me with the comforting sense of belonging and being home.

"I didn't expect retirement talk to come up for years!" she adds robustly.

"Guess they're not as young as we think they are."

"It's early retirement. And he is only *talking* about it—considering it—I guess."

"It is weird to think about." I ruminate on the prospect of my father's no longer working. He's been an architect at the same local firm since before I was born. Since before Gracie was born. It seems like such a final step, retirement. Like the mark of an ending and a beginning, a milestone you meet with nothing expected to follow. I furrow my brow. *God,* I think, *it's like the beginning of the end.* I say this to Gracie, and she just erupts into laughter.

"You're ridiculous, Jules. Dad's in his fifties. I'd *hardly* say it's the end."

"I know, but. *Retirement?* It's so . . . permanent."

"Not necessarily." She sets aside her piece of the newspaper and enjoys her coffee some before saying, "Besides, he said he's only considering it. He wouldn't retire for a few years, if he does decide to early."

"True."

"And even then he could do contract work or consulting or who knows what." She takes one more sip before setting her mug on the step below and reopening her paper. "I couldn't picture Dad as the type to retire early, completely step out of the game, and, what? Join Mom at home?"

"I guess."

"You know if he did that he'd totally try to jump in on her work." She giggles. "He'd probably get all flowcharts and business model and whatnot on her."

I laugh at the image of my dad, always busy with some project from work sprawled out in the home office, getting the itch to work as soon as he retired early. He might take that big cruise he's been talking about, where you cruise for a month or something when the ships are preparing for the season, making the lengthy trip from a Nassau home port to Europe. Then after that he might do a few handy jobs around the house, like replacing the rain gutters or redoing the downstairs bath, which he and Mom have talked about for years. Then he'd find some way to dive back into work. Mom's stationery design work would eventually fall victim to micromanagement, new business strategies, emerging markets, God knows what.

"You're probably right," I say. "He'll do some more thinking about it, and I bet he won't."

"Or he'll contract."

"Maybe." I exchange the front page for Op-Ed.

"You don't think they'll move, do you?" she asks.

I laugh in disbelief. "What? Move?"

The picturesque home in the ritzy Lower Riviera neighborhood is the only home the Bennett clan has known. It's gorgeous, it's prime real estate, it's *home*. For my parents to move would be as unheard-of as it would be for Gracie and me to agree to put Mimi's place up for sale without giving it our best shot at living together to keep it in the family.

"There is no way they'd move," I say, confident. "They've been here forever."

"Exactly why they may want to move. Do you think they'll want a change when they retire?"

"Gracie." I abandon my paper and coffee and turn toward her, one leg pulling free from the warmth of my sweatshirt. "What's with the concern? What's going on?"

"I just don't want them to move. I don't want . . . change." She makes a small shrug with one shoulder. "I like having them practically down the street. I liked having Mimi down the street, too. I like having you here. You know me, Jules. I'm a homebody, and I like having everyone in one place."

"I know. But Gracie, you can't expect everyone you love to live within one square mile of you for the rest of your life." I raise my brows in an expectant way and try to meet her eyes. Her gaze is cast downward at her coffee mug.

"I know." Her voice is small.

"For now, at least, you have everyone here."

"Physical distance can mess things up, Jules. When you went off to New York, eventually we barely talked. We never saw each other. And David—him being up north certainly never helped our relationship. It just sucks."

"Okay." I give her thigh a little shake. "Stop borrowing trouble. I'm not in New York anymore. Mom and Dad are still here. None of us is going anywhere."

"Not yet."

"Eventually someone might move, and that's life. You can't control that, Gracie," I say. She nods. "If I start to think about 'what if' too much, I get down."

"Yeah . . ."

"Let's just enjoy the here, the now. It's pretty good, you know?"

"It is." She forces a smile, a weak one, but a smile nonetheless.

"And as for David?" I sigh. "There was more than distance to blame for why things ended up the way they did. I mean, I'm sure long-distance relationships are hard and all, but—"

"I don't want to talk about him."

"All right." I nod understandingly. "If it makes you feel any better, I think about what will happen next spring a lot. I worry a little, I guess you could call it, about what's next."

"You do?"

"Yeah. I mean, I suppose we can just go on living here in the house. I haven't really given much thought to what we do *after* spring. I do think about the fact that something has to be decided."

"Stay here or go back? To New York?"

"Maybe. I don't know. It's a possibility. We'll just have to see." I am about to say that I want to live where I feel needed, where I feel at home, where I can try to find my star and shine. Who knows what the future holds? We can't predict it, and while it's daunting from time to time, the uncertainty and array of possibilities can be pretty exhilarating.

Before I can say anything else, Gracie says, "I like living with you, Juliette. It's nice having you around." She then claps her hands, stands, and says sprightly, "My nerves are shot over today. I think that's why I'm all in a worrywart mode."

"What time are you meeting?"

"Two."

"You going for lunch?"

She shakes her head. "He offered, but I'd rather not talk in a public place like that, while eating. I want to have a serious and open talk and not be distracted."

"Where are you meeting?" I shuffle the newspaper pieces into one pile.

"Hendry's." She glances at her watch. "I have some work I thought I could do before then. To keep my mind occupied."

"Sure."

"I want to go for a ride, too. Clear my head. Relax. You want to join?"

I'm enjoying the lazy morning. Aside from filling out the job application and doing the *Times* crossword, I was looking forward to a wide-open day with absolutely no plans. But Gracie's face is pleading. Her rosebud lips are slightly parted, a faint smile of positive anticipation on them, head cocked to the side, eyes opened a bit wider as she awaits my answer.

Knowing she would appreciate the company (and I the bike ride after all that pie I ate yesterday), I leap up and tell her I'll be ready to go just as soon as I get changed.

Shortly before two o'clock, Gracie knocks on my bedroom door. I roll from my prone position on my bed and prop myself up on an elbow, head in hand.

"Well, this is it," she says. Her voice is tinted with timidity and a courage that, I can see by the way one fist is balled and one hand is loosely on her stomach, fingers spread, is a forced kind of courage. The kind any woman would summon as she prepared to face the man she loved, not knowing if this would be the last time she would ever see him again.

"How do I look?" She holds out her arms, gestures to her outfit. This afternoon Gracie is going as no one other than Gracie. She's not dressed to kill, nor is she dressed down so casually you might think she was heading to a picnic on the beach. She's just Gracie, dressed in her modest pair of fitted black slacks and a cashmere, baby blue, short-sleeve sweater, wearing black ballet flats.

"Beautiful," I say, giving her a thumbs-up.

"I don't know when I'll be home." She begins to twiddle her fingers nervously.

"You take as much time as you need." I sit up. "And remember, if you need anything, you *call* me. Period. No matter what."

"Thanks."

"I mean it. No matter what. Advice. Encouragement. A slap in the face. A slap in *his* face."

She smiles for the first time, smooths her hands across her sweater. "Wish me luck."

"You don't need luck." I make a *psh* sound. "But good luck anyhow." I hold my arms open and give her an encouraging embrace. "You can do this, Gracie. Follow your heart." I kiss the side of her head, then look her in the eyes. "But take it from me, sometimes you *also* need to listen to your head." I tap her forehead, and she laughs.

"Speaking of which, I wrote a check for those parking tickets. Can you mail them?"

I roll my eyes. Leave it to my sister to pull the responsibility card at a time like this. Her mind should be nowhere near such trifles.

"Yes, yes," I say, rushing her out the door. "And I'll pay you back. You're not paying my tickets."

"I just wanted them taken care of ASAP."

"You've got other biz to attend to, my dear. Scoot-scoot."

"All right," she says after she's gathered her purse and jacket. "Here goes nothing."

"Or everything," I say. "You've got it. Remember: follow your heart. *Your* heart, *your* terms."

22

Gracie

The moment of truth has arrived, I tell myself as I pull into a parking space. The lot is wide open, save for David's BMW. I park, leaving three spaces between us—a symbolic gesture to remind myself I am in control of this situation. I am not going to be that girl who in a flurry pulls into the parking spot right next to the man she loves and runs out of her car and into his arms, pleading, *Choose me! Love me!*

I give myself a quick once-over in my rearview mirror. I check the backings of my silver post earrings, adjust my watch, make sure my keys are in my purse. I am both stalling and making sure I touch all prep bases.

When I look at myself in the mirror once more, I'm suddenly awash with concern that I'm dressed all wrong. We're meeting at the beach, not at a romantic French bistro. I grumble under my breath and brush away the lint on my dark pants.

Seeing David slowly approach my car out of the corner of my eye causes me to disregard my last-minute worries. *I look fine,* I try to convince myself. I take a deep breath, step out of the car, and think, *There's no going back. This is it.*

David is a sight for sore eyes. He's wearing slacks; I try not to grin at the similarities in our attire, at our mutual misunderstanding of what is best to wear for a meeting at the beach. I'm in my ballet flats; he's in his leather loafers. It's uncanny, really.

But that cable-knit sweater of his, the same navy-and-cream turtleneck he wore when I saw him last, is perfect for any occasion, the way it makes his blue eyes shine. It fits his form—wide shoulders, slim torso, thick chest—perfectly, hugging and hanging comfortably in all the right places. His dark hair is slicked back save for a few stray strands the ocean breeze has caught. There's no other way to sum it up: David Nichol is classically handsome.

And the way he walks over to me. Both hands in his pockets, his gait—a mixture of easy saunter and confident strut—is arresting. That familiar shaky sensation hits my knees.

David removes a hand from his pocket as he nears. His head tilts to the side and one corner of his mouth turns up. I have to force myself to take in another breath, exhale . . . breathe.

Before he can have the first word, I say, "David. It's good to see you again." I keep my greeting platonic, neutral.

I give myself one point for the absence of a quiver in my voice. My goal for the afternoon is ten points. If I can give myself ten points, I will walk away the victor. It sounds silly, childish even, but the heroine in my latest romance novel did this when she had to encounter "the one who got away." Who says what works in fiction can't work in real life? It's worth a try at least.

I remind myself that I should be filled with confidence I'll make it through. Not even one minute into our meeting and I've already earned three points—one for the parking job, another for the first word, and now a strong voice.

You can do this, I think as David nears. We are now only inches apart, and my heart is beating so hard, so fast. *You can do this.*

David's arms open wide, a smile coats his thin lips, and we embrace. I take the moment to breathe in his warm and familiar scent: Calvin Klein's Obsession. It's the only cologne I've ever known David to wear. Its notes of clove and mandarin, a hint of nutmeg, send me into a euphoric journey down memory lane—all the nights he held me in his arms in bed, when he embraced me just like this to say hello, to say good-bye, and just because. I don't want to let go, but breaking from the hug first will earn me point number four.

Point earned. I ask how his Thanksgiving went.

"Oh, you know the Nichols." He slips one hand back to his pocket and rests the other on the small of my back as we walk away from the parking lot. His touch sends tingles up my spine. Good tingles, familiar tingles. "Father and his incessant talk of yachts and regattas, cups and all that."

"How could I forget?" I gesture to the beach, ask if he wants to take a stroll.

"Read my mind."

"How's your mother?" I ease into comfortable conversation. David's hand is still on my back, but the tingles are thankfully subsiding as we continue our gentle banter.

"I'm afraid she got a little too sauced on the sherry last night." He flashes me his charming grin.

"Oh no!" I laugh, recalling that Mrs. Nichol has a habit of getting a bit loose in the mouth when she hits the celebratory beverages. One Christmas she was in such a jovial brandy-induced mood she told me about Mr. Wuggles, the stuffed toy turtle David slept with until he left for college. While she thought the attachment to the toy was adorable (evidently the turtle was still on a bookshelf in his bedroom, and I did eventually coax David into showing it to me), David did not. Mr. Nichol just groused about how his wife needed to stop embarrassing herself, to say nothing of her son.

"Oh yes. All in all, it was a perfect evening. Mary brought a boyfriend for the holidays," he says of his little sister. "Mom thought he was the best thing since sliced bread. Marcos is half-Portuguese, so . . ."

"Ah, of course." Mrs. Nichol is herself half-Portuguese. "I bet she loved that."

"So much so, she decided to dance the fandango with him. Turned on the music and just danced, right in the middle of the family room."

"That's your mother," I say with a laugh and shake of the head.

"You should have seen Marcos's face. Poor guy. He did loosen up. Mary was mortified."

"I bet."

"He seems like a good guy. Makes my sister happy." His eyes lock with mine for a brief moment when he says this.

"That's nice," I murmur.

"How about you?" He clears his throat. "Bennett Thanksgiving the usual festival of fun it always is?"

"Far from a dancing festival. Just the four of us this year. Small but nice."

"I'm sorry. It's the first Thanksgiving without Mimi."

"Yeah." I stop to take off my shoes, and David does the same. "It was nice, though. Easygoing. What the family needed, I think." The cool, soft, lightly damp sand feels good between my toes.

We approach the shore but keep a good twenty feet or so from where the water rushes upon the sand. Hendry's Beach is empty, a rarity for this wide, sandy stretch. Though not a touristy spot, it is one of the most family friendly in town and is often the ideal place for a picnic, kite flying, light bodysurfing, or sunbathing. I suppose the Black Friday chaos or the exhaustion of yesterday's holiday can be to blame for its unexpected emptiness.

David and I continue our light conversation, catch up about family, work. I give myself one point for beginning our reunion with a friendly chat and carrying on with it for thirty minutes. I do not want to be that girl who blurts out a million and one questions and accusations and pleads about our relationship straightaway.

When David asks if I am seeing anyone, a question I think comes a little out of left field, I give myself another point for treating the question casually—a simple one-armed shrug, a slightly flirtatious grin, and a shake of the head.

A point awarded for putting my hands behind me when David makes a motion to hold my hand. And another point for being brazen, interrupting his talking about one of his high-stress cases with the question, "So why'd you want to see me?" It is finally time to get to the crux of our meeting. Now that a reasonable time has passed, I am determined to be the one to initiate that conversation.

"You know I always love seeing you" is his sly (and wholly unexpected) response.

"No." I'm still brazen, and I award myself another point for it. "You're not getting off that easy, buddy." I tiptoe around jocularity. I may want to have the upper hand here, but I don't want to come off as a bitch or as if I'm eager to give him the third degree. I won't get anywhere with that. Neither David nor I would recognize me if I'd agreed to meet him today only to cut him down, grill him, or inflict some kind of vengeance. And then I'd lose all my cool and be no better off, no closer to answers and hope for closure (if that is what is to come of this meeting).

I stop, turn to face him, and take one of his hands in mine. "David, I will accept only honesty. You've hurt me. I'm not here to have myself get hurt again. So no more lies."

"I can do that." His eyes bore into mine; his hand grips mine tightly. "Caroline and I have called off the wedding."

"It's still off?"

"You told me not to come here if it were back on."

"Good."

"It was a lot of on-again, off-again."

"Why?"

"First, I think it's because everything happened so quickly." We begin walking. "We dated for not even five months before I proposed." He glances at me and says, "Way too fast."

I ask him why he rushed things.

"It seemed the thing to do. I don't know." He rubs a hand along the back of his neck. "I like the firm I'm working for, but I'm kind of gridlocked there. Dreaming of becoming partner is just that: a dream. It's such a big firm, and there's just no chance in hell, what with the top competition and so *much* of it . . ." He rubs his neck some more. "Caroline's an attorney. Met her at a birthday party for one of the big-shot partners at my firm. Her father's a big shot himself, has his own firm, in fact. They were longtime friends, he and my colleague, and . . . Anyway, that's how Caroline and I met. She works at her father's firm." He glances at me, checking to make sure I'm still following, still interested. I am. It's the first wave of honesty I've had in a long time with David. The topic isn't exactly my cup of tea, but the honesty is refreshing nonetheless.

"We started dating, things moved kind of fast. We had a connection that—" David stops midsentence. A sheepish expression overcomes him, and he wags his head.

"Anyway," he says, "things were fast, we move in together, she mentions I should try for a spot in her father's firm. Of course, I have to think about my career. If things with Caroline go sour, how is *that* going to work out with me at her father's firm? With me working alongside her?" I nod. "No way in hell. Too much of a risk. Plus, I have a good gig where I'm at. Yeah, room for growth isn't really prime right now, but it's good. Safe. I have some important cases." I nod again.

"Turns out Caroline's sister's husband, who's an attorney at their father's firm, was fast-tracked up the ladder as *soon* as they got engaged. Married two years and he's a full partner. Crazy."

"So . . ." My brow crinkles, and I look from David to the sand. Up until now I've been unable to keep my eyes off him—his handsome profile, strong jaw that's peppered with the early growth of a five o'clock shadow. When he reveals what sounds like *motive* behind an engagement . . . The bile begins to rise. I'm feeling light-headed.

"Caroline and I had danced around the marriage topic," he says. "Then we got to talking about my career, our future, how her father would certainly fast-track me. I mean, Gracie, they're loaded. They're connected. Her family's a legacy of high-powered attorneys, municipal court judges, and she's even got an uncle who is a member of the California State legislature." His tone is thick with enthusiasm. "The career opportunities would be unbelievable. The power, the wealth, the influence."

"Didn't know they taught corporatism in law school." I can't help myself. David's always had a knack for being a little full of himself. I chalked it up to confidence, but now that I'm hearing this, I almost don't recognize him.

"That's what I'm saying, Gracie." He stops, reaches for a hand, but I refuse. I keep them both firmly locked together behind me. His whole face, once lighted by the ecstatic talk of power, greed, and marrying up, is now soft. The David I know is back.

He reaches for my hands again, and this time I concede, but with caution.

"What *are* you saying exactly, David?"

"Back and forth Caroline and I went, arguing about getting engaged so soon. She'd accuse me of marrying her for a job with her father, I'd accuse her of wanting to get herself married off so she could get her share of the family wealth. Vacation home in Nantucket, a dowry, all sorts of craziness. We were convenient for each other, for each other's careers."

"I'm surprised you didn't pan out, then."

He sighs. "Eventually what attracted us to each other started to get so muddled by trying to make names for ourselves. We were so focused on building our careers. We'd fallen in love and then . . . became blinded."

There's a pause, and I nod slightly, hoping David will take the lead and continue.

"I don't know," he breathes out at last. "When I told Caroline you and I'd gotten together, that was the final straw." He gets a far-off look in his eye as he gazes out at the water. "It wouldn't have been a marriage of love anyhow."

"That's what marriage is," I say. "At least what I think it should be: for love."

"I thought I loved her." He rubs a thumb across my hand, squeezes it a little more tightly. "I've had some time to think about all this."

"And?"

"I haven't been able to get you out of my head."

Butterflies fill my stomach. I have to try with all my might to keep from smiling.

David squeezes my hand harder, locks his eyes onto mine. "I don't know if what we had in the past could ever be had again, Gracie. Or repaired, or whatever." He inhales deeply. "I don't really know if I'm ready to dive into something again after what's happened." I nod quickly, understandingly. "I just know that I was in love with you. That I did love you, Gracie. Maybe I still do. I don't know." He pauses.

"I'm really confused, Gracie. I wanted to see you to tell you the truth, to come clean. It's a fresh-start kind of thing." He squints. "You know?" He steps nearer, slipping his other hand around our clasped ones. "I don't know what I want or if I can even have whatever it is that I want. I just know that right now I'm happy to be with you. I'm happy to see you. To talk to you. Like the old days."

What David is telling me isn't what I expected, but then again, I honestly didn't know what to expect. I came here today with no real expectations, nothing other than wanting to make a step forward in the right direction, following the path that *I* want.

What the path is I'm not really sure. I've always thought I had a clear picture of what it is I want in life, a very clear picture with relatively defined goals and ways to go about achieving them. Bumps have happened along the way, but I find a way around them. This bump, though, I have no idea how to handle.

If I follow my head, I might tell David he should take more time thinking about what it is he wants. Because if I'm standing here before him, his engagement is broken off, and he knows that I have never stopped loving him, he admits he's loved me, then he could very well say that he wants me, that he chooses us. *I'm here!* That would be the most rational and logical approach. If this were a deposition, I would ask the most straightforward questions so as to avoid objections, murky answers.

If I follow my heart, I might tell David that I still love him, that I don't really know where to go from here, but that if I listen to how I feel about him, then the answer is clear as crystal. If he feels the same way, I'm here. If he needs more time, I'll be here.

But then is that Gracie going back to living on David's terms? Is that a recipe for a half-lived love life? Is this the best I can do—live on a hope and prayer that David will eventually (on his terms) love me as I love him?

Feeling conflicted, I decide to take the rational approach and earn myself that tenth and final point. "I love you, David." My words come out shaky. "I don't know if I love you as much as I used to. You've hurt me a lot."

I look at him straight on, square back my shoulders, dig my toes firmly in the sand. It's going to take every gesture of confidence I can muster to say what I hoped I would have the chance to say today.

"My head's a mess," I say. "My heart wants you. But since you don't know what you want, and this is all so overwhelming and new, all this information, this honesty . . ." I pause for a breath and a swallow.

"Since moving quickly didn't do you any good . . ." He nods, eyes closed. "We have to decide. We're either all in or we have to part ways. I don't think I can love you as a friend. I can't be that in-between girl anymore."

"Do you want to give us a try?"

I think long and hard on this for a minute. I do want to give us a try, but not like this. Not now. Not under these circumstances. David's recently come out of an engagement, our history is gritty, and, as much as I love him, I'm not ready for a relationship. And I don't think he is, either. When I tell him this, he just nods slowly.

"Trust me," I say with a shaky laugh. "It's taking a lot of restraint for me to not dive into this and say let's give us a go right now!"

"Oh really?" A smirk glosses his lips.

"Don't do that." I playfully push his shoulder back. "You know the effect you have on me."

"Oh, do I?" There's that smirk again. He pulls me into his arms.

"David. I'm serious."

"So am I." He rests his forehead against mine, and his cologne overwhelms me. I'm melting, right here, in his arms, all alone on the beach.

"Fast won't work for us," I whisper.

"Slow," he moans. "Slow and steady."

His sexual innuendos are doing nothing for my levelheaded stance, my resolve to approach a reconciliation and take a step forward with maturity and as much foresight and caution as possible. If a relationship is to come about and work, we have to be more vigilant than ever. The journey will not be an easy one, if, in fact, we choose to take this path.

"David?"

"Mmm?" His eyes are closed, forehead still pressed to mine, both hands now wrapped around my waist.

I am following my head and standing strong. "Slow," I repeat. "I don't want to define what it is we're doing, what we are. You need time and I need time to think this through, to get used to an idea of us."

"Okay."

"I mean, the logistics alone . . . Long distance isn't what I want. There are more pieces to the puzzle than 'I think we should give us a shot and see how it works.' Okay?"

"Okay."

I am following my heart and choosing to live my love life on my terms. It's an intimidating venture, but that somehow feels right as I lean into David, my face pressed to his chest. I close my eyes, and my arms find their way around his waist. "Slow," I say once more, this time in a whisper.

His embrace is familiar and warm, tinged with contention as much as passion. My head feels fuzzy, but my desires are clear. My knees are weak, but my stance is strong. I feel precisely how I've always felt about David: we are that on-again, off-again couple, at variance with each other but somehow still in harmony. It's a wicked and beautiful enigma.

David moves one hand to my waist; the other gently grazes my rear. "Slow," he says, also in a whisper. "We can do slow."

And since what we have is such a wicked and beautiful enigma, and since I consciously and of my own volition choose to follow my heart right here, right now, I lean in and press my lips to David's. Our kiss is intense, hungry, all consuming. My eyes are closed, my tongue comes into contact with his, my fingers dig into the back of his head, and his fingers tangle in my hair. It doesn't feel wrong; it doesn't feel right—it just feels good.

Juliette's encouragements to follow my heart flood my mind, mixing with the thoughts of how good it feels to have David's arms wrap around my body, how good it feels to run my fingers along the waistband of his pants, remove his belt, look into his intoxicating eyes, and nod.

"I'm sure," I tell him, actually feeling confident about the first thing in a long while.

In that blissful moment, as David pulls my sweater free and places a trace of gentle kisses along my nape and shoulder, Juliette's encouraging words aren't the only thoughts rushing forward. Her inclination to follow her heart and live on *her* terms when it comes to relationships, her free spirit and exuberance for life, are added encouragements as David draws himself near me on the sand. I am exactly where I want to be right now, and that makes me incredibly happy.

As David and I move together in our own enigmatic rhythm, I can hear the rushing and crashing of the waves in the distance. The water floods up the sand, pauses for a moment, then returns to the sea, taking with it all my hard-earned points of the day. And I'm all right with that. I followed my head, and now I'm following my heart.

———

"You're beautiful, Gracie," David says. He pulls his sweater back on, adjusts the thick half collar. "Thank you."

"'Thank you'?" I clap my shoes together to loosen the sand. "I don't think I've ever heard *that* after sex."

"Not thank you for sex." He gets an embarrassed blush. "Thank you for seeing me. For talking."

We make our way from the desolate beach to our cars. Making love on the beach was something I never put on my bucket list, seeing as it's an unimaginable, risky move. We'd found the shelter of some rocks and then just relied on a bit of luck that the place would stay deserted for a while. I had nothing to worry about. We had the beach to ourselves, and David made me feel safe and comfortable, happy.

"You sure you don't want to do dinner?" he asks, following me to my car.

"I'm sure."

"I'm leaving town tomorrow."

"I've lived without you for months on end, David. Years have passed since we were exclusive." I shoot him a you-should-know-better glance as I unlock my car. "I think I can handle one month. Besides, we're supposed to go slow."

He grins, a grin that says exactly what I'm thinking: *Sex on the beach is slow?*

Well, I think, *slow starting now.*

"So Christmas?" he says. Wrapped in each other's arms on the beach, watching the waves come and go, we talked about where we would go from here. The next step is relatively simple: we don't want to define what we have right now (and I don't think we could if we tried). So we'll both go about our lives, he in Sacramento, I here. We'll keep in touch—phone, e-mail, text—but only minimally. We agreed to spend some time really thinking about where we want things to go. Then, in one month, when he'll be back in town for Christmas, we'll take it from there. See what the new year could bring us, I guess you could say.

"You want to do anything special?" he asks. "Do some Christmas shopping at the outlets? Go on a little getaway? Catch *The Nutcracker* in LA?"

I appreciate his attempt at pulling the boyfriend card, or at least the dating card. "We'll see," I reply casually. "Right now I want you to go back home, work hard, think about me from time to time." I bat my lashes, overtly flirtatious. He laughs. "And text me or something now and then. Get your thoughts straight." I have to admit that I'm incredibly proud of how resolute I am.

"And you?"

"I'm right as rain," I tease.

He gives me a kiss, his lips moist and soft. "I'll miss you."

"Good. I'll miss you, too."

"You take care, Bennett." He holds open my car door, and I slip in. "You, too."

In a queer effort to earn back one of those washed-away points, and since I told myself I'd do it before I set out on this visit, I pull out of the parking lot first. I cave and look in my rearview mirror, though, just before I turn onto the street. David's still standing where I left him, one hand loosely in his pocket, the other waving long and slowly overhead.

I smile and look at myself in the mirror, feeling proud, brave, genuinely happy. I drive back home with one more thing I can be grateful for this Thanksgiving.

23

Juliette

December has arrived. As the autumn leaves fall and turn in the wind with the nearing of winter, so too do Gracie and I, in poetic fashion, turn over a new leaf. Only yesterday did I finish filling out the Anthropologie application, then turn it in with a broad smile, a hearty "Thank you for the opportunity" (as solicited as it may have been), and an unfamiliar feeling of assuredness that somehow this will all work out. A fresh step in the right direction.

For the past week and a half, Gracie and David have kept in touch; Gracie's been in an uncustomary upbeat mood since their meeting over the Thanksgiving holiday, of which I know next to nothing.

She's kept mum over the details (perhaps worried that overindulgence will cast a jinx on their new step). She's shared with me only the news of David's broken engagement, the indefinable friendship she shares with him, and the agreement that they will keep in touch and take things slow. They want to see where things go, if they go anywhere.

Gracie seems to think it all innocuous. I'm not so sure. David's hurt her plenty of times before, their whole "seeing where things go" never having really worked out so well in the past. He has a manipulative pull over her; where things go always seems to be in David's favor, Gracie's heart a shredded mess. I hope whatever new leaf they're turning over is as innocuous as Gracie believes.

Whatever is currently churning between them and whatever went down over the holiday weekend, Gracie seems happy. I can't begrudge her that, as skeptical as I may be of David, as much as I may question his character. There's a lift in Gracie's step, a smile on her lips, and a relaxed air about her since she met with him. At first glance you might mistake her, with all her glow and pep, for a woman in love.

While that may very well be the case, Gracie's glow is that of a woman in a new stage, a new chapter in life. It's exhilarating when you're turning over a new leaf, when you almost don't recognize that bold and cheerful person who looks back at you in the bathroom mirror. Be it a new man, a new career, a new city, a new apartment, a new friend, a new venture you've personally dared yourself to take on, it's something *new*, and that often brings unbelievable exhilaration, confidence, and a sense of peace.

Gracie isn't sure where things will go with David, but she's hopeful, she's taking a step forward, and she's refreshed by the possibilities. I don't know what will come of this job application, but the step in a new direction—going after something I've been thinking about for a while—is empowering.

Like Gracie, I can't help but feel uplifted, as if things are going right and I've got ahold of my life. Winter may be the gloomiest of seasons, but I think this year's winter will be brighter than usual if Gracie and I carry on the way we're going.

———

"You ready?" I ask Gracie as I enter the living room.

She's seated at the dining table, a chair already pulled out for me directly across from her. She's got a pencil behind one ear and her hair tied back in a tiny ponytail, engrossed in the latest copy of *Better Homes and Gardens* she picked up at her favorite bookstore the other day.

Some of the flowers and shrubbery in the garden are looking pitiful; a few we fear have just downright died. Winter is to blame for the state of some, our neglect of the garden for that of many. To say we've tended to the garden this season with Mimi-like care would be a gross understatement.

"Ready when you are," Gracie trills.

"This is a *huge* favor, Gracie."

"No problem." She trades her magazine for the blank piece of paper I hand her. "I did this all the time when I worked at the Student Affairs office in college."

I heard back from Anthropologie. I was rather shocked that they called to schedule an interview. Sure, I'd been positive that my application was as polished as possible. And sure, I'd been so fueled by determination that I was almost convinced I'd get at least an interview. But still, when you're given the initial green light on something you're passionate about, especially when you royally screwed it up last time, the moment can knock your socks off.

"You're sure you want me to be tough?" Gracie crosses a leg over her knee, holds up my mock application.

"Bring it on."

Just then a vibration sounds, Gracie's cell phone atop the dining table the culprit.

"Lee probably reminding me about those memos." Gracie grabs her phone.

"Always taking work home. You deserve a break sometime."

Gracie's lips curl up into a smile as she hungrily reads whatever riveting text has just appeared on her screen.

"Ooooh, let me guess," I sing. "David? Lovey-dovey David?"

"Stop it." She finishes reading the text, the apples of her cheeks turning pink. "It's work time, not playtime."

"A little phone sex later today, eh?"

"Jules." Pink turns to red.

"I can't help it. You get all sparkly eyed when you hear from him."

"I know. I love it."

Though Gracie insists they're strictly maintaining their slow speed, I can't count how many times I've caught her glowing as she reads or eagerly types something on her cell phone. And it sure as hell isn't Lee who's getting her panties in *that* kind of a twist.

"Back to business." Gracie clears her throat and turns her attention to my mock application.

"Hey, I'm not the one getting all hot and heavy in the middle of an interview," I razz.

Gracie clears her throat again—louder, more dramatic. "Even though," she draws out slowly, "I don't know the specific interview questions they'll ask, I'm sure of the standards. And I'll throw some others out there just to get you used to being comfortable, to acing them."

"Totally." I sit up tall in my seat, cross my legs just like Gracie. "I want to be prepared. I am *getting* this job."

Gracie begins the mock interview with the usual questions and topics: "Tell me about your most recent employment." "How would you fit into our business?" "What is your experience with working retail? Fashion? Design?"

I answer all of them with ease, mentioning that I had a friend who was a part of their visuals team internship program and loved it. I, of course, also run on about how I love the store's style and its eclectic fashion, which is always mirrored in its displays and floor design.

"What do you think?" I say to Gracie, interrupting the mock interview. "Playing it up is good or . . ."

"Great," she encourages. "Don't brownnose compliment, just stroke-the-ego compliment."

"Was I stroking or nosing?"

"Totally stroking."

"Good." I beam. "Okay, back to the inter."

"Jules." Gracie sets down the blank piece of paper. "The internship program? Is this what you're applying for?"

I scratch at my eyebrow in an evasive way. "Not really."

"But you mentioned window display design . . ."

"They don't just hire for those positions, Gracie. Like—" I'm jumbling my words. My face is feeling flushed. "Like. They have a visuals team who does all that cool design-y stuff, and they have an internship for it." She's nodding interestedly. "And like—like—they have regular sales positions, too. Like, you help girls shop and clean up the floor and . . ."

"Well, if you want to design the displays, then I think that's what you should try for. You said that was something you were interested in because a friend did it and—"

"Gracie, please!" The volume of my voice rocks Gracie some in her seat. "I'm sorry," I spit out immediately. "Sorry, I just . . ." I pinch the bridge of my nose in frustration. I didn't want to have to dig up more past dirt, relive more failures, but I have no choice. I don't want there to be secrets and lies between us. They've built the divide in our relationship before.

"This isn't the first time I've applied for a job here, Gracie." I tuck a leg securely into my chest. "I applied back in New York City, my senior year."

"You didn't get it because you ticked the felony box?" She tosses a limp hand in the air. "If only you would have told me, I would have cleared up this felony-and-misdemeanor difference in a split sec—"

"No. This is before that happened."

"Oh. Well, what happened?"

"Don't judge me."

Gracie gets that look about her, that look like she's about to do the Juliette eye roll and tell me to stop being so ridiculous. That she isn't *always* a judgmental, take-the-high-road kind of girl.

Before she can defend herself, I say, "It was awful. Just awful. And I swore I'd put it behind me and forget all about it. But I can't. I want to be honest with you. And . . . I really *do* want this job. My past mistakes are keeping me from moving forward."

"You can't let that happen."

"No."

She scoots her chair closer to mine and tells me that she's here to listen.

"There's a special internship program, for college students," I start. "A friend of mine from my art history classes got it. It was totally kick-ass, and she encouraged me to try out for it the next term. So I did."

"Good!" Gracie's smiling.

"Well, not really. I applied, got past the initial interview, and then passed this thing where they have you pull clothes and style different outfits. Then the general and visual managers interviewed me with a couple of other girls and I made it—the final round."

"God, I thought fighting for low-level status as a paralegal at a firm was competitive!"

I laugh. "That's not half of it. We also had to submit these inspiration boards showing we understood the company's vision and yada-yada. Anyway, they said my board was truly *inspired* and I'd make a great addition to the team. I was so high!"

"I bet!"

"Well, no, like . . . I got *literally* high."

Gracie gets a puzzled look about her.

"I nail all those first inters and tasks and then come the final interview—the one where they decide who makes the team—I totally sleep through."

"What?" Gracie's jaw drops.

"I know. Class A loser move, huh?" I roll my eyes. "I went out to a club the night before the final interview, celebrated that life was *finally* on track—oh, the shitty irony—and I got baked. Passed out at some guy's apartment—I don't think I ever got his name—and walk-of-shamed like thirty blocks. No money left, my cell phone and keys in Cassie's purse. I was a mess."

"Jules!"

"I just lost total track. I was so high I forgot all about my interview. By the time I got home and was able to call, they said that they were sorry my purse was left in a cab, but I still could have found a way to contact them to let them know I'd miss my interview. Needless to say, I didn't get the position."

"All that *and* you lost your purse in a cab?"

"No. I had to lie to try to save face. Couldn't very well tell them I was high as a fucking kite and slept late."

"No." Gracie shrugs one shoulder. "Suppose not."

"Anyway, I totally ruined that one. It was an *awesome* position and I, like so many opportunities, gave it the finger."

Gracie takes a few long breaths, as if she's trying to process the pile of typical little-sis-Juliette behavior I've unloaded on her. At last, she says, "The past is the past." I nod. "I doubt the Santa Barbara store compares notes with its New York City ones, so just try again."

I make the sound of a game show buzzer: game over.

"What?"

"Can't exactly," I say. "Not enrolled in college. A requirement for the special internship."

"Oh. So this job application—"

"I have a plan." I hold up my index finger, ready to assure her that I'm going to figure something out. "I'm going to apply for a regular position, sales or whatever, and let them know of my intentions of window design, and . . . well . . ."

"Work your way up?"

"Something like that," I say with a grin.

"You can do this, Jules." She picks up the blank piece of paper.

"You think?"

"Definitely. Like you said, you've grown from that phase. You're searching for what you want, and . . . that's all you can do."

"Yeah."

"A tip, though."

"Yeah?"

"If they ask if you've ever worked at one of their stores before, or even applied, I wouldn't exactly mention any of this," she says with a comical wrinkle of her nose.

"Really?" I guffaw. "You think that's TMI?"

"A little." She shakes the paper in front of her. "Shall we carry on with the mock interview? Do you think it's helping?"

"Gracie," I say through an exhalation of relief, "you have no idea how much this is helping. Thank you."

"Sure."

"I know you have some of your own work to do, and you're spending time on something *not* so highbrow—"

"Don't put yourself down." She pats my arm. "You're going after what you want. Anyone would respect that. I respect that. It's encouraging."

24

Gracie

"I aced it!" Juliette screams as soon as I walk through the front door, home from work. She barrels into me, wrapping her arms around me. "I am *so* in! And all because of your kick-ass prep!"

"The interview went well, I assume?" I say with anticipation.

"Better than well. I aced that sucker!" She releases me, smiling from ear to ear. "They said they were impressed with the interview, my enthusiasm, how I was interested in not just another retail position like they usually get. Even though that's what they would hire me for, at least initially. Anyway, the interview was a success!" She claps her hands.

"That's awesome, Jules!"

She eagerly pulls me onto the settee with her, then hands me a thin sheaf of papers. "Look! Tax form, legal docs, info sheet. Like, legit employment stuff!"

"You're hired?"

"Well, practically. The manager said she'd get back to me to figure out schedules."

"That's *great* news! And you didn't tick the box?" I cast her a quick, skeptical glance. "A misdemeanor is not a felony . . ."

"I know." She rolls her eyes. "No box ticking."

"And a background check?"

"Nope. No check."

I smile and tell her I knew things would work out.

"But," she adds with a pointed finger, "if they did do a check, I was already prepared to be totally up-front. Honest."

"Nice. See, I told you things would work out."

"Oh! And you know the visual team deal? Well, the team is already in place, and I don't qualify for the internship. Obviously." She scrunches up her face in mild disappointment, then she's quickly back to her enthusiastic self. "But no matter! It looks like I'm going to be a sales team member, working the floor and fitting room and stuff. It gets me in!" She bounces up and down, excitedly clapping hands atop her thighs. "This is the happiest I've been about work in *forever*! And all because of your help, Gracie." She pulls me into another hug. "Thank you, thank you, thank you."

"It wasn't *me*. *You* rocked your interview; *you're* the one with the enthusiasm for the job."

"Yeah, but . . . I wouldn't have had the courage to apply if you hadn't helped me with the whole misdemeanor mix-up. I don't think I would have ever given this shot at window design a second chance, you know? Without your encouragement?"

"Without my bugging the hell out of you to get a job?" I give her shoulder a playful nudge.

"Yeah, well, maybe some of that, *too*."

"Congratulations, Jules." I briefly look over her paperwork. "When do you think you'll start?"

"Manager said she'll call in the next week or two. The holidays make everything slower, and they've already got their holiday team in place. I wouldn't start until the new year." She barks out a jubilant shriek. "I'm just so fucking excited!"

I chuckle at her colorful excitement and tell her that this is definitely a time to celebrate, then. "I think we have a bottle of sparkling wine somewhere in the pantry. Can stick it in the freezer for a quick chill?" I make my way to the kitchen, then pause and turn back toward Juliette. "Or we could go out and celebrate?"

"Rain check." She makes a pouty face. "I've got a date tonight."

I groan. This better not be the guy she picked up at the coffee shop and drove to Ojai with. Does she not know how dangerous that could have been? She didn't even know the guy, and he was an out-of-towner at that. Sometimes Juliette lives too perilously. I tell her I hope the date isn't with whom I suspect.

"Josh," she says in a flurry, and to my dismay. "He's a super nice guy. So laid back. A filmmaker."

"Pornos?" I can't help myself. I give her a toothy grin.

"Ha-ha."

"Well, I'm sure Josh is a nice guy." I try to lighten the mood, be positive. "He's probably harmless, what am I saying? I mean, you already went out of town with him, and he didn't rape or murder you."

She laughs sarcastically. "Yeah, thanks. That's encouraging."

I decide to change the subject altogether. I'm probably inserting snippets of skepticism not only because I do think there's *some* inherent danger in taking up with a complete stranger, getting into his car, and just hitting the road, but also because I'm not in the most chipper of moods, especially when it concerns the opposite sex.

It's been days since I've heard from David. It's not that unusual that we go days without texting or e-mailing, a week without a phone call. Although we had hit a stride of pretty heavy texting recently. But the last text David sent, he said he was on his way out of town for business, somewhere up north, for a few days. Said he'd have downtime in the evenings and would love to talk, to help pass the long, boring evenings.

Though I have not received a single promised call, text, or e-mail—nothing—I've decided not to be *that girl*. I've thrown myself headfirst into distractions instead.

I dedicated nearly my entire day to focusing on the stack of work I have to complete for the firm before the Christmas holiday. Over my lunch break, I focused on coming up with menu ideas for the Christmas brunch Juliette and I are doing for Mom and Dad, our affordable, joint gift to them this year. I read, cover to cover, the latest *Better Homes and Gardens* issue in preparation for next weekend's garden project. And I evidently spent some time worrying about Juliette's new beaux, concerned that she could be so flippant about her suitors and her sex life. Yet I'm relieved that her impulsive trip to Ojai was not the impetus for a missed interview.

Of course, when she regaled me last night about the "amazing, brilliant, *so*-fun evening!" with the transient filmmaker named Josh, my guard was up. I know Juliette's an adult, she handles her business, and in the end her life is her life, but I know what this job means to her. I'd hate to see some guy muddle things up. I'm ecstatic, to say the least, that she's more or less gotten the job, that she's following her path.

"I'll put the bubbly in the fridge, then," I say on my way to the kitchen. "We can have some when you get back tonight, or tomorrow. This is fantastic news, Jules. I'm really proud of you."

Before I can ask about more job details, about the interview, and if they lobbed any hard questions her way, Juliette's off to her bedroom to get ready for her date.

I slip the sparkling wine in the fridge, and then, not because I'm *that girl*, but because curiosity is only natural, I steal a glance at my cell phone. I've successfully distracted myself all day. I deserve this peek.

The screen, unfortunately, reveals only a text from Suzanne: 10 am mtg. with new client. Lee wants us both there. Instead of responding, I limply toss aside the phone, wondering if this text will be the last of the evening.

———

I'm back on his terms, I just know it. I can feel it. I've turned into that insecure, questioning, doubting woman—precisely *that girl*—wondering if and when David will contact me. It's nearly eleven o'clock, and still nothing. I didn't want to get my hopes up, but I did expect something by tonight. Surely if he had all that supposed free time at night, he would have called by now.

Then a horrible idea comes into my mind, and I'm racked with guilt. What if something happened to him? What if David was involved in a three-car pileup on the freeway? What if the stress of his job has gotten to him and he's had a heart attack? I try to laugh at the absurdity. *David's too young for that,* I think. But the car wreck?

Filled with worry and despair, I decide there's no harm in giving David a call. Who says I can't contact him, anyway? I figured his saying he'd call when he had the free time negated the need for me to be the next one to make contact. It was also a prime opportunity for me to practice not being *that girl*. But when I think of something happening to him, my gut aches. I could never forgive myself for playing the high school game of he'll-call, she'll-call.

Filled with resolve, I pick up my phone and dial his number. After five rings, it clicks to voice mail.

"Hi, David. Gracie here. Just wanted to see how it's going. Hope work's going well, traveling's all right. Umm . . ." I tightly twist some hair around my finger. "Call me when you get a chance. Or text. Or e-mail." I suppress the urge to sigh at the desperation in my voice, my words. "Bye."

Then, a horrific image of a car wreck flashing before me, I blurt out, "I love you. I hope everything's fine." I hang up and slowly set my phone down on the coffee table, wondering if a car wreck really could be the reason for his lack of contact.

I thought I'd feel better after making the call, but I don't. I actually feel worse. Why didn't David pick up? Could something be really wrong? If not a tragedy, could something *else* be wrong?

This careless behavior is distinctively David. How could I have forgotten? However, since we met over Thanksgiving, things have changed. No text, e-mail, or voice mail between us is ever left unanswered. In fact, a voice mail is rarely necessary, because we often pick up when we see each other's name pop up on the screen. Kind of like new lovers, we want to be around each other, under each other's influence, thinking about each other as much as possible.

I send David a brief text, just in case the voice mail doesn't go through. Then I decide to call it a night, waiting up neither for Juliette to return home from her date (she did text me, as I'd asked, to say she was safe and having a blast) nor for David to respond.

———

When I awake in the morning, for a brief moment I think it is Saturday. Then I remember Suzanne's text. It is Friday, nearly the weekend . . . but not quite.

I briefly consider calling in sick, something I never do, even when I am sick. I just don't feel like getting out of bed, getting all dressed up in a pantsuit, and then sitting down for what will surely be a lengthy meeting with the new client.

I'm disappointed I don't feel any different after a night of sleep—if you can call it that. It was like sleep after a night of heavy drinking. Though I can probably count on one hand the times that's happened, I've never forgotten the painful feeling of the mornings after. You feel as if you went to bed, knocked out and sleeping like a baby, but you never got enough of that much-needed REM thanks to the alcohol, so you awaken feeling as if you've been up for twenty-four hours straight.

Nevertheless, I stumble from my bedroom into the bathroom, knowing that Suzanne and Lee are counting on me. I love the work that comes with signing a new client—getting the chance to help another person, from start to solution.

I rub some sleep from my eyes with one hand and fumble for the bathroom light switch with the other. The light is already switched on, and I push the door open wider. I'm met by the unexpected running of the shower water and a wall of steam.

Juliette is never up before I am, I think. I cast a glance at the vintage alarm clock on the shelf above the toilet. It's barely past six. Nothing could wake Juliette this early in the morning. Nothing.

Rubbing the last of the sleep from my eyes, I step farther into the bathroom, the door creaking behind me. I am about to ask what's got Jules up so early in the morning. Before I can, a male voice says, "Juliette?"

I can't think fast enough. My mouth remains shut, and I tighten the belt of my bathrobe, then gingerly take one step backward. I move too slowly, still overcome by sleep. In the next instant, a man's wet head pops out of the shower curtain. "You want to hop in and hop on?" he says.

"Omigod!" I clap a hand to my mouth. The man's eyes widen, and he abruptly pulls the curtain closed. An "Oh fuck!" escapes from behind the curtain as I dash out of the bathroom, heading straight for Juliette's room.

"Jules!" I burst through her door unwelcome, unannounced, completely disregarding the rules I'm such a stickler for. "Juliette, *who* is in the bathroom?"

Juliette shoots up in a panic. "Wha—what?" Judging by her sleepy expression and disoriented response, she was still in dreamland.

"There's a man in the bathroom!" I point behind me. "Explain yourself!"

She scratches her ratted blonde mane of hair. "Is it morning already?"

"Jules!"

She makes a calming motion with her hand. "All right, all right. Don't scream."

I groan, telling her that this house isn't hers alone, that she can't do as she pleases and let anyone come and spend the night, much less use our shower.

"Sorry. I wasn't thinking when I said he could shower." She yawns. "Must have been half in a dream."

"Honestly."

"Chill." She pulls on a pair of what I'm sure are his boxers, followed by what I'm sure is also his Burning Man T-shirt. "He'll be out of here before you know it," she says, disappearing into the bathroom.

I sigh, completely beside myself, then drop down on the edge of Juliette's bed. When I spy two condom wrappers on her nightstand, I leap from the bed.

I contemplate whether I should go back into my bedroom. Seeing or hearing the two of them slink down the hall from the bathroom would be very uncomfortable, so I decide to retreat to the kitchen until the coast is clear.

As I walk down the hall, past Mimi's open bedroom door, I can hear Juliette kittenishly shriek from inside the bathroom, "No, stop it. You have to go."

As uncomfortable as I am made by the situation, as upset as I am at waking up to a strange man in my bathroom in the morning, I feel a pang of longing. I miss David, I realize. I'm lonely.

When I spot my cell phone on the coffee table where I left it last night before going to bed, not wanting to be tempted to continuously check my screen for missed calls and messages, I miss him even more. I check my phone now, but the screen reveals nothing.

"I'm sorry about that, Gracie," comes Juliette's authentic apology twenty minutes later.

I heard her surreptitiously send her date on his way, and then she appeared in the kitchen, sheepish, obviously embarrassed about the run-in, and apologetic. She's now dressed in a pair of sweatpants and a wrinkled NYU T-shirt. "We got back so late, and then we hooked up here and . . ." She tucks a matted lock of hair behind one ear as she pours herself a cup of the coffee I just put on.

"Some warning, Jules." I don't really want to talk about it. It's behind us. We both know it was awkward, but we can avoid its happening again.

"Not the first time that's happened to you, right?" She takes a seat next to me at the kitchen table. "Sure you had a college roomie or two who had to sneak out a frat boy now and then?"

I ignore her jesting and say coldly, "I take it that was Josh?" I turn my Daisy Duck mug in a lazy circle.

She pulls a leg to her chest and rests her chin on her knee. She looks as if she's been up all night doing exactly what the wrappers on her nightstand suggest she was doing.

"Mmm-hmm," she says, sipping her coffee. "Banged so hard I have bruises."

The way she somehow pulls off the look of a child—messy hair, sleepy eyes, posture slumped, knee tucked close, wrapping her fingers around her childish Minnie Mouse mug—despite last night's activities, makes me smile, soften toward her. Juliette knows how to get under my skin, but I can hardly stay angry with her for long.

"You're insane, Jules," I say with a grin. "You like this guy? Think you'll see him again?"

She shrugs. "Maybe. He's in town for only a week. To be honest, I'm so sore I don't think I *can* see him again before the week's up." She giggles.

"Don't want to hear that." I reach for the bottle of fish food and give a pinch to Harold.

"It's fine," she says. "We had our fun. No need to get hung up on details." She cavalierly takes a sip of her coffee.

"I envy your relaxed attitude."

"You can totally get some just for fun, Gracie. Nothing's stopping you."

I give her a discerning, sideways glance.

"I guess you and David are trying to figure things out. Sorry." She brushes away the thought.

"That's not exactly my style, anyway," I say, and she just shrugs. "I guess at least one of us is doing things on her terms."

"What are you talking about?" She winces. "You and David are doing your slow thing. You've got your terms. So what if we're different?"

"I don't have my terms."

She looks puzzled. "You're seeing each other at Christmas, right?"

"I don't know."

"What?" She sets down her mug, leans over the table. "Gracie, what's going on?"

"Nothing. That's just it." I explain how I haven't heard from David yet, that I don't want to be *that girl*, how I really *am that girl*, that I'm having second thoughts. In hindsight what David and I are trying to do doesn't seem like a very good idea. It doesn't even really seem all that different from what we used to do. Why would David and I suddenly work out *now*?

"He's probably busier with his business trip than he thought he'd be." Juliette tries to lift my spirits. It helps some.

"Maybe."

"That's most likely it. And if not . . . fuck the bastard." She crosses her arms over her chest and leans back in her chair, smug.

"Jules."

"I'm serious. I have no patience for him breaking your heart again, Gracie. Uh-uh."

I take a small sip of coffee. "Thanks for the support."

"I'm serious."

I look at the wall clock across the room. "I should get ready. Have a busy day today."

"I'm serious, Gracie," she says as I pass by her. She grips my arm. "I won't tolerate him hurting you. Not again."

"You and I both."

———

If someone had told me that this Christmas would be the worst in the history of Christmases, I wouldn't have entirely believed them.

I'd known of Mimi's advancing cancer, and as last Christmas approached, I was as prepared as one can be for it to be the last one we'd share with her. I thought *that* Christmas was hard. This year's, though? The first without her? Impossibly difficult.

Had I been told that David would not only come back into my life but rattle it with the power of a 6.5-magnitude earthquake, I would have found it hard to believe. First, I thought it next to impossible that David and I would ever have another chance. Then, once that happened, I certainly didn't think that what we started would end the way it has, and so abruptly.

It's midafternoon, shortly after the meeting with the new client, when David's long-awaited call comes through. I'm ecstatic! Relieved!

Even though I'm in the middle of typing a draft that has a fast-approaching deadline, I pick up my cell phone to take David's call before the second ring can be completed.

"David?" I excitedly answer. I'm grinning from ear to ear.

"Hey." His response is short and heavy.

"How are you?" Still grinning.

"I don't really have much time."

I furrow my brow. "Okay. Do you want to just call back later?" I give a sigh of relief. "I'm just *so* glad you're all right. I've been worried about you."

"Look, I said I don't really have much time." Though a longer response, it is still just as heavy as his greeting, if not more. "I can't do this," he finally says.

"What?"

He repeats himself—the heaviest words yet.

"David." My voice is a whisper. I can feel tears form. I grip the phone so tight I begin to lose feeling in my fingers.

"I'm sorry, I just can't anymore."

I lower my head, trying to find shelter at my open desk behind my computer monitor. I shamefully shade my face with a hand pressed to my forehead, as if shielding myself from the sun.

"I don't understand," I whisper into the receiver. "What's going on? What happened?"

"What more can I say? I'm sorry."

"That's the best you can come up with?" I bite down hard on my bottom lip.

"I'm really sorry."

"I don't understand. I. Do. Not. Understand. How can you do this? How?"

"It was worth a try. We gave it our best."

"Bullshit." My voice is raised. I forget for a second where I am, caught up in the familiar torture of one of David's "breaking it off" conversations. "That's bullshit and you know it," I whisper, yet with so much fury there's spittle on my computer screen.

And then he delivers the blow, as if I haven't taken enough of a beating already. "It's not working for me," he says in even, determined, cold tones. "I'm sorry."

No explanation of *why* it isn't working, just a bomb delivered from nowhere! Followed by a weak, pathetic apology.

Amid more empty apologies and half-thought-out, tossed-out phrases like *we tried* and *we failed*, I feel myself fall down into oblivion, like Alice gone down the rabbit hole. There's no end, I'm stuck in some weird void, and despite the voice over the phone, I'm all alone.

"David, this isn't making any sense." I force myself to come to, to coax him into giving me an explanation that isn't half-assed. He cannot just leave it at *It isn't working out.*

"What we had was special," he says, still noncommittal. "It was worth giving a try. We owed it to each other to try."

"That's just more bullshit." I squeeze my eyes shut, trying to abate the tears. All it does is bring the already-formed ones cascading in a rush down both cheeks.

I gather the little strength I can find and leave my desk, trying to walk quickly but not so quickly I draw attention. I flee down the hall, holding my breath and holding back my tears until I reach the bathroom.

"Bullshit," I cry as soon as I lock the single room's door. I angrily bite the side of my hand, hot, burning tears now freely running down my cheeks. "You're a liar!"

"It wasn't working out, Gracie. I'm sorry. I didn't mean to hurt you like this."

I give a guttural sigh in response to his pathetic attempt at apology, at explanation. Bullshit he didn't mean to hurt me—that's all he's reliably been able to do!

"If it's any consolation," he has the gall to say, "I hurt, too." He has to be kidding! "Gracie." His voice is soft, smooth. How can he be so calm at such a time? I suppose this is the blessing of being the dumper. Always the dumpee, I wouldn't know. "You'll be fine, Gracie. You're bright, beautiful; you'll find someone right for you."

"Spare me the false compliments." I give a Juliette-style eye roll.

"Well, I've got to go." He clears his throat. "Please know how sorry I am."

"I don't care about how *sorry* you are. You're a liar. A cheat!"

"Don't say things you'll regret."

"How about you don't *do* things you'll regret. *Start* things you'll regret."

"I don't regret what we shared, Gracie." His tone is imploring. "I loved you, but I love Caroline."

My greatest fear is confirmed: Caroline is back in the picture.

"So that's it?" I spit. "You two back together?"

There's a long pause before he says, voice weak, "Yeah."

"Yeah, all right. Good luck with that." I'm seething, sarcasm my only reliable friend.

There's another long pause.

"So are you two getting married?" I bark at last. "Is the wedding back on?" Part of me doesn't want to know; I want to hang up the phone after telling David he can go to hell. Another part needs to know in order to approach that awful little thing called closure.

"I didn't plan on talking about this." He sighs.

"A lot you didn't plan on, huh? I think you owe me an explanation, David. An explanation for why you keep barging back into my life, turning it upside down, leaving——" I stop and bite my hand again, images of the two of us wrapped in each other's arms on the sandy beach. My stomach churns; I'm so sick with myself, with my stupidity, with my desperation.

"Caroline called *me*." He says this in a defensive way, as if it could lessen the pain of their reunion. "Said she had some time to think about my infidelity. The time apart made her realize she still loved me." I resist the urge to hurl all over the floor. "When she told me this, told me she wanted to give us another chance, that she wanted to get married after all, I couldn't say no."

"Couldn't say no to making partner at her daddy's law firm, right?" I shake my head in disgust.

"Gracie."

"Come on, David. Be honest for once!"

"Marrying Caroline gives me the life I want. Gives her the life she wants."

"You're pathetic."

"You have no idea the kind of stress I'm under from my family. My *father's* a successful attorney, a full partner. Do you know what it looks like for me to be just a number at some firm? Like some first-year or paralegal pissant?"

His words cut like a knife.

"I *deserve* to be at the top of a firm."

"There's dignity in actually *working* for something, David. Not using someone to get there."

"I'm not like you, Gracie."

"No. No, you're not. You're heartless. You're cold."

"Whatever. I wouldn't expect you to understand. Look, we shouldn't have gotten to talking about Caroline. I've got to go."

"Have the last word." I roll my eyes some more, tears flooding forward. "Yeah, fine. I've heard enough anyhow. Confirmed everything I hoped to God was *not* true about you. You bastard!"

"Whatever. If it makes you feel better to hate me, to blame me for all this, *fine*. I have to do what I have to do. Marrying Caroline is the right thing for me. I'm sorry things had to wind up like this for you, but . . ."

I cannot believe he can be so calculating, so cold. It's as if our years of history mean *nothing* to him.

I take in a quick breath. Our years together, I realize, *do* mean nothing to him. We are over. Gracie and David are over.

"David." I muster the courage to say what should have been said long ago.

"Gracie, let's just hang up and—"

"Listen to me! I wish I could say I hate you, but I can't. I don't love you, that's for sure." This is only half-true; anyone knows that when you love someone so deeply, however much an asshole and cheat they turn out to be, falling out of love takes time, just like its counterpart. I say this anyway, though, because I know that I am, for the first time, going to allow myself to fall completely out of love with David. I have no choice. He has hurt me too many times, and today will mark the very last time.

"I'm *so angry* with myself for letting us carry on like this again," I say. "But I am livid with you for doing this. You have no character, David. You're so selfish. So cruel. I'm sick that I ever loved a man like you."

"Gracie."

"You used me." I think back to that moment on the beach again. "You used me. On the beach . . . All these years . . ." Fresh, stinging tears fall.

"What do you want me to say?"

"Nothing." I am in a state of disbelief. I do not know this man on the other end of the line. Or, as I painfully consider, this is *exactly* the man I've known all these years. This is David Nichol, my greatest mistake. I can finally see him for precisely who he is.

"I've got to go," he says.

I refuse to be the one left hanging helplessly on the other end of the line. I will fight to be the first one to hang up, as childish as that may be. It's all I can do at this point to keep from screaming at the top of my lungs and cursing David till kingdom come.

"Do not *ever* contact me again. Do you hear me, David? Ever! Under no circumstances are we to ever talk to or see each other again. Got it?"

He is silent.

"I've said it before, but I mean it this time. We are through, David. Through."

"It's understandable you're angry."

"Fuck you!" I yell before hanging up abruptly.

His manipulative comments burn long after we've disconnected, still burning when I find myself back at my desk minutes later, tears wiped, eyes trying to focus on my blurry computer screen.

"Asshole," I mutter under my breath. I suppress the urge to hurl my phone across the room. I grip it tightly before releasing it. The orange sitting on my desk, the remainder of my lunch, catches my eye. All at once I begin to grow calm.

"It's going to be all right, Gracie." I hear Mimi's comforting voice. "This *too* shall pass."

I take in three long breaths and count to ten. For a brief moment I consider returning my attention to the draft, the cursor blinking in its reminding way at the document's last word.

My heart is aching, and I can feel a headache coming on. I decide to call it a day, scooping up my things and blocking out my calendar for the remainder of the afternoon. On my way out, I grab the orange.

———

Meadows Memorial is its usual tranquil self, the lawns crisp, the palms swaying in the winter breeze. There's no one in view, save for a groundskeeper tending to the planted flowers atop the graves. In the quiet and loneliness, and at the sight of the orange I've just placed atop Mimi's headstone, I find some much-needed solace.

"Why did I set myself up for this, Mimi?" I ask, seated on the grass next to the large Christmas wreath Juliette and I placed here a week ago. I finger one of the shiny gold globes Juliette artfully glued onto the pine.

"I either play by his rules, and he breaks my heart, or I decide to go Gracie! Cast caution to the wind, give this a try, but not get too invested and hung up on hope."

I shrug one shoulder. "Then again, sleeping with him wasn't exactly *not* getting too invested." I wag my head, dismissing the notion. "But that was part of it, just letting go, go Gracie! Choosing things on my terms for once. It all was shot to hell, Mimi."

I sit in silence for a moment, looking about the grounds, watching the geriatric groundskeeper slowly moving from one grave to the next.

"How does he take my breath away and knock me down, all at the same time? I'll tell you what, my first mistake was agreeing to this little test. This little wait-until-Christmas thing. What was I thinking? That he'd move down here? That he'd give up his career and his chance to make partner at some fancy firm? You know, Mimi, that's why he's marrying her. Only a characterless man would marry a woman so he could make partner at a firm." I scoff.

"Suppose they are made for each other. You know she's marrying him for some dowry? Jane Austen all the way, but minus the sweep-you-off-your-feet romance. He's a cad, that's what he is. The biggest cad Austen could have written!"

I jam my hands in the pockets of my coat. "Saint Nick is *not* exactly doing a stand-up job this year. Christmas is totally blowing." I chuckle, picturing the look of confusion Mimi would have over my choice of words. *Christmas is totally blowing* would have her stumped, pursing those rosebud lips of hers.

"Totally blowing," I say under my breath, before choosing to enjoy the remainder of my time with Mimi in quiet contemplation.

———

"You were right, Jules," I say later that night. "I should have been more cautious."

"No." Juliette's been pacing the living room floor for several minutes, wearing a hole in the rug. "You were cautious. You had a plan. You had terms."

"See how well all that turned out?" I was surprising myself, making jokes, keeping a droll tone despite what hit the fan earlier today.

Ordinarily I'd be a total wreck, mascara running down my cheeks mixed with gushing tears, my stomach churning, head throbbing, screaming over yet another wretched breakup. Perhaps I'm just in shock, or maybe I am finally fed up with the lies, the games. Maybe I've grown immune. Maybe my outrage in the office, followed by the quiet time to think with Mimi, has already considerably helped me along the path of healing.

Or perhaps I was, somewhere deep down, all right with this final departure from my chapter with David Nichol. He did not treat me well; he took advantage of me on many occasions, advantage of my love and feelings for him. He was, as Juliette pointed out, manipulative and selfish. When that kind of man breaks your heart for the last of many times, when you realize moving on is only going to spare you many more years of heartache, it's kind of hard to be overcome with longing and desperation for yet another chance. What's done is done, and it's probably for the best.

"Damned if I do, damned if I don't," I say. I can't deny the pain, however, that comes with a breakup, especially one as convoluted as David's and mine. We had years together, many good times and good memories. This past month there was a seed of hope. It won't be easy to let go, to fall out of love and move on.

"Damn him!" Juliette exclaims.

"If you don't put your heart out there, how can you expect to fall in mad love?" I say glumly. "If you guard your heart, you'll never share it. But why must it get broken before it can be loved?"

"I don't know, Gracie." Juliette comes crashing, deflated, onto the space next to me on the settee. A pop from underneath sounds, a warning sign we may need to treat the old piece of furniture with more care, maybe even get it tuned. "I don't know what to do in situations like this." She gives me a crooked grin. "Neither the guy nor I are ever around long enough to get to this stage."

"Damned if you do, damned if you don't," I repeat. There is no one right, guaranteed answer when it comes to matters of the heart.

"I will say it's taking all my strength *not* to get in my car, drive up to Sacramento, and give him a piece of my mind," she says hotly.

"Thanks, Jules." I pat her knee. "I appreciate the support. I'm afraid your car wouldn't make the long journey."

"I'll take your car, then," she says. "Take a train, a bus, a plane."

"Calm down, Dr. Seuss." This makes her smile, and she returns the pat on my knee.

"So it's done?" she asks. "No more David Nichol? Forever?"

It's hard to believe. I will never see David again. I will never talk to him. I will finally move on, put him behind me. I'd be lying if I said he didn't still have some kind of a hold over me. Our last time together, on the beach, is still so fresh in my mind, fills my heart with such sadness. No matter how much I may come to try to deny it, no matter what David may have thought or said, I am convinced there was a love between us shared on that beach. There had to be! The way we kissed, held each other, made love—neither of us could deny the passion.

"No more David forever," I say, and that familiar burning in my chest returns as the words sink in.

"You swear?" Juliette's child-like pressing helps the pain abate some.

"I swear."

"Pinkie-promise swear."

"Oh, Jules. Pinkie-promise swear." I hold up my pinkie, and we shake. "I'm moving on," I say. "He's marrying what's-her-face, and I'm going to focus on work, get that garden in shape . . ."

"Dates?" She wiggles her eyebrows.

"Too soon. No."

She shrugs and leans back into the settee.

"I am saying good-bye to David and all things David forever," I state with resolve. "He's broken my heart for the last time."

Juliette folds her arms over her chest and sighs. "Merry fucking Christmas, right?"

I take the pillow I'm hugging to my chest and hit her with it. "Don't say *fuck* so close to a holy word."

She just rolls her eyes, as she always does, then leans over and smacks a kiss on my cheek. "Don't ever change, Gracie."

Winter

❄

25

Mimi

Dear Gracie and Juliette,
Winter! It is winter right now as I write you these letters, my dears. And, as you now read this, you are a
brief few months away from completing the challenge.

Since it is winter, the days are shorter, the air is
colder, and if not for the holiday cheer that comes
with the season, we might all get a bit Scrooge-like. I
imagine a foul mood might catch you both now and
then, lead you two to henpeck each other. Maybe get
down on yourself because life's not quite going according to plan. The sooner you learn that it never will, the
less you have to worry about. (And less worry means
fewer wrinkles, my dears.)

But this too shall pass. In even the most trying
of days, as mine have become, there are lessons to be
learned—often those are the days when you can learn
the most. Each day is a gift, a chance to grow, so never
stop believing in yourself or in each other. I will always

believe in you, and I believe you can make it through this final homestretch.

I do hope you're not angry with me for devising this challenge. You may be wondering why I didn't just leave it to these letters to encourage you to get to know each other again. Why I didn't just pull you both close during my final days and tell you how important it is to me—how important it is to the both of you—that you not take for granted the special relationship that can be had between two sisters.

You see, there's no time like the present, and I've found that when you're faced with a decision to make, here and now, you can't fall back on procrastination. You can't weaken, you can't question, you can't escape it. You have a challenge before you, so you must decide and move forward. Move left, move right, but move forward.

When you were away at college, Juliette, I can't count how many times Gracie and I chatted over tea or a Sunday brunch, and how often she voiced her concern for you. She would say you two hadn't talked in weeks, months. I'd encourage her to just pick up the phone then, find out how you were doing. Maybe even allay her fears. No time like the present. I can't count how many times I told her to value sisterhood, to not just feel her love for her sister but to show it.

When you were away at college, Gracie, Juliette beamed with pride over her big sister going off to school. She, too, wanted to grow up and follow her passion. She'd tell me how you'd paved the path of the Bennett sisters, an example of going to college, making something of yourself. Though Juliette's never been too sure of what it is she wants to do, your example gave her the motivation to get out there and try. I'd remind her that even though you were no longer one room away, she could still lean on you, learn from you. She could pick up the phone and call her big sister, her friend.

Those months between phone calls and visits grew. The distance between was rooted deeply, each of you just as stubborn as the other about making that move. About picking up the phone, digging below the surface, moving past whatever troubled you, whatever excuses you had, and truly being there for each other. About motivating each other and leaning on each other as you used to. There is no time like the present, but when each is too stubborn, what's a grandmother to do?

Every woman has her secrets, her reasons for keeping things close to the heart. Every woman has her crosses to bear, her reasons for doing what she does. Every sister, though, has a friend in the other—a chance for a friendship unlike any other. To find that friend, to foster that friendship, sometimes one has to bare her secrets, lay down her crosses, set aside all her reasons for a moment to examine what is really at stake, what really matters.

Gracie, Juliette, I do hope you are not too upset with me over your inheritance conditions. I hope that you can understand why putting you two in this position is so important. Why I felt it was my last chance. If this challenge and my letters do not bring you encouragement at times when you think you cannot rekindle your relationship, talk to your mother. Like me, she does not have a sister. She's never had the chance to experience such a true and unique friendship. You may think she would then be the last person to talk to about sisterhood, but trust me. She will understand. She will encourage. I am certain that if she could wish just one thing for her daughters, it would be that you two could have what she was never able to.

I am afraid my sentiment and this sickness are getting the best of me now. I will close this letter and the year with the warmest of hugs and kisses and a promise that I will always be with you. When your crosses become too heavy, your reasons too many, pull out one of these letters or take a walk in the garden or just talk. I am here.

And your sister is, too.

Until spring,

All my love,

Mimi

26

Juliette

Christmas came and went in an unfortunately uneventful flurry. What with Gracie's breakup, my preparation for the new job that has been confirmed, and the general busyness of the holiday season, we shamefully didn't make it to Mimi's at the start of winter, as we'd planned to do, to read her letter. Gracie and I agreed that she'd understand, that she was the kind of woman who believed tending to a broken heart and following your passion were the ultimate trump cards. We made it two weeks later, after the New Year's holiday, which was even more uneventful than Christmas.

Gracie and I did ring in the New Year with some sparklers, sharing a bottle of cheap champagne in the backyard, wrapped in blankets underneath the orange tree. The tree always makes us smile, makes us feel Mimi is with us. We both know she still is, her spirit filling the home, her memories something we can rely on when feeling lonely or nostalgic.

Something about seeing the tree, though, provides such repose, such encouragement that what Gracie and I are doing here is important. Though the coming spring will mark a full year—will bring the final letter—Gracie and I eagerly await the season both for the arrival of new garden blossoms and fresh fruit and because time has the magic of healing wounds.

The time off work for the holiday, though Gracie then didn't have near the distraction she preferred, seemed to do her some good. She started jogging nearly every morning, saying it was the best way for her to clear her head, distract herself. Once work recommenced, she continued her routine. I accompany her some mornings, when I'm not working at Anthropologie.

I'm scheduled for a few weekdays, and every other Saturday, starting at nine sharp. It wasn't as difficult as I'd thought it would be to drag myself out of bed in time to get ready for the workday—I'm finally really liking what I do, doing something I choose, even if I'm not doing window design. I'm sure I'll get there, some day, some way.

When I join Gracie on her jogs, I can tell she appreciates the company. That once-familiar pep in her step returned when we talked about things like the lousy lay I had with the new guy working in Gracie's favorite bookstore or how hilarious the comedy we spontaneously decided to watch at Metro 4 on a weeknight was. It's as if my company is as much a healthy and welcome distraction for Gracie as her morning jogs. It is my pleasure to help; it is a rare moment when I feel as if my sister really *needs* me, her little sis. Though she doesn't say it, and though she seems just as happy to jog on her own, I feel this is true. And it feels *good*.

Clearing out the dead foliage one long afternoon in the garden before Christmas was another great escape for Gracie, as are the Friday nights out together, which we picked back up after a brief hiatus. Sometimes I'll hear her crying in her bedroom. I figure those moments are for her and her alone, moments to grieve. If she were to ask for a hug or a comforting word, I'd dash in there immediately. I'm grateful, though, that these somber moments are becoming fewer and further between.

I may not have experience with the pain of losing a boyfriend I loved with all my heart, but I am not unfamiliar with the feeling of loneliness and emptiness that can overwhelm you when your world is rattled. Going through my misdemeanor, having to step back and reevaluate my life and choices, was the greatest eye-opener. Not that I immediately bounded in the right direction, eager to pick up the pieces and start a new path. It took time and Gracie's help for me to make a real change, to feel confident and move forward. And it will take time for Gracie to heal, to find out where to go from here. Letting her know that I am here for her, as she has been for me, is all I can do at this point. And I think that's all she needs. With my help and some time, she can get through this.

"I was thinking of going for a ride," I say to Gracie as I put on a pot of water to boil. "After dinner?"

Gracie eyes the box of spaghetti with a look of disdain, then says she's not in the mood for it.

"We've got enough Chinese leftovers for one, if you'd like that instead," I offer.

She opens the fridge, stands in its coolness and light for a long while before shutting the door with a sigh. "I'm not all that hungry after all. Don't have much of an appetite."

"You sure you don't want to go for a ride with me, then?" I lean back against the counter.

Gracie seemed to be in happier spirits this morning when we shared the bathroom getting ready for work. Tonight she's like a different person.

"Could feel nice to get some fresh air," I say. "It's unusually warm."

She shakes her head and mutters, "I'm not up for it."

"You sure? Could feel nice . . ."

She shakes her head some more before disappearing around the corner.

"Okay," I say to myself. I stand and watch the pot of water come to a slow boil.

———

It's my second week at my new job, and I love it. I'm tempted to put an end to the lawn jobs, determined that I'll do so well at the store I'll get more hours, become practically full-time. I choose the responsible route and decide that the money is still good, the lawn work still decent exercise, and there's no need to put all my eggs in one basket. It is only my second week, after all. Although if the first one is any indication of the rest, I will be a shoo-in for a promotion and more hours.

I'm working strictly retail, no floor or window design. I rotate through greeting customers, taking shoppers' choices to a fitting room and assisting the fitting room stylist, running pieces back and forth, and helping people coordinate outfits.

Charlotte, the stylist, says I have a real knack for suggesting pieces that complement one another, and Margo, one of the assistant managers, says I'm a fast learner and have an infectious positive attitude. I feel welcome and encouraged here. Everyone at the store is really nice and helpful.

For the first time in a long time, I am doing something I really want to do, not because I am expected to or think I should or have no other choice. My new position may seem like menial work or a small dream to some, but to me this is a job that symbolizes overcoming my fear of judgment for a past I thought would hold me down. It is a job that provides a chance for me to grow and be responsible, to seize an opportunity and just run with it. To stick to something, despite my flighty tendencies.

I may not be doing design now, but I'll never know if I don't try, if I don't take that step forward. I just know Mimi would be proud. Gracie never fails to tell me that she is, and that means the world to me.

———

"Juliette?" Charlotte asks. She's holding up a pair of dark-wash skinny jeans in one hand, in another a flowing floral print shirt from one of my favorite lines. "Could you get Elizabeth here one size up in the jeans, and see if there's still the darker pattern of this shirt?"

"Absolutely." I flash Elizabeth my welcoming "customer smile," which has quickly become second nature.

"Thank you," Charlotte purrs, returning her attention to Elizabeth, a dishwater blonde with doe-like baby blues who can't be more than twelve.

I've always known the clientele here could be well stocked with cash, women dropping thousands on relatively few pieces just like that. Some, however, come in and scour the sale alcove, like me, and maybe occasionally swipe their card for a couple hundred that they probably *shouldn't* be spending. Like the store's style, the mix of customers is eclectic.

I don't mind the juxtaposition of clientele. I don't even mind running back and forth pieces that I would much rather keep for myself than watch go into the pretty cream-colored bag, wrapped neatly in tissue paper. I feel needed here; I feel I have a purpose. And it's fun!

"Hey, Juliette?" Margo says, stopping me as I make my way to the stack of just-in skinny jeans. I haven't tried on a pair, tempting as they may be, the $225 price tag keeping me at a dreamer's rather than buyer's distance. Even with the employee discount, I couldn't justify the splurge.

"Yes?" I spin on my heels.

"We're getting in a shipment tomorrow. New first-round, spring season stuff." Margo presses a hand to her décolletage in a dramatic fashion. "To-*die*-for pieces. Employees get the first chance to scope out the goods, buy up to three pieces on discount." She returns the stack of jeans in her arm to the pile, ordering them neatly. "We have to leave *some* for the customers, right?" she says in a low voice, with a sweet, girlish giggle.

"Oh, right. Thanks for letting me know." I swap out the pair of jeans for Elizabeth. "I don't think I can buy anything, but I'd love to look."

"Definitely! It happens once the shop closes, when we restock. Are you closing tonight?"

I'm not scheduled to close, working only the opening shifts and until midafternoon. When I was hired, the manager, Shelley, said that if it went well the first few weeks and I got a handle on things, I could add in a closing shift once a week.

That was the shift, as Shelley said, when things could get really fun. Girls either hated closing because they wouldn't get home until midnight or even later, depending on inventory needs, or they loved it, getting to restock, paw through new sale items (and evidently new season arrivals), even snacking and turning up the music as they worked. "Sometimes it's sorority row here," Shelley said, only half-kidding.

I tell Margo I would love to close, but that I may still need a few more weeks of work under my belt.

"Oh, fiddlesticks." Margo looks my mother's age, acts my age, and has a vocabulary like someone Mimi's age. She is a hoot—to use one of her favorite phrases. "I'll talk to Shelley," she says. "I've never seen anyone work so hard so early and catch on so quickly."

Charlotte's voice crackles over my headset. "Juliette?"

"Yes?" I answer, and Margo gives me a smile before dashing to the registers.

"Can you also grab one of the new lavender knit pulls that we have in the front? Size extra small."

"You've got it," I say eagerly.

I grab the darker floral print shirt on the way to the front of the store when Charlotte adds, "And if you can find Elizabeth a beautiful necklace, something with a wide bib, to go with it, that would be wonderful."

I'm getting to style, I think with a flush of pleasure coloring my face. It is one of the many fun perks of my new job. Even if I don't get to do window or floor design yet, I can still explore my creativity, play with fashion, experiment. *Last year was rough,* I think as I pad across the store, *but this year things are really looking up.*

———

I haven't been scheduled for any closing shifts yet, but Shelley's invited me to tonight's closing, both to view how things work and to check out the new spring arrivals. Ten minutes to closing, I lock up my bike and grab the notebook I've used to take notes of protocol, things I want to remember. When Margo sees this, she giggles in that sweet Southern way of hers. She says all the girls who wielded a notebook like me during training moved on to more senior positions or were transferred up and to another location. "You're a keeper," she says with that dramatic wink of hers.

Closing is usually left to a small number of employees. When there is a major stocking ahead, especially when a new season's line is in, there can be a dozen or more working. Tonight, me included, there are an even dozen.

Though everyone is excited to look through the fresh designs, some scooping up a few things for themselves, it is widely agreed that the goal is to get this done as fast as possible. Some of us, me included, have to work in the morning, and no one likes watching the clock strike past midnight while hard at work on the floor.

It turns out to be a lot of fun, probably very much like a sorority sister get-together, as Shelley said. We turn up the radio, toss back some sodas, mineral waters, Red Bull for those needing an extra boost, and work to return the store to the pristine order it is in each morning, but filled with some fresh, beautiful designs.

One of the sales associates, Gina, a freshman at UCSB, shows me how to reorganize the sale items. "It's like flotsam in here," she says, shaking open a ruffly nude-colored scarf. "People come in and tear this place apart. It's the worst part of the store after a day. Worse than the break room."

"I can imagine," I say with a sly smile. "I'm one of those scour-the-sales kind of girls. It's like an invitation to go haywire in here, dig through piles of things."

"I totally know what you mean!" Gina neatly folds the scarf. "I'm so one of those girls, too. Always shopping the sales racks." She neatly sets the scarf back on the wooden shelf above a long line of clothes hanging about in a dysfunctional way.

"There isn't necessarily a particular order to things," she says. "Obviously keep the same items together, by size. Items like scarves and belts, jewelry . . . stationery, home items . . . try to make them look appealing."

I pick up a mug with the head of a rhinoceros as the handle. "Appealing?" I say in jest. "Oookay."

Gina laughs. "Some things are on sale for obvious reasons." She points at a corner behind her. "If you want to put that on the shelf with the other mugs . . ."

I situate the quirky rhinoceros mug on the appropriate shelf, where I spot a simple mug with the letter *G* on it in a vintage typewriter font. The other mugs like it have the letters *Z, Q,* and *U*—uncommon and therefore understandably sale-shelved. But *G*?

"Okay, maybe working closing isn't the best," I say.

"Why's that?" Gina pushes about tightly packed clothes on hangers, sorting rapidly like a pro.

"I end up shopping," I say with a snicker. I show Gina the mug.

I realize she might want to nab it, what with her name starting with a *G*. Finders keepers, but I don't exactly want to incite a stupid catfight over a twelve-dollar mug, less the employee discount, right as I'm getting into the swing of things.

"I bought that when it was full price," she says. "Who would have thought a common *G* would go on sale, right?"

I may not be going home with any of the expensive items from the new spring line, but the mug is mine. Well, sort of.

———

When I arrive home a hair past midnight, I want to rush into Gracie's bedroom and tell her all about my great first closing night. I learned a lot; I met some new girls—girls who usually work the last half of the day or the closing shifts. Shelley complimented me on my suggestion to bring a mannequin wearing new spring pieces into one of the bedroom displays on the floor. It wasn't a conventional setup, but it sure made me see myself in the room . . . and the outfit. I explained how I thought it took the customer out of the shopping experience and put her in the living experience. Margo, not surprisingly, gushed that my idea was pure poetry.

It may be late and I may have an early day tomorrow, having offered to come in an hour early to help finish up with the bit of inventory no one had the energy to finish tonight. But I can't wait! I have to tell Gracie all about my night.

I press an ear to her bedroom door, listen for any hint that she's still awake. Nothing. *Drat!*

Careful not to wake her, I push her door open a crack. I wait to see if she stirs as the golden light from the hallway cuts into the darkness of her room. Nothing.

I pull the new mug from my bag and set it on her nightstand. It isn't much, but it made me think of Gracie. A mug can't heal a broken heart or really help someone move on, but it is a small way of saying I'm thinking about her, that I've got her back. Or at least her coffee.

———

"Gracie?" I ask the following morning as I knock on the bathroom door. "Gracie, you in there? I've got to get ready for work. You got my text, didn't you?"

Why am I asking that? I texted her last night that I'd be going in to work an hour early today and therefore needed the bathroom at seven. She confirmed, saying she'd be out for a morning jog then. Seeing as how it's ten past seven now and she's occupying the bathroom, I wonder if she thought I meant tomorrow morning.

"Gracie?" I say again, this time trying the doorknob.

"Don't come in!" she growls, taking me completely by surprise. I can hear her clunking around in there. It sounds as if something's fallen, maybe broken, as it bounces on the Spanish tile floor.

"Gracie, what's going on? Are you okay? Did something break?"

"It's just the damn water cup," she says in that same offensive growl.

I hold up both hands in surrender. *Someone woke up on the wrong side of the house,* I think. I don't remember hearing Grouchy Gracie since we were in high school, during that two-year stretch when her PMS was at its absolute worst.

"I'm sorry to bother you," I say, bracing myself for a barked retort, "but I really need the bathroom. I have to go to work in less than an hour." I lean my head back, mouth open wide, and exhale. This is not the time for Grouchy Gracie, of all the mornings. "I thought you were going for a jog?"

"I changed my mind, all right?" She mutters something indiscernible.

I don't want to ask, but I don't have a choice. "Do you know when you'll be out? I really need to shower."

"Dammit, Juliette. I'm in the bathroom!"

"Okay, sheesh." I take a reluctant seat on the edge of Mimi's bed. I drum my fingers against my knees, dangle my feet, and let my heels hit the wooden frame in a constant beat.

Gracie continues rumbling about in the bathroom. The sink runs. The toilet flushes. The cup falls again, and I can hear her muttering to herself, even throwing out a rare F-bomb.

I tap my knees some more, click my tongue softly, wondering how I'll be able to explain my first tardiness at work. Only my second week, it won't look good, and I've surprised myself that I, ever-tardy Juliette, have not been late once. *Guess it was only a matter of time,* I think as I lean back on my elbows.

A nasty thought occurs to me. *Did David contact Gracie again?* My stomach nearly flips at the thought. I have to ask.

"Gracie?"

She doesn't respond.

I brace myself for what I fear is the inevitable. "Did David call you?"

Still no response.

I'm not sure what to make of her silence. Deciding to wait until she emerges to get to the bottom of things, I lie back down on the bed. But as my head hits the comforter, a crinkling noise sounds. It's a plastic bag. I roll onto my stomach and take a peek inside.

"Omigod."

"Jules?" comes Gracie's voice. "You still there?"

The bathroom door opens, Gracie emerges clad in nothing more than a pair of panties and a sports bra, and I'm caught holding the contents of the bag, breathless, pale faced, but nowhere near as gobsmacked as Gracie.

Head dropped, both hands over her face, she wails, "I'm pregnant!"

27

Gracie

I peek through my hands, press my palms tighter to my face. My head continues to hang low as my eyes follow the mess on the tile floor—bobby pins, hair ties, Q-tips, a package of floss.

In my nervousness and haste in discovering those two faint pink lines, I knocked the items atop the bathroom counter to the floor. I practically upended the trash can in my panic-stricken search for the First Response box, unsure where I left it, desperate to make sure two pink lines didn't mean what one pink line meant. The tightly folded paper instructions that I cast into the damp sink confirm my worst nightmare. I was grasping at straws thinking the back of the box could offer an alternative explanation for what those two daunting lines mean.

"Are you . . . sure?" comes Juliette's timid voice.

I nudge aside the mess on the floor with my bare toes and can respond with only a dreary nod.

Next thing I know, Juliette's got her arms around me, her hand on the back of my head, and she's telling me everything will be fine. "We'll figure this out," she says. "Together."

"You want to talk about it?" Juliette says some minutes later, once the tears and initial shock ebb. We sit on opposite sides of my uncharacteristically unmade bed. It is the first sign of what I fear has become the upended, chaotic life of a single mother.

Juliette glances at the front, back, and sides of the First Response box. "There were two in here. You take them both?"

I nod. "And they're both positive." I pull myself into a cross-legged position.

"I'm sure it's not what you want to hear right now, but are you sure?" She knits her brow in consternation, and I give a breathy sigh of confirmation. *Yes, I am pregnant.*

She quickly disappears into the bathroom, a second later returning with the peculiar *G*-lettered mug in hand. She's wearing a bemused expression. "Gracie! Is this . . . *pee*?"

I can't stifle my laughter, although nothing about this situation is even remotely funny. "That *is* what you have to do with those little sticks, dip 'em in pee," I say.

"I have to say I never thought, when I saw this mug at Anthro last night, that it would *ever* be used for this." She peers at the two sticks soaking inside the pee-filled mug.

"Oh, Jules." My voice is whinier than I expected. Surely the pregnancy hormones aren't already kicking in. "That's so sweet of you to have thought of me. I love it. Really, I do. Explains why I've never seen it before."

I had been in such a panicked flurry over the fear that I might be pregnant that I didn't hesitate to grab the mug sitting conveniently on my nightstand and use it to try to dispel my sneaking suspicion.

I'd woken to my alarm just after six, ready to go for a jog, and then from nowhere I found last night's dinner coming up. Once the nausea subsided, I suited up for my jog, and not five minutes after I headed out, what little was left of my dinner found its way to the corner of Laguna Lane and Malcolm Drive.

It was that, coupled with the fact that I had missed last month's period and was going on nine days late this month, that made me fear the worst. I'd chalked missing last month's little visitor up to the agonizing stress of my breakup with David.

But now I am certain I am pregnant, with two positive test sticks sitting in a mug full of urine, the letter *G* intricately inked on the mug that seems to be shouting, "*Yes*, these are *your* sticks, Miss Gracie with a *G*! *Your* pregnancy test sticks. Positive!"

"How does this happen?" Juliette says. She crawls back into my bed.

"Ha! The sperm meets the egg—"

"Gracie, now is no time to whip out the dry humor."

I hug a pillow to my chest. "Oh, now's the perfect time. When life's gone up in smoke, a little humor is *always* needed."

Juliette smiles, then leans near and says, "So just whose sperm *did* meet this eager little egg of yours? And *when*?"

"Whose do you think?" I put on my best deadpan expression.

Her face goes long in what I really can't believe is surprise. It's not as if I have any other suitors knocking on my door . . . knocking me up.

I give a small grin, impressed that I'm managing to handle this with such a great deal of much-needed humor. To be honest, with those two tests, the breakup, and the difficulty of such a rough year compounded, I don't think I have many tears left in me.

"But *when*?" Juliette's in full gossip mode—eyes wide, mouth agape, fingers tightly clutching my comforter. "Thanksgiving?"

"When else? That's the last time we saw each other." When I thought back, from time to time, on the way David and I ended things, I began to discover that our shared moment of intimacy on the beach no longer felt romantic. Not even in a dramatic sort of way. No. Now it just feels . . . depressing.

"I didn't know you two hooked up! Where? Here?" She stops her rapid-fire questioning, saying she'll shut up, that it's none of her business.

"On the beach," I say in a lackadaisical kind of way.

She's totally flabbergasted, and as I give her the basics of how it happened, I can sense she's trying her hardest not to grin, not to say, "I know you're knocked up and that's so not cool, but go Gracie! Prudish Gracie goin' at it on the beach!"

"The one time I let go," I say with a sniff, "have fun, cast caution to the wind, I'm fertile and fucked." I hug the pillow tighter to my chest. This is the permission to let Juliette have her laugh. And since I can't really think of what else to do at this point, and since crying or fretting is just too damn exhausting, I join her.

———

Juliette asks a dozen times if I'm sure I'm all right with her going in to work. She's already running late to help with inventory, but she says she's still willing to stay home today and help me—call my ob-gyn, pick up a book or two on pregnancy, even research other alternatives and make an appointment if that's what I want. I insist that she go to work, touched though I am that she's willing to help and sacrifice the good name she has going for her at her new job.

Besides, it's not as if I'm incapable of picking up a few books or scheduling a visit to my o.b. myself. And there are no alternatives to this pregnancy that I need to research, no appointments that I need to make ASAP. As soon as I saw those two pink lines, as soon as I was able to process that I, Gracie Dawn Bennett, was going to be a mother, two things flashed across my mind. All right, two things *after* the barrage of expletives. One, I was keeping my baby. And two, I was going to do this by myself.

I am not as definitive on two as I am on one. I want to spend some time to rationally go over the pros and cons of bringing David onto the scene. Having a baby is a big deal; deciding single-handedly whether the father will play a role or even be advised of his entry into the paternal world is a decision just as large.

I have always said, when watching episodes of *16 and Pregnant* with Juliette during the lazy summer afternoons when there was nothing else on television, that it is the guy's right to know he is going to be a father. I was a fervent believer in these equal rights. Though he doesn't carry the child for nine months, the father is as much a parent to the baby as the mother. If he doesn't want to play an active role in the child's life, he still has the inherent right to make that choice, just as the mother does.

Now that I've stepped into this new pair of shoes, I can't say with such finality that I believe that. Quite simply, David is an asshole. He does not love me. I do not love him. I may have loved David that moment on the beach, and I may have been trying to convince myself for weeks that he, too, loved me then. But the fact is that this baby was not conceived in love. He or she is an accident, one I cannot imagine being made better by involving someone as cruel, characterless, immature, and self-absorbed as David. He is marrying for financial and career convenience. How would he view fatherhood?

However, the fact remains that David *is* the father. How can I not tell him? Is it fair to him, to the baby, even to me, to keep such a secret?

Once Juliette's gone to work and I've called in sick to the office, I pull out a legal pad and pen, make myself a cup of chamomile tea, and sit down in the den to make a list. I'm conflicted, no idea where to go from here, an old-fashioned pros-and-cons list seeming like the most rational step forward. Within minutes, it is quite apparent how I feel.

I stare, dazed, at the legal pad. "Telling David" is written across the top of the page, and underneath is a weighty list.

Pros

1) *He IS the father*
2) *It is his right to know*
3) *Child support*

4) My baby will know his/her father
5) A chance he will marry me, out of duty

Cons

1) He IS the father, and he's an asshole
2) He will likely demand a paternity test—don't want to deal
3) He will likely tell me I've done this on purpose (I've trapped him)
4) My baby will know his/her father; will learn what a disappointment he is
5) A chance he will marry me because he feels obligated
6) We don't love each other and have no business raising a child together
7) He is getting married to another woman
8) Visitation and joint custody, a best-case scenario, means a child born into a divorced-parents situation
9) I will love my baby; David is incapable of honest love
10) I do not want David as a part of my life, and I do not want him as a part of my baby's life

The cons continue in this vein, ending with number twenty-two: "David is my past; this baby is my future."

As I look over the list, it suddenly becomes clear that I am *finally* making that move forward, away from David, away from the past. Getting over a love takes time. Sometimes you think it might even take an eternity. *This list,* I think with a weak smile, *is proof that it is possible.*

Emotionally conflicted and exhausted, I set aside the list and head out on some unpredicted errands: going to the drugstore for prenatal vitamins, going to my favorite bookstore for some informational books about pregnancy and infant care, making a phone call to the ob-gyn. It is the most surreal morning and afternoon of my life. Even more surreal than when David called to seal the fate of our relationship.

Juliette sends me a text that I should make a doctor's appointment, and that if I want the company and support, she'd be happy to join me.

I'm so lucky to have a sister like Juliette at a time like this. She hasn't cast judgments on my hooking up with David, although I am sure she wonders just what the hell I was thinking. (She's not the only one.) Even for someone like Juliette, who isn't one for rash judgments, it must be difficult to look at me, someone who tends to tout virtue, consideration, and rational action and thinking, and not see me as a hypocritical fool. Who's laughing now?

How can she keep from saying out loud what she must be thinking, that I am a victim of a one-night stand gone bad? A victim of something I always frowned upon *because* of the situations just like this that can arise: broken heart, feelings of being used, pregnancy.

In one fell swoop, I feel like the poster girl for Planned Parenthood, warning young girls and women what not to do. Just because you love a man and you are convinced he loves you doesn't mean he does. Just because it feels good to let go in the name of passion doesn't mean you should. Just because you're all alone on the beach doesn't mean you should make it your bedroom. And for God's sake, just because you think it's only one dynamic, fantastic, and perhaps once-in-a-lifetime moment doesn't mean you dive in. It sure as hell does not mean you forget the condom!

Halfway through one of my new books, as I catch my mind wandering down the self-critical road, I am no longer feeling I can do this. No matter which side of my pros and cons list I choose, I can't have a baby. I feel shame, which turns into frustration, which becomes an anger bordering on rage. How could I be so stupid? How could I let this happen?

When I envisioned becoming a mother, I did imagine I would be in my mid or late twenties. In fact, there were plenty of times over the past few years that I found it mildly surprising (and a tad disappointing) that I was not already a mother.

Life doesn't always go according to plan; I'm not that naive. But I'd be lying if I said I didn't think that by now I would be married and a mother of one, maybe two, living in a modest but picturesque home somewhere around West Downtown that my husband and I had meticulously chosen. I never pictured this: single, freshly broken up with the worst ex-boyfriend of the century, feeling pitifully foolish, living in my late Mimi's home with my little sister.

It could always be worse, I can hear Juliette say, which helps keep my spirits slightly elevated. But having to think on that isn't the way I want to start my pregnancy. These aren't the thoughts or the situation I want to have to deal with as I prepare to bring a new person into the world.

Hopelessness settling in like the thick grey clouds that hover ominously over the wharf in the winter, summoning heavier ripples and waves than usual in the harbor, I decide to close my book and go for a walk. Maybe the fresh air and exercise will help calm my rattled nerves.

I take my cell phone with me to make an appointment with my ob-gyn. I can be upset with the situation. Ignoring it isn't responsible. It won't solve anything, and it certainly won't make me feel any better.

———

"So, Tuesday?" Juliette asks, consulting the calendar on the kitchen wall. "I don't work Tuesday, so that's good for me . . ."

"Tuesday it is," I answer.

It was bizarre when the receptionist asked, after pulling my file, "Are you scheduling for your annual, Ms. Bennett?" By rote I nearly said yes, but this next appointment would not be for preventative measures, would not be a simple checkup, wouldn't even be the pre-natal appointment I'd imagined having some day, my husband by my side. This made my heart heavy again, and I couldn't help but wonder when the fear and the anger over what had so swiftly become my new life would subside. Perhaps, as with falling out of love, it will just take some time.

"That is, if you even want me to come along?" Juliette says in a cautious tone.

"Of course I want you there." I point at the calendar and tell her to flip ahead to August. She does and shrieks giddily at the sight of the red circle around the twenty-third. Discovering that date made my heavy heart feel lighter—another rush of emotion, this time positive. *I can do this,* I told myself as I made the thick, colorful circle.

"You know your due date already? That's what that means, right?" She pulls herself onto the counter.

"It's a guesstimate. I picked up some books." I point to one of the three on the counter near Juliette. She immediately picks it up and fans the pages, curious. "The doctor will be able to better tell at my appointment."

"Holy crap, sis, this is for real."

"Yeah." I give an affected smile. "Those tests weren't a game."

She closes the book, her thumb between two pages. "You know?" She looks upward. "I know this isn't exactly how you planned it, I'm sure."

"You've got that right." I pull a Sprite Zero from the fridge, the first of what will be many on this long decaffeinated road.

"But it's going to be really neat, really great, Gracie. I bet Mimi would have loved to have a great-grandchild here." She runs a hand along one of the hanging cupboards. "I'm proud of you for having the baby, for doing this alone. I mean, of course you're not *alone*-alone.

I'm here!" She darts a glance my way. "Or have you decided to tell David?"

"I still don't know yet."

I've been coming up with one additional reason after another I *shouldn't* tell David. The pros side of the list is really coming up short. A part of me feels incredibly selfish for keeping something like this from him, and part of me wonders if I would be doing more harm than good, to both me and my baby, if I were to share this news with David. What if he were to feel a sense of obligation (highly unlikely) and rush back into my life, maybe try to work things out between us again, even offer to marry me? What kind of lie would we be living? Worse, what kind of life would I be stepping into? He's made his bed with Caroline—his deceitful, power-hungry, money-driven decision—and I want nothing to do with someone who values greed above love.

"That pros-and-cons list suggests one way over another." Juliette sets aside the book.

"Yeah, I should have made that kind of a list *long* before we got back together . . . after our *first* breakup." I sniff, disappointed in my lack of discernment. Or was it just desperation all these years? False hope? I take a drink of my soda and decide it's a messy mix, a question that isn't even worth an answer.

"Mimi would be proud of you, Gracie. It takes a strong woman to have a baby like this."

"I doubt Mimi would be proud that I got myself knocked up."

She just shrugs off my comment.

"Can I ask you something?" I furrow my brow, poised to ask a question I'm not sure is couth. "Have you ever . . ." I look to my stomach to hint at my question. Juliette doesn't pick up on it. "Have you . . . ever been in this situation?"

"Pregnant?"

I nod.

"Can't say that I have." She scoots along the counter before finding a prime spot so she can put her feet in the sink. "Although one of my roommates was."

"Yeah?"

In a cavalier tone she says, "She had an abortion."

"Did she tell the father?"

She turns on the sink, runs water over her feet. "Nah. What was the point?"

"You don't think he should have known?"

"Ha!" She lathers soap in her hands, then rubs her feet clean. "He was a junkie, Gracie. Total cokehead. His apartment looked like Brooklyn on a white Christmas." She laughs to herself in a deprecating way. "He had no business being a father, and she knew that. She didn't exactly want to be a mother! It was a mess." She finishes washing her feet, telling me offhandedly that she shouldn't have worn her Converses without socks.

"Look, Gracie." She turns to face me, wet feet dangling and dripping dots of water on the kitchen floor. "David was a manipulative SOB. You have my unflagging support to keep him uninvolved. If you want him involved, I say be cautious. *Very* cautious. This is up to you. I really don't subscribe to that whole equal-partners-in-this number. Maybe that makes me a bad person or ass-backward, but I don't give a damn. David hurts you, and you're very vulnerable right now. Don't go beating yourself up over this."

"Yeah. I know."

"When you decide what you want to do, I'll stand by you either way." She asks if I can toss her a towel.

Not wanting her to use the dish towel for her feet, I give my goofy sister a wad of paper towels. I'm about to tell her what she's doing is unhygienic and rather gross, but I let it go.

"Thank you," I say as she wipes her feet dry. "Thanks a lot, Jules."

The next two weeks pass by agonizingly slowly. I am a mere week away from my prenatal appointment, and I feel as if I've been pregnant for months. My morning sickness does not abate. I have had to call in sick to work on three mornings, two of which were back-to-back. I am drowning in paperwork and looming deadlines. I've tried to jog in the evenings when my sickness is at its lowest, but more often than not, as soon as I make it two blocks, I'm dry-heaving and light-headed. I don't have any cravings, other than for sleep, although I am put off by the smell of hard-boiled eggs, our fabric softener, and evidently the brand of ultra-musky cologne worn by one of Juliette's overnight dates.

What makes my fresh pregnancy feel even more as if it's been carrying on for ages is the mounting pressure to let the firm know of my bun in the oven, to tell my mother and father that they will be grandparents. I don't know what will be harder to take, Lee hitting the roof when he learns that his go-to paralegal will be taking a maternity hiatus, or Mom and Dad learning that their good girl Gracie has put her future in jeopardy. And they'll be less than pleased to hear who the father is.

I should rip off the proverbial Band-Aid—better to deliver the news now than dwell over it in this anxious way. I decide the most appropriate time to share the news is after my first prenatal appointment. If the doctor discovers there is a complication, or I have a miscarriage, what would have been the point in getting everyone at Donoghue, Sterling & White in a huff or telling Mom and Dad that it turns out it isn't wild Juliette and all her dates they have to worry about?

I decide that I will tell Lee and Suzanne in person and send out a memo to the rest of the office after my appointment. Then I'll break the news to the grandparents-to-be in person. How? I'm not quite sure yet. I'll do it with Juliette by my side, if she won't mind. Surely there's strength in numbers. The presence of support and the hand to hold will be emboldening.

It should come as no surprise that even the best-laid plans can be shot to hell. I slipped up at work today when Suzanne offhandedly asked if the reason I was calling in sick so often was that I was secretly interviewing with other firms.

"Ha!" I laughed. "Lee isn't *that* impossible to work with."

"Well, you're not pregnant, are you?" she asked, half-joking.

"Yes," came my wholly unexpected response. I clapped a hand to my mouth, eyes like saucers, and Suzanne told me I must be lying.

"No. Way!" she huffed.

The cat was out of the bag. Suzanne's mouth is even looser than mine. If I didn't pull Lee aside right away and tell him my news, come lunch break everyone in the office would be abuzz. A week ahead of schedule, I grudgingly sent out a memo to the office after I told Lee that I'd be putting in for maternity leave at the end of the summer.

Once the office knew, I felt my parents had to. They're the grand-parents, after all. But this isn't the kind of news you casually share over the phone. I wasn't sure how to share it yet, but a phone call prompted by the firm's premature discovery was not the answer.

It is already ten o'clock at night, and my body is exhausted from the combination of morning sickness and a successful, although brief, early-evening jog. I was pacing the living room, my bedroom, even the garden until the chilly air drove me back inside, where I proceeded to resume my pacing in the living room.

My cell phone clutched in my hands, I am trying to come up with a way to set up Mom and Dad for my news. Over a spontaneous brunch this Saturday? Maybe Juliette and I could invite them over on Sunday? I look down at my phone, helpless and exhausted.

Hoping Juliette can weigh in on the situation, impart some of that fiery, determined advice of hers, I head to her bedroom. I pause just outside her door.

She warned me that she'd have a date over tonight, a guy she met at work—or was it at the coffee shop? The beach? I don't know. I can't keep them straight. She also promised he wasn't going to stay the night, because she has work in the morning. When he'll be going home is a question I don't think Juliette knows the answer to.

There's muffled laughter and voices on the other side of the door, making me feel like a creeping Peeping Tom. I retire to the living room . . . and wait.

The waiting makes me anxious. I'm biting my nails, something I never do, and I'm having horrible thoughts about the injustice of my sitting here, pregnancy books spread about, that stupid pros-and-cons list bookmarking one of them.

I don't have time to think of something called a birthing plan. I didn't ask for this. I've got a deposition to prepare for on Monday! Needing to enroll in birthing classes and inform myself of the dos and don'ts of infant care has swiftly and unwelcomely usurped the mounting pile of work at the office. God, where is the justice? Where is the loving boyfriend who just might make this all a little more manageable?

I loudly clap shut one of the books with a grunt. "How is this fair?" I mutter, eyes closed in remorse.

Where is the justice in my making the single mistake of neglecting to use a condom, the *single* mistake of giving in to passion and sleeping with a man I loved, and winding up single and pregnant? Where is the justice when cautious Gracie plays with fire *one* time, while the Juliettes of the world get off scot-free, dating with abandon, having the kind of Friday night a single, twentysomething woman should be having?

I'm burning with fury as Juliette and her date emerge from the bedroom at last. Seated with crisscrossed legs on the settee, one pregnancy book in my blanketed lap, another to my right, and some contract drafts I've been intermittently working on to my left, I summon all the strength I can find not to bark out a response to Juliette's date's lazy wave and greeting: "Hey, there."

"Nate's going to be going now," Juliette says sheepishly.

She leads this Nate guy by the hand to the front door. The two linger on the porch for a while, and I can hear her seductive giggle. From where I'm sitting, I can see her stand on tiptoe on one foot, leaning gently into her date. I see his hands come around her back, one hand cupping her rear. I clench my jaw. I think of how David used to touch me like that.

"Good night," Juliette whispers. She leans into Nate some more.

"I'll see you around?" Nate drawls out.

"Maybe." She giggles. "Call me sometime next week?"

"Maybe," comes his nauseating reply. I really believe there was a high school class on flirting that I either slept through or neglected to enroll in. These two obviously aced it.

"Hey," Juliette says once she shuts and locks the door. "You still up, Gracie? Shouldn't you and that little jelly bean be getting some rest?"

"I don't get it," I say with a sigh. I toss aside one of the books, feeling indignant.

"Mom and Dad?" She waves a hand dismissively as she walks to the dining table. "They're not uptight conservatives. All right, maybe Mom can be." She holds two empty glasses between her thumbs and index fingers. "You're worrying over this *way* more than you need to, hon. And I'll totally be there with you when you tell them, help lessen the blow." She titters. "Although it's totally not that big a deal. You've got a safe job—a career! You're not a teenager, okay? Being a single mom isn't the end of the world."

She waltzes into the kitchen as she says, "Plenty of women have babies without men—single women, single moms who adopt."

She returns, still holding one of the glasses, but it's now full of red wine. She takes a pull. "Know what I mean?"

"It's not just that," I say, although she does have a point. She makes me feel slightly better, but it isn't enough to tamp down my frustration, the nettling feeling of injustice.

"What else? That you told your firm before them?" She makes a motorboat noise, eyes rolled upward. "BFD. You don't even need to mention that part."

"Jules." I push aside the rest of my books and tear away the blanket.

"Hmm?"

"Don't take this the wrong way, but how is this just?"

"Just what?"

"*Just!* Justice and injustice."

"Huh?"

"This! You, me. God, this is going to sound so bitchy. Where's the justice in my being pregnant, you know?"

She squints, confused. "Justice?"

I angrily stab a finger in the direction of her room. "You're with a different guy every night."

"Whoa, wait a minute." There's a note of indignation in her voice. "Not *every* night."

"It might as well be. You shack up with practically every guy you meet."

"What?"

"I'm sorry, maybe it's these hormones. Or I'm just so angry I have to deal with this."

"So throw *me* under a bus?"

"Come on." I laugh tightly. "You have to admit it's ridiculous, terribly unjust. I play by the rules, the laws. And *I'm* the one who gets pregnant."

"Unprotected sex on the beach is playing by the rules, Gracie?" She makes a clicking noise with her tongue, taps a finger to the side of her mouth. "Yeah, *that* was brilliant!" She slams her glass of wine onto the table. "Where do you get off insulting me like this? This is like something out of a history book."

"Huh?"

"Judging me! Like you did when I was in high school."

"What?" I gasp.

"Don't act like you don't remember. When I smoked, you judged. When I got drunk, you judged."

"You were practically *always* high or drunk! Always getting into some sort of trouble."

"That's not the point! You were always judging me, Gracie. And now, after all this time"—she shakes her head—"nearly a whole year, we're back to fighting, judging, saying these hurtful things. I thought we were really growing past that."

"I just think it's unjust that you get to sleep around, have your fun, and get off scot-free."

"Scot-free? Scot-*free*? Ha! I've had my *own* shit to deal with, Gracie! I don't get off scot-free, and you *know* that!"

I press my lips together, cast my gaze to the floor.

"I may be doing something I really love for once, but I'm working a part-time, minimum-wage job, okay? I'm mowing lawns, for Chrissake! I don't have a boyfriend, a relationship that *means* anything. The friendships I have are weak. Some of my choices have set me back. To say nothing of the guilt I feel! I do *not* get off scot-free."

"Whatever."

"You know, Gracie," she says, clenching her jaw, "I was hoping things were changing with us." She yanks her messenger bag free from across the back of the dining chair and flings it over her shoulder. "Thought Mimi was really right about all this." She waves a hand about. "But it turns out you're still the same self-righteous, judgmental bitch you've always been."

Her words cut like a knife, and all I can do is watch in astonishment as she charges for the front door.

"I thought we'd moved past this shit." She yanks open the door, and I finally blurt out her name.

"Where are you going?" I leap out of my seat and follow her to the front door.

"I'm leaving! I don't have to stand for this. I don't have to stay here with someone who thinks so low of me."

"You can't go."

"Like hell I can't." She pulls her keys from her bag. "In fact, consider me already moved out."

"Juliette!" I chase her across the lawn as she storms to her car. "Juliette, you can't be serious."

"Watch me."

"You're moving out?" I gasp. "Where are you going?"

"What's it matter? You can stay here, live your perfect little rule-abiding, judgmental life, and I'll go elsewhere where I can shack up with every man I meet!" She narrows her eyes. "That's what I do, isn't it?"

"Jules!"

"Well, I may shack up with every man, but at least I'm not stupid enough to get *pregnant*!"

She leaves me speechless, and all I can do is watch her charge to her car.

"Consider me gone!" she hollers, flipping a rotating wave with one hand. "I won't cramp your style anymore." She unlocks her car, tosses her bag into the passenger's seat.

"Wait!" I finally yell. I'm angry, I'm hurt, I'm confused, but one thought shines through clearly. "What about Mimi? What about the challenge?"

Poised to open the driver's side door, she stops, rests a forearm on the roof of her car, and says, fixing me with a steely gaze, "We both know the whole point of the challenge was to bring us closer together. Mimi's made it abundantly clear. Tonight—" She rolls her eyes. "Shit. Tonight we've torn each other apart. We're doing more damage than good." She half sighs, half snickers. "I'm outta here."

"But . . ."

She gets behind the wheel and starts the car, and before I can pull open the passenger door and plead with her to reconsider, she gasses it down Laguna Lane, blowing through the "Stop" sign without so much as a timid brake, her taillights fading into the dark winter night.

28

Juliette

After all this time, all we've been through, all the progress we've made, and only two months away from making it a whole year, Gracie's true colors show. She has insulted me before, made me feel foolish for choices I have made that she deems wrong. But this one takes the cake.

"Juliette, what is going on?" Mom demands as I angrily stalk from the living room and up the stairs to my old bedroom.

"I told you, Mom," I shout. My fingers grip the wooden stairwell tightly. "I don't want to talk about it. We just had a fight. Can we leave it at that?"

"Janey," Dad says to my mother, putting a comforting hand on her shoulder. "Let's let her calm down for a bit."

"She's been tight-lipped nearly the whole hour she's been here, George!" Mom gives Dad a disapproving glance. When it comes to dramatics and heated arguments, Mom is queen. Dad is a humble, silent guest whose hands are tied, who is usually not participatory.

"Juliette!" Mom snaps. "You are not staying here until you tell me what is going on."

I stop halfway up the stairs. I turn my head sharply and look at her. "I can't stay in my own *bedroom*?" My tone is reminiscent of those teen years. This whole scene is, in fact: me on the stairwell, stomping to my room, refusing to talk to my parents, shouting, protesting, Mom casting threats, Dad trying to make peace.

"Jules—" Dad says, but Mom cuts him off.

"You can't barge in here, mumble about how you can't live with your sister, grouse on the couch, and say you don't want to talk about it. Flee to your room and what?"

"I'm tired," I lie, trying the easiest tactic to avoid further discussion.

"No. No, Juliette." Mom crosses her arms over her chest, the ultimate maternal stance, with her shoulders squared, head high.

"This is between Gracie and me, Mom. God! When will you understand that?" I throw my hands up into the air, exasperated. "When will you understand that sometimes it's *just* between sisters? That we have to learn to grow up and handle each other ourselves?"

"I'm not trying to get in the middle—"

"Well, you are!"

"Listen to me, Juliette Kay." Mom walks to the bottom of the stairs, eyes boring into mine. "I know you and I haven't always seen eye to eye, and by God that's fine—that's the way it is, and I've come to accept it. But I will *not* stand here and watch you and your sister fall further apart."

"We're not falling—"

She holds up a finger, halting me as she nears. "And what would you call this?"

"Uhhh, *bullshit!*"

"Watch your mouth." She now wags her finger inches from my face. I want to smack it back, just as I did when I was younger. I want to scream at the top of my lungs that it takes two to end up in a shit pile like the one Gracie and I are in. She is just as much a part of the problem here as I am . . . More, I'd argue! Here I am, being supportive of her getting knocked up, and she has the audacity to judge *me*, to wave the flag of injustice?

I'm so very tempted to scream all this to my mother, to tell her that for once fucked-up Juliette *isn't* the one who's in trouble, *isn't* the one who cast the first stone, *isn't*—

I catch my breath. I grip the stairwell tighter. Tighter. And tighter, and tighter . . .

"Whatever you two argued about, you can fix through talking," Mom says. Her voice is calm and steady. It, surprisingly, invites me to a place of peace.

I steady my breaths and slowly nod. I am hearing my mother. By nodding, I am acknowledging that I hear her, that I am willing to listen. But! I am *not* prepared to take her advice. Not yet, anyhow. What Gracie said was just . . . low. Too, too low.

"How bad could it have been?" Mom says with a weak grin.

I take a seat on the stairs and watch as Dad, a hand running through his thick mane of grey, leaves the front room.

Mom takes a seat three steps down from me, one hand on my knee. "How bad, Juliette? Really?"

I raise two very inquisitive eyebrows, the ultimate defiant glance of my teen years. "You don't want to know."

"Really so bad that you can't face her? Can't talk it out? That you have to storm over here and—"

Heat flushes my face as my brief sense of peace dissipates with Mom's continual prodding. "I don't have to keep company with someone who thinks I'm a slut, Mom. Okay?"

"Juliette." She sighs heavily. "Language."

I roll my eyes. "Whore. Cheap. Easy."

"Juliette!"

"She's being a judgmental bitch, and I don't have to stand for it."

Mom rubs at her temples, head wagging in that familiar disappointed fashion of hers. "Please." She holds up a hand in front of me.

"No name calling. Please. You're much too old for that. Much too good of sisters for that."

"Whatever. Nothing's changed."

"You and Gracie need to apologize and work things out." She says this as if it's so simple. As if there isn't a valid reason for why I've run over here.

"I don't want to."

"Juliette."

"I don't!" I shout, standing. Before I can get out another word, Dad reappears. He says nothing. He doesn't have to. My allotment of words, my volume, have reached their limits. "I'm going to bed," I grumble.

"Jul—" Mom calls out, but Dad makes a hushing sound. As I reach the top of the stairs, he has her by the hand and is leading her, reluctant though she may be, to the bottom of the stairs.

"Good night, Juliette," Dad calls out. "We'll discuss this in the morning."

———

"Good morning, Jules," Dad says cheerfully as I make my sleepy way into the kitchen. "How'd you sleep?"

He and Mom are seated at the breakfast nook, mugs of coffee in hand, a copy of the *Wall Street Journal* in Dad's other.

Mom gives Dad a quick, pointed look, as if admonishing him for his pep when I should be scolded after last night's events.

"Fine." I mumble my response.

"Morning, dear." Mom's voice is small.

My initial response of a close-lipped smile elicits a cleared throat from my father. *Try again.*

"Morning, Mom," I then say, voice just as small.

"Fresh pot of coffee's on, if you like. Dad also has some French press."

"Thanks." I pour myself a mug of coffee, take note of the time indicated on the wall across the way, and prepare to return to my bedroom to dig something out of my old closet to wear to work today.

"Juliette?"

I turn and face my mother.

"I want to talk to you."

"Mom, I've got to go to work," I say with a heady sigh.

She just stares at me, a deadpan look on her face.

"I know, I know. Juliette's got a job. Surprise, huh?" I give her the same deadpan expression.

"It's too early for attitude, little girl." Dad folds his paper, eyes me, and tells me I can give my mother five minutes. "She's your mother," he says. He kisses my forehead as he makes his way through the kitchen. "She deserves at least that much." He turns back to Mom and says that he's going to get ready for work. "No catfighting," he adds.

I blow on my mug of coffee, lean against the refrigerator. "So . . ." I tap my fingers against the mug.

"First, Juliette." Mom smooths down the lapels of her bathrobe. "Drop the attitude. I want to have a serious discussion with you. All right?"

"In five minutes? Wow. Okay."

"Attitude."

"Fine." I tell myself to check the immature behavior. Mom doesn't seem to be in the scolding mood, doesn't seem to be wearing those worried-mom pants of hers. She's surprisingly very composed, determined.

"I obviously don't approve of Gracie calling you . . . those names." She wags her head. "I don't know what it is you two argued so heatedly about, and, quite honestly, I don't care."

"Mo—"

"I don't give a damn."

Taken aback by her language, I clap my mouth closed and listen.

"Your Mimi was very explicit in her plan. You and Gracie are to live together for a whole year. Now"—she makes a halting motion with her hand—"I am not saying that one night apart, or two or three or whatever it is you feel you need away from each other, is going to break the deal. The whole point is for you two to live together and appreciate each other. To grow close again."

I open my mouth to mention that we have made it nearly one year. Isn't that impressive already? Don't we get some points for that? Some recognition and praise for not having ended up where we are now so much earlier?

Mom is on a path, though, and she won't deviate. "This challenge of Mimi's," she presses, "isn't just something she wanted. *I* wanted it. *I* loved the idea! Get my two girls under the same roof, make them work out whatever it is that's kept them at such distance all these years."

"Uhh, California? New York?" I have to cut in, point out the obvious.

"*Emotional* distance."

Mom's right. The last thing I could have imagined doing before this whole challenge began was calling up Gracie and admitting my legal troubles, my dirty drug habits. She'd never understand. She'd judge before I could finish. And I'm sure the last thing Gracie could have imagined doing was letting her little sister know how foolish she felt hanging on all this time to David, an engaged man. She'd probably think I wouldn't understand how she could love an asshole who used her like that. She'd be embarrassed, insecure.

After nearly a year now together at Mimi's, all that temporizing and worrying does seem a bit ridiculous. Sure, Gracie hasn't hesitated to judge me before, and sure, I've told her more times than I can count that she shouldn't be such a prude and hold out for David. But when I finally came clean and turned to Gracie for help, when I turned to my big sister as I used to when I was younger, I realized how silly I'd been for thinking she'd tear me apart, try to give me a lesson on morality and responsibility.

When Gracie told me what really happened between her and David all these years, the first thought I had was to defend my sister, not to rebuke her. We may have grown apart over the years, but this challenge *has* brought us closer together. No one can deny that. Not even me, sitting here still brooding over last night's blowout.

Still, what Gracie said last night was awful. Does she really mean those things?

"Juliette?" Mom meets my wandering gaze.

"Sorry." I set down my mug of coffee and join Mom at the nook.

Then again, what I said last night was pretty awful, too. And deep down, I don't mean those things. Yeah, so Gracie made me angry and can get under my skin, but I truly didn't mean those hateful words. They were just words, stupid, hurtful words, spoken in the heat of an angry moment.

Mom pushes a strand of hair behind my ear. "Sisterhood is so important. The relationship you can have with a sister is unlike any you can have with another."

I groan, long and loud. "I love you, Mom, but seriously. How would you know?"

"I wouldn't." A look of regret covers her face, and her hands fall to her lap. "That's exactly why."

"What do you mean?"

"Juliette. I've never had a sister like you and Gracie have each other."

"Exactly! It's not all roses, Mom."

"I used to have a sister."

I set my mug, halfway to my lips, down with a thud.

"I was five."

"Mom," I gasp.

"I was five when she passed." Mom looks to me with glossy eyes. "She was only a baby. Not more than a few months old. I don't have

349

many memories of her, but the one that stands out the most is how genuinely *happy* I was to have a sister."

"Oh, Mom." My fingers blindly search for hers, wrap around her hand and squeeze it tight.

"But I've always wondered what it might be like today, if she were still here." She squeezes my hand. "What kind of special friendship we would have formed. Having two daughters myself was all I wished for. I wanted you and Gracie to have what I couldn't, what I knew was so very special that I had missed out on."

"Wh—what happened?" I'm hesitant to ask. All my life I've gone on believing that my mom was an only child, that Mimi and Grandpa only ever had their Janey. And now, all this time . . .

"It had only recently been given a name then, and we weren't really sure." She presses her lips together tightly. "It was SIDS." Her voice cracks. "Your Mimi only explained to me that the angels decided it was Lori's time to join them." A single tear rolls down her cheek and she quickly wipes it dry. "I was five. Confused. Heartbroken. I asked Santa every year for a new baby sister for Christmas. I even asked for Lori to come back."

"Mom." I pull her into the tightest embrace. "I'm so sorry."

She leans her head against mine. "We can take for granted what we have, Juliette. Until it's taken away, and then . . ."

"Yeah."

"I may have had a sister for only a short while, and I know that it's completely normal not to see eye to eye on everything. Sisters argue. Friends argue. I understand that." She dries away the last of her tears and sniffs. "But I *do* know what it's like *not* to have that friend to argue with, that friend who will always have your back simply because she is your sister. There is a special place a sister can have in your life if you'll *let her*, Juliette."

"Why didn't you or Mimi ever mention Lori?"

"A painful memory," she says. I nod. "And I suppose that's how it was back then, for Mimi." She shrugs one shoulder. "Mimi lost her father at a young age. Her mother never talked about it much, and Mimi never did. You don't air your dirty laundry, don't talk about a painful past. I guess sometimes you just bury your secrets, you move forward. Just do what you can to survive."

"Did you and Mimi ever . . . talk about Lori? Together?"

Mom gets a far-off look in her eyes as she glances across the kitchen. "No, not really. At least never directly. I think it really was just too damn painful for her."

"And for you?"

"I was only five. It hurt a lot then, and a day doesn't go by that I don't miss her, wish she were here." Mom looks to me and I nod. "Losing a child is the worst thing that can happen to a mother."

"I can't even imagine." I sigh. "You would never know Mimi had a second daughter. She was always so full of life, so kind and warm."

"She loved you and Gracie fiercely. Like her own children. She wanted nothing more than for you two to be sisters, friends. And"—she exhales a loud, long puff of air—"as she would always say, this *too* shall pass."

These words sink in with a greater strength and import than they ever have before.

"You and Gracie will argue. And you will overcome it." Mom kisses the side of my head. "In your time." She flashes me a small smile. "You have no choice, right?"

Gracie and I shared some hurtful words. While the damage we've done isn't irreparable, it can't be reversed with a quick fix.

"Remember," Mom says. "You two don't need to have everything in common. Not even that much."

I roll my eyes. "That's for sure."

"But you're sisters. That connection is something you do have in common, and it's something that most sets of friends don't share. It's special, that bond. You don't have to be similar or share every interest. You just have to . . . love each other."

Just then, a gruff sound breaks the silence. Dad cautiously enters the kitchen, making sure he is heard so as not to startle or disrupt too badly the intimate one-on-one between mother and daughter.

Mom and I exchange understanding smiles. I give her a wink, just like Mimi, and she pats me on the leg. "I love you," she whispers to me.

"I'm going to work, girls," Dad says as he fastens his cuff links.

"You're not the only one," I sing, leaping from the barstool.

"Looks like you girls are in good spirits." Dad is all grin as I make my way across the kitchen floor. He nears Mom, his back to me.

"Something like that," I say, turning around to look at Mom once more. I mouth an "I love you, too," drawing a tiny heart in the air with two fingers.

"Janey?" Dad refills her coffee mug before slipping his into the dishwasher. "You all right?"

"I am," Mom says, smiling at me. "I really am."

———

After work, I consider returning to Mimi's to talk to Gracie. But as soon as I enter the empty living room, I decide I'm not yet ready to face my sister. I haven't given any thought to what I'll say, having barely made it to work on time this morning and been nonstop busy on the floor. When we do talk, I want to say the right things.

I do stuff a few clothes and bathroom products into an overnight bag before leaving, and just in case Gracie's forgotten, I run around to the back and give the orange tree and other drying plants a quick watering.

Perhaps tonight I will gather the nerve to give Gracie a call, or find the courage to hop back in my car and return home. Perhaps.

———

Another day passes without a word from Gracie, without the nerve arriving for me to make the first move. Dad's already said in that endearing yet direct way of his that if we don't kiss and make up by tomorrow he's going to intervene. I believe his words were, "I'll lock you two in the garage and make you clean it until you get to talking."

No longer one to think the garage all that great a place to hide out in one's free time, and certainly not one to find the appeal of approaching an apology under such circumstances, I cross my fingers that one of us will man up and make that move forward soon. As the older sister, does the responsibility rest on her shoulders? As the one who ran away, does it fall on mine?

Enough time has passed for me to calm down, to no longer feel incensed over our words. I've been focusing on work and trying to find the right words to say to Gracie. Unfortunately, I'm making real headway only on that first one.

The next morning, no word from Gracie, and, fearful that Dad is going to intervene any minute, I almost decide to just hop in my car, pajamas on and all, and drive straight to Gracie. Go to her and tell her all about Lori, all about how childish we've been, all about how Dad is going to put us through serious torture if we don't get our acts together and figure shit out.

I convince myself a cup of coffee and the morning paper, albeit the dry *Wall Street Journal*, are deserved before I attempt reconciliation.

Beating Dad to the morning ritual, I open the front door to retrieve the paper. Instead I find something else. I find not the *Wall Street Journal* but the *New York Times*. And atop it, an orange.

"Son of a—" I mutter under my breath.

I set the orange on the counter, plunk down on a barstool, and listen to the drip-drip-drip of the percolating coffee.

I can't believe it. My sister. My one-of-a-kind sister. A smile coats my lips as I unfold the newspaper and read the Post-it Note she's stuck to it: "I miss you."

Not many words, but just the right ones.

"What's going on in the world today?" Dad asks, gesturing to my newspaper. "Hey, that's not the *Journal*." He turns to look back at my mother, who's right on his heels. "Do we get the *Times* now?" He glances at my paper again, and before I can explain myself, I grab my purse.

"Where are you going, dear?" Mom asks.

"Somewhere I should have gone days ago," I huff, stuffing one arm into a sweater.

Without another word, I make a beeline for the Citroën. I'm so ecstatic to have heard from Gracie that I can't think straight. I'm sure I've got sleep in my eyes, my hair's a real rat's nest, and I'm not even sure I have on matching flip-flops. As Gracie would lovingly kid, since I've at least remembered to put on underwear and a bra, I'm halfway to a Juliette kind of Sunday best. I realize, as I so clearly picture her making such a comment, that I miss my sister terribly.

I get behind the wheel and chuckle to myself. Gracie's absolutely right to miss me, because I miss the hell out of her. Sisters need each other. I need my big sister. How childish and stupid have we been, fighting like this, letting distance do again what it's been so horribly grand at doing all these years?

I sail down the street, passing my alma mater Santa Barbara High, rolling through one "Stop" sign, waiting horribly long at another. Finally I approach Laguna Lane, make a screeching turn onto the street. I leap from the car almost before I set the parking brake and run up the steps to the front door.

"Gracie! Gracie!" I make quick rounds in the house. "Gracie, you home?"

She must be jogging, I think when I consider the early arrival of today's newspaper.

"Gracie?" I give a try in the garden, but nothing.

Still no more sure now of what I will say to Gracie than I have been these past few lonely days, I jump back into my car and decide fate will have to step in here. Gracie's reached out, and in her gesture I've realized just how much *I* miss *her*.

After all, Mimi said Gracie's loyalty would see her through trials, and my tenderness would see me through. Without another moment's thought, I restart the car and begin the journey down one of Gracie's more frequented jogging routes, ready to embrace those very qualities that will see us through not only the next season but hopefully the rest of our lives.

29

Gracie

"Gracie! Gracie!"

The shouting draws nearer, and now I can hear my name being called out.

"Gracie! Wait!"

I slow down before coming to a halt. I turn around.

"Gracie!"

It's Mimi's Citroën, stopped in the middle of the street behind me, and my goofy sister, hair a mess, one arm waving wildly overhead, is charging out from it. "Gracie, wait!" she hollers.

I try to catch my breath, wipe the sweat from my brow. "Jules," I gasp.

"Oh, Gracie! I got the paper. The orange. The note."

Before I can say another word, Juliette has me wrapped in her arms. She's gripping me so tight, pulling me so close to her. "Oh, Gracie. I've missed you, too."

My heart still pounding, sweat still forming, I catch my breath enough to say, "Juliette, I've missed you *so* much. I'm so, so sorry."

"No, no. *I'm* sorry, Gracie." She appraises me for just a beat before pulling me close once more. "I didn't mean what I said. At all."

"I didn't mean it, either," I rush out. "What I said was horrible. So bitchy. Unforgivable."

"I forgive you. We both said things we didn't mean."

The time that Juliette's been away, I've been so clueless, so lonely, relentlessly running over what to do next. Who was supposed to make the first move? How would I tell my sister I hadn't meant what I'd said, that I had been stupid and hotheaded? That I was frustrated and had wrongly taken it out on her, and that I was so sorry? Would she even want to see me? Had we really done the kind of damage that couldn't be undone?

I talked to Mimi under the orange tree, trying to clear my head and figure out where to go from here. I even drove to Mom and Dad's the night of our fight, fairly certain that's where she'd run off to. When I saw her car in the drive, I froze. I didn't know what to do, what to say. I was anything but prepared. No audacity whatsoever.

And the last people I wanted to see were my parents. I felt as if my pregnancy would somehow be brought up in all this mess, and I didn't want to deal with that. There was enough on the table, and what was on the table was already such a seemingly insurmountable mountain that neither Juliette nor I knew how to approach it.

But this morning, I didn't care anymore. I wanted my sister back. We could get through this. We've gotten through so much already. Uncertain how best to let Juliette know that I need her and that I want to talk—that I miss her—I took the cue from Mimi.

It happened during one of my conversations with Mimi under the orange tree, a ripe orange in hand and with an overwhelming sense of loyalty to the only sister I've ever known, ever loved. It wasn't as bold a move as a phone call or a knock on the door, but I knew it was the right move. The kind of move where you show exactly how you feel.

"We have to work on that," I say, wiping the sweat from my upper lip. "Saying things we don't mean." She nods. "And, like, *bitch* and *slut* can*not* be the first words out of my baby's mouth."

Juliette laughs loudly enough to wake up the whole neighborhood. "No, but that would be pretty funny."

"So not." I roll my eyes, full-on Juliette.

"Gracie, let's not fight like that again."

"Deal." I hold up my pinkie finger.

She holds hers up and says, "Fighting's unavoidable. That's obvious."

"True."

"But not like that. Not again." She locks her pinkie with mine.

"Deal," I say as we shake. "No more bad names or insults. No more fights in garbage piles or nights spent apart in anger."

She laughs some more, her head flying back. "God, you're so right."

A honk-honk sounds, then a car swerves around the Citroën. "This isn't your private driveway!" the offended driver shouts from his Porsche convertible.

"Suck a lemon!" Juliette yells, giving the driver, a man who could very well be experiencing his midlife crisis, the bird.

"Oh dear God," I say with a laugh. "My poor son or daughter is going to learn *so* much."

Juliette winks, then tells me she'll give me a ride home. "We've got lots to talk about," she says. She hangs an arm over my shoulders. "And it's more a doughnuts-and-coffee kind of talk than a jogging or bike-riding kind of talk."

———

I'm in shock. When Juliette said we had lots to talk about, I never imagined she meant Mom, Mimi . . . and *Lori*. How could Mom and Mimi have kept this a secret for so long?

"Mimi *did* say every woman's got her secrets," Juliette points out. "And I guess this one she decided to deal with in her own way."

"The challenge." I gesture around the living room. "It all makes so much sense now."

"Well, I think anyone would argue that saving sisterhood is kind of a big deal."

"Yeah." I pause before I say, "Do you think Mimi would be upset about these past few days? That we didn't exactly . . . erm . . . *live* together."

"I think she would have expected it. This hasn't been easy."

"It hasn't exactly been the hardest thing, either." I can't help but look down at my stomach. A stomach that now does not reveal the clear future ahead of me, but in a few short months will be a reminder every day of the difficulties ahead.

"That won't be easy, either, Gracie," Juliette says, leaning near me. "But it won't be the hardest thing to do."

"If I'm honest with myself—" I start. I'm not sure if I should go on. What I have to say could insult Juliette again. She is the one who says that my feelings deserve to be acknowledged, though.

"Go ahead," she says, as if reading my mind. She gives me a reassuring touch on the knee.

"If I'm *really* honest, I do think it kind of unjust that this is happening to me."

"Instead of me?"

"It does seem awfully unlucky, doesn't it?"

"Gracie." She raises high one eyebrow. "I don't mess with a guy unless he's suited up. Even *I*, wild and fancy-free Juliette, have *some* rules."

"We'd been together for so long," I try to rationalize. "I just . . . didn't think about it."

"And you were caught up, in the moment, in passion." She squeezes her eyes shut, purses her lips. "I get it, honey. It happens. But you've got to just move ahead now. You know?"

"Yeah. God, I love you, Jules. I'm really sorry. I want you back home. It's totally sucked without you around."

"Quieter, I imagine?" she teases.

"Yes, but that's not always a good thing."

"I guess my bringing guys over all the time can be a bit insensitive. I talk about how we're changing and growing, and *psh*, I haven't changed a bit. Still wild and irresponsible."

"You should live the life you want, Jules. I only worry about you."

"I know. And I've heard moms"—she points to my stomach—"make the *worst* worriers. So, well . . . there's that." She flashes me a teasing smile.

A calm washes over me, a calm that I haven't felt in the longest time. I could never turn my back on Juliette, even when she drives me batty or does the stupidest things. She's my sister; she's my friend. I know she'll always have my back and she accepts me for exactly who I am, baby and all.

I realize, even though I am calm, I am tired. Not only physically tired, obviously; I am tired of arguments, of saying things we regret, of beating each other down when we need to raise each other up, support each other. If we don't have each other, whom do we really have?

"So," I say, "you're not moving out?"

"No! That was Rash Juliette talking. No way. I wouldn't do that to Mimi. To you." She pauses. "To the baby."

"Ah, gee, Jules. You're going to make me cry."

"We've both done enough of that for a while." She gives me a pat on the back.

"So . . ." I'm dying to ask.

"Yeah?"

"Did you . . . tell Mom and Dad?"

"About the baby?"

I nod.

"That's not my news to share, Gracie."

"Thanks."

"When are you? Going to tell them? You know, I honestly don't think they'll be all that upset."

"Psh! Single and pregnant?"

"Successful career? Always responsible? Except for, like, *one* time." She rolls her eyes. "You were made to be a mother. No one has anything to worry about. And I really think that given our fight and time apart and all that drama, they'll be really happy about this."

"You think?" I can't imagine.

"Even if it isn't ideal right now, I'm happy for you. I know Mimi would be."

I stand from the settee, tuck my sweat-soaked hair behind my ears. "Then, if you want, I'm going to hop in the shower and then head over to Mom and Dad's," I decide. "Want to come along?"

"To tell them?"

"Yeah. I . . . need you."

She's glowing. "You need me?" She's smiling so wide, as if I have never told her that I needed her.

"More than you know."

"Definitely." She nods emphatically. "I'll definitely be there with you."

As we make our way to our bedrooms, I feel myself rise, uplifted by the knowledge that my sister and I need each other, and we know we need each other.

Before slipping into my bedroom, I spin toward Juliette and say, "You know, I think we're going to be all right, Jules."

"I think we *are* all right, Gracie."

———

My news didn't break Mom or Dad, as I feared it would. Instead, my parents were ecstatic. Sure, under different paternal circumstances things could be brighter, but Mom and Dad embraced me, congratulated me.

They congratulated Juliette on becoming an aunt, congratulated themselves on becoming grandparents.

Mom began the predictable barrage of a million and one questions as soon as I delivered the news that I'm happy about the baby, as unexpected as it may be, as worried as I am that the road ahead will be rough. I answered most with candor and confidence.

As for the ones I couldn't stomach ("Are you going to raise this child alone, as a single mother?") I just looked to Juliette, wearing a tight, helpless smile, and in that telepathic sister way invited her to help allay the fears, the questions, the worry. "Gracie's never going to be alone," Juliette said. "She's got us. She's got me."

But before Juliette and I walked into the family room to deliver the baby news, I clutched her forearm and said, "Let's not talk about our argument."

"That's fine by me," she said, visibly relieved to put it behind us with her loose shoulders and tired smile.

We would put it in the past enough to move beyond for bigger, brighter, and better things. The past is the past, and we move on. But we'll still keep it somewhere, fresh, in the back of our minds, so we remember how pointless it is to argue like that, how much unnecessary pain and strife it can cause. I know it won't be the last time we go at it, but I'll endeavor to make those times as infrequent as possible.

"I'd love to not talk about it," Juliette added. "But Mom'll hit us until we cave."

"I don't care." I had an air of indifference about me. "It was between us, between sisters. Let's keep it that way."

"Okay, Gracie." Neither of us could fight our growing smiles as we realized the circle was closed. The circle was . . . not a circle. My sister and I have a relationship with our mother, and the three of us together make up the Bennett ladies—the female force of our family.

But Juliette and I also have a one-on-one relationship. There is a mutual understanding, a trust, a love between two sisters, like two links in a chain that cannot be broken.

————

At last, on an unseasonably warm day filled with abundant sunshine, my prenatal appointment has arrived. I'm grateful I am not plagued by morning sickness today. I don't test the waters with a jog; rather I rise early and take a long, warm shower. I dress for the workday, for the meeting with a client I have this afternoon. It is a meeting I refuse to miss even if morning sickness arrives later than usual. And so begins the balance of career and motherhood.

Juliette and I are both relieved that Dr. Portland's office is not full, the wait to be seen not long. Juliette was asked to fill in for a sick employee later this afternoon, and I'd hate for her to miss it. She proudly told me this morning that she's been late only once since she started her new job, and we both know to what morning she's referring. She won't be late again on my account.

Dr. Portland shakes both our hands as we enter the small, sterile examination room. He asks me, with a broad grin, if I'm excited about the baby and have been anticipating the pregnancy.

I glance at my ringless left hand, feeling a sense of shame that a woman in this century really has no business feeling. I feel it nonetheless and slip my hand underneath my thigh, which rests coldly on the examination table I'm perched upon. I'm clad in one of those skimpy patient aprons that barely close at the back.

"It's a surprise," I say with a forced smile. I'm not here to make small talk. I would like to go through the regular checkup motions, whatever they may be for a first-time prenatal appointment.

"And you think you're about ten, eleven weeks along?" He motions for me to slide down the table, feet in the medieval-like stirrups.

"Mmm-hmm." I look to Juliette, and she gives me a thumbs-up.

"Well, we'll be able to tell you for sure today." Dr. Portland slaps on a pair of latex gloves. He tells me he's going to do a routine gynecological examination, and I recoil at his swift touch.

Uncomfortable and exposed, I look over to Juliette. She's playing with the plastic baby from the anatomical model of the pregnant belly on display. She waves the plastic baby's hand at me and silently mouths, "Ma-ma," wearing a very creepy face.

I smile through a deeply suppressed laugh, grateful for her humor in all of this, impish though it may be.

"How about we take a look at that little baby, all right?" Dr. Portland says when he's finished with the examination. He's all smiles. I feel obliged to mirror him. I am supposed to be the happy mother-to-be, after all.

He squeezes a blob of gel onto my relatively flat stomach. Dr. Portland tells me that at this early stage, it is normal for my stomach to remain unchanged. My breasts, however, could already be noticeably larger, the aureoles darker, sensitive. He doesn't have to tell me this, though. I feel pubescent all over again as I wake up and go to bed with breasts so tender you'd think I forgot to put on a sports bra before a run.

"Oh! Doctor?" I say as soon as the thought comes to mind.

"Yes?" He holds an ultrasound probe on top of my stomach with one hand, the other keying in something on the keyboard adjacent.

"I was wondering—is it safe for me to jog?"

"Is that already part of your exercise regimen?"

"Yes."

"And cycling," Juliette adds.

"Absolutely," he says. "I wouldn't recommend training for a marathon. Your first trimester is your most precarious. But if you're already a runner, I see no harm in continuing your exercise routine. Unless you feel light-headed or unusual pain."

"I have been, sometimes."

"That's the morning sickness." He types something into the computer. "Take it easy, slow. Don't get your heart rate up too high. I say, if you can still have a conversation while you're jogging, you're at a good rate. Only increase your time and distance so long as you feel up to it, and don't overheat."

I look down at my stomach, wet with gel, the probe poised just above my belly button, and I have the first urge to cup a hand to it, like pregnant women who actually have a basketball belly to cup. My baby is in there. A tiny, living, growing person is inside me. A being that I'm already caring for, that I'm already concerned about. It is another surreal moment.

Casting a glance at Juliette, who's intrigued by the clouded black-and-white image on the screen, her hand now holding mine, I realize this year is going to be filled to the brim with one surreal moment after another.

"All right," Dr. Portland says in a long, drawn-out way as he slowly moves the probe about.

"Omigod!" Juliette gasps. "Is that the head?" She waves a finger at a stark white cloud amid a sea of grey. Suddenly it disappears. "Where'd it go? That was the head, wasn't it?"

"Was that the head, Doctor?" I'm curious myself. It seemed too white, so . . . empty.

"Maybe it was his butt," Juliette says. "Oh, is it a boy? A girl?"

"Can I find out the sex today?" I look to the doctor.

I hadn't even given a thought to learning what I was going to have. The realization that I could have a son or a daughter crashes over me like a tidal wave. Even if I can't learn today, as Dr. Portland quickly tells me, knowing that there is a little boy or a little girl, a son or a daughter, inside me fills me with glee, with a genuine happiness over this wholly unexpected pregnancy.

"What is that?" I ask as more black-and-white images dance across the screen.

"Hold on there." He moves the probe some more. "I'm going to take some measurements, make sure everything's healthy, coming along just fine, and then we can get a due date for you."

He tells me that he's measuring the head, brain, heartbeat. Everything checks out, and I exhale in relief when he's done calling out the numbers his assistant diligently jots down in my folder.

He moves the probe about my gel-coated stomach and points out where the head is, the heart. His explanations turn into babbles as I lose myself in the euphoric moment. I am going to be a mother, and this is my child. This tiny human on the screen, this little jelly bean, is my baby. I am in love. I thought I knew what love was, what unconditional love was, but I didn't. Not until now do I feel that the only thing in the world that matters is my baby, the health of my baby, the well-being of my baby, raised in a happy, warm, enriching home.

"Beautiful baby," Dr. Portland says. "And a clean bill of health, Gracie!" He removes the probe, powers down the screen. "Congratulations."

"Yeah, congratulations, Gracie." Juliette gives my hand a tight and encouraging squeeze.

———

"How about Jagger if it's a boy? Or Slade? Oh, wait! Tito or"—Juliette belts out a loud laugh—"Zeus!" She turns the page of the baby name book Mom gave me over Sunday dinner last weekend, a pleasant visit Juliette and I made after a relaxed afternoon at the movies.

"Those names are not for real," I say disbelievingly.

She holds the book open for me to see, leaning nearer in her seated position on the thick blanket we've spread out on the beach. Reclined comfortably, head on a balled-up mess of beach towels, I curiously look at the opened page.

"Of course they're absurd names," I say, incredulous. "You're looking under *Macho Names*. Give me some real names."

"For a girl we've got Dagmar, Gudrun, or Iselin."

"Jules." I close my eyes, pull my hands into my oversize sweatshirt sleeves as the crisp March sea breeze picks up.

"Noomi, Saga, Tuva . . . ," she prattles on.

"What is this, a *Game of Thrones* character guide?"

"Close." She pages through. "Female Nordic names."

"What kind of book did Mom give me?" I query with a laugh. "There have got to be some names in there that aren't so obscure?"

"There are," Juliette says in a tone that suggests this is obvious. "But these ones are so much more fun to look through."

She pauses in her exuberant search, setting aside the book. She pulls a towel from the oversize beach bag and wraps it around her. It is not the warmest evening, but spring is around the corner, the sun's light lasting longer, the thermometer slowly rising.

Carrying beach towels and blankets, outfitted in oversize sweatshirts, Juliette and I are among the growing throngs of locals eager to treat approaching spring as if it has already arrived, awoken from its short winter hibernation and ready for lazy Santa Barbara summer days on the sand.

"Isn't it weird?" Juliette says in a far-off way. She's looking out at the ocean, knees pulled into her chest, towel draped like a cape about her body. "That you're doing *baby name* searches?"

Instinctively, I drop a hand to my stomach, only a faint bump. I am now in my second trimester, nearing the halfway mark. "It is hard to believe," I say.

Though "single and pregnant" is a situation hard to believe, I find it nearly as odd that I am sitting here, on a beach at home, on a Friday night, with my little sister, and we're researching baby names together. All right, she may not be taking the research too seriously, but she is here by my side, almost as if nothing has changed since we were kids.

Things have changed, though. We have been through an interesting year, to say the least. A year filled with tumult and tragedy, difficulties and misunderstandings, but a year also filled with humor and consideration, love and growth. It's been a year of challenges, and in two short weeks, Juliette and I will have crossed the finish line our Mimi set out for us. It's hard to believe a year has passed, harder to believe we've done it.

"Jules?" comes a deep, raspy voice. "Is that you? Juliette?"

Juliette and I both look in the direction of the voice, our eyes following the tall, bleached-blond, olive-skinned man with the bodyboard under one arm who approaches, lumbering in that beach-bum-in-the-sand kind of way most guys who hit the beaches year-round do. He chucks his board to the sand before sitting back on his heels next to Juliette.

"Cary?" Juliette says, sounding surprised. "What are you doing here?" She turns to face him. "Aren't you supposed to be at Brown?"

He pushes back stringy strands of wet hair, then replies with a casual, "Cornell."

"That's right," Juliette purrs. "Cornell."

"Last midterm was on Wednesday, so that makes for a *looong* weekend before spring break." Cary smiles a warm, gap-toothed grin.

"Cancún?" Juliette guesses. "Cabo?"

"Cancún. You should come."

"Yeah. Right." She rolls her eyes.

They continue their banter for a few minutes after I'm introduced. Cary presses Juliette for a second and third time that she should come along to Cancún, or at least to his buddy's party tonight. Juliette plays with the invitation coyly, neither shooting him down nor committing, while I toy with the idea of either taking notes on their tête-à-tête or writing this off as an uncomfortable third-wheel moment.

I never do decide, but it's no matter when Cary gives Juliette a seductive wink as he stands, telling her to "look me up or give me a call or somethin'."

My eyes go straight for his washboard abs as he stands and brushes sand from his shorts. Juliette does not need to explain the attraction.

"Or I'll give you a ring, if you like," Cary adds with a sly, cool-guy kind of grin.

"Maybe." Juliette quickly glances at me, then back to Cary. "But I'm pretty busy this week. You know, work and all."

"Yeah, cool. I, uh, yeah, I'll be back this summer."

"Oh yeah? Can't resist Cancún and the good SoCal parties, huh?"

"Actually, I've got an internship." He runs a hand through his wet hair.

"Oh!" Another surprised look from Juliette.

"Yeah, got to eventually take life seriously, right?"

Juliette smiles. "Not *everything* in life, but . . . some things, I suppose."

"Yeah. Some things." He nods slowly, then claps a hand on top of a fist. "Well, maybe I'll see ya round sometime, Jules."

"Yeah, maybe."

"Nice meeting you, Gracie." Cary gives me a casual wave before fetching his board. "See ya, Juliette," he calls over his shoulder.

Juliette moves to a prone position, telling me that we really should get to some serious work on figuring out baby names.

"Wait a minute," I say, pointing at Cary, who's making his lumbering way across the beach, back toward the ocean. "You don't want to talk about Mr. Washboard Abs who *so* has a thing for you?"

"Oh, Cary?" She flutters her lashes. "We had a thing last year. It was fun, that was all."

"I remember him. Cary, from the summer."

"Yeah."

"Thought he wasn't your type," I say. "A stoner or something?"

She rolls her eyes. "Yeah."

"Thought you guys went your separate ways?"

"We did."

"But he seems to *still* be into you . . ." I playfully nudge her arm. "So you think you'll go to the party tonight?"

She turns onto her back, reclining on her elbows. "Nope. I have work tomorrow."

"I see."

She flips some loose strands of hair over her shoulder. "Cary's fun and nice . . . and I'm not opposed to fun . . . or nice. But fun is all he was, you know?"

"Miss Jules looking for substance?" I tease.

"Something like that." She gives me an equally teasing wink.

"Well, he's talking internship in the summer, not Cabo. Maybe he's turned from stoner to substance."

She rolls her eyes again. "I don't know about that. Besides, I've got work. I've got you."

"Hey, I may not approve of every guy you date, but don't let me stand in the way of your social life, Jules."

"It's not like that," she says. "Things at work are great, really moving. I think if I keep up the hard work, I might really get a shot at helping with some design. *Maybe.* I've got to stick to the job I have and see."

"I'm proud of you."

Juliette said things have been going so well at work that she's been given more hours, more responsibility. She regularly closes the store a couple of nights a week and assists with styling in the fitting rooms. Her boss even wants to "discuss future possibilities" next week.

"I don't think running off to Cancún would be a prime example of responsibility," Juliette says.

"Well, obviously not that," I say. "The party, though?"

"You pushing me to go to the party, Gracie, or what?" she says, a hint of jesting in her voice. "Someone want the house to herself tonight?"

"No. I don't want you to feel—" I break off.

"Feel what?"

I sigh, discomfited. I come right out and say what's been on my mind as my pregnancy advances, as the time to read Mimi's final letter nears, the time for our challenge to officially come to a close. "I don't want you to feel like you have to make your life accommodate mine."

"What are you talking about?"

"I'm going to have a baby, Jules." I sit upright.

"I know." She looks perplexed.

"Just because I'm having a baby and my life is changing doesn't mean you are, doesn't mean your life has to."

"Yes, it does."

"No, it doesn't."

"Gracie—"

I rest a hand on her knee. "You don't have to suddenly become a nun and change your whole life because you think I might be sensitive to your dating or want to be there for me in my delicate situation or—"

"You're babbling," she says with a shake of her head. "You're being ridiculous. And whoever said anything about becoming a nun?" She points to where Cary wandered off. "I may not be interested in some stoner—reformed or not—who's minoring in women's studies because he thinks that's a surefire way to get laid." She chuckles.

"There's an MO."

"Yeah, but it works," she says with a kittenish flick of her hand. "I may not be interested in that, but my date with Tad next week is totally on. He may not have a body like Cary, but he's an artist. I'm sure his hands can work some serious—"

"Okay," I spit out with laughter. "Point taken."

"Gracie, listen. I'm going to live my life the way I want to. Granted, things may not always go my way, and obviously I have to exercise caution or choose the more responsible route over impulse." I nod. "And sometimes I'll probably need a reminder to get my mind out of the gutter. I want you to know, though"—she takes my hands in hers—"that I have my life, and that includes dating. Maybe not casting *such* a wide net, but still dating."

"I know."

"And that life also includes *you*. It includes this little guy or girl." She touches a hand to my stomach. "It's a juggling act, but what life isn't?"

"That's true."

She falls back on her elbows again. "Besides, it's the life I want." She casts a glance my way. "And if you're not living the life you want, what the hell's the point of all this?" She waves one hand loosely about.

She's right. Life is a juggling act, you are not always dealt the cards you want or know how to play, but stepping up and playing them is what it's all about.

"We've done exactly that," I say to her with pride.

"We have," she says enthusiastically.

"And we've got only two more weeks," I point out.

"The next two weeks will be a breeze. And the rest of the year a real adventure."

"The year?"

She casually shrugs. "Yeah. Why not? I love my job, things at Mimi's have been great." She quickly adds, a finger held up, "Yes, we've had some fights and clashes, but siblings fight. That's normal. I think all in all we're pretty damn fine roommates."

She's absolutely right. In Juliette I have found more than a sister, more than a well-matched roommate. I have found a friend—my best friend.

"Why wouldn't I stick around?" she says. "Why wouldn't we just keep doing what we're doing? Gracie and Juliette, plus one."

"You're serious?" In recent days, namely since the news of my pregnancy, I haven't given much thought to what happens after spring. It was a miracle I finally came to a decision regarding David and the baby.

"Why not?" she says. "I'm sure you'll want the help with the baby."

"I will need the help." I look down at my stomach.

Juliette looks at me for a long, silent while before saying, eyes glistening, "You're always rescuing me, Gracie."

"I'm the big sister."

"I've always wanted to be needed *by* you. Silly, huh?"

"No. No, not at all."

"I'm always getting into trouble, needing *you* and—"

"I need *you* now more than ever, Jules." I take hold of her hand. "I've *always* needed you. Having you in my life this past year has made me realize all that I've been missing. We need each other. God." I wag my head. "David sucked the fun out of my life, making me think badly of myself, my ability to love, made me a panicky mess. And *you*! You make me laugh, and you make me see that catastrophes aren't always as catastrophic as I make them out to be. You've been my rock with David and now the pregnancy. You may be crazy, but I can use a bit of crazy in my life. You're my sister, and I'll always love you. We need *each other*."

"You're about to have a *heavy* dose of crazy in your life, Gracie." She giggles, gesturing to my stomach.

"Yeah, that's true." I look from my stomach back to Juliette. "I'm going to be a single mother, Jules."

"You've decided?"

I nod. It wasn't an easy decision, and it's one I'm sure Mom will tell me I should reconsider. But the David I discovered during our last conversation—the *true* David Nichol—is no man I want to know, no man I want my baby to have anything to do with. If all he is after is his legal claim to fame, wealth, power, and achieving it without a care in the world about whom he hurts along the way, then turning to him with something as precious as another human being—*my* baby—would be the most foolish decision I could make. It would be suicide, and I've endured enough damage. It's time to finally follow through with changing things. David is gone, and it will stay that way.

"I hope it's the right decision," I say through sudden tears. "I think it is. I feel in my heart that it is."

Juliette wraps me in a tight embrace. "Then it is, Gracie." She rubs my back. "And I am here for you. I can totally help you with this little bundle." She wipes away my tears and tells me this is no time to cry. "I'll help you out with diaper changing and feedings, if you use a bottle, obviously." She smiles broadly. "And we can go to the beach together, and I can babysit!"

I laugh. "When you're not out on a hot date?"

"That's right. When I'm not and *you* are."

"Oh, Jules." I wave her off.

"Of course, I don't know much about babies, but I'm sure it isn't rocket science."

"You're serious?"

"Yes!" She groans. "Besides, it's good for me, being here in Santa Barbara with you. You help keep me grounded. We have our fun together. And you're right, we need each other."

"Bringing a baby into this will change a lot of things. It won't be fun twenty-four-seven, I can assure you."

"What life *isn't* filled with changes?" She gives me a knowing sideways look.

I can't argue with that. "So we stay in the house?" I ask, befuddled by the suddenness of our decision. "After the year's up? Like nothing's changed?"

"Like nothing's changed," she says with a wide smile.

"Except, of course, a *lot* has changed . . . is changing."

"Except a lot has, is, and will forever change."

I wrap an arm around her, and she points out at the water. "Except for a few things," she adds. "One, this view will *never* get old. It will never change. I must have been daft to leave it for the chaos of the city."

"Oh, you love New York."

"I do," she says with a giggle.

"What else will never change?" I draw closer to her, feeling her warmth.

"The taste of Mimi's oranges," she says in a noteworthy way, her lips puckered, five fingers pressed together in a similar pucker brought to her mouth. She closes her eyes and inhales deeply, as if she can smell and taste one of Mimi's sweet oranges right now.

"Definitely."

"Our memories with Mimi."

I moan an agreeing response.

"And this." She rests the side of her head against mine. "Us. Sisters and friends."

I squeeze Juliette tight. "Friends."

"Best friends," she says.

After a while, Juliette pulls the baby name book back out, insisting that she'll get serious about name searching, but only after she runs down a list of names that sound like the lineup at a strip club. She defends her activity, saying that I need to make myself aware of names *not* to choose.

As Juliette entertains herself, snickering at some names and wielding a highlighter for others that are worth consideration, I lie down and close my eyes. I think on change and the cards life deals us. I think of Mimi and her last days, the days when we knew that the cards we'd been dealt were the ones we'd hoped would stay at the bottom of the deck, permanently.

Yet we also knew that sometimes the cards you hate the most and expect the least are the very cards you need to move forward. I would like to think that if Mimi were still here with us, living, breathing, dancing to Simon and Garfunkel in her living room, Juliette and I would have the rekindled relationship we now have today. We would not have had to find each other in the face of tragedy.

Whether that is true or not I will never know. What I do know, though, is that in a tragic event, Juliette and I did find each other again. In Mimi's loss we have gained, and because of that I am confident that the cards we were dealt were the cards we needed, the cards we were always meant to play.

Spring

30

Mimi

Dear Gracie and Juliette,
Congratulations! You've done it. Of course, I always knew you could. There was never a doubt in my mind. And there was never a doubt that you two would reconnect, finding the very near and dear and unique friendship that can be found in sisterhood.

I know the year has been filled with challenges. Life can be difficult. It can serve you lemons, but it can also be very, very sweet, like an orange.

I've never said thank you for accepting this challenge, but now I will say thank you for completing it. Thank you for giving each other another chance. For looking at each other and discovering that one helps the other get to where she needs to be, to be the person she is supposed to be, to reach for her star and shine in her own way. You have always needed each other—when you thought you didn't, when you thought the other wouldn't understand, and when you thought you were on your own.

Though this is my final letter, my final words, it is not good-bye. This is not an end. It may have felt like that one year ago, but that will never be the case. You know that now.

There are still many more days, more moments, more conversations we will have. More memories to be made on Laguna Lane, from one generation to the next. I look forward to being a part of them in my own way.

I miss you and I love you, my darlings. Always.

All my love forever,

Mimi

31

Juliette

"You ready?" I ask Gracie, holding out to her Mimi's fifth and final letter.

She fixes her eyes on it as she loosely wraps a lightweight peach-colored scarf around her neck. "You've got the other letter?"

"In my bag."

"Then yup, I'm ready." She opens the cherry-red front door and steps out onto the porch.

Greeted by a warm burst of morning sunshine, the salty sea dew still hanging limply in the air, I motion for Gracie to take Mimi's letter.

"No," she says as she trots down the porch steps. "You're reading the last one."

I've never been the one to open and read Mimi's letters. Each letter was one step closer to finality that I was not ready to take. That was a task I charged Gracie with, as the older and sage sister.

I follow Gracie down the steps and to my car, picking up from the lawn the morning's *Times*, its plastic bag soaked from the sprinkler's pre-dawn shower. Chucking the newspaper onto the porch for later shared reading, barely missing the steps with my pitiful throw, I say to Gracie, who's waiting patiently at the passenger door, "Why me when you're so good at it?"

"I think you should." Her tone is insistent.

"For a lawyer, that's not much of an argument."

"If I were a lawyer, then maybe that would be true."

"Morning, Juliette! Morning, Gracie!" Mrs. Frazier, our neighbor directly across the street, jubilantly calls out and waves.

"Morning, Mrs. Frazier," I say as I unlock the car doors.

"A beautiful first day of spring, isn't it?" She retrieves her newspaper, the plastic bag also soaked judging by the way she's holding it out at arm's length and giving it a shake.

"It is!" Gracie and I say in unison.

As I pull onto the street, I give Mrs. Frazier a quick wave. She waves back, crossing her lawn and returning to her front porch. I'm happy to see that her lawn is freshly cut, green, well taken care of. It's been less than a week since I last mowed it, less than a week since I stopped caring for all the lawns in the neighborhood.

I'd been wanting to focus more attention on my new job for a while, so when Shelley broke the news that she could offer me full-time hours, I was ecstatic. The hours would still be spent on the floor, in the fitting rooms, and behind the cash registers, with plenty of late-night stocking and opening shifts. Shelley explained that she couldn't place me in any official design position, as there was already a set visual team for our store. She did say, though, that I would be her first recommendation for the team in the event of an absence or the need for a replacement, or if it needs an extra hand during the busy season. Until then, I've decided my assigned roles will fit like a glove.

Shelley did have one more interesting thing to share before she assigned me more hours. Months ago I would have jumped at her offer. Today, though, things are different. It wasn't easy to turn her down, but I knew it was the right thing to do, and at its heart, it was what I wanted.

At first I considered not telling Gracie about Shelley's proposition that I take the internship opportunity in New York City. It was a rare opportunity for a non–college student to participate in the visual team internship—the very internship I messed up when at NYU. College graduates with degrees in the arts could apply. My lucky ticket to get into design at the store! The position didn't pay, which would pose a bit of a problem, especially given a move back to the city, but, as Shelley said, I'd have glowing recommendations and an excellent track record to help me land the position.

I didn't want to share the proposition or my decision with Gracie because I knew how she would react. Of course, I was spot-on. When I ended up telling her, she said I was holding myself back, that I was not thinking clearly and maybe feeling guilty because of her situation with the baby and all. None of that was true, of course. I had made a decision, and it was because it was what I wanted, believed was right for me. And for us.

I told Gracie about the opportunity because I remembered that one of the things that made our relationship—our friendship—work was that we didn't keep secrets. Not anymore. We are each other's support system, and that means sharing the exciting news as much as the not-so-exciting news.

Though New York City isn't in my sights right now, there are other options. How I feel about them I don't yet know, but that's nothing a little chat with Mimi and Gracie today won't be able to fix, I'm sure.

"You read it," Gracie says. Her hands are jammed in her coat pockets, refusing to accept the letter with SPRING scrawled on the envelope, which I am holding out to her.

"You've read all the others," I say, about to tell her that she should just read them all, but she cuts in.

"All the more reason for you to read this one."

I look at Mimi's headstone and sigh. "We've come a long way, but we still bicker like the best of sisters," I say to Mimi.

Gracie looks on at me, expectantly.

"Fine," I say at last. From my bag I pull a second letter, the letter Gracie and I wrote for Mimi together last night, and I suggest to Gracie that we read our letter first. "Together?" I say, opening the double-sided folded sheet of paper.

"Together."

Gracie begins, the older sister dutifully taking charge, that same charge that has allowed her to dictate that I read Mimi's final letter. The thought of peeling open that envelope—of reading that first line, that last farewell—sends tingles up my spine, makes me feel cold and suspended somewhere between an end and a beginning.

"'Dear Mimi,'" reads Gracie. She eyes me for a second—a small smile, a quick swallow—eyes swiftly back to the letter. "'One year, four seasons, full circle. We took on your challenge, with some hesitance and a bit of resistance, but we took it on and we completed it. We not only accepted your challenge to live together for one year in the place that we have called our second home, but we accepted the challenge to rekindle our relationship, to know each other again, to learn that we have taken our sisterhood for granted.

"'It wasn't done without tears and fights, words we now regret. We are sure you, wise Mimi, figured as much. We think you would be proud of us. You always said we could do whatever we put our minds to, that this too shall pass. Well, we didn't give up. We've made it. And our grief has gotten easier, but of course we miss you like crazy.'"

Gracie pauses and looks to me. She hands over the letter and wipes a tear from the corner of her eye.

I clear my throat and finish the letter: "'The year was a rough one. We know this next year is going to come with its own set of adventures and trials. We're better prepared for them, though, not only because we've learned so much from the past year, but because we have each other. We've decided to stay at Laguna Lane, living as roommates just like we have been. Some things shall pass, but this isn't one of them.'" Gracie and I share a small smile.

"'Gracie's going to have a baby. A little girl, we just found out.'" Gracie takes my hand in hers. "'And I was offered a chance to try for an internship in New York. It's funny how things seem to have a way of working themselves out. It isn't a fit for me right now, but maybe taking some art and design classes at UCSB will be. Maybe I can try to get into the program that way.'" I look at Gracie for reassurance, and she nods, squeezing my hand.

"'Santa Barbara feels like home,'" I continue, "'so the three of us, including baby Bennett who will be stealing hearts when she arrives this summer, will continue to call 1402 Laguna Lane home. No longer a second home, but our home.

"'We wish you were physically here with us, Mimi. But we feel your spirit all around us, guiding us, always in our memories, forever in our hearts. We want to say thank you.'" I hand the letter to Gracie for her to finish.

"'Thank you,'" she picks up. "'Thank you for letting us see that to be sisters means more than sharing a set of genes. It means so much more. It means having a friend—a best friend—who's been there all along. Whose place is not just in your heart but by your side. We send you our love, our thanks, and a promise that 1402 Laguna Lane will stay in the Jones-Bennett family for years to come. Neither of us has claimed your old bedroom as ours. We think it will make the perfect nursery for the baby. Don't you think? We love you. We miss you. Love, Gracie and Juliette.'"

Gracie folds our letter in half. She pulls an orange from her purse and sets the letter underneath it, atop Mimi's grave. "Thank you, Mimi," she whispers.

With my orange for Mimi in one hand and Mimi's final letter in the other, I compliment Gracie on the letter we wrote.

"She would like it," Gracie says. "You know what else she would like?"

"Hmm?"

"You enrolling in some of those classes you love so much. Those art and design classes."

"At UCSB?"

She nods.

Shelley offered an alternative to nabbing a spot on the local visual team at the store. I could try for the internship again, just as I did in New York, as a student. I could take some art classes while working full-time at the store, apply when the program opens up, and see where things go.

"Maybe," I say to Gracie, and to Mimi. "It wouldn't hurt to try, right? I mean, being a student again, even if just part-time, is the last thing I thought I'd be doing now, but . . . maybe." I shrug and look to my sister, who only warmly smiles in response.

"Well," I say with a sigh, "I guess it's time to read the letter." I wrinkle my face in discomfort and timidity. I knew this time would come. I never really thought about its actually coming, though. It was one of those far-off things that happen *eventually*, like turning thirty or getting married.

"You know what?" Gracie puts a hand on top of mine, my fingers tentatively poised at the center point of the envelope's seal. "I've got an idea."

"We have to read it," I say.

"Of course. That's not what I'm suggesting."

"Oh?"

"I think we should read Mimi's last letter at home, in the garden, under the orange tree."

It's a brilliant idea. I tuck the letter into my bag. The overwhelming weight I've felt all year with the opening of each letter melts away as I realize that it is not misfortune that visits me each time. That I'm not counting down the seasons to when I have to say good-bye to Mimi. Mimi physically left us a year ago; we've already said good-bye. Opening each letter has been a symbol of moving forward, of moving in and out of life's seasons, life's changes, the unexpected *and* the expected. It is not misfortune that visits, but simply life. Life in all its twists and turns, spontaneity and routine, highs and lows.

Gracie pulls her purse higher onto her shoulder, brings one hand to the small bump of her stomach, and says, "Back to the house, then?"

"Back to the house." I rub a thumb across the smooth orange in my hand.

"Do you mind if we stop on the way for some frozen yogurt?"

I chuckle. "Another peanut-butter-and-strawberry fro-yo craving?"

She rubs her stomach. "Sadly, yes."

"Sure. If you don't mind if I make a stop."

"At?"

"Maybe the university." I shrug one shoulder. "To pick up a course catalog?"

Gracie's beaming. "Deal." Then she turns and begins her way back to the car, a peppy, very pregnant sway to her step.

I set my orange atop Mimi's grave. It gently rolls in place, leaning against Gracie's. I kiss my fingertips, touch my fingers to Mimi's name, and whisper, "Thank you, Mimi. For everything."

I look to Gracie as she ambles in a slow and contented way across the grounds, stopping just at the peak of the hill before turning around. She smiles. It's a smile that says she's ready when I am, that it won't be difficult to read the letter. And if it is, she's got my back. She always has.

And then, with a sense of calm and assurance that this is the beginning of something beautiful, something special, I walk across the lawn and meet my sister. And together we find our way home for what will be one of many more conversations under the orange tree.

Acknowledgments

As always, my endless thanks to my family and friends for telling me I can do it. For believing that there was always a book waiting to be written after the Girlfriends. (And for pushing me to finish what I started.)

Many thanks to those who contributed to getting this book from concept to actual book: my editor, Liam Carnahan of Invisible Ink Editing (here's to many more books together); the kind girl at Anthropologie who let me hit her with a million and one questions in the name of book research so I could reliably spin the truth as any writer endeavors to; all my dear friends who listened to me dither about plot and character development so much they're probably questioning my tether to reality; and my readers, who have waited far too long for the next book and who are constant reminders of why I do what I do (and why I love it).

Deepest thanks to my sister, my friend, who not only inspired this story, gave Juliette her name, and is probably grateful its genre is not autobiography, but who loves me unconditionally. A true sister's sister, a friend's friend.

And, as always, forever and ever and ever thanks to my husband for never letting me put the pen down. *Ich liebe dich*, Christian.

About the Author

 Savannah Page is the author of the When Girlfriends series, heartfelt women's fiction. Sprinkled with drama and humor, her writing celebrates friendship, love, and life. A native Southern Californian, Savannah is currently living in Berlin, Germany, with her husband; their goldendoodle, Hurley; and her collection of books. Visit her at www.SavannahPage.com.